Sheila Curran

Diana Lively Is Falling Down

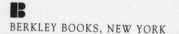

BERKLEY BOOKS, NEW YORK

THE BERKLEY PUBLISHING GROUP
Published by the Penguin Group
Penguin Group (USA) Inc.
375 Hudson Street, New York, New York 10014, USA
Penguin Group (Canada), 10 Alcorn Avenue, Toronto, Ontario M4V 3B2, Canada
(a division of Pearson Penguin Canada Inc.)
Penguin Books Ltd., 80 Strand, London WC2R 0RL, England
Penguin Group Ireland, 25 St. Stephen's Green, Dublin 2, Ireland (a division of Penguin Books Ltd.)
Penguin Group (Australia), 250 Camberwell Road, Camberwell, Victoria 3124, Australia
(a division of Pearson Australia Group Pty. Ltd.)
Penguin Books India Pvt. Ltd., 11 Community Centre, Panchsheel Park, New Delhi—110 017, India
Penguin Group (NZ), Cnr. Airborne and Rosedale Roads, Albany, Auckland 1310, New Zealand
(a division of Pearson New Zealand Ltd.)
Penguin Books (South Africa) (Pty.) Ltd., 24 Sturdee Avenue, Rosebank, Johannesburg 2196,
South Africa

Penguin Books Ltd., Registered Offices: 80 Strand, London, WC2R 0RL, England

This book is an original publication of The Berkley Publishing Group.

This is a work of fiction. Names, characters, places, and incidents either are the product of the author's imagination or are used fictitiously, and any resemblance to actual persons, living or dead, business establishments, events, or locales is entirely coincidental.

PRINTING HISTORY
Berkley trade paperback edition / July 2005

Library of Congress Cataloging-in-Publication Data

Curran, Sheila.
   Diana Lively is falling down / by Sheila Curran.—Berkley trade pbk. ed.
      p. cm.
   ISBN 0-425-20242-9
      1. Arthurian romances—Appreciation—Fiction. 2. British—Arizona—Fiction. 3. Women architects—Fiction. 4. College teachers—Fiction. 5. Amusement parks—Fiction. 6. Married people—Fiction. 7. Billionaires—Fiction. 8. Widowers—Fiction. 9. Arizona—Fiction. I. Title.

PS3603.U768D53 2005
813'.6—dc22   2004062730

PRINTED IN THE UNITED STATES OF AMERICA

10   9   8   7   6   5   4   3   2   1

To my parents, Ranger and Celia, and to my brother, Thomas Patrick Curran, whose grace while dying taught the rest of us to live.

* * *

Acknowledgments

I must begin by thanking the wonderful faculty wives I've met in Oxford and other places, very few of whom are actually married to professors like Ted, but whose stories gave me the idea for this book. Your contributions to academic productivity are vastly underrated.

To the multitude of dear friends who have fed my soul in Ohio, Chicago, New York, Charlottesville, Boston, Keene, Phoenix, Oxford, and Tallahassee: I count my evenings with you as some of life's greatest joys.

Speaking of joy, it is an embarrassment of riches to have grown up in a family like mine. My parents built their own Taj Mahal in the desert, a tribute to the happy childhoods they hadn't had, a moveable feast of love and support for their ten children. This network has blossomed exponentially to include relatives by blood, marriage, friendship, and the great sport of fine dining. The shelter I have enjoyed within this nurturing and ever-growing brood is an inheritance that I *can* take with me. For all you've done to support my writing, from cheering me up to sending a check to comping my bar tab, I am forever in your debt.

To the enthusiastic first readers of this book, Mary Anne Hudnall; Ranger and Celia Curran; Tere Clarkson; John Corrigan; Bob Clarkson; Cathy and Larry Dorfman; Ranger Curran II; Martin Blank; Jack Hudnall; Stephen Hudnall; Tasha, Casey, and Joan

Clarkson; Mary Finnegan; Beth and Mike Curran; Rhian Miller; Myrtis Meyer; Jane Crawford; Jane MacPherson; Jane Ulrich; Orla Kennedy; Barbara Murphy; Susan Estes; Aline Kalbian; Tracy Fessenden; Deborah Susser; Joy Sirinpin; Charlotte and Michael Morrissey; John Curran; Dede Curran; Emily Cutrer; Julianna Baggott; Paul Shepherd; Tracy Sumner; Julie Patterson; Michele Schiener; Ellen O'Daniell; Carolyn Scarborough; Lynn Bush; Tim Race; and Nancy Morris: I loved your suggestions.

To Larry Dorfman, whose CEO insights helped me enormously. To Tom Cutrer, for his guns and ammo information and Charley Scarborough for his help with probate issues. To Alex Alienikoff and Jill Breslau for legal insights. To the many websites I visited in search of information about killer bees, stock trading, and environmental technologies. To the authors of "Who Owns Water?" in *The Nation*. To William McDonough and Robert F. Kennedy Jr., both of whom I heard speak to the National Press Club on NPR and whose ideas helped create the environmental backdrop for this novel. To my professors at the Western College of Miami University, especially Terry Perlin, and at the University of Chicago, and to all the great writers whose work I have inhaled.

To my agent, Laura Gross, for loving this book, and getting it to Susan Allison at Berkley Books. Having heard so many bad-agent/bad-editor stories, I was unprepared for the generosity, wit, intelligence, beauty, and vision of these two incredible women. Susan's suggestions and prodding created a far better book than I could have imagined on my own, and Laura's insights were spot-on, each time I needed advice. To Julia Fleischacker at Penguin, for your work on publicity; to Kathy Kleidermacher, who came up with such a great title; to Cathy Dubowski, who superbly edited the copy; to Julieanna Lambert, who helped get it through production, thank you. To the sales staff at Penguin, for getting this into stores, you are golden.

To my husband, John Corrigan, whose companionship and support have allowed me the safety I needed to write, for urging me on and making me laugh. To my children, Curran and Helen, for helping me discover the wondrous mayhem of the domestic sphere, and the glory of unsung devotions. My love and thanks to all of you.

One

Diana Lively is naked under her bright yellow raincoat. Water streams down the shiny Mackintosh, carrying clouds of lather from her daughter's hair. Eleanor, age four, wails to the shampoo gods, but it's not the soap in her eyes that's making her cry. It's the indignity of having been caught with her brother's new packet of Walking Stick Insect Eggs before she's had time for a proper look. Worse, five of six eggs have gone missing and Mummy's put Bunny in the washing machine.

The raincoat is ludicrous. This Diana knows. Still, better this silly shield than the possibilities that suggest themselves in venomous twigs hatching in unexpected places, for despite her intellectual powers, Diana has an uncommon aversion to insects of any kind. The thought of one, even the childishly drawn Walking Stick on the front of William's packet—much less the two hundred offspring promised—is enough to cause her feet to move of their own accord. And so it is, that here she stands, in this shower, on a late summer afternoon, wearing her raincoat. Diana's heels rise slightly off the ground; her beautiful mouth twitches with each movement of her daughter's head. To put it kindly, she is alert. Highly alert.

Diana's eyes are blue-grey and slightly Asian-looking in their elongated shape, though she is fifteenth-generation English aristocracy, a fact which she ignores and her husband discloses with equal amounts of daily exertion. Even when she's had a full night's sleep, which she hasn't for three days—having stayed up to finish a dollhouse for Mary Colville's daughter's birthday—Diana's eyes have a slightly smudged look. Her mother and eldest son are constantly after her to wear a concealer, or as Humphrey puts it, "Well, at least put on some bright lipstick, Mummy, to distract the eye! If you'd just take the time!" Then he'd tsk, tsk and plead with her to let him just take five minutes each morning. The things he couldn't do.

A knock sounds at the bathroom door and eighteen-year-old Humphrey peeks in, his wet hair slicked back like a blond Elvis. "I'm done, Mum. No cooties. How's Eleanor look?"

At the sound of her name, Eleanor clambers over the side of the tub, dripping water on the hexagonal tiles.

"Eleanor!" Diana's voice carries with it her phobia and exhaustion, and she repeats her daughter's name in a softer tone to reverse the effect. Humphrey swoops his sister back into the tub and kisses her neck until she giggles.

"Come now, I can't do this if she's moving," Diana murmurs, but she, too, is laughing.

* * *

IN Arizona, Wally Gold is known as the Ammo King. Here in England, he's just another rough-around-the-edges American tourist, except to a small group of professors in one of the Oxford colleges, who have been told of his visit and the money it might bring their way. Wally is trying to find the Porter's Lodge at this fine college, alma mater to prime ministers, NATO chiefs, and Nobel laureates. Part of the problem is that Wally's not sure what a Porter's Lodge is, or for that matter, a porter. He is thinking of a lodge, as in Elks or Moose headquarters, and walks directly past the small stone anteroom next to the yawning arched gates with their Latin inscriptions that, were he able to read the language, would have told him where he was.

Wally is six feet, but he looks taller, with the physiognomy most often associated with meat carvers and longshoreman. His face is a broad-planed tribute to Slav, Italian, and Jewish ancestors, with a wide forehead, high cheekbones, hawk-shaped nose, cupid lips, and pointed chin. He's wearing an ill-fitting black suit that his wife had bought four years before, on sale at Barney's in New York.

"Hey, babe, on sale or not, it doesn't do me much good if it's too small," Wally had said gently. "Now we can't even return it."

"You'll grow into it," Mary Kate had said. "I've already done our New Year's resolutions and we're giving up meat."

Wally laughs; his dark eyes brighten with the hint of tears. He holds his watch out in front of him as far as he can and tilts his head back to read it, before pulling a pair of glasses from his front pocket. The watch is still on Arizona time. Wally mouths the addition— "It's eleven. Plus eight. That's seven"—before quickening his step, hurrying in the wrong direction down the busy Oxford street, away from the College gates.

* * *

Ted Lively, Diana's husband, is a professor at St. Mark's College. He is an expert in Arthurian legend. Ted is very handsome, if a little on the thin side, and he wears his brown hair in the same sculpted Prince Valiant cut he's worn since he was an undergraduate there. Ted's office is a suite, with a large study and smaller bedroom off to one side. Ted's desk—a massive eighteenth-century block of ornately carved cherry—is perfectly clean, save for his new computer. His black leather jacket is lying on the back of a fine burgundy leather couch. The jacket and the computer are the newest things in the room.

A blond undergraduate named Fiona Cheswit is sprawled across the sofa, her brown suede hip boots rising confidently from a jewel-toned Uzbekistan carpet. She is slightly intimidated by Ted's bookshelves, the rows of first editions kept gleaming by the College's house staff, and so opens her long legs just an inch wider, to reverse the power flow.

Ted pretends not to notice that Fiona has neglected to wear her knickers, confirming his hypothesis that her tresses are naturally blond. He is thinking of offering her a glass of sherry, thinking of the single bed in the adjoining room, thinking of England, when a knock shatters his reverie. Both he and the fair Fiona jump up to meet the president, who has entered without waiting for a response.

Behind President Bernard looms an ox of a man, who looks as ill at ease in the College as he does in his suit. He looks like a butcher, looks as though he should be manning a blood-smeared meat counter in the Covered Market, but Ted has been forewarned. This must be the American. Ted looks at his watch. "Terribly sorry. We were just dissecting Chetrien De Troyes's thirteenth—suffice it to say, I've let the time get away from me. You must be Mr. Gold."

Wally reaches out to shake Ted's hand. "Wally," he says. He turns expectantly towards the young woman, waiting to be introduced. The professors ignore her as she gathers her belongings and saunters off.

Ted opens an old book and lifts it towards Wally with the expectant triumph of someone who's holding the top-secret code to next year's NFL draft picks. Mary Kate could have explained what all the fuss was about, Wally thinks, if he'd only come that summer she'd wanted. He straightens his back and grinds his clenched fists deep into his suit pockets.

Wally finds his glasses and forces himself to look at the picture that Ted is holding up for him. "It's 'The Troubadour,'" Ted murmurs, indicating the colorful portrait of a reclining knight, adoring a fair-haired damsel. "A variant of the tale of Gawain, who saves Arthur by marrying a hag. He kisses her and presto! She's a beauty, with the complication being that she can be beautiful either by night or by day, but not both. He must choose which. Well, most knights would, of course, choose night, as that is when they see their women most. But Gawain is an impulsive fellow, and he generously tells the woman that she can choose the time herself. By showing compassion, which arises from his natural spontaneity, he releases the hag from her spell and she remains beautiful round the clock. Amusing twist on paradise regained, eh?"

Wally's eyes have a faraway, distracted look. "Kind of about faith, if you think about it," he whispers, almost to himself.

"Oh, Lively, speaking of beauty," President Bernard interrupts. "I saw Diana at Boots this morning. Invited her to dine in tonight."

"Brilliant," says Ted, but even Wally can see that he is anything but pleased.

Ted reluctantly closes the book, his hand imperceptibly caressing the colorplate before he brings the binding together with a snap.

* * *

HUMPHREY is brushing his mother's hair and working it into a simple French twist. Hair pins protrude, fanlike, from his clenched lips. Diana is trying to do something about her fingernails, which are bitten down to the quick.

"A pity women don't wear gloves to dinner these days," mumbles Humphrey around the pins. "Your nails are a disgrace."

"I'm shattered they let poor Gordon go. He always made me feel better, one friendly face in that stuffy—"

"So who's the new butler then?"

"I don't know—"

"Eleanor, come back here right this second! I saw you take them. Now bring them back! This instant!" Eleanor steals into the room on all fours, Diana's diamond pendants hanging from her mouth. She slowly makes her way to her mother, who pets her daughter's head before bringing her up to her lap for a smooch.

"Really, Mum, this hoarding business has gone on eons longer than is developmentally appropriate. I wonder if she could use some psychiatric attention."

"Maybe you can get a two-for-one scheme for Eleanor and Humphrey!" laughs William, aged ten, who has entered the kitchen from the back door. William plops down on the chintz-covered cushions of the window seat.

"Out! I just finished washing those," scolds Humphrey, pointing at his cherished Laura Ashley fabric. "Put your trousers by the sink in the washroom and then up to the shower. Mum's off to High Table and you aren't to spoil it for her."

"Who *wants* to go to High Table?" mutters William, taking a scone from a basket which Humphrey has swaddled with a napkin of the same blue and white fabric as the cushions. William rolls his eyes and leaves the room, trailing crumbs behind him.

* * *

Though Humphrey couldn't have known it, and would have been crushed if he had, William's pants are full of mud because a Year Eight boy has pushed William down on the football field. It is his first term at middle school, and William wants desperately to fit in with all the other Year Five students. But Marcus Graves, whose older brother, Spencer, had lost last year's fencing competition to Humphrey, tripped William and held him down. "Your brother's gay. Must be gay too."

"Is not!" William had shouted, tackling the older boy's legs and pulling him down with him. "He pummeled your brother!"

"Only 'cause Spencer didn't want to touch him!"

At this, William had seen red and kneed Marcus in the testicles, hitting Marcus's cup. The pain in his knee brought tears to William's eyes.

"Bloody unnatural family!" shouted Marcus, for the rest of the team to hear. "Brother crochets doilies, sister nicks everything, and father is some fag at University!"

As he makes his way up the stairs, William lets the tears come, giving in to them, and prays for something, anything, to save him from this year at school.

* * *

In the kitchen, Diana has been transformed. She has let Humphrey work his magic with hairbrush, concealer, lipstick, and a "spot of color" under her cheekbones. She wears a deep blue shimmery dress that whispers as she moves, sheer black stockings, and a pair of slim black leather slippers. She moves with the natural grace of a dancer, though it's been years since she's had the time for ballet.

Her eldest son has prostrated himself at her feet as she heads out the door holding her bicycle helmet.

"Take a taxi! Your hair will be ruined!"

"It's not far and I'm late. This will get—"

"We're not into the overdraft again, Mum?"

"I'll get the cheque for the dollhouse next week. And I've another commission next week. Really, I prefer to cycle, darling."

"While Ted takes cabs and buys himself a new computer?"

Diana sighs. "That's his money, from lecturing. I'm late, darling."

"Mum, what's his is his and what's yours is ours?"

"Humphrey," Diana says sternly. "We all do what we feel we can. He needs the computer for work."

"Then why did he interrogate you about the blueprint you bought the other day?"

"Because I've never practiced my architecture, Humphrey. This is enough. I appreciate your concern, but these things are between Ted and me. I've told you before: Marriage doesn't tolerate mathematical analysis. If it makes you feel any better, I'm looking forward to the exercise and fresh air before I settle down for the evening next to some bloody old bore bursting with the effects of pre-Raphaelite syntax on postmodern diction among Bolivian expatriates who wear feathers to bed on Tuesdays and Thursdays."

Humphrey snorts out an involuntary laugh. "Promise you'll fix your hair?"

Diana holds her palm up to her firstborn in a solemn finger-matching ceremony before Humphrey slips a small comb into her evening bag and kisses his mother goodbye.

* * *

PRESIDENT Bernard opens the door to the Senior Commons room after he and Ted have donned long black robes. They usher Wally through the door ceremoniously. The room is palatial, with two-story ceilings, fifteenth-century tapestries, seventeenth-century chairs, and paintings of stern-looking men wearing historically appropriate black garments. Something about the setting invites reverence, or in Wally's case, intimidation. He lowers his voice to match the hushed tones of the rest of the room's occupants. At the same time he represses a cliff-jumping impulse to yell out a Southern football cheer. President Bernard pours three small sherries and offers one to Wally. Wally has never in his life tasted sherry, but as it looks like the only alcohol available, he takes the tiny glass and sips it, shuddering at its unexpectedly sweet taste. Paul Bernard looks at his watch. "As soon as the rest of our group arrives, we'll process to High Table." He inflects the verb so that it sounds like *procession*.

"I'd better use the men's room then," says Wally, feeling like he's back in first grade raising one finger at old Mrs. Humberside.

* * *

DIANA stands in front of a huge gilt-framed mirror, around the corner from the College Senior Commons room, where she is expected to join the College Fellows and their guests for sherry. She has set her bicycle helmet on the floor and is frantically trying to get her hair back into a smooth roll before one of her husband's colleagues come round the corner. When Wally lumbers into view of the mirror, she jumps, startled. Her hair falls out of the bun she's worked so hard to create and she frowns, ignoring Wally completely.

Wally wants to ask her where the men's room is, wants to ask her where he can find a real drink. He wants to tell her that she's the first beautiful woman he's seen in England. Instead, he says, "Sorry."

"That's all right. I thought you were one of the Fellows, 's all. Look, sorry to ask you this on your first day, but could you possibly find a place to stow my helmet? I tried to get into my husband's office, but it's locked. And he'll be disgraced if I walk in as though I haven't alighted from a golden chariot, manned by footmen—" At this point Diana smiles at Wally before she puts three hairpins in her mouth and whips the comb through her thick black hair, getting snagged almost immediately on a batch of tangles.

Wally obediently picks up the helmet, thinking that even Mary Kate hadn't been so bossy to complete strangers.

Diana eyes tear up, but she continues to yank the comb through her hair, ripping it and scowling at herself in the mirror. Wally hides Diana's helmet behind a potted plant and strides over to her, taking the comb in one meaty hand and enveloping her tresses with the other, gently working the comb through to the ends.

Diana's face has gone several shades of pink as she tries to think of the correct response to the new butler's extreme familiarity.

Wally speaks first. "You need to start at the ends and work your way slowly backwards towards the scalp. I used to do this with my daughter."

The man's American accent stops Diana in her tracks. This one's not long for the job, not here. Too bad, really. There's something in the ease with which he untangles her mane that makes her feel as Johnny did, at home in this unwelcoming place.

"You have children?" Diana asks kindly, already imagining this man thrown out on the street with his family.

"Just one. She's seventeen."

"And how is she liking Oxford?"

"Oh, she couldn't come. She's got school."

"Oh! You must miss her terribly!"

Wally is glad to have someone read his mind. "God! I do. But she insisted I come and do this for her mom."

Now Diana truly pities the man. "Are butlering positions so scarce in the United States?"

Wally looks puzzled. "I— Oh!" His laugh is low and ragged. Diana is suddenly put to mind of a large Kodiak bear she saw a few weeks earlier on the BBC. Wally catches his breath and picks up the comb from where he's dropped it. A glint comes into his eyes as he takes Diana's hair and twists it expertly into a pretty close approximation of Humphrey's handiwork. He sets the comb on the table and places a trembling palm in front of her for the pins. "I used to do hair before they hired me to wait on the Oxford Dons. Might Madam hand me the pins, please?" he asks, shaky with the effort of trying not to laugh.

Diana senses a sudden change in his demeanor. The man appears unstable. She can see his hand is beginning to shake. What if he's not the new butler after all? What if he's just wandered in off the street?

"I've got it," she says, commandeering her bun as she spins away, out of reach. "Thank you," she adds as she edges backwards towards the opposite wall, knocking over an ivory stag umbrella stand. She sticks the pins in quickly, so that only one side of her hair is secured, the other half falling in a Dutch Girl wave against her shoulder, as she uses the outside of her foot to lever the white stag replica upright. It teeters gently before penduluming back to the ground.

Wally moves instinctively towards her, his arm coming up to help her fix her hair, but Diana ducks out of his reach and runs towards the Senior Commons door.

"Your purse!" offers Wally, now nearly dancing with his need to find the men's room. He jogs manfully towards her holding her small beaded bag.

"Keep it! You'll find I've got no money!" cries Diana, vaulting through the large oak doors and into the room, where a dozen esteemed professors are drinking sherry and quietly chatting. They all turn to gasp at Diana, who—having loudly pronounced to the world the universal truth of being an academic's wife in Oxford—stumbles through doors that were in the process of being opened from the other side. In her struggle to regain her balance, Diana grasps at the nearest gray-flanneled knee in her vain attempt to stay upright.

The pants she's yanked are those of the new College butler, Joseph, who is carrying a small tray of sherry glasses. Though Joseph's pants are pulled past the Calvin Klein waistband of his boxers, he manages to keep his tray and its contents in teetering balance, proving his stripes in the brotherhood of English butlering. He helps Diana up and tucks his head down towards her with a patronizing bow.

"So sorry," offers Diana, to the group of black-robed Fellows, whose spines have registered her Venusian one-sided hairdo with the slightest of readjustments towards Heaven, "but there's a man out there!"

The president's wife, who is far more clever than anyone credits her with, is the first to offer Diana her hand as she chuckles, "That *would* give one a turn, dear, in these halls."

Celia Bernard's barb is wasted on Ted, who is strenuously shepherding Diana towards the stairs to the women's powder room door, hissing, "What in God's name have you done with your hair?"

* * *

HUMPHREY needn't have bothered with the "spot of color." Throughout the evening, Diana can be observed, her head turned with unswerving, focused interest towards the sub-Saharan linguist on her right, or at table turn, to the physicist on her left. Her cheeks are emblazoned with the scarlet patches of a woman who has been slapped. And, metaphorically speaking, she has. This man, whom she's taken first for the butler and second for a thief off the High Street, is seated between her husband and President Bernard.

It is the linguist who explains his identity: a rich American who is dedicating a small library of texts on Arthurian legend to his late wife's memory. The wife, it seems, was an enthusiast of Camelot, and Wallace Gold is being cultivated to endow a chair in Arthurian studies. "Which," Victor Lesh adds, with a leer, "would of course benefit *your* mate, considerably. Not that you need it, being royalty and that."

"I'm afraid my royalty has as much to do with legend as any of the tales of King Arthur," Diana says, distracted by the hiccup of annoyance she feels at her husband, who continually puts her in the awful position of having to choose between carrying on the inflation of her bloodlines or contradicting him publicly. She shakes her head and doesn't notice Wally, who is trying to catch her glance, in between trying to figure out which fork to use and wondering what that gray gelatinous mass is that Ted has heaped on his plate.

"You see, as we know it," Ted continues on Wally's right, "the Legend of the Grail first appeared at the end of the twelfth century. Most people associate it with swordplay and gore, but it is very much about the quasimystical exaltation of Woman. This myth countered the Church's stranglehold on the definition of Woman as the temptress Eve, who'd caused so many problems with her apple. But of course, in these tales, I argue, Woman isn't really woman at all, she's the Earth goddess, she's Fertility, she's a way to reclaim barren lands decimated by the Crusades."

"Sounds like you dons could use a dose of that."

"Beg your pardon?"

"Where's all the women?" Wally asks, spreading his hand out to indicate the splendid eating hall studded with Renaissance portraits, the luxurious candlelit tables, the wines, the food, the tapestries, the glorious architecture of the room, the rows of black-robed professors. "And where's your wife? I thought the president said she'd be here."

"You didn't meet Diana?" asks Ted, ignoring Wally's larger question, as he flicks his pinky towards the linguist and the physicist, who are leaning forward, speaking around Diana, obscuring all but a patch of blue sleeve and a set of tapping nail-bitten fingers. "Of course, some know her as Lady . . . but you can see how that might have caused confusion when the Princess was alive."

"I'd like to meet her. After losing my wife, I find I'm . . . well, women, they just cheer me up."

* * *

THE travel agent booked the largest suite at the Old Parsonage Hotel, but Wally's presence still overwhelms the sweetly decorated room.

It is one a.m. and the lights are off. French doors admit the milky moonlight of the garden. Wally wears blue-and-white striped pajamas and kneels to the side of the bed, hands folded on its coverlet. He is praying, something he's come to only recently. Outside, in the garden, a sudden brightness appears and recedes so swiftly, Wally can't be sure if he really sees it or not.

It is in that slip of moment, between the knowledge and the question, that Wally understands what it is he must do.

The next morning he calls Arizona, waking Guy, his best friend and Chief Financial Officer, who tries to change his mind. After reminding Guy that he's the boss and the boss is always right, Wally hangs up the phone and heads to the College to have lunch with President Bernard.

* * *

DIANA is wearing headphones and singing along with the Captain & Tennille as she hangs microscopic voile curtains in the upstairs bath of her latest creation, a miniature French country house of yellow stucco with tiny granite sills inset across the Provençal facade. She is crouching and singing and shaking her booty every time the Captain hits a high note and thus does not hear the doorbell. Eleanor is only too happy to usher the friendly giant into the house, only too happy to relieve him of his passport while he moons at her mummy like Jack in the Beanstalk the first time that goose laid its golden egg.

Wally leans over awkwardly to tap Diana on the shoulder. She jumps up, yelping, swiping at the creepy crawly that has landed on her shoulder while stamping at the ground in a way that is completely involuntary, so that as her face registers the presence of a human, her body is still hopping away from the horde of huge jumping Malaysian cockroaches that have attached themselves to her twitching carcass. Wally is so empathetic that he steps back, too, right over the spot that previously held a minuscule, perfectly fashioned French Provencial sofa, but now holds a crushed scarlet velvet blob punctured by broken wooden splints. The Captain & Tennille are now crooning in the general vicinity of Diana's collarbones, and she looks at Wally like he is some bill for which she is being unfairly charged at a rate that was exorbitant in the first place.

"I guess this isn't the time to tell you that Captain & Tennille went out with Earth Shoes and were last sighted at the Peoria Dinner Theatre, opening for Engelbert Humperdinck and the Lennon Sisters?" asks Wally, reaching for his wallet.

"I don't suppose this is the time to tell you that I don't follow fashion when it comes to music," retorts Diana. "If you're looking for my husband, you've missed him. He's meeting with Paul at the College."

"I was just there and they told me he was here," says Wally, distracted by the fact that his large wallet seems different somehow. He pulls out a fifty pound note and clumsily offers it to her. "Sorry about the doll furniture. Can we get another?"

"No, *we* can't. It's all right," Diana sighs. "To tell you the truth, I wasn't too happy with the rucking on that settee. It must be a sign from God."

"Don't laugh. I believe in those."

"Oh, so do I. But if He's truly involved Himself in the rucking on that settee, this is a deity with too much time on His hands."

"I'm serious."

"So'm I. Quite serious. I barely find the time to *floss*. And He's got an entire universe to maintain."

"Do you ever feel like it's not God talking, but maybe . . . some-one you . . . knew?"

At this, Diana meets Wally's eyes.

She softens, taking his hand, and gently rolls his fingers over his currency, as though to say, *Take your money, it's all right.*

"I lost my first husband, twelve years ago."

It's all she has to say.

* * *

WHEN Humphrey and William return to the house, they find a large man sitting at their mother's kitchen table, a pair of reading glasses leaning off of his nose. Wally is examining a splinter he's pulled from his thumb, remnant of his futile attempt to fix the tiny *settee* he's crushed.

"Hullo?" asks Humphrey, dropping his knapsack and edging William back towards the still open door.

"I'm Wally. Your mom'll be right back. You guys hungry? I could make you a sandwich."

Humphrey warily begins emptying his pack onto the kitchen counter: pine cones, purple dried flowers, scarlet leaves. "That's very kind of you, Mr. . . . eh . . . Mr. Wally. But we're not hungry."

"I am!" says William. "But there's nothing in the pantry—Mum's dollhouse lady's coming soon—"

"William," warns Humphrey, pinching his brother beneath the elbow.

"Hey. Tell you what," offers Wally. "I saw a Pizza Hut downtown. You guys ever had pizza? Gimme the phone."

Wally has dialed 192, but in a heartbeat, Humphrey has leapt across the floor and pressed down the Reset button. "It's very expen-sive in this country to call Directory Enquiries," pants Humphrey, his cheeks reddening. "We—"

"It's not that we're *cheap*," volunteers William. "But Daddy tweaks

Mum if he finds one on the bill. He wants her to walk to the public call box, on the corner, where Directory Enquiries are free. It's awright, though, I can dial their number."

Wally looks back and forth from Humphrey to William a few times, as if to digest these nuggets of information. "I guess you *have* had Pizza Hut," he laughs.

"It's numbers," says Humphrey. "William's got a part of his brain that's dead on with numbers. We've never ordered takeaway pizza, but if William says he knows the number, he does."

William punches in the telephone number, his brother's praise and the prospect of real food pulling his lips into an upside-down smile.

Wally takes the receiver and is ordering as Diana comes into the house. "Hello? Pizza Hut? You deliver? Okay. How about one cheese, one pepperoni? The biggest you got. And how about some Cokes? I'm gonna hand the phone to my friend William. He'll tell you where the hell we live."

* * *

"You must be joking! I shall be the laughingstock of Oxford! I won't do it!" shouts Ted.

"Could you not use the money?" asks the president. "I know the College can."

"You know I desperately need the money! But why not ask me to dance naked through France for it? You know I'm shortlisted for the Fletcher Prize! If they hear of this, I'll be out! I've worked too hard to have it snatched out of my fingers at the final moment by a sentiment-driven Neanderthal from North America!"

"The consulting fee is ten times what you'd get from the Fletcher, Ted."

"The King Arthur Theme Park and Museum! In Lake Havasu, Arizona! Where in God's name is that?"

"Three hours by car from Phoenix. A short plane ride. Where the London Bridge is, Lively. You've seen the pictures."

"No, I can't say I have, Paul. I'm not a masochist who delights in the Americans' appropriation of our culture. And you're asking me to help the man create another abomination, a theme park in the desert, but it's not just any theme park. It's one that takes what I consider to be one of our national treasures, my field of study, and turns it into a Technicolor nightmare!"

"It doesn't have to be that, Ted! The man wants to create a monument to his wife. Why not use your influence to prevent the nightmare? Create a real tribute, that educates visitors—"

"Paul, have you taken leave of your senses? What sort of person drives through a desert to look at a bridge that belongs to another country? Americans on vacation don't want to learn. They want a Mac-experience. I can see it now—sand, plastic, and fat Yanks covered with sand."

"You don't have to live there, Ted. You can live in Phoenix."

"Stop! Don't you think it's bad enough that one rich American steals our bridge? Do we have to add to the insult by allowing another to erect a monstrosity—"

"Look, he didn't steal it. The London Bridge was sinking into the Thames and our government sold it to him."

"Paul, that bridge is our history."

"Lively, why are we arguing? You will have leave of teaching, you can write your next book living in—I'm certain—a beautiful house in Phoenix that he's providing, free of charge."

"Paul, you can't force me to do this. I won't do it. The King Arthur Theme Park? Just a hop, skip, and jump from the London Bridge? If I weren't so insulted, I'd get a good snigger out of this! Paul, you can't force me to do this. I won't do it!"

"Think of the money. Think of your family. And he's willing to pay, whether the project is completed or not. For all you know, the Americans Against Amusement Parks are banding together right now, to bring this down around his ears. Still, he's so eager to construct this monument to his wife that he's willing to pay you a generous consulting fee *and* endow the chair in Arthurian studies. All this even if something unforeseen prevents him from actually building his park. The Arthurians at Edinburgh were chomping at the bit for this endowment and we won it away from them. I'd think you'd be delighted."

"If you're so happy about it, why don't you do it?"

"Believe me, if I were an Arthurian scholar, I would. I could think of many ways to spend the money whilst enjoying the sunshine. But he's insisting on you. Think of it, man! All expenses, for you, Diana, and the children, six thousand pounds a month for consulting that won't take the sweat off your brow. Think of it as an adventure for the family. The chance to live in America!"

"You are actually managing to keep a straight face as you suggest I sacrifice the education and manners of my children so that I can help to bequeath the universally acknowledged sphincter muscle of Western civilization with yet another blistering pustule of popular culture?"

Paul Bernard shifts his weight from the balls of his feet to his heels and back again. He clears his throat. "Your mortgage, with which the University helped. That balloon payment coming due."

The president clears his throat again.

Ted bangs his fist down on his desk and sits in the chair, defeated. He delicately places his brow in the cradle of his slender fingers and ruminates, Rodin-like. "And I'm to be paid whether the park is built or not? I'd have to have that in the contract, you know."

* * *

DIANA sprays more Fairy Washing-up Liquid on her sponge. She scrubs at the plates. "William," she calls. "Time to get started on your homework!"

"It's not due till Thursday," says William, who is sitting on the floor, relacing his shoes in an intricate double-cross pattern that Andrew Macmillian started two days ago and now the whole Year Five is imitating.

"I want homework!" four-year-old Eleanor cries mournfully, as though she is being deliberately neglected, as though what is being handed around is a tray of chocolates.

"I know just the thing," says Humphrey. He sets a sprig of dried flowers next to his gold-painted foam wreath and hops up to pull out an old *Vogue* from the kitchen junk drawer. "Where are your safety scissors, Eleanor?" Humphrey answers his question by extracting the scissors and some pink construction paper from the drawer. "Now! Here's your assignment. Barbie has been invited to the Savoy for tea with Fergie. What's a girl to wear? Find me three outfits that wouldn't cause the Queen to drop her teeth you-know-where, and I'll give you a special glitter Spice Girl sticker! Awright?"

"William," repeats Diana. "Tomorrow *is* Thursday. What's the assignment?"

"I have to write something important that happened when I was little. I was thinking maybe of Johnny."

Humphrey stops all construction on the Harvest Festival wreath. He stands watching his younger brother, his Adonis-like body completely still.

Diana creases the folds of the Pizza Hut box, pressing down on the square's sides. Her voice is gentle as she fixes her gaze at her younger son. "Darling, you weren't born then."

"Well, I was somewhere, wasn't I? And I wouldn't exist if he hadn't been so brave. I don't have any stories like that. Tell me again?"

"You know, I remember something wonderful that happened when you were little," says Diana, leaving the box on the counter where she's folded it. She sits next to William on the window seat. "When I brought you home from the hospital, your father didn't know what to do with you. You were so tiny and he was so awed, he was afraid to hold you. Afraid to change your diapers, for fear of hurting you. I'll never forget; Humphrey was only eight and he showed your father how to do it. No one could believe that an eight-year-old boy knew how."

"Mum, let me get this right. You want me to tell my whole class about me wearing nappies? Are you completely off your head?"

"Oh. Well—"

"Mum, what's the use? I can't think of anything. I ate too much pizza. Are we really moving to America?"

"Of course not! We can't possibly—"

"Why not? It's fantastic!" says William.

"Well, for one thing, it's halfway around the world. Two, the schools are—you may *not* miss school. Third, my work is here. Fourth, this house. Fifth, rattlesnakes, sixth, black widows, seven, scorpions." Diana presses vigorously at the edges of the pizza box.

"Fantastic!"

Diana shivers.

"I hear the front gate," says Humphrey.

"Daddy's home," sings Eleanor, cutting out a green fake-fur mini-skirt. William quickly opens his knapsack and retrieves his pencil case and paper. When Ted enters the room, each member of the family is busily working.

"Hullo, darling," says Diana, using tweezers to stuff cotton into the red velvet backing of the new miniature sofa.

"Eleanor, how many times do I have to tell you not to leave your Wellingtons by the front door? I'm going to kill myself tripping over your things. I work hard all day. All I ask is safe passage through the front hall when I return."

Eleanor resolutely looks away from her father and cuts off the feet of a Ken-like model wearing corduroys and brogues.

"Bad day at work?" asks Diana sympathetically.

"You might say that," mutters Ted. He has suddenly noticed the Pizza Hut box on the counter. He counts to ten while he pours a glass of vodka and tilts it back in one swoop. "You know," he says, in a deadly quiet near-whisper. "It astounds me, the colossal stupidity of short-term solutions. Those advertisements are your siren song, Diana. It's been a few years, but you *were* once educated. Just yesterday, I was being pleaded with for twenty pounds to get you through the week and—" Ted sweeps his hand towards the Pizza Hut box. "Why not just sauté the money with a few capers and feed that to the children? That's why we're in the trouble we're in and that's why I am being forced to throw my career down the loo, so my children can grow pudgy on fast food?"

"Ted."

"Don't you dare shush me in my own kitchen. Well, the College's kitchen, but I'm the *serf* they've assigned it to, for the next month, at least."

"What *is* the matter?" asks Diana. "We didn't pay—"

"I know that. You *never* pay. I do. You're all doing arts and crafts while I—"

"What Mum's trying to tell—"

"You know, Humphrey, have I given you the impression that I'm interested in your input? Is there something in my demeanor that shouts *Oh please, tell me your every thought, I'm so interested?* Because—"

Diana has risen and gone to stand beside Humphrey, taking his hand. "That's enough, Ted. I can see you've had a very bad day. But you won't take it out on the children. Or me." Forcing a smile on her face and a lilt in her tone, she chirps, "Time for baths, children! Chop, chop! Last one up is a beastly Tory!"

"I'll do it, Mum," says Humphrey. As he leaves the room, he turns to Ted. "In answer to your question: not to worry. You haven't given me the impression that you're interested in me at all."

Humphrey turns, his eyes bright with angry tears, before leading Eleanor upstairs to the bath.

They are followed by William, who brings his homework sheet with him. William's handwritten essay reads *I was five years old when my father was killed, by a strey bullet from a shooting party in the woods near our house. My mum and I would have surely died as well if Daddy haddent jumpt in front of us.*

Ted pours another vodka and quickly drains it. He pours a third and caresses his finger along the outside of the Waterford glass, as if measuring the level.

Diana stands and faces him, her hands gripping the counter behind her.

"I hope you have an explanation for your behavior, Ted. I really do."

"I. What would you like to hear first? The bit where Paul holds the mortgage over my head as a cleaver to force me out? The bit where the Fletcher Committee dies of laughter at their near-miss in awarding the book prize to hired help for an American theme park? The bit where Humphrey decides not to take his University spot at Cambridge next year because he's six thousand miles from any hint of civilization? Just stop me when you feel the urge, as I tend to bubble over with the good news of the day. Oh! The bit where we've rented the house to a visiting Fellow from India, who will, no doubt, build cooking fires in the middle of the parlour, fueled by my now-worthless manuscript."

"But how could you rent the house without consulting me! I don't understand any of this."

"Well, *that* gives us something in common. And I didn't rent the house. Paul, who holds the note, arranged for *that* between executions."

Two

Diana—late for her appointment—is rushing about. "William, will you ring me a taxi? And Humphrey, have you seen my tape measure?"

Eleanor sits at the kitchen counter playing "Office" with a stack of papers and her Barbie stamps. When William reaches across her for the phone, he notices a small photo of Wally, surrounded by official-looking stamps and three hot pink outlines of a Barbie Princess. "Mum," warns William. "I think—"

"Just ring! I'm so late, William! Please."

William dials the cab company as Eleanor fixes a sparkle unicorn to the left-hand bottom corner of Wally's picture. "Mum, I—"

"Humphrey! Humphrey! My tool bag!"

Humphrey, usually so helpful—is entranced by the television—from which Martha Stewart is describing how to make new terra-cotta pots look as though they've been sitting in Grand-Mamá's potting shed for decades. Despite her legal difficulties, Martha has long been Humphrey's idol, transforming the ordinary with her exquisite, almost Zen attention to detail.

Humphrey backs up, still watching as Martha slathers a white paste on the brownish pots, and reaches around the door to extract his mother's tote bag full of small tools. He stands like a coatrack, holding the bag, imagining suddenly a tasteful armband, moss flowers perhaps, or a sea grass bracelet, to be worn by Stewart supporters the world over until Martha has been restored to her rightful place in domestic affairs. He thus does not notice that his younger sister has just chosen a Barbie negligee trimmed in ermine to stamp under Wally's passport photo.

"No taxis, Mum, I've rung three different places," interrupts William. "Shall I get your cycling helmet?"

As Martha gives her recipe for inciting mold on clay surfaces, Humphrey moves to the kitchen island, for a piece of scrap paper. It is now that he sees what his younger sister has done.

"Oh my God! Oh my God!" Humphrey takes both of his sister's hands and holds them down, causing the artiste no end of anguish.

"Mine!" she wails, the purple Changeables in her hand, poised to add some amethysts to the bright yellow crown on Wally's head.

Diana is already out the door when Humphrey breathlessly catches up with her. "Mum—Eleanor's nicked Wally's passport!"

"I'm so late, Humphrey!" Diana pleads, jamming her bag into a side basket of her bike. "I'll drop it to him after my meeting. Call the Old Parsonage and let him know I'll leave it at the desk, round four o'clock."

"There's more, I'm afraid—"

Diana grabs the passport and tucks it into the pocket of her jacket. "I've got to go! God, it's hot! Just call, love!" Diana shouts as she wobbles away on her bicycle, her tools clanking away in the basket behind her, unsettled by the dimpled pavement of the street.

* * *

DIANA leans her bicycle against the dun-colored stone of the hotel's courtyard. As she opens the door to the lobby, she is narrowly missed by a Scotsman, who appears to be executing a mad Highland fling in her general direction. Wally, whom she's fervently hoped to avoid, is seated in an overstuffed chair, watching her kilt-wearing assailant as he thrusts his right hand towards Diana's chest. Watching, that is, until he sees Diana. Wally jumps to his feet, apology writ large on his features, but the Scotsman pauses only long enough to hold up his hand, nod quickly at Diana, point to the rafters, and say, "Just one moment, if you will. Giving the Yank a fencing tutorial. You see," huffs the man, turning back to Wally, who is too polite, or too stunned, to stop him. "The bout consists of bluff and counterbluff, feeding false information to one's opponent while trying to anticipate his next move."

Diana sidles around the impromptu demonstration, thankful for the distraction. If she simply places the passport in Gold's hand and waves, she'll be back on her bicycle before she has to utter a word.

No such luck, however, for the Scotsman's jacket begins to vibrate. "Oop!" is all the man says before raising the ever-preemptory forefinger to Heaven. Retrieving his mobile phone, kilts swirling behind his chubby red-haired legs, the man disappears through an arched doorway.

"Sorry," Wally says, shaking his head and reaching for Diana's hand. "I don't—even know that guy. Kinda interesting, though. Isn't Humphrey a fencer?"

Diana nods. "Here," she says, offering him the small dark book, avoiding his eyes and his friendly handshake. "You didn't have to wait."

"Are you kidding? I'd have come in a cab, but Humphrey said you'd already left. Let me buy you lunch."

"No, thank you, Mr. Gold," Diana says, her voice flat.

"Oh come on. I feel terrible making you come all the way over here."

Diana shakes her head. "No trouble. I'm sorry, I have to go now, Mr. Gold."

"What's the matter?"

"I don't know what you mean."

"Why are you looking at me like I'm public enemy number one?"

"I truly don't know what you mean," Diana says crisply, edging back against the heavy door. "I hope your flight goes well."

Wally barely seems to move and yet he is somehow too close, leaning over her as he pushes open the door and takes her elbow. "Look, come with me across the street and get something to eat. Before that guy finishes his call and I'm stuck again."

"Thank you. But I'm needed at home. My life has suddenly gotten very complicated."

"Geez. Can I help?"

"Yes. You can. You can retract your offer to my husband and convince the College that you don't want us to move to Arizona. Then you can persuade the tenant to let me live in my own home. Perhaps *he* would like to build your theme park."

"Geez."

"Stop saying that. You sound like some rustic who's never done anyone a bit of harm. You know—the one consolation I've always had for my impoverished life in Oxford was that my children were safe."

"Arizona's not the moon."

"No, it's a million kilometer shooting park. A fact which is—in no small part—due to your stock-in-trade, and though I'm trying not to cast the first stone, I find the whole concept just a bit much right now."

"Look, if it makes you feel better, I'm selling the—"

Diana holds up her palm, which is trembling slightly. "I'm told the scorpions nest in shoes and are fatal to small children. But not to worry! Between rattlesnakes in the garden and black widows in the cupboard, the scorpions will seem positively *dainty*. No, it's not the moon, Mr. Gold. The moon is *known* to be uninhabitable."

* * *

Two mornings later Wally is packing for the plane. For the twentieth time in two minutes, he presses his hand to the logo on his alligator shirt, searching the nonexistent pocket for glasses that can't be found. Wally's suitcase groans on the bed, overflowing with presents for his daughter, Audrey. He moves to the phone, presses the number for the front desk. He shakes his head at the bleating busy signal, rummages through his things, shakes his head again. He squints at the pad of paper next to the desk and fumbles with the numbers on the phone.

"Diana?" he asks. "Oh, sorry. Hey, you don't know the *Livelys*, do you? No. Sorry. Sorry."

Wally presses 192, England's version of 411. "Hi there. Hey, do you have a number for Lively? Ted? Theodore? Theodore! Jesus, *that's* perfect."

Wally scrawls the number in huge letters and then waits while the operator connects him.

"Hello, Diana? Diana?" There is a pause while Wally listens to the rest of the recorded message. The beep startles him. He clears his throat. "Hi, uh, Wally Gold, here. I'm leaving in a few minutes. Just thought I'd say thanks. For tea the other day. And for getting my passport back to me." Wally shakes his head and hangs up the phone.

"I'm a moron!" he mutters, bringing his hands up to grab his temples. He dials the front desk, gets a busy signal, and throws the whole phone against the pillow.

A slight crunch reports that his glasses have now been found.

Wally reaches under the pillow case to retrieve them. One side is a spiderweb blossom of cracks, but the other is virtually unchanged. Wally sinks to the couch and looks gratefully up to the ceiling. "Mary Kate?" he wonders. "Mary Kate?"

When he picks up the phone again, and dials the front desk, Wally is jubilant. "Look, send me some biscuits and gravy, Room 112. Right, that's right. It's an American breakfast thing. You just pour the gravy over the top of the biscuits and that's it. Look, miss, you're not *eating* it, are you? I don't care if you have to send to London for 'em, just get me them before the car gets here and I'll throw in twenty pounds for you." Wally hangs up the phone and shakes his head, but this is an entirely different bend of neck, chin, and chest. This is a head shaken in wonder and awe. He sits lost in thought, smiling broadly.

He continues to grin, even when his breakfast arrives and the plate cover is lifted to reveal six chocolate cookies displayed in a crescent pattern and covered in thickened veal stock. He hands the waiter twenty-five pounds, for Wally is nothing if not a man of his word.

And so it is that Wally spends his last few minutes in Oxford, winking piratelike through his half-damaged glasses and daintily wiping the chocolate biscuits free of gravy with a white linen *serviette* before popping them into his famished mouth.

* * *

DIANA's mother, Charlotte, is helping her daughter pack up the kitchen. She lets out a frustrated breath at the crumpet cosy she is attempting to fold. Made of white linen, trimmed in lace, and trailing lace-bordered ribbons, it is an unmanageable dirigible of wrinkled cloth.

"P'raps if you roll it, Meemaw?" asks Humphrey.

"I've tried that. Honestly," murmurs Charlotte, "p'raps this should go to Oxfam, darling."

"Loan me a match, I'll put it out of its misery," snorts Ted. "Celebrate Guy Fawkes Day a bit early. Where on earth did you get this *thing*, Diana?"

Ted, at the window seat—ostentatiously idle—looks like Lord Byron splayed back poetically on a set of blue-and-white pillows, his neatly creased pants forming a triangle: the bent knee its apex, the straight leg its hypotenuse. Ted's hair spins the sunlight into golden edges.

Diana cannot help but notice her husband's physical beauty. The more attractive he gets, though, the less she seems able to *feel*. *Why can't I simply give thanks and enjoy?* she asks herself as she sorts cutlery into piles. After all, most of her friends seem to be married to paunchy caricatures of the overfed Oxford professor, whether thick-limbed or thin. Even Mary Colville's husband, George, once so utterly gorgeous, has greyed with time: hair, beard, skin, teeth, blending into the same transparent pallor. Diana's keen visual sense cannot help but register her good fortune, cannot help but register Ted's glow, his chiseled languorous expressions. Nevertheless, there is this growing sense of distance, of a remove she cannot master.

"Diana? Are you with us?" asks Ted, causing his wife to jump.

"The Markesons, I think," offers Diana, who has become adept at following her husband's queries while veering off on her own tangents. "Wedding gift. Or your aunt Lizzy, p'raps?"

"Elspeth would *never*," laughs Ted, quickly scanning Charlotte's expression for any suggestion of disapproval awakened by the working-class taint of "Lizzy." "Mother, you must rest," he says, letting his tongue caress the word *mother*.

As Ted is prone to see things, use of this endearment confers Charlotte's august lineage on him, in a hand-in-marriage sort of way. "You've been working too hard. We'll sort all this out."

"Well, I don't mind pitching in with Diana and Humphrey, Ted. I love them and I'd like to lighten their load," Charlotte says pointedly.

"You do know that my patron is paying for this move, Mother? I keep telling Diana that, and yet *she* insists on duplicating the movers' efforts."

"We *do* have to decide what to take, Ted," Diana murmurs.

"Why? I say, let Mr. Gold move our entire household. We should not lift a finger. You heard him insist that this not be hard on you or the children. So take him at his word."

"Have you any idea what moving our entire household would cost, Ted?"

"So what, Diana? He's got it. And he wants me. I think I've been inconvenienced enough."

"A bit tricky, taking everything, Ted," Humphrey says evenly. "We don't know what the house'll be like."

"I think we can imagine," snorts Ted. "You saw his suit. Picture *petit bourgeois* overstatement and multiply it geometrically."

"Whatever you might say about Wally, Ted, he's not *petit bourgeois*."

"Oh, we're on a first-name basis with the man, are we? I'd have thought your tastes a bit more refined, Diana. Allow me to be more precise. Take a Blackpool soccer yaboo, cross him with a Cockney fishmonger, throw in too much money, too few manners, and wrap in something cheap and cheerful. He's Donald Trump on a stocky scale. Or who's that awful chap who narrates *Lifestyles of the Rich and Famous*? Robin Something?"

"You know, I thought his clothes were rather nice," ventures Humphrey, rolling a set of shrimp forks in a yellow napkin. "Probably an American cut that threw you."

"My point precisely. You'll notice your *daughter* abstaining from discussing my employer, Charlotte?" Ted winks conspiratorially at his mother-in-law, who is now helping Diana fold a damask tablecloth. "He's besotted with her, poor man."

"Ted, the poor man is grieving for his wife," Diana says sternly, bringing the cloth's edge to her lips.

"How did she die, again?" asks Charlotte.

"A drowning accident. A river boat," Diana says.

"Raft, Mum," offers Humphrey. "River-rafting. Nigel Thompson did it last year in America."

"Right. He was booked to go, too, but had to cancel at the last minute. So on top of losing her, I imagine he feels if only he'd gone, he might have prevented it."

"That's awful," murmurs Charlotte.

"When did you discover these bits, Diana?" asks Ted, eyeing his wife. "It sounds like an awfully intimate discussion to have with a virtual stranger."

"Wasn't a bit intimate, Ted. The day he bought takeaway pizza for tea, he was talking about it quite openly. William asked how his wife had died. That's all."

"Say what you will. He's clearly infatuated with you. Ever since I mentioned your bloodlines."

Charlotte is surprised to see her daughter's neck blotch crimson as she drops one corner of the tablecloth. "Honestly, Ted," snorts Diana. "Would you *please* give this a rest. You couldn't be more mistaken about him. He wouldn't give a fig about the English caste system. Why should he? He's what the Americans call a self-made man."

"Have you forgotten how this man's money was made, Diana?"

No, I haven't. But we don't know—"

"How's that, Mum?" asks Humphrey.

"Oh, she's neglected to mention it to you? Very interesting, Diana. You normally have very little tolerance for merchants of death."

"As I said—"

"How's that, Mum?"

"I believe he's involved—"

"Not just involved, Diana. I ran a search on the Net. The man has no shame. His Web site calls him 'The Ammo King.' 'Involved' is an understatement. The man is the largest ammunitions consolidator in the Wild Wild West. So he's self-made, all right. Self-made on a heap of corpses. That's our benefactor. Wallace Gold, the Ammo King. Not surprising, really, that he's so taken with the King Arthur legend. A chance to heal the land after the slaughter of war and destruction."

"Well, at least he's penitent," stammers Humphrey, watching his mother's troubled expression.

"I doubt it," Ted snorts. "But he sees the tide is turning, wants to tuck into a wave and come out smelling of something better than blood. Bathe himself in the waters of forgiveness. If he compensates us well enough, we'll confer him with new status. Who better than the child and widow of a slaughtered man, who better than the world's leading scholar on Arthurian legend? All he needs do is throw money at the College, and Paul will sacrifice our family's reputation to purchase a new soul for Wallace Gold."

"Is this true, Mum?" asks Humphrey, setting his palm on Diana's shoulder. "Mum?"

Diana waits until she's finished counting spoons, then sets them into their case and turns to her son. "I don't know, Humphrey. As I understand it, his firm is rather like a trade union that brings the small shopkeepers together to negotiate rates with the large ammunition vendors. He was in the Vietnam War, and when he came out of it, it was what he was trained to do."

Ted wipes his brow theatrically. "Oh, so he's an altruist now? Look, I feel no compunction about spending as much as I can of his money. No compunction at all!"

"Why don't you simply refuse to go?" asks Charlotte, noting that her daughter has turned her back on Ted and is straightening the fringe on the kitchen carpet.

"I've tried! The president of my College won't take no for an answer! So much for academic freedom."

"So," muses Humphrey. "Would you refuse a Nobel Prize then? That's arms money, too."

"That's completely different and you know it, Humphrey. I'm surprised at you, having done so well on your A-levels, turning to sophistry. Especially in defense of America's Ammo King. I should think you'd have more respect for your father's memory than that."

"I'm not defending the man. It's just that bit about not casting the first stone."

"I never thought my wife and children came so cheaply. The man buys one takeaway pizza and they're willing to—"

"Honestly, Ted! I think I speak for Humphrey and the rest of the children as well when I say that, much as we wish we could stay in our cosy home, we've accepted the fact that we are going. We might as well make the best of it."

"Baa . . . Diana, baa! Perhaps when you have less to lose, you can be philosophical, but my whole academic career is in jeopardy because of this man's insanity. Sorry to say: It's not so easy for me to go along. In fact, while I may be forced to accompany the man on his fool's errand, there's nothing to say I will not do my best to insure we're not held there a moment longer than it requires to bring this goose chase to a screeching halt and return the Livelys to their rightful place in the south of England."

* * *

EXITING the automatic doors for Terminal Two, Wally notices first the press of heat rising up from the sidewalk, and second, Audrey's 1972 VW van at the curb. She is standing in her Catholic school uniform of pleated skirt and Peter Pan–collared shirt, pleading with a cop, who is writing her up. "Daddy!" she shouts, running towards him, her beaded earrings slapping back at her poker-straight blond hair, the fringe on her knee-high moccasins keeping time with her stride.

The cop is grinning as he hands Wally a ticket. "Hey, I saw you at that Diamondbacks game last spring. Aren't you the Ammo King?"

"In a past life," says Wally, squinting at the ticket. "How's the Squaw Peak lookin'? Traffic still up to here?"

"Nah. They finished the construction last week. Sorry about the ticket."

"That's okay. Audrey's got this sense that rules don't apply to her. Not your fault."

Wally heaves himself into the passenger side and hands his daughter the ticket. "Another for your collection," he says. "That's fifty bucks less for EARTHCARE."

Audrey refuses to acknowledge the piece of paper in her peripheral vision as she pulls out onto the expressway. She and Wally both know that he'll end up paying it. Her allowance will not be diverted from starving children and the hole in the ozone to line the pockets of a useless bureaucracy enforcing the brutal dictates of a status quo.

"How was your trip?" Audrey asks, patting her father's hand just vigorously enough to push the ticket back onto his lap.

"Good. You okay?"

"I missed you. And Guy woke me up in the middle of the night, hitting the redial button. 'Sorry, Audrey. I'm just so out of it in the middle of the night.' What's that about? You can't call your friends during daylight hours?"

"I'm selling the business, kiddo."

In twenty-two seconds they are on the shoulder of the road. Cars whiz past, shaking the van. Audrey's bright blue eyes are fastened on the worried deep brown of her father's. "Don't toy with me, Daddy."

"It's true. We're getting out. Guy is full of doom and gloom, so don't you start."

"*Moi?* I'm thrilled! I knew if I just planted the seed, you'd realize that—"

"The thing is, Audrey, I like the idea of the kibbutz and all. But—"

"You *can't* sell the business and not do the kibbutz. You've got to even out the yin with the yang or the whole thing's useless!"

"Look, honey. I'm gonna do good with the money. Just, this is for your mom. She loved all that King Arthur stuff. Remember how she used to read to you at bedtime? In the hotel—" Wally raises his hands. His voice catches. "Look, you know selling the business has been a long time coming. And making a fun place for kids . . . I know this sounds crazy, but I was praying to your mom when—"

"Dad. Mom is *gone*. This is not healthy."

"Listen, sweetie, this is gonna sound crazy, but your mom's been giving me signs. Not just one, either. You know how she used to stick my glasses between the pillowcase and the pillow when she made the bed? And I'd keep getting into bed and breaking them? Well, look!" Wally fishes his glasses out from his briefcase and presents them to his daughter.

"Dad, you're scaring me. If you would just read my proposal—"

"She did it in England, Audrey! And that's not all." Wally reaches into his back pocket and pulls out his passport. "You know how your mom was about the Ammo King campaign. How it was *her* idea and how she used to play Barbies with you and you'd dress Ken up like the king? Well, look at this." Wally opens the page to reveal his picture, clotted with royal symbols, a crown jauntily attached, an ermine negligee that doubles nicely as princely cloak. "Audrey, I swear to God, I have *no* idea how this got here. I opened it at Customs and there it was."

Audrey shakes her head like a dog getting rid of water. She takes her father's hand and gives it a sympathetic squeeze. "Okay, so I get it that you have to sell the company. I'm all for that. But what's stopping you from doing the kibbutz? I think you'd see that the Israeli model could transform the lives of the tribe in a way that—"

Wally reaches over and gently places his oversized hand under his daughter's chin. "Audrey. You know, we're never gonna know whether or not—"

"Paperwork doesn't matter, Daddy. I know right here," Audrey whispers, pointing to her heart. "Every time I see those Indian kids downtown without any shoes, I know. Like you always say, there's knowing and there's *knowing*. I just know."

* * *

DIANA is pacing in the sunroom. A large table holds her latest project, a three-story Tudor, commissioned by her friend Evelyn for her husband's birthday. It's a copy of Simon's childhood house, which Diana has reconstructed down to the tiny stone lions at the entrance.

Evelyn and Diana have been friends since boarding school when they were seven, the standard age for upper-class British children to be yanked from their happy homes and taught a thing or two about stiff upper lips and the many-splendoured textures of porridge.

Both girls had been sent to England on the same plane from Afghanistan, where Diana's father was in the foreign service and Evelyn's ran a large manufacturing plant. They had arrived at the terminal exhausted and frightened, all the more so when no one from the school had arrived to meet them. In the two hours of waiting and uncertainty, the girls had moved progressively closer to each other, finally sharing the same undersized Lucite seat. Evelyn—one month older and taking her seniority to heart—had offered Diana half of her last bag of sweets. Through the first bleak year of grey Church of England rituals, the two girls had become inseparable, made all the more so by a forbidding, undemonstrative school staff and a pack of flint-hearted schoolmates. Years later Evelyn introduced Diana to Johnny, whom she'd met at University. At their wedding, Evelyn had drunk to her two best friends, who'd done her the honor of cutting her phone and petrol costs in two by residing in the same location. When Diana had gotten pregnant with Humphrey, Evelyn had shamelessly hinted that first, *Evelyn* was a genderless name of literary and historical value, and second, that the baby's parents would never have been so happy were it not for her matchmaking. When Johnny was killed, Evelyn had mourned him with such dramatic ferocity that Ted—seeing her for the first time at the funeral—had mistaken her for the widow. This misunderstanding—and Evelyn's misplaced fury when he'd offered his condolences—he'd never forgotten. "She has to be the center of attention, even at Johnny's funeral. She outwept you, for God's sake."

"You just don't understand Evelyn, Ted," Diana had said. "She's always been high-strung and she's always spoken up for me when I've been too shy to express myself completely."

It hadn't surprised Diana when later, Evelyn objected to her marrying Ted, nor when Ted had vetoed Diana's plan to name Eleanor after Evelyn.

"You two will fight at my funeral," Diana had said to Evelyn recently, when Ted had precipitously deserted a dinner party after Evelyn had beaten him at bridge.

"First off, if you die first, I shall hunt you down and kill you," retorted Evelyn, with tears in her warm brown eyes. "My only hope for you and the children's happiness is a swift but painful death for that man. He is insured, Diana?"

Diana had given up trying to bring Evelyn and Ted to any sort of rapprochement in their continual warfare. She knew that Evelyn never saw the more vulnerable side of Ted, a side made all the more remarkable by the fact that he'd chosen to reveal it at the very time that Diana had needed it most, shortly after Johnny's death, when most of the people she knew were preoccupied with her tragedy. She'd become everyone's pet charity. Their bleeding-heart eyes said it all: *Poor Diana Sennett, what an awful thing.* Ted, though, breezing through the door with a packet of sweets for Humphrey, never wore that look. He saw her as a whole person, someone who wanted to be needed, not simply pitied.

In fact, many of Diana's early conversations with Ted—whom she'd met for the first time at Johnny's funeral—had centered around an epiphany he'd undergone the moment he'd seen his classmate's coffin. Ted had realized that since his own father's passing, he'd been repressing any memories of his childhood, a time dominated by the uncertainty of living with a gambler for a father, a time of constant want, inadequate food, housing, or clothes, to say nothing of education. Ted had begun to stop in regularly, to check on his classmate's widow and, with a candour that was refreshing, had shared his emotional journey without reservation. Diana, glad of the chance to focus on someone else's sorrow, had given him the name of the grief-support group her mother was insisting she attend. Diana had been touched by the fact that Ted treated her normally, without the kid gloves of horrified sympathy with which others seemed to approach the grieving widow. Over time, as more and more of his childhood emerged, she'd come to admire the ascent Ted had made, from public housing to Oxford's most prestigious college, and where others saw flaws, such as his frugality and controlling behaviour, Diana had glimpsed a five-year-old, desperately trying to create order in a life where predictability was scarce.

Now, Diana forces herself to move back to the table, away from her senseless pacing. She picks up a tiny brush and begins to stain the wooden cross-hatching with cocoa-brown paint. She is expecting Evelyn, who is bringing a remnant of flocked wallpaper for the tiny sitting room walls. Though Diana tells herself she's calmer now that she's begun to work again, she knows better.

Rather than providing Diana the relief she'd hoped, being nearly finished with this last dollhouse has only heightened her anxiety. The trip yawns before her, a chasm of unknowns. In a week she will step out of a plane into a landscape she expects to look like the American Westerns she's seen as a child. Dust will be blowing into a brown nothingness, coiled snakes and large furry spiders will scuttle before her feet like herds of cattle. The sun will be blindingly, screechingly hot. It makes her thirsty just thinking of it.

When the doorbell rings, Diana is carefully sawing the head of a toy antlered deer away from its plastic body. She will mount the head on the dollhouse wall for the billiard room, one of a select menagerie of endangered beasts. Diana trots downstairs holding the saw and almost-decapitated animal. She unbolts the front door, expecting Evelyn.

"Mummy!" shouts Eleanor, whose hand is being held tightly by her playmate Anna's mother. Anna's mother is wearing a Body Shop T-shirt protesting the use of animals as research subjects. "That's Charley!" Eleanor reaches out for the deer and only a quick gasp from Anna's mother causes Diana to move her hand up quickly, pulling the razor-sharp saw with a nearly decapitated deer out of Eleanor's reach.

"Eleanor! Never, ever come near Mummy's tools!" Diana kneels down to deliver this stern message, taking Eleanor's chin in her free hand, her other raised above her head with saw and nearly headless animal. "And it's not Charley, darling. Charley's an antelope. Isn't he? Oh God, it's not Charley, is it! Oh God, I hope not!" Diana stands up, tottering a bit as her knees are stiff. "Thank you so much for having Eleanor, er . . ." She has forgotten Anna's mother's name. She cannot, in her panic, snatch even a surname from the recesses of her stress-drenched brain. "Would Anna like to stay and play for a bit?"

Anna's mother gives an alarmed chirp. "Oh! Better not. I've tea to put—"

"Diana!" interrupts Evelyn, who is coming through the gate. "I've just realized! What will you do with Johnny's ashes? Shall I have them while you're off? I'll put them next to Mummy's on the mantel?"

After Anna and her nameless mother have nearly fallen down the front steps in their rush to go, Diana lays tea. She pours Ribena for Eleanor and scotch for herself and Evelyn. "I'm taking Johnny with me," she tells her friend, after an unladylike gulp of whiskey.

"Bloody selfish of you. What if he gets lost?" says Evelyn rhetorically. "These biscuits taste awful, like someone dipped them in petrol."

"We always talked about going to America."

"Are you all right?"

"No. I'm really not. One *is* supposed to recover from the death of one's spouse after twelve years. So why do I feel so awful?"

"There," soothes Evelyn. "Have a biscuit. They're not half bad if you hold your nose. Here." Evelyn cradles the taller Diana in her well-clad arms and gives her a quick squeeze. "Sit down and I'll pour us more scotch."

"I just feel so guilty. It's unfair to go off like this. He won't know where we are."

"Who? Johnny? You don't give the him much credit, Diana. If the dead can walk through walls, they can bloody well read your travel itinerary. Besides, don't you think he'd have wanted you to enjoy . . . Oh my God! I can't believe it!" Evelyn looks at her friend, horror-struck.

"What?" Diana jumps up and simultaneously swipes an imaginary spider off her chest. Normally, this would amuse Evelyn. Instead, she is still looking at Diana as though she has just announced she has a terminal disease.

"You married Ted as an act of penance."

Diana's eyes widen and she kicks her friend under the table while rolling her eyes dramatically toward Eleanor, who is laying salami slices like flower petals across her plate.

"Ow! Why are you kicking me? Ow!"

"How *can* you be so thick?" asks Diana.

"Naughty Mummy, use your *words*," scolds Eleanor. "Evelyn is your friend. We don't kick friends."

"You're right, darling. We don't kick friends." With this, Diana reaches over and gives Evelyn a ferocious pinch on the cheek.

"Don't kill the messenger, darling. Look at it this way. Starved of love here, starved of love there. What's the huge difference? What is it you're afraid of? That you'll actually enjoy yourself?"

"That's it. Brilliant, Evelyn. I'm terrified of having any sort of fun."

"You said it, darling. And you think our dear departed would want that of you? Do you?"

"I have lots of fun. I love my children. I love my work. I love— you. My life is lovely. It's just a bit of a drain going off and leaving everyone who knows me, for a place where I'll just be another faculty wife with a useless hobby."

"Would you please stop taking yourself apart? Ted does a perfectly good job of that all by himself, without you butting in and mucking up the desolation."

"Evelyn. Enough."

"I must say one last thing, before you flounce off to the Land of Large Servings. I believe what you do with the dollhouses is high art. To say nothing of the drawings for Johnny's book, which I remind you—lest Ted has permanently erased it from your memory—won the Newbery Award. And I know that when you decide to go back to architecture, you'll make a name for yourself. This is genuine, Diana. You've a brilliant gift."

"You're not the least bit biased, Evelyn. You think *anything* I manage to do a bloody miracle!"

Evelyn picks up Diana's glass and inspects it, to see where all the scotch has gone. "Using words like *bloody,* are we? And let me tell you something. You are marvelous. You are a miracle. How can you believe Ted's appraisal of your talents, and not mine? The man wouldn't know art if he stepped in it."

"I'm not sure I appreciate that metaphor."

"You know what, darling, believe me or not"—Evelyn leans forward, tugging slightly on her friend's sleeve—"you're going to adore America. I just know it."

"You do, eh?"

"Yes. Trust me. Sometimes I just know what's best for you."

* * *

TED is grinding away at Fiona, who lies beneath him with the rapt expression of a true devoté. He licks one pert nipple, then its twin, before his next inquiry, which, because of his motion, is tapped out in a pounding staccato. "And Arizona's environmental laws were enacted when?"

"In the early nineteen seventies, with a blow at the mining and logging industry by ahhh . . . assorted groups from Prescott and Tuscan."

"That's Tucson, not Tuscan," corrects Ted. "Not to worry, my fair Fiona. You are an exquisite researcher. Now, which authority controls new construction in the state?"

"It depends on where one is, and the effects."

"You minx. Don't be coy. I want the answer and I know you've got it."

Fiona leans her head back against the pillow, her beautiful chin trembling as she luxuriates in the attention this eminent professor is bestowing upon her. "American civil law is based on the code that one is free to do whatever one needs to make a living, *unless* by doing so, one harms others in the process. *Now,* if you could establish that by building a park, this Gold chap is likely to create pollution that seeps into the watershed of the Colorado River, that might be enough to get the locals in a dither."

"Brilliant. And what's the catch?"

"Who—how did you know there'd be a catch?"

"I can see it in your eyes. So, what's the catch?"

"Well, first off, they're a highly unpredictable lot across the pond. Most Americans see water as absolutely abundant and not worth their while to quarrel over. They've been so blessed with so much in the way of resources, they've come to see water as something completely infinite and expendable. Furthermore, the legal authority over this river is your proverbial rat's nest, with eight states, several federal agencies and at least four Indian Nations involved. And the commission created to govern the watershed spends most of its time fighting among itself, rather than watching out for the common interests of their body politic."

"Oh, speaking of body politics," whispers Ted, nuzzling his tongue into Fiona's left ear. "I'll show you an uprising that you won't soon forget."

* * *

WALLY stands outside the large oak door, shielding his eyes from the sun. He stares at his shoes, looks at his watch, and sighs. He looks at the key he's holding and sighs again. "I hope this is okay with you, Mary Kate. It's time we used the place, don't you think?" he asks, turning and looking up at the cobwebs in the doorjamb.

He opens the front door and strolls through the empty house, writing notes to himself, a new pair of reading glasses slipping on his nose. In the kitchen he leans his elbows over the granite island, looking outside, remembering Mary Kate's insistence that the kitchen windows take up the whole back wall. "I know Audrey's a big girl," she'd said. "But I still want to keep an eye on her when she's in the pool." So she'd found a custom window designer to come in and do the work.

The windows alone had been sixty grand, almost as much as the custom cabinets. The carpenter, a bent old Mexican guy from Apache Junction, had bid thirty, but that was before Mary Kate checked the man's references. The previous client mentioned Mr. Ramirez was in foreclosure for unpaid medical bills. Two days later Mary Kate had typed up her own invoice for the man, doubling his fee. She'd then bullied Guy into running interference at the bank, and had driven Mr. Ramirez downtown to Veterans Affairs, where she sat with him and filled out the mountains of paperwork documenting the man's World War II service. All this without Wally knowing a thing about it until the old man had come up to him after the memorial service. Ramirez had told him the story, clutching Wally's arm like if he didn't hold him up, the bigger man might fall. He'd told Wally he'd pray for Mary Kate, though she wouldn't need it because people like her, they went straight to Heaven, no purgatory.

Wally lifts himself up from the counter and measures the space for the fridge before proceeding outside. He moves past the empty pool, walking the perimeter of the yard, past pink bougainvillea bushes, whose thorny tentacles thrive on neglect. These have flourished during the family's absence.

Wally unlocks a padlocked gate and crosses a long grassy field, a precious desert amenity otherwise known as a "greenbelt," though in neighborhoods like this, it's less like a belt than a boulevard, allowing golf carts, horses, and bichon walkers a place to meander. About sixty yards of emerald turf separate this house—where the Livelys will live—from the one Wally inhabits with his daughter. He opens the arched wooden gate and enters his backyard, where Audrey is tending a twenty-square-foot crop of sugar cane that's planted behind the cabana.

It is Audrey's dream to go to Africa with UNICEF. "I'm not planning to show up like Daddy's little rich girl, who doesn't know how to cut it. I'm gonna know my way around a machete," Audrey has vowed.

Audrey is also experimenting with certain environmentally friendly insecticides, having read that last year's famine had been caused by a particularly stubborn sand-mite carried in on foreign missionaries' shoes. Her solution is made of jalapeño peppers distilled in human urine, then mixed with crushed insects, cobwebs, and tequila. Audrey sprays it out of an old Lalique perfume mister of her mother's, taking special care with the leaves. She catches Wally's reflection in her mirrored aviator glasses.

"Dad?"

"Mornin', sweetie. Sleep okay?"

"Dad, were you . . . did you just come through the gate?"

"This English family I told you about—they need a place to stay. I thought we might as well get some use out of the other house."

Audrey reaches up on tiptoes to feel her father's forehead. "Dad?"

"Hey, you've been after me to sell it."

"I know. But, I don't know. I mean, it's okay, I guess. But it feels funny. All that time thinking we'd live there, and then we didn't. It'll feel weird to have someone—"

"I know. But it—if this guy's gonna help with this tribute to Mom, then maybe he ought to live in her house? See what she was like."

Audrey snorts. "Maybe he can let *us* know."

"Audrey. Don't talk that way."

"What way? Honestly? What're you afraid of, Dad? The Committee to Canonize Mary Katherine Gold might get wind of the fact that she—"

"Audrey, honey, why do you keep going on about this?"

"I won't hide my head in the sand, Dad. "

"Sweetie, your mom got depressed sometimes, but she would never have taken her own life. I swear to you. For one thing, no one was a bigger baby about pain. And another, she loved you too much to ever do that to you."

"Yeah, well, maybe, but, Dad, Mom hated the outdoors. Doesn't it strike you strange? She chooses a class-three river to change her mind?"

"Honey, she did it 'cause she was searching for a way to get—healthy. And she thought I'd like it. If it's anyone's fault, it's mine. Honey, just try and remember what the shrink said."

"If I have one more person tell me about closure, I'm gonna have to throw up."

"Sweetie, you came home from middle school one day and your mom was missing. We had to bury an empty casket. That's not easy, no matter who you are. So stop beating yourself up."

"I'm not."

"But you are, baby."

"Am not."

"Are too," Wally says, drawing his daughter close for a hug. He sighs, knowing that nothing he can say will penetrate the barricades that Audrey has created against a world of uncertainty. Better suicide, with its appearance of volition, than the pull of rapids, the blink of an eye, the swirling confusion of real-time events and missed opportunities coming to the same vanishing point; a hot day gone pointlessly, relentlessly cold, just like that.

* * *

"WALLY?"

"What time is it?"

"I'm paying you back for those calls from England, you asshole."

"What time is it, though?"

"It's only eleven-thirty in Indianapolis."

"Guy, I got up at four-thirty. What is it?"

"I just talked to the CFO for Huntington. They're gonna float an offer tomorrow."

"How much?"

"Forty."

"Holy shit. Guy, remember when the stock was a buck eighty?"

"Look, there's still a lot can go wrong, Wally."

"Forty! I can't even do the math."

"That's why you got me."

"Unbelievable."

"Yeah. But listen, friend. I want you to consider something. The stock sounds high now. But the ammunition division prints money. You sure you wanna do this?"

"Guy."

"No, I'm serious. What the hell do you know about theme parks? I bet you never even went to one. Am I right?"

"Guy, I told you before. They're a place families go to get away from the world. Wouldn't you rather be a part of that than some gangbanger's funeral?"

"Wally, come on. Guns don't kill people, people—"

"Guy, this is me, Wally, not some reporter. You know what the business does to people's lives. I don't need it."

"Okay, so get out. But put your money somewhere safe."

"Safe's not me. You know that."

"Look, if you're gonna throw your money away, why not just give it to Audrey and let her distribute it to whatever tribe she thinks she's descended from this week. At least somebody'd be happy."

"Guy," Wally warns.

"Look, Audrey's like a daughter to me. But she's gone wacko with this Indian thing. She's got blond hair and blue eyes, for Christ's sake!"

"Look, you lose your mom at fourteen and we'll talk. I think you'd be rewriting history, too."

"Wally, all I'm saying is if you're gonna risk your nest egg, why not make the kid happy?"

"I would if I could. But life on the reservation—even if it turned out that Mary Kate's family *did* have Indian blood—Audrey doesn't have a clue. They'd be about as happy with a poor little rich girl trying to save them—"

"Exactly!" interrupts Guy.

"Look, did you call me up in the middle of the night to talk about Audrey?"

"Wally, it's only nine-thirty in Phoenix."

"Guy."

"I'm just saying: You sure you wanna sell? You're throwing away your bread and butter for a merry-go-round in the middle of nowhere. I'm your friend. There's a risk to even *saying* you might sell. If word gets out that Huntington wants to buy you, and they get cold feet, the stock price'll tank. And other buyers won't come near you with a ten-foot pole."

"Warning taken."

"Bullshit. You're gettin' off on the risk."

"Guy, look, do me a favor. You know I never had a religious bone in my body. Something happened to me over there. I don't want to— I'm not so sure now about anything, except one thing. I gotta get out of this business and I gotta show Mary Kate how I feel about her."

"Jesus, Wally. Like Audrey keeps telling you: She's *gone*."

"That's the thing. She is, but she isn't. You can think what you want. You haven't been there and you wouldn't have gotten it if you were. But somehow, I gotta follow through on this."

"Okay, just don't say I didn't warn you. You *poquito loco*, mister, but I love you anyway."

"Look pal, I love you, too. And don't worry about me. I may be crazy, but I've never been more certain of anything in my life. Sometimes you just *know*."

"Yeah, and sometimes you should just *say* no."

"Funny."

"Yeah, laugh now, mister. Laugh now."

Three

Mary Kate's house—soon to be the Livelys'—has a Spanish feel to it. Despite the best-laid plans of Mary Kate's designer friend, the one who'd worked for Glenn Campbell, this house is a haven of simplicity. Its floors are a warm terra-cotta *saltillo*, its walls a sunlit yellow. Arched doorways lead from a two-story great room into a low-ceilinged dining nook complete with fireplace and views of the pool. All the main rooms open onto the U-shaped courtyard where the blue of the newly filled pool reflects a wall of climbing pink bougainvillea. This wall backs to the green belt, which leads to the wall surrounding the Gold's original house, where Wally and Audrey have remained the last three years.

To call it Mary Kate's house is not quite correct, because the very features which Wally loved were the ones that had made Mary Kate shriek for a refund.

"It looks like a Mexican restaurant!" she'd cried, the first day she'd returned from Europe, having left Wally in charge of the contractor. "What happened to my Italian marble? Where's my silk wall treatments?" The fight had gone on all night long, with Wally standing by the architect's advice to "shitcan the fancy stuff " and Mary Kate screaming they'd move into this house over her dead body.

Three weeks later they'd been standing at her memorial service and Wally had begun the intensive daily labor of forgetting they'd ever disagreed. About anything. If it meant locking up a house and never moving in, these were small prices to pay for the trove of good memories he'd been treasuring ever since.

Getting the house ready for the English family had meant hiring cleaning crews and painters and shopping for furniture. Wally had spent a small fortune in the past week, filling the house with massive rough-hewn oak tables and armoires, overstuffed chairs and sofas, comfortable beds. He'd stocked the library with Mary Kate's favorite books and found brightly colored paintings at a charity auction: large Mestizo women carrying water jugs, farm workers hoeing rows of beans, the backgrounds dwarfed by the giant brown bodies. It was an inversion of the way most people felt about the desert.

"I feel like I moved to the planet Neptune!" Mary Kate had complained, the first time he'd met her, all those years ago, at the Small Business Start-Up Course run by the Department of Labor. "I'm used to seeing trees around me. Protecting me. Here, I'm just sitting out, waiting for the spaceship to plunk down and fetch me for their latest experiment."

Wally—already smitten—had laughed and swallowed his usually vehement defense of the desert. "I love seeing the horizon. It's like the beach."

"Yeah, except where's the water?" she'd said. "You *poquito loco,* mister, but I like you anyway. I might just do a party for you, at cost. How else you gonna let your vendors know what you got to offer?"

Wally still remembered the way his stomach had cramped up when Mary Kate suggested that party. He'd passed the anxiety off as withdrawal from weed, which he'd stopped smoking a month before. Later, though, he realized he'd gotten nervous because he knew Mary Kate's party would put his idea out there for vendors to shoot down. Up till then he'd been in the ozone of planning, driven by the vision he'd had that last day at the store.

Guy's dad had been in the gun business for twenty years, and Wally had worked the front counter up to the end, the day the bill from Viking Ammunitions had swamped the boat with so much water they couldn't float anymore.

Six grand when Wally had figured three.

"Hey, I don't get it. I ordered these same supplies in the Army and I know the unit costs by heart. What's the deal?" he'd asked the Viking rep.

"Oh, they get a special price on account of how much business they do with us," the rep had smirked, avoiding the sound of Guy's dad's oxygen tank rumbling in the back room, avoiding Wally's eyes.

Wally had gotten mad enough to start thinking: If all the little old men in their tiny little shops got together, they could put this twerp in their own special headlock and give him what-for. He'd stopped smoking pot that day and had started going downtown to talk to the men in the Senior Corps of Retired Executives about how to start his own business. Mr. Fauntleroy had been a consolidator back East, and he'd given Wally enough information to get started. The banks wanted a business plan before they'd loan him money, though, so he'd taken this course, met Mary Kate, and that was that.

Before the end of the first week, she'd decided on the party and he couldn't figure out how to get out of it. Later, even Mary Kate had admitted that endive stuffed with salmon aspic and *kir* cocktails hadn't been the way to go, but at least by the time Guy got back with beer and pizza, his prospective clients had stayed sober long enough to see Wally's presentation. The idea was simple: If they banded together, they'd have more bargaining power and they'd get more for their money. It was simple and when their network grew big enough, they'd see the price of ammunition decline to what the franchises got.

Wally's business, by the end of the first year, had already signed two hundred stores. Mary Kate, on the other hand, couldn't seem to find her niche. Rich people met party planners at their country clubs, and the middle class couldn't afford to hire someone to tell them what they could read in *Good Housekeeping* on their own. When he saw she was having trouble making ends meet, Wally invited Mary Kate to move in with him. She'd decorated his apartment with white couches, white carpets, ficus trees, chrome-framed glass coffee tables. The day he'd come home and found an army of these German Hummell things all over the tables, he'd told Mary Kate it was time they looked for something bigger.

"How did you know?" she'd asked, her eyes bright with tears.

"Know what?" he'd asked, poised to deny every detail of his true feelings about what she'd done to his apartment. She'd had nothing but one disappointment after the other lately. This wasn't the time to confess he felt like he was living in a hotel with his aunt Elsie and the Seven Dwarfs.

"I'm pregnant," she'd whispered back and Wally had whooped and swept her up and carried her around the apartment in a victory dance. Two months later they'd closed on a new house on Camelback Mountain, where they'd lived happily ever after, or at least that was how Wally saw it, until fifteen years later the helicopters stopped searching, and Wally had to admit that sometimes, things didn't turn out for the best, after all. It was a longstanding argument he'd had with Mary Kate, who was always calling him the last great optimist. That awful day, just to prove her right, when she'd finally made her point, not even all the king's horses and all the king's men could bring her back home to enjoy her final Pyrrich win.

*   *   *

"ALL my bags are packed, I'm ready to go!" croons Humphrey as he lovingly secures a sheer collar of navy chiffon round a nosegay of forget-me-nots. "I'm standing here, outside your door! I hate to wake you up to say goodbye!"

"Too late for that, by half," mutters Diana, smooching her son on the cheek as she scoots past him towards the kettle.

"Where's the pater?"

"In my carry-on."

"Sorry. Not Daddy. I meant Ted."

"Oh. Sorry. Spent the night at the College. One last chance with his first editions. That's pretty."

"Isn't it, though?" says Humphrey, cinching the chiffon evenly into pleats around the tie. "It's for the Jenkins. They're so good to take the Royal Mother."

"I know. William's beside himself that she'll not know why we've left her."

Humphrey responds with a short sniff.

"It doesn't bear much thinking, does it?" asks Diana, dropping sugar cubes one by one into her cup. "Poor dear."

"Oh, stop. She has barely acknowledged our existence except to sleep in William's bed from time to time. She'll not know we're even gone."

"I'm not sure about that, Humphrey. Cats are far more dependent than you think."

"Mum, you are a hopeless romantic. That cat has as many emotions as . . ." At this, Humphrey casts around the room for an example. "Ted."

"That was uncalled for."

"Sorry. I do hope the poor cat didn't hear me."

"Humphrey!"

"No. I mean it. I've taken a vow to be kinder to animals."

"It's not his fault, Humphrey."

"What's that?"

"It's not Ted's fault you're being dragged off to America."

"Are you joking? I'm thrilled. Now I've got something to say to all those dreadful people who ask what I'm *doing* with my gap year. Arizona has a lovely exotic ring to it. Perhaps not quite as good as cycling through Azerbaijan or coaching illiterates in Africa, but it's got that lovely capital A at the helm. So what if all I do is watch telly and loll about."

"You do *so* much, Humphrey. You mustn't think of yourself that way. I'm just worried you'll be bored."

"Yes, well, don't you worry about that. With your hopeless self-concept, William's table manners, and Eleanor's shrieking thievery, I'll have blood, sweat, and tears to fill my every waking moment."

* * *

IT's one a.m. in Arizona. Way past Wally's bedtime, but he can't get to sleep. The Huntington offer is in. Hard to believe, enough to pay everything off and then some. Enough to build a smallish King Arthur Museum and Fun Park, if the estimates from the themed entertainment consultants were anywhere close. Enough if he is careful. He can hear Mary Kate now. *You, careful? Not in this lifetime, mister.* Not like she was any better with money. They'd made Guy crazy with the way they didn't keep track of things, so much so that even after Mary Kate was killed, Guy had raised hell about a million-dollar account she'd closed out without telling him. She'd written a check to herself, with "furnishings" on the memo line. Nothing ever shipped in that would have explained the cost, just like Wally could have told him. He could see from the state of her handwriting where she'd been when she wrote that check, and it wasn't anywhere in *this* universe.

That night when Guy had gone on about the missing money in Mary Kate's account, that had been the closest Wally'd ever come to hitting his best friend. The only thing that kept him civil was Audrey's presence in the next room with three of her classmates. That, plus the fact that Guy had always had a soft spot for Mary Kate, no matter how bad she got. How many times had Wally gone to bed and left the two of them up talking, knowing Guy'd laugh at her stories no matter how many times she repeated them? Complaining was just Guy's way of showing he cared. Every time Wally'd dipped into his line of credit, every time they'd expanded the company, Guy was bent over, holding his stomach and crying in his beer. So why was Wally letting what Guy had said the other night keep him from sleeping?

So what if he'd never been to Disney? So what? He'd been busy pulling up the stock to friggin' forty dollars, and he'd be damned if Guy would make him feel guilty about it after all this time. With this last thought, Wally rolls over and forces himself to count the ways he'll make things right.

* * *

FIFTEEN pieces of luggage are piled in the cloakroom, waiting for the arrival of the taxis. The passports and tickets are with Ted, who hasn't yet returned from the College. Humphrey and William have taken Eleanor on a last walk round their tiny street.

Diana is glad of the quiet. She removes a small framed picture from the carry-on, removes an egg-shaped bronze urn, and holds them cupped, one in each hand. A smiling young man stares back at her. She returns his gaze, mirroring his affection. "Another adventure, Johnny," Diana whispers. "We always planned this." She secretively folds the frame and returns it to her bag just as Ted bursts into the room.

"What are the children doing chatting up the neighbors? I thought I said to have them ready!"

"They *are* ready. We've been waiting for *you*. I just sent them out for a bit of fresh air. P'raps you'd fetch them, while I ring the taxi?"

"I have things of my own to do," Ted says, leaning down to tie his shoes. "Sorry, but I do," he adds, as though trying to convince himself that, otherwise, he'd be ever so happy to help.

Five minutes later the family is crowded onto the stairs inside the front door, at Ted's insistence, waiting for two oversized taxis that will take fifteen minutes to arrive. William is using his forefinger to jiggle a molar that's loosening. Eleanor is seated at her father's feet, playing with his shoelaces. Humphrey is quietly going over the checklist he and his mother have drawn up. Their voices have an almost elegiac rhythm as they recite the familiar items one last time: lights, lights, gas, gas, rubbish, rubbish, list, list, sheets, sheets, books, books.

"Please!" scolds Ted. "I can't concentrate on the fare if you prattle on. Those Hindi taxi drivers are likely to fleece—Eleanor. Sit! Could you please stop fidgeting! Do not move a centimeter. I know you're able to behave as should a proper child, if only certain parties wouldn't *insist* on spoiling you. Let's just stay at Daddy's feet and concentrate on how we might stay still for two seconds. Think of the upcoming trip, for God's sake."

When the taxis finally arrive, Ted bolts out the door like a general into battle. He is shouting orders behind him, his arms powered like windmills against the imponderable odds of moving quickly with shoelaces that are tied tightly together. It is as though his brain cannot accommodate the notion that Eleanor's pickpocket skills are equally suited to other surreptitious ends.

He chugs forward despite his daughter's handiwork, in a frenetically accelerated, ankle-tied waddle, grasping desperately for the railing before diving down the steps, headfirst. He lands in a clumsy push-up and shouts "Eleanor!" Diana, Humphrey, William, even the two taximen, are caught in a slow-motion pantomime of wanting to help, trying to catch him, while Eleanor—proud of having learned to tie shoes at such an early age—daintily jumps past his prone body, shaking her fists in the air together like a triumphant pugilist. This is a competition and she is the rightful victor. With that, she runs for the open taxi doors. "I call jump seat, William!" she cries happily. "Last one in is a beastly Tory!"

Four hours later the Livelys are belted into the middle aisle of the jumbo British Airways jet, flying from Gatwick to Sky Harbor Airport in Phoenix. Ted, William, Diana, Eleanor, and Humphrey, cosy as peas in a pod, excepting the fact that Ted is glumly inspecting his scratched palms and refusing to speak to Eleanor.

His daughter appears singularly untroubled by her father's snub. She pulls at Humphrey's sleeve and cries excitedly, "We're falling! We're falling!" As Diana has taken a tranquilizer, Eleanor's antics cause her mother only a mild shiver. Each member of the family has a small water bottle in front of them, to avoid dehydration. Diana drains hers before falling asleep. She wakes with William tugging at her arm.

"Mum, my tooth!" William holds out his molar proudly, its smooth white surface clotted with a stem of bloody tissue. "Where'll I keep it?"

Diana hands him her empty water bottle and goes back to sleep. The next hour is punctuated by visits from flight attendants bearing trays, drinks, pillows, blankets. The noise of Eleanor whining for Tubby-tubbies, as she calls her favorite program, the soothing sounds of Humphrey offering her his water bottle to pour into hers, so she can play scientist. Diana closes her eyes, thanking God and the urn of his late father's ashes, that Humphrey is so inventive.

She falls back to sleep, jostled now and then by Eleanor's appropriation of all arms-reach cups and bottles for her pouring project. Diana is dreaming of Johnny, dreaming he's alive. They are in a car, and he is driving on the wrong side of the road, singing a Talking Heads song in his public school accent. Suddenly he is pinching her arm. "Stop it, John, that hurts!" she scolds.

Ted pinches her arm again and Diana pries open her eyes, wondering what Ted's heard. Has she revealed herself?

Apparently not, as Ted's expression hasn't a trace of the wounded puppy. More like cat in mid-hiss. "Where's my water? I left it here right before I went to sleep and now it's gone."

"I don't know," says Diana. She offers a silent prayer of thanks that she hasn't blurted Johnny's name aloud. Ted's equilibrium is already off kilter. He has convinced himself that the larger academic universe is focused solely on enjoying the spectacle of his humiliating ejection to the wilds of Arizona. "Here, take this," Diana murmurs soothingly, appropriating a nearly full bottle from Eleanor's tray table. "Now, may I *please* go back to sleep?"

Too late she notices William's tooth bobbing in the upside down wake of Ted's water. Ted—in his thirst—has quickly drunk half the bottle. How will she explain herself?

It is at this moment that William's eyes widen with realization. He is looking at his father with a mixture of fear, admiration, disgust. William and Diana exchange wide-eyed glances, then both close their eyes and wait for the eruption that is sure to come.

"Auughh! Auughh!" explodes Ted, spraying water across the back of the seat in front of him. Two flight attendants are nearby. They rush over, wiping their hands on cocktail napkins. The tall Whitney Houston look-alike asks, "Are you all right, sir?"

Ted holds up his British Airways bottle indignantly. "Auughh! Would you mind telling me how this got into my water?! Auughh!"

The two flight attendants crouch forward to squint at the bottle before involuntarily backing away.

"Euew!" Whitney is wincing apologetically, as though she herself has shed a tooth and squirreled it away in Ted's bottle of mineral water. "Might we get you another?"

"Or a cocktail, perhaps?" offers her blond companion.

"There's a free chair in First Class, if you'd like," adds Whitney.

Ted is still harrumphing about hiring a solicitor as they escort him to the front of the plane and away from William and his mother, who have been holding hands rather fervently during this whole exchange, their squeezes a Morse code of *Omerta* as well as a kinetic tactic to freeze their expressions of solemnity against the sparks of hysteria igniting within.

* * *

"BRENNER? Got a wrench in your hand?"

"You know it. But I can talk. We're waiting on a tow truck anyhow."

Brenner, like Guy, is one of Wally's friends from Vietnam, someone who knew him before he made his money. Brenner lives in northern Arizona, in a town named Dreamy Draw. His real name is Frank, but no one calls him that, not since the day he shaved his head and rubbed it with baby oil in 1973, in the long-haired days when the only bald man anyone knew about was Yul Brenner, from *The King and I.* "So, how's it hanging, Wally? How's Audrey?"

"Great. She got an A on her community service project up at your place."

"That's great, man. Ravenna hated to see her and her friends go. The town square never looked so good. I love this free yard work concept, specially when it's a bunch of good-looking white girls from the city. So," Brenner asks, after a pregnant pause. "Why you calling?"

"Can you keep a secret?" Wally asks.

The question is rhetorical. Like Guy, Brenner is someone Wally trusts completely.

Unlike Guy, Brenner listens to Wally's plans without a peep, and when he's done, all he says is "Sweet. Mary Kate woulda been all over that. But you gotta make the food better than in most of those parks, or you'll have her turning over in her grave."

Mary Kate had taught Brenner to cook, the year after he'd tried to kill himself with an overdose of Percoset. Everyone else, including Wally, had been so nervous, always trying to figure it out, why his friend would do something like that, but Mary Kate had this ability to just sit and "be" with somebody in pain, whether it was Wally's mom with the cancer, or Brenner with his black depression. She'd sent Wally back to work and let Brenner spend time with her and Audrey, who was just two years old. One day she took him to the mall and bought him a black lab puppy that shed all over her white carpets. On any given day Wally would come home for lunch and find the three of them, sad man, happy dog, and bouyant toddler, within two feet of Mary Kate, no matter what she was trying to do, whether it was paying bills or talking on the phone or painting her nails. This would have made most people crazy, but not Mary Kate. She just hugged Brenner, let him be, and fed him good food. When he was ready, she taught him how to cook for himself. From there on in, Mary Kate could do no wrong in Brenner's eyes, and even when he'd gotten back on his feet and bought the Harley dealership up north, he'd made it a point to return to the Golds' kitchen whenever his energy flagged, claiming there was something about Mary Kate's coq au vin that mended him. When Mary Kate had been lost in the river, Brenner had led the search parties, tracking the scent with Marvin, the black lab she'd bought him. It was only when Brenner showed up at his back door, shivering from the icy rains that had turned gullies into raging canyon rivers, that Wally could be convinced that his wife was truly, truly gone.

"She'd have liked what you're planning, man. She was nuts about that Camelot stuff. So, where are you thinking to do this?"

"Well, that's the thing I wanted to ask you. You know anyone on the city council over at Lake Havasu City? Someone who could tell me how to approach 'em."

"Wait a minute, I got a better idea. Come check out some property above us on the hill."

Brenner's home, Dreamy Draw, is a tiny town situated in the foothills across the lake from the London Bridge. Brenner is the mayor, so chosen because he's the only middle ground in a town that's equally divided between the old bikers on the right hand and old hippies on the left. Brenner, who owns the Harley store, is married to Ravenna, who owns the bead store. Enough said.

"The lot is totally beautiful, man. Just like Mary Kate, beautiful inside and out," Brenner tells Wally. "Twenty-six acres of plateau, otherworldly plant and animal life, just sitting up in the trees. And the view of the lake'll knock your socks off."

"I don't know, Brenner. It's too far from the Bridge, don't you think?"

"That's the golden part, my friend. We have a perfect view of it, plus, we can have a little ferry business that runs people back and forth. It'd be a gas, man. Part of the attraction. Think about it."

"I will. But hey, I thought the Draw tarred and feathered the last developer who rode into town."

"Not anymore. Them's early days. Right now, we gotta have a new pumping station, a storm water system, you name it. We got seven hundred people, about two of who pay taxes. The rest mostly barter their goods. Somehow, I don't think the backhoe company's gonna accept homemade alpaca Sherpa hats as payment. Long as you don't come in and pave paradise, which we know Audrey's not gonna let happen, I think we can do business. Hell, we could do a lot worse. "

"I'll come up and look around, Brenner. But listen. Don't say a word about this."

"I won't. Last thing I need is anything gettin' out before I figure out how to finesse it. I can make the council come to Jesus, but it won't be automatic. I gotta lay some groundwork, get 'em to understand the severity of our situation."

"Now, you know we're just lookin', Brenner. No commitment till we've seen the land and thought it through."

"Hey, I'm not worried. This piece of land'll sell itself."

* * *

WHEN the Livelys arrive in Phoenix some eleven hours after their departure, Ted is the first to deplane. Never one to pass up a bargain, Ted has done his best to eat and drink everything offered as well as anything passing through the aisle towards someone else's seat. When he leaves, the first-class attendants thank their lucky stars that Oh-Might-I-Try-Some-of-That? is finally on the ground. The attendants are joined in gratitude by Ted's seatmate, a middle-aged lawyer who'd fled to London for her first vacation in six years only to be grilled for eight hours on her way home by If-You-Don't-Mind-My-Asking? about Colorado River water rights and the various ways in which the Arizona Corporation Commission could kill or cut a deal, depending on whose strings were pulled.

Fueled by a half-bottle of champagne and six Absoluts, Ted waits, looking every bit the cat that ate the golden canary as his family straggles through the gangway towards baggage. Humphrey wears his uniform of Oxford-cloth shirt and khaki pants. His blond hair is shiny and curls against his fine-boned features. William, dark like Diana, gives his father a close-mouthed nod before brushing his bangs with the back of his hand. Diana brings up the rear, carrying Eleanor, who is wrapped around her mother like a small blond Kewpie doll with the agile grip of a monkey.

Diana is wearing an elegantly tailored shirtwaist dress that once belonged to her mother and has now come back in style, at least in England's better hotel lobbies. It is a heathery violet color, shot with a faint navy plaid. It looks like the same material as a shirt Mary Kate had gotten for Wally in England. It doesn't seem a fitting question to ask, though, where she got it, not when Diana and her kids have that look of stunned and stranded deer waiting for the bullet.

"Mummy, I want cowlads," moans Eleanor, burying herself into Diana's neck.

William, who's been thinking along the same lines, is disappointed when Diana strokes Eleanor's back and says, "I don't think they have many cowboys here anymore, darling."

"When you get settled in, I'll take you to Rawhide, Eleanor. You, too, William. It's a Wild West town, and they've got cowboys, gunfights, everything," says Wally.

"We'll see," says Diana, shooting Wally a blistering look.

"No, it's all pretend," says Wally. "Not real guns. The kids'll love it."

Wally strides over to help Humphrey with the family's luggage while Ted circles the carousel clutching his laptop and monitoring exiting octogenarians to ensure they've not stolen any of the Livelys' battered suitcases. Diana, stubbornly standing at the row of black leather seats near a window, wants nothing other than to sit down, though she's been sitting for hours. She wants nothing other than to disappear into the nearest dark-paneled cocktail lounge until the next flight departs back to Britain and she can return to the sheltering green-grey mists of normality.

This airport is screechingly bright, lit by sunlight, fluorescent overkill, and neon lurid flashes of clothing. The predominant attire appears to be beach wear, except she has it on good authority that Phoenix is nowhere near the sea. In fact, it is, according to Ted, nowhere near anything.

This geographic remove doesn't seem to have deterred hundreds of travelers hefting golf bags as they shout to one another about the rental car, the limo, the currency exchange, Aunt Sally, jet lag, and a thousand other jauntily broadcast bits of trivia. It is so bright, so loud. William looks as though he would like to sit on her lap and tuck his head into her dress. She wishes she could suggest it, wishes he weren't too old for such things.

She wishes she could sit on her own mother's lap and do the same.

Wally is leading the family out through automatic doors, towards a bright red Suburban, which looks to Diana as though it might be something safari drivers use to fend off elephants. It is huge. Though she doesn't notice it at the time, the pickup zone is littered with these vehicles, which the Catholics call "Mormon station wagons" and the Mormons call "Catholic station wagons," the point being that neither group is known for its concern with overpopulation or global warming, for that matter, which a vocal minority of the locals regard as a hoax perpetrated by East Coast intelligentsia for reasons not yet revealed, but nevertheless compellingly perceived as "special interests." Diana cannot notice the other vehicles because she is far too busy surreptitiously scanning the pavement for rattlesnakes, scorpions, tarantulas, and black widows. She is far too busy trying to mimic a normal relaxed walk while at the same time preparing herself to fend off a lateral attack of slithering monsters. This puts a little bounce in her step, a gait which Wally misinterprets as excitement.

You see, he tells himself as he starts the engine, *it'll all be all right.*

Wally awoke this morning with an uncharacteristic sense of doom, a mood not helped by the sight of Diana, almost catatonic, as she waited to go through Customs. Though it is Ted that Wally has hired for his project, Wally finds himself focusing on Diana, craving her approval.

Wally had forgotten how beautiful she is.

"I hope the house is okay," Wally says, conversationally, to Ted, who is in the passenger seat next to him.

Wally can see Diana in the rearview mirror, clutching the looped handle above her head with both hands, eyeing the bleached rise of the highway like it's the Whale and she's Jonah. She's unbuttoned the top two buttons on her dress, rolled up her sleeves. A fine sheen of sweat has formed on her brow. Her pallor is ghostly white.

"My daughter Audrey's getting some last things for the bedrooms and the pool area," Wally continues. "Hey, William, you like to swim?"

"Yes, sir."

"How about you, Eleanor?"

Eleanor burrows her head into her mother's shoulder.

"She's new at it," Diana murmurs.

"Well, there's a wrought-iron fence between your house and your pool. I had it installed last week. You gotta keep it locked. You boys understand that?" asks Wally, suddenly focused and intense.

Humphrey nods distractedly. His main concern, on the ride from the airport, is how bad the house will be. Though he knows Wally is rich, Humphrey can't rid his mind of an image that keeps rolling in front of his eyes like a fever dream from American sitcoms: mud-orange carpet, mustard walls, avocado tweed furniture. Much as he loves his family, Humphrey doesn't think he could live in a place like that. He'd have to run away to Connecticut and camp on Martha's doorstep, a pilgrim seeking sanctuary from the irredeemably ugly.

At least he's brought his favorite flowered sheets from home, a little something familiar to tide him over. At least his bedroom will be a haven, assuming the walls are a nice soft color that doesn't clash with his favorite designer's soothing pastels.

Humphrey's fears about aesthetics escalate as they drive through neighborhoods in which the gardens appear to be sandlots onto which a handful of boulders have been dropped by careless giants. Here and there a huge totemlike cactus sits like a neglected snowman, nonplussed by the brutal heat. The whole lunar tableaux is backdropped by long, low houses with wrought-iron trim and Moorish-looking archways. The houses are planted out in space, plunked down on the horizon, unrelieved by sheltering trees, naked under the bright sun, waiting.

Little does Humphrey realize, as he recoils from this alien landscape, that they are driving through prime Paradise Valley real estate. This is a neighborhood known for its median home price of nine hundred thousand. Here, art galleries outnumber churches and gardeners work around the clock. Here, in cloistered backyards where Versailles meets Vegas, hired Major League players refine Junior's pitching throw and exercise cabanas vie with in-pool bar facilities as the freshest, finest New Best Thing.

Humphrey is already calculating the mileage between Phoenix and Connecticut when Wally pulls up the mountain, past cascading rock gardens lit by bougainvillea, into the driveway of a large butter-colored stucco house, three intersecting rectangles centered around an oval portico. Lush desert plants caress the base of this house; their blossoms sprout purple, yellow, hot pink.

"This was my wife's project," chats Wally. "She never got to see it finished and I never had the heart to move in. Time the place was used."

This is the first Diana has heard of this house having a personal connection to Wally. She remembers those first few years after Johnny was killed, remembers the cottage they'd shared on his father's friend's estate, remembers the numb, robotlike move with Humphrey, away from the memories. Suddenly she is near tears, feeling the weight of Wally's sadness.

"It will be lovely, I'm sure. We're grateful," she says. She wants to cry, and she wants to comfort this huge man, but Ted has brushed between them on his way to the door, carrying his laptop and his own suitcase, which he's extracted from beneath the rest of the family's in the trunk of the Suburban. He stands at the door, raising his body's weight up on tiptoes and down again, while Wally unloads two suitcases and escorts Diana and the children up the flagstone walk to the oversized door.

* * *

AUDREY and her friend Stacey are in Bed, Bath & Beyond, a thirty-thousand-square-foot retail space devoted to merchandising the good life through sheets, towels, and soap dishes. Stacey has stopped to look at some Laura Ashley sheets, tiny pink rosebuds against a background of creamy white.

"Oh, aren't these adorable?" squeals Stacey.

She fingers the sheets for a minute before slapping herself across the face. "As if! I keep forgetting he's a guy."

"Wait," says Audrey. "That is an *excellent* idea."

"Audrey! He'll hate this."

"Exactly. Those little kids, they can't help what they're doing. But this Humphrey guy is old enough to think for himself. If he's going to insist on helping his parents in their colonial attitudes, then let him suffer."

"Audrey! That's so mean!"

"Hey. My father *finally* liquidates his company and somehow gets talked into this King Arthur bullshit instead of my Native American kibbutz. This is for my people I'm being mean. That's different."

Audrey loads the shopping cart with a comforter, pillow shams, bedskirt, sheets, curtains, and matching towels. "Look, as soon as we get them to go back to England, I'll give this set to you. Help me pick out a girlish towel rack and laundry hamper. The sweeter the better. Oh, I can't wait to see the look on this smug imperialist's face when he sees his room!"

* * *

WILLIAM is putting away his toy soldiers, having brought along an entire infantry from England. Each of these metal figures is freshly painted, touched up before they left, by his mates at Warcraft, who didn't want Yanks to think that British boys were shabby in the fighting department. Will they even play war games here? It's a question William's afraid to ask, afraid to find the answer.

The soldiers are lined up next to William's bed, on the thin ledge of a chair rail. William reaches into his suitcase and takes out the Manchester United calendar, opening it to September, what's left of it. Ten months before they go back, ten months in this place where the plants are spiky and sparse, ten months in a heat so thick it moves over the body like marmalade.

William takes a crayon and carefully edges in from the borders, filling the first day's square with red, stopping to ask himself whether that's cheating, as it's not quite done yet. The sun is low in the sky, Mum and Humphrey are laying tea. "Cheer up, old lad," William whispers. "Think of the swimming pool. Maybe you'll teach Mum to swim this year. Make her try."

* * *

HUMPHREY has just finished making up his bed with his favorite Laura Ashley rosebud sheets. He is grateful for the simplicity of his room, its soft green walls edged in creamy trim. He is straightening the angles on this bed of roses when the doorbell rings. Seconds later Eleanor bursts into the room. Behind her stand two blond teenage girls carrying large shopping bags. The closest blonde, the one with a triumphant grin on her face, whose fringed short brown suede skirt matches her fringed knee-high flat boots, is starting to apologize for being late when her mouth simply drops open.

"Ohmigod!" whispers Stacey, her head craning over Audrey's shoulder at the small pink rosebuds covering Humphrey's bed. "This is too unreal!"

"Oh, I hope you don't mind," says Humphrey. "I brought my own sheets from home. I like to have something familiar. I hope you didn't go to too much trouble."

Audrey is still standing there, shocked, trying to put together this room with the handsome boy standing in front of her, when the glimmer of an insight overcomes her features, and with it, a strange loosening of her limbs as she comprehends that Humphrey is from an oppressed class in his own right.

It is almost visible, this change of heart. She brings the shopping bag forward, laughing and opening it so that Humphrey can see its contents, the familiar print of pink rosebuds shielded by the plastic packaging.

"Great minds think alike. Do they have that saying over there in England?"

* * *

DIANA stands at the French doors separating the kitchen from the back garden and pool. The pool light is on but she doesn't know where the switch is, doesn't know how to open the gate, wouldn't go near it if she did. At age four Diana had been left at swimming lessons with an instructor who threw his pupils in the pool and made them swim to the edge. Diana still remembers the shimmering glass of the water above her, the cast of blue it gave everything, the bodies moving above the surface, and her sudden sense of time as elastic. She'd waited at the bottom of the pool, holding her breath, hands clasped over her mouth and nose, wondering who would notice if she disappeared. She had no memory of being rescued, though she'd been told it was an older child who retrieved her, not the swimming master who'd come up with this lovely sink-or-swim notion. What *had* remained was the intestinal certainty that she wasn't cut out for the water, was one of a minority of her species who didn't have a natural prehistoric memory of aquatic survival encoded in her muscles. Just looking at this pool outside her door was enough to add gravity three times her own body weight, was enough to tighten every nerve to a paralytic pitch.

It had been simple in England, to avoid mentioning this infirmity. Diana told people she was allergic to chlorine. It wasn't so much shame, as an evasion of the advice that seemed to flow from natural swimmers, a fountain of reassurance and perplexity that anyone so grown-up would have such a childish dysfunction.

"Nearly a full moon," Ted says, startling Diana into a small jitter.

"Mmnn," says Diana, forcing her body to relax as Ted's hand caresses her spine.

"Look, I know I've been a beast. It's very wearing on me, as you know. But I will try that stiff-upper-lip business." Ted nuzzles the back of Diana's neck with his lips and brings his hand to her waist.

"That's all right," whispers Diana. She eases forward slightly and clasps his hand with her own in a platonic friendliness. "They can see us, Ted," she explains, nodding her head towards the Golds' lighted windows.

"And your point?" utters Ted, jerking her back to his embrace and moving his fingers up to cradle her breast. "He may have all the money in the world, he may have bought and sold my College, but he doesn't possess you. Let him see us and weep."

* * *

UPSTAIRS, Humphrey is putting Eleanor to bed.

William pokes his head in the door. "Did you bring the book?" he whispers.

"Of course, silly. Are you all right?"

"Don't you think you should read it to Elly?"

Humphrey crosses the room and checks the hallway. "Elly, can you be very quiet while I fetch Mummy's book? William, why don't you crawl in with her and rub her back?"

Humphrey tiptoes out into the hall and down the stairs. When he sees that Ted is mixing another martini, he knows he's got time. He takes the stairs quickly and reaches underneath his mattress for a thick padded envelope. In Elly's room the children are lying with the covers to their chins, uncharacteristically silent in their exhaustion. Both have their mother's eyes, both peer out at him with the glazed excitement that is one step short of tears. It is an uncertain place—this Arizona—and even the thrill of such new and luxurious accommodations can't undo the children's unease at so much to get used to. To say nothing of the fact that they are jetlagged. *Continuity is just what they need*, he tells himself. *Let Ted take a flying leap.*

Carefully Humphrey extracts a large hardbound children's book from its protective casing. The cover is blue and green and purple, his mother's artwork. It features a small knight on a large horse approaching a lovely young maiden who appears to be rising out of a deep dark lake. Humphrey fingers the gold medallion of the Newbery Award and opens the book to the authors' dedication page. William and Eleanor always insist that he read this first. "To Humphrey. With all our love. Mummy and Daddy." He turns the page and begins the story. Eleanor's fingers trace the pictures as he reads, dropping off at page three. Her eyes are closed now. Humphrey pretends not to notice Elly's departure, for he knows

William believes he's too old for bedtime stories. Despite this fact, Humphrey can see that it is William more than Elly who needs to hear the familiar words. It is William who yearns for the story of a young boy and his quest to undo the curse on his kingdom, a blight begun by his father's plunder of neighboring lands.

Humphrey continues to read and tries to ignore Ted's voice, playing in his head with the same waspish sting, over and over. "Look, if you must know," he'd exploded one night, two years before, somewhere in what Humphrey remembers as the beginning of his stepfather's descent into heavy drinking. "It's shit. An overly romantic and uncritical acceptance of mystical nonsense that perpetuates an outmoded and Eurocentric view of the Middle Ages. I'm sorry, but I can't have the children exposed to something that so completely contradicts my work, to say nothing of the rigorous revisionist history that's been undertaken at this University as well as others. Look, it's not your fault, Lady Di. You didn't know what you were doing. It's Johnny who should've known better. How he got the Fletcher, after that tripe, I'll never know."

The next morning Humphrey had overheard him apologizing to Diana. "Look, I had too much to drink last night. I hope I didn't say anything too . . ." There Ted had let his volume taper off, and Diana had rescued him by suggesting they forget the whole thing.

The problem was, of course, that much as his mum might pretend otherwise, forgetting had been the very last thing she was capable of doing. From there on in, reading the book had become an almost sacramental form of remembering, not just for Diana or Humphrey, but for William and Eleanor as well. The fact that they must hide their devotions from Ted only added fuel to the fire of a parthogenetic universe where wishes were horses and beggars and would-be orphans did indeed ride.

Four

When Diana wakes the next morning, she delicately removes the Baggies tented over her Italian loafers and bangs them against the floor. After squinting fiercely into the toes, she forces them onto her feet and adopts a rather strange position, a tiptoed crouch, the better to scan the perimeter of the master bedroom floor. After repeating this vigilant inspection in each of her children's rooms, Diana ventures downstairs.

Ted is in the kitchen, watching the small television mounted under the cabinets. His breakfast debris is visible across the granite island: An open bread bag cascades slices into a puddle of orange juice and several bits of eggshell are scattered within a small blizzard of salt and pepper. By the time Ted's program goes to commercial, Diana has put on the kettle, sponged up the juice, put away the bread, and wiped down the counters.

"Ted?"

"What?" The irritation in her husband's voice carries over the sound of the advert, an epic, symphonic celebration of nature that—for some reason Diana cannot grasp—includes a large snub-nosed truck hurtling through pristine unspoiled wilderness. This rampaging machine is clearly "matter out of place," a concept with which she feels a bit too familiar at this juncture.

"I know you've got to go to Gold's meeting," she says, pulling her eyes from the commercial and towards Ted's jutted chin. "But I need to run out for something. Could you spare some of the dollars you collected at the currency exchange?"

"Honestly, Diana, not to be *mean*, but what could you possibly need? Gold's left the refrigerator overflowing with food, and it's the size of Lebanon."

"Just—"

"Look, there's no point in my coming here if the money is going to be frittered away. You've been here less than a day and already you're going shopping?"

"That's hardly the—"

"What's important is to distinguish between what we *need* and what we simply *want*. You must put up your defenses against these adverts, though I find them a bit too blatant—"

"There are things I need—"

"No, *want*. That's the point."

"How would you know?"

"Precisely. If you don't tell me what it is—"

"But I shouldn't have to, Ted. I'm a grown woman."

"What have you got to hide? Just explain to me."

"I have as much right—"

"Well, actually, Diana, that's not precisely true. You know how *wet* you are with money. Do you really want to let go of a system that works well for us? After all, I did the accounts before we left. By the time we pay off your Visa credit account, we'll be behind for the month."

"But that Visa covered food and things for the children! I didn't buy myself a thing."

"Did we not agree that your credit card was for your sole use and responsibility? And that it wasn't to be used—"

"But you were never home! And there were things to be done. I was forced to—"

"Don't get yourself into a state. I will be happy to give you some money. I'd just like to know how—in the midst of this abundance—you might want for anything! Not to be Shylock, but you'll thank me later for exerting some discipline. You know you will." Ted reaches into his pocket and extracts a wad of bills. He carefully separates out a dollar bill squeezing it between his fingers to make sure it's not joined to another. "Here."

"Ted. You've just given me less than a pound."

Ted rolls his eyes and extracts two more singles, laying them before his wife with a flourish.

* * *

AUDREY is sitting in front of her new iMAC, firing off a quick note to her favorite chat-room buddy. Skygyrl had entered the EARTH-CARE chat room shortly after Audrey did, three years before. Despite the fact that they've never met, or perhaps, *because* they've never met, Audrey has opened up to this person, whom she knows only by screen name, in ways she hasn't with other people. They can talk about anything from acne gel to Pearl Jam to global warming. They even get into stuff Audrey can't be straight about with her friends, like what happened to her mom. Skygyrl knows when to give advice, and when to just shut up and listen.

> EARTHGYRL: Sorry they all came down so hard on u last night with their "animals are people, too" crap. Like my mom used to say, "If God wanted people to be vegetarians, She wouldn't have made cows."
>
> SKYGYRL: LOL. So what's this playground petition about, anyhow?

EARTHGYRL: You know Baby Face, my friend from the community garden? Well, his uncle Roger is a carpenter who built playgrounds all over the city out of wood treated with pesticides. Anyway, last year, Roger was up in Prescott, working on a lakefront project, where he had to stand in the water all day, building this raft thing. One day he collapsed and had to go to the emergency room. They told him he was just tired, so he went home, slept through the weekend, and when he went back to work, after half a day of standing in the toxic soup, he blacked out again. Anyway, it turns out he's got bladder cancer from exposure to all the chromated copper arsenic in the wood he was working with. Not just, like, in the water, but breathing the dust for all those years. Anyway, long story short, now he's in a wheelchair, basically with a death sentence. His doctor says it's too late. He's only thirty-eight! Anyway, the experts agree the wood is BAD and it's getting pulled off the market, but still, most of the kids in the city are on these playgrounds that were built with the stuff, and nobody's even doing anything about it! So we're putting together a petition to the city council to pull the wood with CCA out and put nontoxics in. Baby Face's uncle's all psyched about helping us get signatures.

SKYGYRL: Poor guy.

EARTHGYRL: I know. He's really sick and still willing to help us.

SKYGYRL: I bet it helps him feel better to DO SOMETHING. Good job, gyrlfriend!

EARTHGYRL: I haven't done anything! Elizabeth is still reviewing the petitions and she's been in D.C. so I haven't heard back from her. I've been crazed helping my dad get ready for these English people.

SKYGYRL: Oh, I forgot. How are they?

EARTHGYRL: Mr. Lively's a butthead. The kids are okay.

SKYGYRL: What about the mom?

EARTHGYRL: Nice. I can't see why she's married to that creep.

SKYGYRL: Maybe she should marry your dad.

EARTHGYRL: Why do you keep beating that way-so-dead horse? He's still in love with my mom.

SKYGYRL: But your mom is GONE. What's his problem?

EARTHGYRL: That he couldn't save her.

SKYGYRL: But he wasn't even there.

EARTHGYRL: I know. But not from the accident. From her illness.

SKYGYRL: Oh. :(Maybe he needs a shrink.

EARTHGYRL: He's definitely gone wacko with this King Arthur stuff.

SKYGYRL: Don't tell me he's really selling the business.

EARTHGYRL: DON'T TELL A SOUL!!!!! He hasn't announced it yet. I would be so grounded.

SKYGYRL: Silent as the grave, gyrlfriend.

* * *

DIANA stands at the door of the Circle K. Her face is already red from the heat and the stress of driving on the wrong side of the road. She opens the door, wanders up and down the aisles until she finds the correct section, then reads every box, scrutinizing prices. Finally she carries the small pink box of tampons to the counter, waits in line and sets down her purchase in front of the clerk, next to her three dollars. The clerk scans the box and says, "That'll be $3.20."

"Oh," Diana says, flustered. "I thought it said $2.99."

"Tax."

Diana reddens. At home the taxes are included in the price, but she doesn't suppose this teenage boy is interested. The line behind her has several construction workers waiting to pay for oversized fizzy drinks. "I haven't any more money." Lowering her voice, Diana asks, "Might you have something less expensive?"

The clerk picks up the box. "Hey, Mildred!" he yells to a woman who is stocking milk cartons in the rear of the store. "We got any cheaper O.B.s?"

"What the hell are opies?"

"I don't know ... it says here for women's feminine protec ..." The boy's voice dies down and he looks ready to melt into the bright orange countertop. Diana feels that she would like to join him, right then and there. The men behind her are studying her with increased interest.

"Oh, tampons?" shouts Mildred. "Well, how much are the Tampax?"

The barrel-chested man at the end of the line, wearing a purple tank top, jean shorts, and construction boots, leans over and picks up a box. "It says here three-fifty. Geez. Here, lady. Here's a buck. Go to town. My wife always gets these kind anyway. Says they're more absorbent."

"I couldn't," says Diana, wilting against the counter.

"Sure you can. Here." The man hands the box of tampons with his donated dollar to the man in front of him, who hands it to the man in front of him, who hands it to Diana. The clerk hurriedly makes change and Diana slinks out the door into the morning heat, feeling she may very well have lived the majority of her life in that queue. Even her toes are scarlet, she can feel them pulsing inside her shoes.

It is not until she gets into the car and sits there for a minute that she realizes she is not on the driver's side. By then it is too late for her to open the door, not without attracting once again the attention of all these half-dressed construction workers carrying Big

Gulps and pondering, she is sure, the merits of relative absorbency *vis-à-vis* Diana's period, which has pounced with the vigor of an unspayed feline, and made Diana feel all the more alone in this land of the free and home of the brave. In the glare of the mid-morning sun, in a parking lot from Hell, Diana slides down in her seat and waits, a verse from Johnny's Talking Heads cassette playing over and over in her head. "This is not my beautiful life," she hears herself shouting silently. "How did I get here?"

* * *

AUDREY is in the cabana kitchen, working on her insecticide. She has read that garden slugs and roaches are attracted by the scent of beer, so she adds a half ounce of Foster's to her brew, as well as a pinch of honey. The urine she collected last week looks too gross, even for African sand-mites, so she dumps it down the sink and rinses the collection jar before taking it into the bathroom and refreshing her supply. The knock at the door comes as a surprise.

Audrey looks out the peephole in the front door, the one her dad insisted on, along with a double-bolt lock, after the last big kidnapping story on CNN. Maybe it's that Humphrey kid, she thinks, but there is nothing in view of the peephole except the distorted circular landscape of the backyard. Audrey is turning when she hears another knock. Again, she looks out the peephole. Again, nothing. For a second or two, she can't help herself from getting a crazy idea. Maybe it's her mom. Maybe her dad's been right all along. Maybe her mom is still around, watching over her.

Audrey cannot help but feel her spirits lift in the same way that they do on Christmas Eve, when the nightly news mentions an Unidentified Flying Object spotted over the North Pole. Stop it, she scolds, girding herself for the resignation she flexes like a muscle she is trying to strengthen. She flings open the door, expecting nothing. When she sees the munchkin standing there, she just about hits the ceiling, or would have if it wasn't cathedral-vaulted over the thick wooden door.

"Elly, what are you doing here!" she cries.

"Can Audrey come play?" asks Eleanor, holding a Barbie dressed in evening wear and Ken wearing a hula skirt and boa wrapper.

"Sweetie, you should never be by the pool by yourself! How did you get here?" asks Audrey, swooping the child into her arms and carrying her to the kitchen. "Here, sit on the counter while I finish this and then I'll walk you home."

"What's that?" Eleanor asks, her eyes honed in on Mary Kate's crystal Lalique perfume mister, lying upside down on the drainboard.

"I use it to spray the plants. It keeps the pests from ruining them."

"Elly help."

"No, sweetie. That jalapeño would sting you, bad. Tell you what, though, I'll let you add the tequila when it's time. Okay?"

Audrey shakes her compound in an old Mason jar, allows Eleanor to pour in the contents of a small shot glass, shakes again, and uses a small white plastic funnel to pour it into the clean mister. Eleanor's eyes positively glitter with desire. It's as though nothing is in the room but her four-year-old precocity and a prismatic octagon fashioned in French crystal. When Audrey screws on the lid and attaches the tubing with its balloon-shaped cobalt blue squeeze bag, it is all Eleanor can do to not reveal her intentions.

"Wanna see how it works?" asks Audrey. They proceed to Audrey's garden, which she mists liberally while explaining to Eleanor the relationship between world hunger, crop rotation, and an organic means of controlling pests and weeds. After they've finished, Audrey sets the mister on the doorstep of the cabana and walks Elly into the main house. "In primitive agriculture, now, they do something way cool. They handpick the bugs off the crops, feed them to ducks at the end of each row, and then they've got food coming out the ears, all with no poison to the earth. The lake the ducks swim in is also used to raise fish, while the fish waste and duck shit is recycled to fertilize the earth," Audrey is saying. "But listen, don't say shit. It's not nice."

Eleanor, for her part, has stopped hearing, for she is concentrating on a recycling plan of her very own.

* * *

On Monday morning William is up and dressed well before it's time to leave for school. Audrey has helped to select his first-day-of-school outfit, a baggy pair of tan corduroy shorts and an oversize white T-shirt with the letters AI written on the back.

"Alan Iverson," Audrey explained. "Like, the basketball player?"

Now William stands in front of the hall mirror and tries to pretend he's not really looking at himself. He licks his fingers then dabs them against the ends of his dark hair, which has been clipped into a "bowl cut." "If you didn't know me, would I look all right?" he asks his mother.

Diana looks up at her son, casting him an indulgent smile. "If I didn't know you, I'd be blind with emptiness, darling. You look fantastic. Smashing."

William rolls his eyes. "I mean it."

"So do I. You look marvelous."

"Mum, I don't *want* to look marvelous. I want to look normal."

"Well, you look very American. Is that better?"

"I hardly think so," interrupts Ted, descending the stairs. "When I was a boy, only babies wore short pants to school."

"I told you, Mum!" shouts William, near tears. He runs up the stairs, towards his bedroom. Diana shoots Ted a quick blistering look before running up the stairs after her son, whom she finds sitting at the end of his bed, his arms crossed over his knees, staring at a Geronimo poster and looking every bit as fierce as the great warrior.

"Remember what Audrey said, William? That even the teenagers wear short trousers here? Remember the boys you saw at the shopping mall? Whatever you wear, you'll be fine, darling, but I don't think Audrey would lie. You'll be fine," pleads Diana.

They arrive at school before the bell. As they cross the threshold towards the fourth grade wing, Diana reaches for William's hand, a move which is rewarded by a look of utter horror from her son, a quick dig of his fists into his pockets, and a return of his features to the expression of complete impassivity with which he seems to greet all stressful occasions.

The school is streamlined and clean and completely without character, but inside the small window of Ms. Marsh's classroom Diana can see colorful artwork and several children hanging up knapsacks.

"Shall I go in with you, then?"

William shakes his head and barely looks at her as she whispers goodbye. She'd like to stay and peek in the window, but she knows better.

Inside, William pushes his frighteningly heavy legs forward toward the black woman standing in front. "Are you Miss Marsh?" he asks, handing her a notecard from the office.

"Ms. You must be William. How ya' doin'?"

"Fine-thank-you." William's words trip over one another, sounding completely squidgy to his ears.

Ms. Marsh leads William to the back of the room, gesturing for him to sit at an empty desk. Next to William's seat slumps a skinny red-haired boy wearing glasses and a button-down collared shirt with ink stains on the pocket. "Matthew, this is William. He's just moved here from England. Why don't you help him out today?"

"You from Boston?" the boy asks.

"What?"

"Boston, New England."

"No. Oxford, actually. You see it's not—"

"Whatever."

That is the extent of their conversation until they go to lunch.

"See ya," says Matthew, leaving William standing in line by himself. William feels that everyone is staring dead at him. He doesn't know what to do. Other children take the beige plastic trays out of stacks, so does William. Other children take their silverware, so does William. He follows them as they load food onto their trays, pay the white-haired lady at the cash register, and move on to tables where they are joining their friends. William walks around the tables in a circle, not knowing where he is to sit. Each table has some children and they are all strangers. Matthew has completely disappeared, and even if he hadn't, William would not want to sit with him, having watched the boy pick his nose all morning. Finally, after two circles of the lunchroom, William sets his tray down on top of a window ledge and heads off for the boys' bathroom, where he remains locked in a stall, sitting in his new American clothes and reading the graffiti on the back of the door until the bell rings and it's time to go back to class.

The afternoon is a blur for William, a study of Colonial America, about which he knows nothing. "You see," Ms. Marsh is telling the class. "The colonists thought the Indians were stupid to sell them Manhattan for trinkets, but the Indians didn't believe you could own the land. To them, it was like water or air, something everyone already owned in common. So in their mind, they were putting one over on the white men with funny hats." At one point she turns to William and asks, "Did you learn about this in England, William?"

"I don't think—not exactly," responds William, hearing his words hang like limp laundry in the two o'clock air.

From that point on, every time William says anything, all the children in the front rows turn in their desks to stare at him, their hands gripping their seats, their upper bodies twisted round, their mouths just slightly hung open, mystified by his British accent. William notices Matthew edging away from him, as though his malady might be contagious. He hears Ms. Marsh's "Matthew! Squash it!" and the laughter of the other children as Matthew retracts his V-shaped hand signal from behind William's spanking-new haircut.

When William returns home that day, all he will say is that he's starving. Humphrey makes him cheese on toast while his mother sorts through papers from the school inviting her to join the PTA and volunteer in the classroom. There are two spelling errors in the letter from the principal, as well as a large DRIVE CAREFUL!!! plastered across the top, proud banner to the reckless prescription of adjectives where once only adverbs dared to tread.

Diana rests her hand on top of William's for a moment and asks gently about his teacher. "Is she all right, then?" asks Diana. William ducks his head towards his arm, swallowing the tears that would otherwise accompany any honest reckoning of his day. "Oh, darling, it will get better, believe me," moans Diana, miserable. She comes around the back of his chair and hugs him from behind, kissing his hair quickly. "It's just the first day is difficult, that's all. They've all been in school already for weeks, and it will take them a while to notice you."

"Jesus, Mum! They notice me already. Everyone turns completely around, holding on to the back of their desk to glare at me every time I say the first word! I hate Daddy for bringing us here."

"It's not his fault, William. It's just—"

"Why'd you have to marry Daddy, anyway? If you hadn't, we wouldn't have had to come here. We'd still be in Oxford and none of this would be happening."

Diana just sighs and pulls William up from his chair for a proper hug. No use explaining the truism that plays itself over and over in her brain several times each day, causing Diana to shudder with gratitude for the mixed blessings of a long abandoned dream. If she hadn't married Ted, there'd be no William, there'd be no Eleanor. How could she even imagine such a thing?

* * *

TED, who has been going into Gold Industries for nearly three weeks without being asked to meet with Gold, has nevertheless kept himself busy, ordering transcripts from civil court cases and drafting the occasional letter to government sources entrusted with protecting America's wildlife. Not only has he absorbed thickets of civil legalese, but he's become a dab hand at writing the perfectly innocent enquiry.

September 28

Dear Sirs/Madams,

It has come to my attention that a rather large development is planned for the Lake Havasu watershed. Environmental Impact Studies, with community input, are required for such projects. Might I suggest to you that two constituencies be asked to comment? First, the members of the Amitola tribe, are the original inhabitants of the area. Secondly, might I point out that Miss Elizabeth Stanton of EARTHCARE has been instrumental in protecting the state's pristine natural resources. Furthermore, I would be most grateful if you could clarify the threshold for water usage that would trigger a Tier 4 investigation of the proposed enterprise.

I appreciate your prompt response and your discretion in keeping this letter entre nous.

Yours,
Lance Gawain, Ph.D.
P.O. Box 666
Tempe, Arizona

* * *

DIANA and Eleanor are seated at the kitchen island. Diana is sorting through papers from the children's school, trying to divide it into piles. Every now and then she looks across the island, at an expensive sketchpad that's arrived in the morning post. A small Post-it is placed squarely in the middle of the pad, and scrawled across it, Evelyn's distinctive handwriting.

"Art is more than what we step in, but it's that, too. Off smartly now!"

Eleanor is coloring with a squint of grim concentration, digging her marker into the page. She scowls at her mother and begins to cry. "Mummy! I can't make the mummy's hair yellow!"

"Well, darling, that marker's gotten dried up because you left the cap off. What about brown?"

"No! That wouldn't color good! Yucky!"

Diana's hand reaches protectively to her own dark hair. She smiles at her daughter's vanity. "Color 'well,' darling. *Well* is for verbs, darling. *Good* is for nouns."

"I hate my picture! You draw it, Mummy! For Audrey."

"No, what's wrong with that? You've gotten off to a good start."

"It's beastly!" With this Eleanor takes a nearby pencil and begins to deface the faces of the people in her picture. "I hate it! I shan't color never again! Never, never!"

Diana sets down her papers and picks up Eleanor. She walks her in a circle around the room, making soothing noises. "But you love to draw! You know, Eleanor, being a good artist means making mistakes. You're supposed to. It takes a lot of courage, actually, to make a mistake in the pursuit of art."

"Mummy don't make mistakes."

"Oh yes, Mummy makes mistakes!"

"Not in drawing!"

"But I would, if I had time to draw—" Diana is brought up short for a moment, with the troubled look of someone who can't comprehend what she's just said. She pulls back her head from Eleanor's and stares her daughter square in the face. "You know what, Eleanor, let's start over. You make your picture for Audrey and I'll make one for Evelyn. Awright?"

With this, Diana sets her daughter down on her stool and sweeps the two heaps of papers back into a single mess, which she bends into a mangled cone and stuffs into an empty drawer by the phone. Leaning forward, Diana reaches for the pad, stretching her body over the island. The distance between her stool and the artist's sketchbook is far enough that Diana's feet are momentarily forced to leave the ground.

* * *

EVEN the sand in Wally's Zen box, a gift from Audrey, is muddled. Its normally smooth rows are whipped up like the ocean in midstorm, and the copper rake is pitched in the middle, its staff pointing out like an index finger in rush hour. The frame is made of sandalwood, four times the size and depth of the miniature Japanese garden boxes in the nature stores, and filled with asbestos-free sand from one of Audrey's organic gardening suppliers.

"It'll calm you down, Dad. Just try it," she'd said on Father's Day, unveiling her gift. "I built everything but the rake. Baby Face did that in Metal Work. Isn't it great?"

Wally loves the thing. He really does. Usually, it helps him think, but not today, not with this ad he's trying to get into words.

Guy has already told him not to bother. Personnel has said the same, in their own Human Resources kind of way. He knows he's supposed to be looking over the performance evaluations of his operations managers, which are stacked on his desk at work. Instead, Wally sits in his study at home staring at a yellow legal pad, trying to wrap his pencil around an idea, which, even if he succeeds in writing it, will have to be shelved until later in the process. Despite all these reasons not to, Wally can't get past the need to get it down on paper, to control the flow of words. Unfortunately, there is no flow in sight. Verb won't follow noun, he doesn't know what to say. "Just stop it," he tells himself. "You don't know what the hell you're doing. Let Personnel deal with it."

With that, Wally defies his own instructions and writes: *Architect wanted for themed entertainment park*. He scratches out *park* and writes *enterprise*, scratches that out again and writes *park*. Wally throws his pencil across the room. The eraser bounces off the wall and ricochets into the small architect's model of Mary Kate's house. As he retrieves the pencil from the tiny chimney on the kitchen's east side, Wally cannot help but think of Diana.

Little does he know that at this very moment, near that very same east-most chimney in the house on Gelding Drive, Diana is drawing again for the first time in years, proving Feng Shui's maxim linking eastern location with Creativity.

No, for Wally, it's not so complicated. He sees the model of the house, thinks of Diana, and instantly Wally arrives at what he wants to do. *Dinner*, he concludes, with all the gratitude that would accompany a major life epiphany. *I'll ask them to dinner*.

With this, he reaches for the phone.

*   *   *

TED's Prince Valiant is suffering a Magna Carta of its own. His sideburns have become tributaries for sweat he was promised would not materialize in this dry heat. No matter what he does, the bounce has fled from his crown, and what remains is lank and listless.

"Bedraggled, I am. That's what I am."

"Excruciating drive home again?" murmurs Diana, edging past

her husband to latch tight the door, which resists staying shut, pushed forward by the heat that snakes in from the shaded garage.

"I keep getting passed on the wrong side of the motorway by overfed youth in hideous purpose-built vans, who look as though any minute they'll take out a weapon and begin to defend Garth Brooks to all who shudder."

"I don't envy you, darling."

Diana crosses the kitchen, returning to the table. Any fool watching would see what Ted apparently does not, that Diana is hastily closing her sketch pad to cover her work.

"Some lemonade?" she asks, pointing to the tray she's arranged: tall glasses and a pitcher glistening with condensation. "I made it the way you like—"

"Love one. A lemon-vodka."

"It's just half-four, Ted," Diana murmurs. She tries not to mind the trip to the grocery for the lemons, the careful removal of seeds, the hopes she has pinned on her attractive display of glasses around the pitcher.

"It's the middle of the night in Oxford, Diana." Ted takes a lemonade glass and lovingly plucks ice from the Sub-Zero.

Diana cannot help counting while he pours vodka, automatically calculating the beverage weight. Ted's splash of lemonade takes a fraction of a second to the four point five he's taken with vodka.

Ted takes a connoisseur's sip, shuddering with pleasure at the taste. "I'm feeling rather useless. Gold's got me segregated in a part of his building that no one but his secretary ever goes. She's a disagreeable old bitch, too. I had to actually beg for postage today. Slag. Gold won't meet until the announcement's made. I haven't the foggiest what he wants."

"P'raps if you talked to him, Ted."

"P'raps if he stood still long enough to be talked to, I could do that. P'raps pigs will fly and the Fletcher Committee will actually award Britain's top academic honor to the hired help for a recovering arms merchant."

"I'm sure they aren't seeing it that way, Ted. You do have the visiting professorship in the Renaissance Center. I'm told it's quite good."

It's here that Ted gives Diana the Look. White heat from stern blue eyes. The arms folded across the chest. "Diana. Stop."

"No, truly. Evelyn's chum at Princeton says—"

"Look, I know you're just trying to comfort me, but you know absolutely nothing about my field. This isn't even close to the caliber of Princeton and Princeton's quite a few steps down from Oxford. Gold actually sent me a note suggesting I integrate the work of Sir Walter Scott into my thinking, as his wife was quite taken with that *oeuvre*, too. I didn't know how to break the news that it was a different century, different language, entirely different genre. What an ignoramus the man is! And now I'm at his beck and call. So, please. Don't trivialize the very real sacrifice I've made by trying to pretend this isn't thoroughly detestable."

Ted smiles forgivingly at his wife before letting off a vodka-scented sigh. "It's all false in this godforsaken Land of Bad Grammar. One minute there's nothing, the next, they've slammed up plastic buildings atop sand and called themselves a university. A fellow at the Renaissance Center invited me to lunch last week and we ate in a "food court." On the grounds of their campus! Clock's ticking on the moment they commence naming professors after their fizzy drinks. Oh, good day, I'm the Sprite Professor of Paranormal Psychology. And allow me to introduce my colleague, the Diet Pepsi Chair of Eating Disorders."

Diana laughs and slips her sketch pad from the table onto the small kitchen desk. A quickness in her movement attracts Ted's attention. "What's that?" he asks.

"Nothing, really. It's frightful. Just keeping my arm in practice."

"No, let me see."

"I'd rather not, Ted. It's that bad," says Diana, backing up towards the wall, hands held tight behind her, gripping the pad.

"No, let me see how you've spent your day." Ted kisses his wife hungrily while tugging the pad away from her hands. She struggles hard enough to scratch her finger on the adobe wall. Diana licks her wound. Ted opens the pad and says nothing as he looks at the drawing of a very modern building set in a desert landscape.

"Hmmm," says Ted. "I don't know why you'd be interested in doing something local. We'll be heading back to civilization in less than a year."

"I know; it's horrid. Just keeping in form."

"No, it's not *horrid,* Diana. But you haven't practiced since Humphrey was born and it seems like a waste of time to even think about using your time this way here. Not only is any firm unlikely to hire you based on a 1980s degree, but I'm not at all sure it's worth exposing yourself to the aesthetic malady that's endemic in this land of strip malls and car parks. Stay with the classical beauty of England, and someday you'll practice again. You'll just be disappointed if you set your aim on the impossible. Besides, the children need you."

"No, I don't expect . . . just, the light is so different here. I'm trying to capture the—"

Ted lunges towards Diana, bringing one of her hands towards his crotch. His other hand, holding the sketchpad, lets it drop to the floor. "I could keep you busy, you know. If you've got all this time on your hands, I could give you something to occupy yourself, something for which there's a real market. Give me your other hand."

"Ted," Diana warns. "William's in the next—"

"So? We *are* married. And I'm suffering. Why won't you make yourself useful, wench?"

A loud ringing pierces the moment, once, twice, insistent. Though she knows it's the doorbell, it makes Diana think of an ambulance siren, winding its way up the hill.

* * *

WALLY stands at the front door, holding his sunglasses in one hand. His face is flushed. "Hi!" he says. "Sorry about the doorbell. I'll call somebody to fix it. Listen, I think your phone's off the hook. I've been calling all day."

Diana extends a welcoming hand and, flustered by Wally's awkwardness, drops the sketch pad she's rescued from the floor.

Wally automatically genuflects to retrieve it.

He reaches out and gently puts a thumb at the base of the building. "Nice," he says. "You do that?"

"Thank you, but it's not—it's dreadful—"

"Are you kidding? You an artist? Let me see it, Diana. Do you mind?"

"I think she does, Wally," offers Ted. "She's private about—"

At the proprietary sound of her husband's voice behind her, Diana's fingers relinquish her work to Wally. Somewhere in the general vicinity of her spleen, her ego hugs its knees.

"This is beautiful. You're an artist, then. I shoulda known from the dollhouses."

"Architect, actually," corrects Ted. "But she's mostly been a housewife. Architecture's very competitive in England. Very few jobs. Only the top talent—"

"You're kidding, right? You're an architect? In my own backyard?"

Wally leans over the table, inspecting the drawing. "Why don't you put a bid in for the project?"

Diana is almost bent double by a sudden cramping pain in her abdomen. "I—I need to—I couldn't—excuse me, I'll be right back," she says as she runs from the room, jogs up the stairs, and slams shut the master bath door. She collapses onto the commode and is overcome by a dizzy wave of what-might-have-been until all of her insides have been painfully unburdened. She stands up shakily and looks at herself in the mirror, noticing that her forehead is embedded with crevices, noticing the drawn laugh lines that pull from the corners of her mouth to the line of her chin. She leans forward to turn on the faucet and sees a single white hair in the point of her widow's peak.

* * *

DOWNSTAIRS, Ted is careful with his words. To all appearances, he is protective. "She hasn't practiced since before we met. Was never really serious about practicing that I could see. Much rather move in with Johnny on one of his father's properties, pop out Humphrey, and fiddle with the occasional miniature."

"Johnny?"

"Her first husband. We read for exams together in Medieval Literature."

"So that's how you met?"

"I met her at Johnny's funeral. Not a very auspicious place to find a wife, but I knew the minute I saw her that she'd be mine. Took her a bit to come round, the grieving widow and all that, but she eventually—well, since then we've never looked back. In fact, the thing of it is, Diana's put her soul into her family, into keeping the children and me happy. Think it's relationships that matter to Lady Di, not money."

"How did—you mind my asking how her husband died?"

"A fluke really. He and Diana and Humphrey were walking off their Sunday lunch and a shooting party from the adjoining estate wandered over the property line. Made all the papers in England, the heir to Lord Sennett killed by an industrialist from Germany out on a lark. Child and wife saved by his bravery, and all that, though I do maintain that's a sentimental interpretation by the medical examiner since no one really knows what Johnny was thinking."

It is at this point that William, who has been sitting in the dining room, staring dead ahead at a tiny Warcraft soldier balanced on his homework, finds himself banging the metal toy against the table. "Mum knows!" he whispers.

"Who's that?" asks Ted, high-stepping in a pantomime of secrecy towards the boy behind the wall. "What're you skulking about back here for?" he asks. "Come into the light where we can take a look at you, in your new American trainers. The lad is all foot!"

"Hey, William," says Wally, shaking William's hand. "That reminds me. Did you find out about soccer tryouts?"

"My—I'm not allowed, sir."

Ted places a hand on the boy's shoulder. "The fees are outrageous."

"Don't let money stop you—hell, I'll pay for it! William's got talent. You can't let him sit dormant for a year. Besides, it's a way for him to meet other boys. Let me pay for it."

Ted's tone is icy. "You needn't do that. Diana and I have made up our minds."

"What's that?" asks Diana, entering the kitchen. She's changed into a bright crimson shift and pulled her hair into a loose ponytail. She's wearing lipstick, and even some concealer, which, were Humphrey home to see it, would float his boat for a week or two.

"American soccer," Ted explains, annoyed, resolute.

Wally puts both palms up, like Jesus with the loaves and the fishes. He's pleading. "Look, I brought you here and poor William gets dragged along whether he's happy or not. It's nothing to me: chump change. Don't even think about it."

"Ted worries that William might form bad habits with a trainer he doesn't know," murmurs Diana. "Football is played differently in England, you see."

"Hey, the trainer for this team used to play for Manchester United. He's as English as any of you. I can't see him hurting William's game."

"Oh, Daddy, please . . . I promise—I'll keep up with my schoolwork."

"The trainer's British?" asks Diana, turning to Ted. "Surely that was your objection?"

"Thirty quid a month, Diana. If we're going to fritter away all I'm making, so there's nothing to show for this year, then why don't I cast myself off the London Bridge now and save us all the trouble—"

"Look, I mean it. My treat," Wally mutters. "I can write it off."

"Absolutely not." Diana's tone is heated. "My mother rang today. She's more than willing to pay for William's extras."

"You spoke to Charlotte about this?" Ted's voice is low and flat.

Diana flinches, her neck begins to blotch scarlet. She rambles to cover herself. "Not in any detail. It's just—she rang after Humphrey'd gotten home from that cooking academy. She mentioned that her trust had dispersed more than she expected and she was sending the remainder as an early Christmas gift. There's more than enough there to cover Humphrey's and William's fees and Eleanor's nursery costs."

"You're not honestly thinking about cookery school—"

"Humphrey visited the campus today. It's very well regarded—"

"You must be joking."

"No. Humphrey very much wants to do this. I'm grateful to see him so happy."

"Let me attempt to understand, Diana. What I earn, that goes to the family. But the odd thousand your mother sends, that's yours to do with as you wish?"

Diana's trapped look is more than Wally can bear. He intercedes, clumsily. "Look, it's none of my business, but a lot of the New York chefs train there."

Diana continues. "I was planning to speak with you tonight. Humphrey's so enthusiastic. I haven't seen him this happy in years. This may be his calling, Ted."

"His calling! To be a cook in a restaurant? Lord Sennett's grandson? You must be joking! I won't have him—I'm surprised your mother didn't faint dead away being asked to put her grandchild through trade school."

"He's eighteen, Ted," murmurs Diana, steeling herself. She knows better than to get lost in the labyrinth of argument. Better to concentrate on Humphrey's right to choose for himself than to defend his particular choice.

"Yes, but he's living under my roof."

Wally is preoccupied by a nearly uncontrollable urge to clutch Ted up by his collar and hold him high for a few seconds, close to the roof, which, if he was feeling petty enough to point out, belongs to Wally, not Ted. *Rent free and he's yanking his stepson's chain whenever he can.* Wally counts slowly to ten and repeats his Al Anon catechism: *Can't control other people, places, or things.* "Look, I better go. I just wanted to—to tell you your phone's off the hook."

He exits through the French door to the back, telling himself he'll call later to invite them to dinner, clenching and unclenching his fists all the way to the gate.

Inside, Diana folds shut her sketchbook and straightens papers on the desk, her movements quick, defined, abrupt.

Five

To: Earthgyrl@earthlink.net
From: StantonE@Earthcare.org
Re: Petitions to Pull Treated Wood from the City's Playgrounds

Audrey,
Your petition looks fine, but I'm having our lawyer look at it, just in case. Then we'll print it up and start collecting signatures.
Sincerely,
Elizabeth Stanton
Executive Director, EARTHCARE ARIZONA

To: hotman@hotmail.com
From: StantonE@Earthcare.org
Re: FYI

Dear Mr. Gawain,
While I appreciate getting notice of planned developments up north, there's little I can do but wait to see what the builder proposes for that area. Contrary to popular belief, EARTHCARE does not oppose "development" per se. Our

goal is to urge builders to consider stewardship of the land, water, and surrounding habitats, and to create sustainable, healthy communities. Therefore, you might wait to see the plans before you raise objections. Ideally, you might use your position within your firm to encourage responsible design.

Sincerely,

Elizabeth Stanton

Executive Director, EARTHCARE ARIZONA

* * *

DIANA is grateful for Wally's dinner invitation, eager to escape her crushing sense of déjà vu at hearing the same words, over and over, with William in the dining room, Elly upstairs, and her husband filling his drinks glass. Late afternoon, the sun streaming in the kitchen just as it was when Wally had called, except today she's hidden her drawing and is sitting instead with the brochures for the Paradise Valley Soccer Club, fanned out in her fingers like a hand of bridge. The trouble is, no matter what she cobbles together in the way of argument, she's not gaining a point in this game.

Ted's voice bears just the right dose of rational concern. "You do know I simply want what's best for the children. You do know that?"

Diana sighs. "Yes," she says unconvincingly. She knows that he will win, out of sheer endurance. She is suddenly exhausted. "May we not discuss this right now?" she asks. "I'm shattered."

"Shot your wad talking with Gold on the phone, did you? Or were you drawing again? You know, I've actually found that procrastination is more tiring than actually working. And may I point out that you look charming in that blue dress? I s'pose I might get a bit jealous if I thought too much about it. Rich man invites you to dinner, you transform yourself from dowdy matron to Lady Di."

"Ted, I hate it when you call me that!"

"I can't help it you're titled and named Diana."

"Ted, I mean it. I've never been called—it's humiliating—please don't."

"Why hide your light under a bushel, Diana? It's false modesty, really. Why not be proud of your bloodlines?"

"I'm not a racehorse, Ted. And this is *not* something I earned. Besides, I'm *not* technically a Lady. So it's false, on top of being pretentious."

"So now you'll add prevarication to my long list of inadequacies?"

"No, of course not. But you are too—kind—to me in a way that makes everyone uncomfortable."

"I hardly think you know what makes *everyone* tick, Diana. I, for one, envy you your marvelous mother and father and grandparents and a home that's been in the family for centuries. I never had any of that stability. My father was too busy gambling away his paydraft each fortnight. So forgive me for valuing your heritage. Forgive me for insisting that my adopted son not waste his opportunities by hurling himself off of the mountaintop into the masses, not when I needed to struggle to get to Oxford."

"I told you I couldn't discuss the cookery school anymore, Ted. Please honor—"

"When will we, then? We must twig this early or it will just cause Humphrey more suffering."

"Tomorrow, first thing. Half-eight, we'll have tea and talk."

"You do remember that I work for a living, Diana?"

"But you're never off before half-nine."

"It so happens that I've planned to meet a colleague for breakfast."

"Ted, may we please leave it alone? Honestly, I've got a beastly headache."

"Just how much is this so-called academy? And how much is your mum sending us?"

Diana puts both hands to her forehead and closes her eyes. "I'm going upstairs, now, Ted, to get the children's swimming togs. Then I'm going to take them to the Golds' as we discussed and try to ignore the fact that you so are so completely neglecting my request that we discuss this later. Please."

"Diana, how will you watch them? What sort of watching will it be if you can't save—"

"It's awright, Mum," sounds William, from around the corner, where he's been completely silent, listening and waiting. Protecting his mum is a role he's taken more seriously since the move, here in the land of swimming pools, venomous insects, and snakes that coil in the heat. "We don't want to swim anyway. *The Simpsons* are on."

"Are you sure, William?" his mother asks. "Humphrey's over there and so is Wally."

"No, truly, Mum. It's awright. Elly and I will come with Daddy after the show. You go. Put your feet up."

Diana walks around the corner into the dining room where William sits over his sums. She wraps her arms around her son and kisses his head from behind. She can see the overly neat rows of figures, she can see the pencil at a perfect right angle to the page, but what she cannot see is how this son of Ted's can be so much like Johnny, who had used those exact words every afternoon when he brought her tea and Hobnobs.

Diana musses her son's dark hair, so like her own, and she resolves that whatever it is she must do, her son will play with the soccer league that Wally's recommended.

Already she is planning, already she feels better, so lost in thought that she does not see her husband until his feet, stretched out languidly in front of his third lemon-vodka, nearly trip her on her way out the back door. "You do see," Ted whispers, his voice warmed by the magic of happy hour and the joy of instruction, "how your fear of the water affects the children?"

It is all Diana can do not to kick out at his narrow trouser legs, his reptilian leather pointed shoes. She wants to swat him away with something hard, something fierce, even as she shakes her head and slips past him towards the door. It is not worth responding that Wally would be a suitable lifeguard, for Ted's remark has hit its target, leaving pangs of regret, guilt, and shame. Ted licks the rim of his glass with his pointed tongue and watches his wife edge past the pool gate, cluck-clucking away in his version of amused and affectionate tolerance.

* * *

"Mum! Where have you been all my life? You look absolutely fabulous! Is that the WhiteNight Colourstik, then, that I left for you? See! Doesn't she look adorable, Audrey?" asks Humphrey, twirling his mother with one hand, like a ballerina on a music box, while holding her other.

Audrey smiles shyly and turns her attention back to the Cuisinart. Humphrey has handed her some carrot stumps and casually suggested she "Julie Ann" them with the grating blade while he sears the wok. Somehow, trying to use this machine, which hasn't seen the light of day since her mom spent her entire adult life in the kitchen whipping up covers of *Bon Appétit,* is making Audrey feel like she wants to break down and make a fool of herself. *What the hell is a grating blade and how does Julie Ann do carrots anyhoo?* Why would Humphrey assume she knows how to use a Cuisinart, and worse, why is she letting him get away with this sexist assumption? Why does she feel so pathetic that if she asks for help, it will send her lower lip into a spaz show? Audrey is inspecting the back of each blade, hoping for a clue. She is shutting down her tear ducts by fiercely pulling her pursed lips back through her teeth. Why didn't she ever spend time in here with her mom, like normal girls? Would it have killed her to pretend to be interested?

"What about this kitchen?" Humphrey asks his mother. They are standing in the midst of a polished chrome-and-mahogany galley that has an island overhung with pots of every size and shape, from chrome to copper to bronze and back again. The cooktop has six gas burners, a built-in deep fryer, and a fish poacher. "Isn't it to die for?"

"Beyond," says Diana. "Do you fancy cookery, then, Audrey?" she asks innocently, and it is now that she catches the glint of tears in the girl's eyes.

"How're you doing on the julienned carrots, Luv?" murmurs Humphrey, ignoring Audrey's defeated groan. He is concentrating on smashing garlic with the edge of a knife that looks as if it might have last been seen cutting down bamboo and bayoneting traitors in Okinawa.

Diana gently covers one of Audrey's hands with her own and guides her to the second circular blade attachment. "Here, Audrey, let's see if this is the right blade. You know I think the French enjoy making us all feel really idiotic if we haven't learned their system, which to me is one, inscrutable, and two, of such limited importance in the grand scale of things that I want to say, 'Puh! I *spit* on your silly overblown *système.*'"

Diana mugs the French accent so badly that Audrey cannot help but collapse into a yelp of laughter, salvaging her dignity as she swipes her eyes with the backs of her hands. Diana guides the blade onto its stem, followed by the plastic lid. She swiftly chops the ends of a set of small carrots until they'll fit crosswise in the elliptical funnel of the lid, brings the top hat of the lid to cover, and proceeds to make a shredded melee of the orange stumps.

"Chop, chop, ladies!" chants Humphrey. "So, Mum, this school's brilliant. You must come tomorrow when I deliver my application."

"I'd like to, darling," sighs Diana.

"Oh dear, is that resignation I hear in your voice? Don't tell me: Meemaw's changed her mind, is that it?"

Diana tries to form the words. "No. No. Mum's delighted. It's Ted." She hands her son the bowl full of carrots, as though offering a consolation prize.

Humphrey dumps the bowl into the hissing oil and punctuates his words with great jabs of the wooden spoon, stirring things up. "I won't let him ruin this for me, Mum. I won't."

"No, I know. It's Mummy's money and you're eighteen. It's just—well, you know how he can be. He complains, and I can see his point, I suppose, if you think of it, that my mother's money shouldn't be mine alone to decide what to do with. That if we're a true partnership, well, he ought to have some say."

Humphrey snorts loudly. "That's absolute rubbish! He allows you no say whatsoever with anything he earns."

"We do all live on it, Humphrey."

"Yes and what's wrong with that? He wouldn't be able to teach and write his books and publish his articles unless someone else were taking care of his children, folding his knickers, and cleaning the bloody toilets. To say nothing of cooking his food and hiding the bloody vodka bottles so the neighbors won't see how much he consumes on a daily basis."

"Humphrey, don't—"

"When are you going to take the blinders off, Mum?"

"He's not—it's not . . . You know we entertain quite a bit in Oxford."

"Mum, I've told you before, he's an alcoholic. And—as Auntie Eee-velyn is so fond of saying—that's his most endearing trait."

"Humphrey, he's only objecting to this cookery school because he thinks you'll never go to Cambridge and achieve your best if you're waylaid by something that's temporarily more appealing. And, of course, because he had such a wretched childhood, he yearns for your background. He can't understand why you'd attend a trade school, Lord Sennett's grandson and all that. You have to try and see things from his perspective."

Humphrey holds up his hands, pointer fingers intersecting perpendicularly like a cross. He wields this crucifix against the vampire of understanding that seems to have inhabited his mother's body. "No, Mum, seeing things from his perspective means you never see things from your own. Just once I wish you'd stand up to him, Mum."

"You know it's not at all a matter of standing up for *you*. You're so precious to me."

"It's not that, Mum. I know you'd fling yourself off Big Ben for me. It's what you won't do for *yourself* that troubles me."

"Housewives, unite. You have nothing to lose but your chains," says Audrey, thinking out loud. In fact, it's only when both Diana and Humphrey quickly turn to look at her, a flicker of identical irritation crossing their brows, that she sees she's blurted out the mantra she used to think of whenever she passed through the kitchen and saw her mother fiddling with the Cuisinart, whipping up *creme fraîche* for one of her dad's business clients.

"Sorry. It's just this thing I used to say to my mom," Audrey mutters. When she begins to cry, she is as surprised as they are, though each of them is caught up short for a slightly different reason. Audrey cries because she misses her mother, but she also cries because she has so clearly shown herself as a twit in front of Humphrey, and she cries thirdly because she sees the connection between Diana and her son, so fierce, one she fears that she will never have again, as long as she lives.

Diana quickly enfolds Audrey in her arms and wonders if Wally—who has appeared so chivalrous from afar—might actually be as chauvinistic in his own way as Ted is in his.

Humphrey can't make himself move and he stands there awkwardly, clutching the spoon for dear life, wondering what it is he is feeling suddenly for Audrey, this sense of protectiveness, but of something else, something new. He wants to hug this girl, wants to *hug* her, and it is precisely for that reason that he cannot make himself move, it is precisely for this reason that he reaches for an onion and presents it to Audrey.

"If you're going to cry, Audrey, you might as well chop this next and get it over and done with." Humphrey holds his spoon upside down like a microphone and begins to croon. "Don't cry for me, Audrentina! I could have been delicious! A fancy chef now! With my TV show, I could have been delicious!"

* * *

TED has monopolized the dinner conversation with a play-by-play rehash of the evening news, a swarm of killer bees that had caused an elderly lady's death in nearby Sun City. Ted's color is up, his eyes gleam, and his voice warbles with the fascinated thrill of a voyeur. He enjoys the impact of his story on Diana, whose eyes skitter back and forth between her husband and children with the distracted animation of disbelief.

Ted pours himself more wine, which he's been gulping like water at key points in his monologue. Wally notices a new attentiveness in Diana, an alertness with which he is all too familiar. She is subtle, Diana is, but Wally perceives the invisible string that she wills to operate between her eyes and the neck of the bottle, between her eyes and the ever-pouring hand of her spouse. It is this watchful posture of Diana's, more than Ted's barely noticeable tightness around the lips when he enunciates certain words, that alerts Wally to the fact that Ted is a drinker.

"So, Diana," Wally says, at the first break in Ted's soliloquy. "I've been thinkin'—I'm not gonna let you leave till you promise you'll submit something."

"Pardon?" asks Diana.

"I want you to apply for the architect's job. Maybe you could even help me draft the ad?"

Diana puts down her fork, searching for the right words, but Ted beats her to it.

"Wally, old man. I told you. She doesn't practice."

"What's this?" asks Humphrey.

"I want your mom to give us something of hers to look at. I didn't know she designed buildings!"

Humphrey leans sideways towards Wally and points at his mother, "You know, Mum won the national architecture prize when she was at University."

"Wow. I *told* you you were good. Audrey thinks I'm crazy with all of this, but I swear, it's like I was getting a *signal* to bring you over here."

Audrey winces, catching Humphrey's eye.

Wally is too caught up in his own enthusiasm to notice this conspiracy of concern. "Well, anyway, we haven't even put it out to bid yet."

"And why is that, exactly?" asks Ted, his head tilted, eyes narrowed with the intense focus of a man eager to change the subject.

"Same reason as we had you sign off on that confidentiality agreement. If people find out about this before the Hungtington buyout is announced, it could artificially push up our stock price and then the deal can't go through at what we've been offered. At that point the price will fall all the way to Beijing, at which time we won't be able to sell because the stock's too low. And if we don't sell, then we can't build. On top of that, if we let on where it's gonna be, the land prices'll triple before you can say 'money pit.'"

"So you have to wait?" asks Diana.

"Yes and no. I want to run a blind ad in the trades and get some submissions."

"But how can architects design buildings without knowing what terrain and elevation they're looking at?" asks Diana.

"Well, we'd tier the screening. The first ad'll just request things like their portfolio, outlook, references, that kind of thing. Some sketches just to get a sense of style. I'm gonna want them to work with me on site, anyway. So, Diana, come on, promise you'll put something together."

"Wally, it's very kind of you. But Ted's right. I haven't practiced in—"

"So what? I'm telling you. Something would not let me concentrate yesterday. Something made me come over and see if you'd come to dinner. Just at that same exact time, something made *you* draw a building in the desert."

"Mum, you were *drawing?*" Humphrey's eyebrows lift in a quick vertical jig, and he leans across the table towards Wally. "She's got writer's block about drawing," Humphrey explains. "Or artist's block, I s'pose you call it."

"You have?" asks Ted, incredulous. "Diana, how could I not know such a thing?"

Diana looks back and forth at these conversationalists as though there is a ball they are tossing just out of her reach, and before she can get it in her grasp, the next speaker has batted it away again.

"How did you break it, Diana?" asks Wally. "Your block." He

knows he is being greedy for confirmation, he should just let this go, but a compelling possibility has suddenly occurred to him. That transforming moment in England, when he knew what it was he had to do, sell the company, build this tribute to Mary Kate, bring the Livelys over to Arizona: Maybe it was Diana he was meant to bring all along, not Ted.

"It's a long story, really," says Diana, hesitating. "Essentially, Eleanor was having trouble with her colouring and I—"

"Mummy! Stop!" warns Eleanor, growling through her teeth, a feral animal ready to bite.

"Sorry," explains Diana. "We're sensitive at this age."

"Eleanor, did you make me my picture for my locker?" asks Audrey.

"It's in Arizona!" shouts Eleanor. "Arizona" is what Eleanor calls her family's new house, just across the greenbelt. "Daddy, can you get it for me?"

"I'm certainly capable, Eleanor. Remember the difference between *can* and *may*. But I will absolutely *not* fetch your picture," says Ted. "You've mistaken me for the parent you've got wrapped around your finger."

"Mum?" asks Eleanor. "Please may you fetch my picture? Please?"

"Eleanor, tell me where it is," Wally says, dropping his napkin on the table and rising. "I'll get it."

"No, Gold. She mustn't think she can bend us all to her will. Besides, her room is a complete war zone," mutters Ted. "I meant to mention that to you, Diana. It looks as though several Pakistani families have taken up residence between the beds. All that's lacking is a goat and some curry and we could bring in *National Geographic* to film."

"But Audrey has no mummy!" cries Eleanor. This thought is

enough to bring her lower lip into an overhanging petal of sorrow that quivers over her chin.

"What's this?" asks Wally, shifting his gaze from Eleanor to Audrey.

"Eleanor overheard me telling Humphrey about the Mother-Daughter Outlet Mall thing. That's all."

Wally's eyes cloud over. "I'd have gone with you, Audrey. Why didn't you tell me?"

"Dad, it's okay. You were in England. It's no big deal. It's just— they had one of those booths where you could do the little pictures with your mom and Stacy has them hanging in her locker. A bunch of the girls do."

"So Eleanor promised to make Audrey a picture for her locker," explains Humphrey.

"Oh, that's what she was going on about?" asks Diana, recognition smoothing her brow.

"Is anyone else finding themselves feeling the slightest bit daft?" asks Ted. "Truly, I got completely blitheringly lost four or five sentences ago. What does any of this have to do with the price of rice in China?"

"I couldn't make Audrey's mummy good. My marker breaked."

"You couldn't make her mummy *well* darling, not *good*. It was very upsetting. No yellow for the hair. I kept telling her to use the brown, you see, because I supposed *I* was the mummy she was trying to draw," Diana tells Audrey.

"So, Mum, I still don't understand. How did Audrey's picture lead to your drawing a building? That's fantabulous!"

"I suppose I just—"

"Diana, I cannot believe you've kept this issue from me, the whole time we've been married. If I'd known, I— Well, I just feel surprised," Ted murmurs. "You've never shown the slightest interest."

It is only a matter of time before this problem of Diana's will become something that has been harder on her husband than it is on her.

* * *

"How can he sleep at night, being so disingenuous?" Humphrey asks Audrey as they walk across the greenbelt to fetch Eleanor's drawing. The artiste is between them, holding on to their hands as a personal suspension bridge by which she can—without warning—drop towards the ground before they must exert an equal and opposite reaction and lift her high. As often marks the behaviour of young people infatuated with each other's company, they are exceptionally tolerant of her gyrations, even grateful, it appears, for the buffer she provides.

"Why does she put up with it?" ventures Audrey. "He's handsome, I guess, but he kind of reminds me of a praying mantis, just the way he sits and massages his hands together, waiting and preening. Why did she marry him, anyway?" Audrey asks.

Humphrey unlatches the wrought-iron gate and carefully leads them through the back garden. "That's the rub. I have the worst feeling that she did it for me. So I wouldn't be a fatherless child."

"Bummer," sighs Audrey.

"Quite," notes Humphrey, pulling his treasured Eleanor up into his arms and giving her a fervent hug while blindly guiding his key to open the lock. He flicks on the kitchen switch and they are instantly bathed in a warm yellow light. "Then along came William and Baby makes three. And we're all here together, just as barmy as can be."

Eleanor runs to the counter and retrieves her picture. She hands it to Audrey, who smiles at Eleanor's drawing of a mother and daughter, neither of which have hair, but both of which have over-sized earrings and necklaces. "The picture," whispers Eleanor. "I couldn't make your mummy well."

"That's okay, sweetie." Audrey smiles as she squats down and en-circles Eleanor in her arms. "Neither could my dad and three hun-dred doctors. I love her anyway."

Six

When Wally dreams about Mary Kate, she is alive, seated in her favorite chair in the corner of the living room, folding herself around a tumbler of Dr Pepper. At a certain point in Wally's dream, his wife inevitably begins to disintegrate. It's only then that Wally realizes: It's not Dr Pepper in his wife's glass, but Johnny Walker Black. Mary Kate is laughing, not maliciously, but sweet, like she always got when she had her first couple of drinks. This is how she was before the words started to slur, before the black hole of self-respect opened up and swallowed her whole, before the morning after, when she'd beg his forgiveness and hate herself with such passion it was impossible not to pull her into his arms and declare his undying, all-forgiving love.

On the night the Livelys have come to dinner, though, Wally is awoken in mid-nightmare. They are seated around the table, just like earlier that evening. Wally has raised his glass, promising Audrey that Mary Kate has stopped drinking, for good. Father and daughter raise their glasses, toasting each other. "Now we can believe her!" they shout giddily. Amid this horrid glee, Wally turns to Diana, but she is no longer Diana. She's Mary Kate. Her eyes spill with the hurt of these words from her husband and daughter, and Wally wants, more than anything in the world, to undo the damage, but he cannot move. He is frozen to his seat, his mouth open in a circle of sorrow, watching his beloved wife, whose emerging wound is too deep for words.

* * *

THE sky of the desert at dusk shimmers with watery blue light. Diana stands tall on a boulder and waves at the unbearably beautiful blond man kneeling next to her son. They are an impossible distance away. Johnny is digging in the sand, showing William something astonishing. He does not heed her cries. Diana is filled with despair. She sees the dust rising in the distance, a shooting party that will find him, even here. Doubling over, an Olympic swimmer on the starting blocks of a sport she's never mastered, Diana counts to three and then lifts herself up in the air towards her loved ones.

This flying, why hadn't she thought of it before? It was as though her muscles remembered what her mind had abandoned. Easily, easily, she rises in the air and feels the updraft of wind beneath her palms, knowing that when she wakes, she'll be unable to remember what she cannot now forget. The déjà vu of it: The sense of having forgotten, then remembered, that this freedom was always at her fingertips, is accompanied by another sharp tug of recognition. This landscape—an unchanged fixture of her recurring dream for nearly twelve years—it closely resembles the Arizona desert, a place she'd never glimpsed before moving to these United States of America.

* * *

TED's breakfast appointment has been an inspiration, preventing him from discussing Humphrey's future at a time when his wife was her freshest and he—nocturnal by nature—was not.

He is now seated in a booth at Naughty Nelly's, just a short block away from the campus of Arizona State University. Last week, when he'd left the office, two flyers for the establishment had been lodged behind his windshield wiper. Through an extraordinary coincidence

that even an agnostic would tuck up and notice, he'd found another
flyer on his car when he'd left the next day. The second delivery was
all the more miraculous in that he'd not seen it until he was driving
up the Squaw Peak Parkway and the sky opened up with heavy wet
raindrops, *plip-plop, plip-plop.* On had gone the wipers, and the next
thing Ted saw was hot pink blearing across his windshield, carrying
the Naughty Nelly's logo *plip-plop, plip-plop* atop a pair of truly stu-
pendous breasts.

After the night he's had, with Diana refusing him the slightest
warmth, Ted feels entitled to something delicious for breakfast.
The Bloody Marys at Naughty Nelly's are actually tolerable and
the waitresses live up to the proprietor's promise, at least in their
sartorial flair. Ted's girl wears a pair of chaps, a thong and a suede
cowgirl vest fastened by a toy sheriff's badge. The vest teeters out,
just barely covering a pair of impressively generous breasts that
are unhindered by any apparent undergarment. Valeen has suggested the Lumberjack Special. When Ted asks if he'll be satis-
fied, she raises an eyebrow to suggest that she is no stranger to
customer satisfaction.

"Must come back here," Ted mutters to himself as he brushes
past Valeen and hands her two dollars on his way out of the bar.
Valeen seems astonished at the amount of money he's given her,
leaving him to wonder if he's overdone it. Perhaps he should have
gone with his original estimate of a dollar fifty? "Oh well, she'll remember me now," Ted thinks, and about that, he is right.

This very moment Valeen is in fact moved to discuss his tip with
her girlfriend. "Asshole gets knighted by the Queen at Mother
Trucking Buckingham Palace and he can't tip for shit. I wish I'd
slapped him when he"—here Valeen stops and punctuates her
words with curling peace signs—"'accidentally' felt my boobs while
I was putting on his ground pepper."

Dolores gives Valeen a sympathetic squeeze. "Those English pricks, they never tip. Think their accent's enough to make our day."

"So that's why you asked me to take your table?"

"No, I swear, honey. I didn't know he was cheap, it's just—I was getting a panic attack. I'll make it up to you tonight, baby. You know *mi casa es su casa* anyhow."

* * *

"Oh sugar! Duh, Duh, Duh, Duh, Duh, Duh! Oh honey, honey!" sing Humphrey and Audrey along with the loudspeaker at the trampoline park. They are both wearing huge white Gurkha shorts that balloon with air each time they descend towards their separate bouncing pads. The music stops for no apparent reason, and Audrey's gravelly out-of-key voice suddenly sounds extremely loud. Ducking her blushing face into her chest, Audrey executes a complicated sit, rise, spin in midair, and sits down facing the opposite way. Humphrey tries to follow along, but as this is his first trampoline experience, he gets only as far as the spin before he lands on his side and folds himself into the shaking surface to rest. "I'm knackered," he laughs. "I love this place!" he exults, rising up on his knees to give praise and thanks before he levers himself up with his arms and begins bouncing again.

"Hey, we had to celebrate," nods Audrey fervently. "It's not every day you defy the evil stepparent."

At this Humphrey flops down on the pad. He had conveniently repressed the prospect of facing Ted. "I just hope Mum won't bear the brunt of it."

"Why would she?" asks Audrey, tiptoeing along the rubber-encased frame of her trampoline. She hops from her frame to Humphrey's and squats before him to pull a eucalyptus leaf out of his hair. "She had nothing to do with it."

Humphrey pulls himself into a cross-legged sit and pats the area of the mat next to him for Audrey. "Technically no, but Ted's massively creative when it comes to blaming things on Mum. The laundry puts too much starch in his knickers, he's got her apologizing."

Audrey is now lying on her side, facing Humphrey. "He starches his boxers?"

Humphrey snorts. "No, but same concept. I don't feel at all upset about what I've done, because I know I can pay you back—"

"You don't have to—"

"Of course I do! But I'm worried Ted'll make her miserable on my account. She's never been a natural housekeeper. I've always helped. Just at the very moment she has a chance at submitting a drawing to your father's committee and she'll suddenly have more housework, less help from me, and a husband from Hell to boot."

"*To boot*'s the right word for it."

"I wish," sighs Humphrey. "I've been after her for years, but the more I say, the more she clings to the role of the martyred wife." Humphrey raises his voice an octave and closes his eyes like his mum does when sighing. "'I've made a commitment, Humphrey, not just at the altar but when I brought William and Eleanor into this world. I can't demolish their lives because Ted's sometimes—difficult.' And there's the money side of things. Mum's always into the overdraft as it is. With two houses to keep, on an academic's salary—well . . ."

"Geez, I thought your stepdad was Mr. Hot Tamale."

"Oh, he is, I suppose, but the University system in England pays everyone the same, from Hot Tamale to lukewarm porridge. And they don't pay well. I've always maintained that the reason the Fellows still wear their academic gowns to High Table is so no one can see their shabby clothes beneath."

"What about your mom's dollhouses?"

"They're perfect but so time-consuming. What's that joke your father made at dinner? 'We lose a little on every sale, but we make it up in volume'? And she hasn't practiced architecture since I was born. That drawing yesterday was the first she's done in years."

"Well, I bet my dad'd pay her big time to do the buildings for his theme park. He thinks it's 'no coincidence' that Eleanor was working on a picture of *my* mom when *your* mom suddenly decided to draw again."

"You never know, Audrey. Maybe he's right. Maybe she is getting some help from the Great Beyond."

Audrey shakes her head. "My dad and this religious crap, it's— it's not like my parents *ever* went to church. Mom used to say people might choose Heaven for the climate, but they'd sure choose Hell for the company. And my dad, Humphrey, he was your total atheist."

"Well, you know what Bertrand Russell said: If there is a God, He surely doesn't have such a large ego that He'd penalize those who hadn't been convinced of His existence."

"He, huh?"

"He, She. It. Don't you sometimes just think there might be *something* out there?"

"I think we all *want* to think that so much, we try to make it so, whether it is or not."

"Does that fact, that we'd like it to turn out a certain way, make it any less likely that it will?"

"Humphrey, think of all the shit that's been done in the name of religion. The Crusades, the Inquisition. Think about it."

"Audrey, what does that have to do with anything? I'm talking about us, here, now."

"That's right. Us, here, now. That's what we've got. And my dad is getting so caught up in never-never land that he's not paying attention to us, here, now. Some New Age shaman bit him in the butt. His life'll go by and he'll not be living it. It's been three years and all he can think about is building this stupid theme park. Which, by the way, my mom would have hated."

"How's that?"

"My mom *hated* Disneyland. If Dad had come with us even once, he'd have a clue."

"Pardon?"

"My dad used to be like, Mr. Workaholic. He'd say, 'Let's go to Disneyland,' so my mom would make reservations, and at the last minute he'd always back out and tell us to go by ourselves. We'd be at the park two hours and Mom would have a migraine. She'd promise to take me back again, so then she'd make more reservations, and then my dad would back out again. We'd go, she'd get her migraine, and back we'd go to the hotel."

"How awful for you."

"Nah, I didn't care. Those oversized characters creeped me out, if you want to know the truth. Mom'd let me order movies at the hotel and I could get anything I wanted from room service."

"And have I missed something? Why doesn't your father know any of this?"

"Mom swore me to secrecy. Admitting we didn't like it—it'd be like admitting defeat. My dad just loved the whole picture: his wife and daughter going away to have fun at Disneyland. My mom'd be so frosted when he'd cancel at the last minute, but by the time she was speaking to him again, she'd have made me promise not to tell. She'd be feeling kind of guilty herself, so it was just easier to tell him we'd had a great time. He was working and she was . . ." Audrey stares off into the distance, her lips pursed around the rest of her sentence. "You know, I even made up rides. I got pretty creative at it."

"You poor thing. Twice burned, twice shy."

"Twice! It was probably at least once a year from the time I was six till I was twelve."

"But you kept returning?"

"I guess my mom kept thinking that the next time she made the reservation, my dad'd actually go with us. Then we could let him see how it was. Then we'd 'fess up. But every time, like déjà vu all over again, he'd beg off at the last second. I'd be upset and think 'It serves him *right* not to know.' Like somehow I was paying him back. Then when Mom couldn't tell him . . ." Audrey waves her hand sideways, and lets it fall without resolution.

"You said she felt guilty? Why? Why would she feel guilty?"

Audrey looks at her hands, and then moves her head sideways towards Humphrey's, but she doesn't quite meet his eyes. "Who knows why people feel like they do?" She shrugs. Though she can't quite put it into words, Audrey knows, or thinks she has put together a reasonable theory. Her mom's high cheekbones, her lank straight hair. A watchfulness about Mary Kate, and at the same time a bluntness. Indian genes—a strong possibility—would account for her inability to drink, or rather, her compulsion to drink and her inability to stop. Audrey has watched the History Channel, knows how the bravest warriors had succumbed to the insidious powers of firewater after resisting the more overt weapons of invading armies. This theory would explain a lot, and though genealogical research has dead-ended at the Missouri great-grandparents, Audrey feels certain this is why her mother couldn't resist the hotel honor bars. Not when her head was killing her and she'd been let down, yet again. It all made perfect sense.

Audrey pulls her knees up to her chest and sticks her pointed chin into the crevice above her calves. "It really wasn't that bad." Audrey's words say one thing, her body language another. She holds herself so tautly against the treachery of remembering too much, or blaming, or hating, or hoping, or wishing. In her fetal crouch, she appears a bow stretched against several simultaneous arrows. The arch of her foot is trembling, and Humphrey cannot help but put his strong fingers down to steady her, at the point where her tan recedes into the pale newborn instep, between the defensive callouses on the heel and ball of her foot, a tiny opening of softness he wants to heal.

"I'm sorry, luv," he says, without even thinking.

"It's okay. Just, I don't—Disneyland isn't exactly a place I think my mom would have liked to be remembered, that's all."

"Audrey, don't you think you should tell your father?"

"No. I'm okay. You don't get my dad. He's like—I don't know—he's turned my mom into a saint. He doesn't want to hear anything that gets in the way of that. And besides, he's been so blissed out. I don't want to burst his bubble."

"But don't you owe it to him to be honest?"

"Too late. The time to be honest woulda been when I was twelve. It's just gonna make him feel guilty."

Humphrey sits for a minute, squinting off into the disappearing horizon. "Why twelve?" he asks, turning to look at Audrey. "What made you finally stop going?"

"I don't remember," Audrey says, a bit too quickly. She stands up and moves back to her trampoline, where she executes a number of flips and spins, demonstrating just how flexible a girl she can be.

* * *

WILLIAM is thirsty all the time. He can't fill up. On his way back to class, he stops at the water fountain, for what seems like the thirtieth time that day, bends over and presses the lever on the side of the drinks fountain. They don't have these devices in England. When he'd asked Humphrey why that was, his older brother had shaken his head and shrugged.

"Well, it's always pissing rain at home. You live in the drink. But Arizona. Crikey, William, you can't hydrate enough! So use that fountain, especially after playground."

An obedient William is eager for the cold water, but his head is suddenly pressed down by a descending hand at the back of his neck. The water goes in William's nose, and he sputters up, coughing and snorting, to see who has pushed him.

As if he needed to look.

Standing nearby, peering at the ceiling, is Austin Wilken. Austin's father is a quarterback for the Arizona Cardinals, and so the boy is revered by one and all, teachers and students alike, despite the fact that he is not very bright, despite the fact that he is worlds brighter than he is nice. Two weeks ago Austin had brought a signed American football to school. When Ms. Marsh took a phone call in the office, Austin had carried it around from desk to desk, taunting the boys with a proffered palm and then whipping it out of sight once his victim declared any sort of interest. William, still seated in the back, had made his decision by the time Austin got to him. "No, thank you," William had muttered, keeping his eyes on the book he was reading, about the war between England and the American Colonies.

"Hey, dickhead," Austin had said. "I'm talkin' to you, English boy. You'd better read that book, han't you? Your freakin' Redcoat ancestors got drilled in that freakin' war."

William had nodded quickly, but he kept his eyes on his book. He was wondering if his mum would let him bring his fencing foil to school. One feint and then before you could say *en garde*, Austin would be cowering in the corner, begging for his life. Austin had reached out and flicked William's chin. "Show some respect when you're in our country."

William wanted to shout that Wilken was a German name,

wasn't it? As in Nazi Germany? As in the German tourist that killed Johnny?

William made himself meet Austin's eyes, and suddenly it came to him, what Johnny would have done. William squinted just slightly, and he carefully brought his hand to his forehead and then directly out above Austin's head. "Heil Hitler," said William, in just the same self-assured monotone that he pictured Johnny having. "Heil Hitler."

Ever since the Heil Hitler day, though, Austin Wilken has been relentless. Now William is Austin's brand of choice when it comes to cruel and unusual punishment. "Wee Willie, you're so small; yo mama drank some alcohol!"

William narrows his eyes at Austin, racing his brainwaves for the proper comeback. The water that is dripping down his upper lip itches fiercely, but to wipe it away would be an admission that Austin has gotten to him. William pretends to himself that he is on the football green, having just kicked a goal. He looks past Austin and walks down the hall, past thousands of adoring fans. He is so bent on rising above his surroundings that he does not see the PTA volunteer who has been standing in the hall, pinning cutouts to a bulletin board.

* * *

VALEEN Johnson née Sweeney lives in a small Paradise Valley apartment so that her son, Adam, can go to this choice school that Dolores has insisted on. Her sisters think she's nuts. She could have a whole house in Glendale for what she pays in rent. Valeen has spent her whole adult life hearing just how mental she is, not just for renting versus owning, but for the way she earns her living, for her needing to work in Adam's classroom twice a week so she can butter up the teacher, for her decision to live with Dolores, who's almost old enough to be her mother, half in, half out of the closet.

The only thing her sisters do agree about is Adam. He's the first grandchild on the Sweeney side and adored by each and every one of them for his Hollywood looks, his trophies in every sport, his straight A's, but most of all because Adam is nice in a way that isn't phony, isn't gooey, and isn't up to his mood du jour. Sometimes he scares Valeen, how perfect he is. It could be like God has sent him down here for some special purpose and then he'll be taken away early in life, like the kid in *Pay It Forward*. You heard about stuff like that all the time.

After she's finished hanging the Oktoberfest display, Valeen heads back into Ms. Marsh's room to work in small reading groups with the children. Today's group includes the two boys she saw struggling at the water fountain, one of whom she recognized as Ray Wilken's son. The other boy is the first to read, and when he starts with his English accent, the other children giggle. Valeen is just about ready to lay into him for mocking her when she sees a glint of tears in the boy's eyes.

"Stop for a minute. Tell me your name," she says gently.

By the time William complies, Valeen has made up her mind. "Oh, you're the kid from England, then? Adam told me about you, how brave he thinks you are to move all the way over here and start in a new school. And I bet you're really good at soccer, 'cause you English kids play from the time you're really little. You oughta come over some afternoon and kick the ball around with Adam. Would you like that? Maybe today?"

William ducks his head in what can be interpreted as a nod. He is blushing furiously and trying to decide whether this woman is in on an elaborate plot to humiliate him. Everyone, even William, knows Adam Johnson is the most well-liked boy in fourth grade. What would he be doing asking William over? "Uh, I'm not certain I could reach my mu— mom," says William.

At this, Austin reaches over and swats William on the back of the head. "Oh, Adam'll be so sad if you can't go!" he cries.

"Please, keep your hands to yourself," directs Valeen. "You must be Austin Wilken."

Austin lifts his eyebrows and points to himself with a debonair shake of the head. "Who me? Adam tell you who I was?"

"No, I don't think Adam's mentioned your name. But I remember you from kindergarten. I was at that Pilgrim party when the first graders made you cry. Boy, were they mean! I felt so sorry for you. But here you are, one of the big kids now. Time flies. So, Austin, why don't you pick up where William left off?"

As Austin reads his paragraph with sudden intensity, Valeen congratulates herself for not blurting out that she knew Austin's dad. Who doesn't? Of course, since he's been such a football hero, but she *knew him*—knew him, back when he was in high school, back when she pretended to be straight and so did he, and dating seemed a good enough camouflage for both of them. She remembers them hoppin' around the homecoming floor to Abba's "Dancing Queen," laughin' their heads off.

Nice guy, Raymond, even if he could never come out of the closet. His wife seemed happy enough on the camera cutaways during the games. A really pretty brunette with a ski-jump nose and smug little mouth. Not hard to see who her son got his attitude from.

After the bell rings, Valeen waits for Adam and together they intercept William. "Hey, William!" Adam yells. "Wanna come play?"

Before William can answer, Valeen pulls a cell phone out of her purse. "Let's call your mom and see if it's okay. Adam and I can follow the bus home and pick you up. How's that?"

"I can give you the number," William manages to say.

* * *

October 7
Re: letter of September 28

Dear Mr. Gawain,

No permits have been filed for the Lake Havasu Watershed. Until such actions occur, we cannot send out for comment.

Please be aware that Tier 4 projects undergo an extremely high level of scrutiny and must show substantial promise as regards job creation, revenue sharing, and other economic impacts. Since 1990, only one Tier 4 project was approved. Twenty-two were not. We suggest that all applicants consider ways in which they might reduce usage and fall below the Tier 4 thresholds.

Sincerely,
Francis Cervantes III

* * *

VALEEN pulls onto William's street just behind the small school bus.

"Shit, he's rich!" whistles Valeen, brushing one of her chestnut hairs from the steering wheel of her Trans Am.

"I told you, Mom. He rides the small bus," scolds Adam, who's already explained the Mesquite Elementary School hierarchy.

There were the Camelback Mountain kids, not too many of them, 'cause the houses were so far apart. They rode the smaller private bus with air-conditioning and seat belts. Next were the Pulte kids, so-called whether their tract house had been built by Pulte or Dell Webb or any of the other builders whose neighborhoods had sprouted up between CraftMarts and Michaelses's and Targets and the Sumitomo Plant just north of the city. They rode the big school buses funded by the district, their lots being smaller and thus producing a more densely packed population of elementary-aged children. Their parents complained now and then about the lack of seat belts, but the answer was always the same: The smaller buses ran on less fuel and could not be purchased without the belts. Furthermore, they had not cost the district one cent since they'd been donated back in the Keating years by a Paradise Valley billionaire whose daughter had gone to Mesquite and who lived, you guessed it, on top of Camelback Mountain. An endowment paid for gas and other operating costs.

Then there were the Apartment kids, most of whom were in walking distance of school, except for Adam and a few classmates in the Dreamy Draw Desert Pavilions, a complex just south of the Sumitomo Plant whose gated pink walls hung flags of all nations, behind which cowered a row of undersized dollhouse-like duplexes flanked by an arched freeway wall.

Adam loved the flags. He loved the sound of the freeway, a soothing white noise whooshing up and down the day. He never complained to his mom about where they lived, never seemed to mind the difference between his Christmases and those of his classmates, never asked for anything, just kept his mom and Dolores laughing with his stories that made his school seem like the Discovery Channel, like some exotic place full of strange and fascinating creatures.

Valeen pats her son's shoulder as they approach the Livelys' front door. "Thanks, Adam."

"No prob, Mom. Austin Wilken is such a loser. Besides, I need to practice my soccer anyhow."

"Hon, you know I'm not sure about getting you there, with work and all."

"I know, Mom. But even if I go to half, the coach'll let me play."

"Oh, sweetie, I feel so bad. It's just been so slow lately, I can't afford to take off."

"Mom, don't worry," soothes Adam, pushing the doorbell.

William pulls open the door, so quickly that Valeen realizes he's been standing there behind it, waiting. He has on one shin guard and hobbles across the floor to get another. "Mum!" he yells toward the kitchen. "Mum says to bring you inside," he says, ducking his head down shyly. "She's laying tea."

"Oh, she doesn't need to do that!" exclaims Valeen, her blood pressure rising at the idea of sitting down and making conversation with some proper English lady while trying not to dribble crumbs on her lap. "Adam should change still and—oh hi!"

"Hullo!" laughs Diana, gliding in from the kitchen, wiping her hands on a dishcloth. "I'm Diana, William's mum. Please excuse the mess, but I've been playing make-believe with my daughter, who's had a wretched day at preschool. Do you have time for tea?"

Valeen cannot believe William's mom is so young and pretty. Not at all like Margaret Thatcher or one of those ladies she'd had in mind. "I'm Valeen," she stammers. "And this here's Adam. We can't—I can't stay. My roommate's making cookies and I've got the brown sugar in the car."

While William puts on his soccer cleats, Diana makes polite conversation, asking Adam how he likes his teacher and whether he takes to homework and how long he's been playing football or soccer as she keeps forgetting to call it.

Valeen is so lost in awe at Diana's fancy accent that she can't help screaming when a small green dragon pounces from behind the kitchen door and stands with her hands on her hips demanding "Milk! Puff must have milk!" before pulling off her oversized dragon's head and sternly chastising her mother for leaving her alone.

"Just a moment, Miss Eleanor. I'm afraid you've forgotten your manners," scolds Diana. "Puff must say hello to William's friend, Adam, and Adam's mum."

"Puff need milk! In bowl on floor like proper dragon."

William looks at his sister, as if measuring where exactly—in any make-believe kingdom worth its salt—he might use his sword to inflict the most damage in the least time. "Eleanor," he warns, and there is something about his accent and manner, that brings to mind Valeen's recent customer-from-hell.

"Oh gosh, William's dad, he's not like a knight or anything, is he?" she asks.

"Not last I noticed," laughs Diana. "Why do you ask?"

"Oh, I met this guy the other day from England who'd gotten knighted or "sir'd or something like that. I know, it's stupid, like sometimes people know I'm from Ohio, they ask me if I know so-and-so from Akron. Sorry."

"Not at all. Coincidence—"

"Nah, you're just being nice. Anyway, that's a relief, 'cause this guy, if he's married, his wife's the one that deserves a knighthood."

* * *

TED sits at his desk at Gold Ammunitions, right hand to forehead. It is something between a salute and a Victorian heroine's preswoon caress. His legs are crossed gracefully, his back is straight, and he is waiting. *Tip-tap, tip-tap,* play his fingers against his brow. He watches the screen, silently urging his new best friends in the Sierra Club chatroom to wake up and smell the roses. Or is it coffee? After giving it a minute, Ted sighs and types IS THERE NO ONE WILLING TO SPEAK TRUTH TO POWER?

For his creative use of activist vernacular, Ted is rewarded with three similarly worded but unbearably condescending reminders that the use of all capital letters in an Internet correspondence is considered hostile and is not in keeping with the peaceful purposes of this e-community. The fourth response, however, is pay-dust. It provides the name of an enormously influential investigative reporter who protects the confidentiality of whistle-blowers, large and small. Ted signs off in a flurry of gratitude mixed with pride at his new *raison d'être*, a solitary knight of right against the corporate behemoth that is threatening his family and ruining his career.

* * *

DIANA looks at her watch and yelps. "Ow, it's half-four. Daddy'll be home in forty minutes. Eleanor, it's time to Zoom!"

"Dragon no Zoom. Dragon pway more with Mummy," whines Eleanor.

"Chop, chop, Eleanor. Get the Zoom bags, darling," whispers Diana, already worrying about how she will make her case to Ted. The last thing she needs is to be caught playing when the house looks as it does, three pence short of complete bedlam. William's school satchel lies open inside the door, pouring papers and sweet wrappers all over the foyer. His shoes are toppled in the corner where he's tossed them, and it is now that Diana sees the black skids on the wall where his missed aim has left its mark. A crumpled T-shirt lies on the floor heading towards the kitchen. Eleanor's toys are scattered from one end of the room to the other.

Humphrey has invented the Zoom game. He and Eleanor run from room to room with the bags, racing to see who can fill theirs faster with toys. "Where're the bags, darling?"

Eleanor shrugs and makes her way towards Diana, a determined snarl signaling her plan to grasp Diana's leg and keep her prisoner. She is already growling loudly. Diana hops out of her daughter's reach and dashes up to Eleanor's room. The Zoom bags are completely full. Diana opens the closet and winces at the chaos within before dumping the contents of both bags on top of the Barbie junkyard on the floor. Dashing downstairs with the two pink gingham totes, Diana sneaks around Eleanor, who is crouched over a stuffed bunny and is shaking it with her teeth. Diana scurries around, filling the bags, ignoring the fact that she is mixing everything—papers, bills, junk mail—into the bag with Eleanor's toys. Later. Later, she will get a moment's peace and sort this all out.

By five o'clock she has returned the living room to its normal post-Humphrey state, at least on the surface. Diana knows that Humphrey would never have gotten his categories so enmeshed. He'd have sorted out the paperwork from the things that went up-stairs, but Diana doesn't have her son's efficient cast of thought. She is so undone by the mess and by the prospect of Ted's home-coming that she just wants to be quickly rid of everything that might displease him.

All weekend long Ted has put off discussing William's soccer and Humphrey's cookery lessons. Last night, right before bed, she had forced herself to raise the subject one more time, and Ted had promised to set aside some time today, before dinner, to sort it out. Whether he'd remember—after two bottles of red wine and several post-dinner martinis—was another question. While part of her hopes not, the other part knows she must face this chat head-on. She has promised William and promised herself. She is determined to calmly state her intentions and to not get drawn into Ted's argu-mental "nettles," as Evelyn calls them. Diana is prompted to call her friend, but before she can reach the cordless, the phone rings.

"Diana? It's me. Listen, there's a truck on its way. I'll be over in a couple a minutes, but if they get there before I do, just have 'em wait."

"Wally?"

"I was thinkin'. You know what: I hate the phone. Just give me a sec, okay?"

Diana runs a comb through her hair and sighs at the circles un-der her eyes, darkened by a night of worrying. She splashes water on her face when the doorbell rings abruptly.

Wally stands at the door with such trepidation that Diana instantly fears something terrible has happened. "Is something wrong?" she cries, taking one of Wally's hands and pulling it towards her as a way of guiding him in. "The children?"

Wally stares down at Diana's hands, so white against his olive skin, and though they are strong, even sinewy, they are also very small. It takes a deep breath to stop himself from clamping his free hand down over hers in a desperation not unlike Eleanor's earlier advances. "No, the kids are fine. It's just—I did something on impulse and I hope you're okay with it."

Diana smiles warily, squinting at the sunlight. "Come in," she says and she pulls the door shut behind him.

"The guest room," says Wally. "It's all wrong. The delivery guys'll take it when they bring the new furniture."

"New?"

"You need a drafting table, Diana. There's not one space in this house that's just for you. You need a studio."

"But I don't even know—"

"You never will if you don't try. And if you're gonna try, you gotta have what you need. Wanna come up with me and we'll strip the bed so it'll be ready when they get here?"

Diana's confusion about the purpose of Wally's business, her shock, even a mild disjointed alarm, all these are outweighed by her embarrassment at the chaotic state of the guest room. She is ashamed of her housekeeping and it is this emotion that propels Diana as she takes the stairs two at a time.

"Oh I'll do it. You needn't. You see, Eleanor was in there a few days ago, and I'm afraid she's colonized the space a bit. I'll just straighten up—"

"Hi, Elly," Wally says, squatting down and patting the girl's head.

Eleanor steadfastly ignores him, concentrating all of her powers on pulling a small-toothed comb through her bunny's tail. Wally climbs the stairs steadily, calling in front of him, awkwardly. "Diana, let me help." Diana has quickly pulled the sheets up to the pillows' edge to resemble a properly made bed, but as she seeks to smooth the lumps underneath, she is met with resistance. She pulls back the covers to find a Montblanc pen of Ted's surrounded by a Rorschach blot of ink, a small hairbrush, a credit card in Ted's name for United Bank of Switzerland, and a hot-pink circular with the name Naughty Nelly's written in script across the otherwise naked breasts of a woman with an abundant mane of curly hair.

Diana folds all of the objects into the flyer and is tempted to throw them in the wastebin, but she knows she'll be asked to account for them later.

"Here," says Wally, taking all of them from her and setting the mess on the counter of the adjoining bathroom.

"I'm so sorry about the ink, Wally. Eleanor is so—Eleanor!" Diana shouts. "Come see what you've done! Oh, Wally! I'm afraid it's leaked through to the mattress!"

"Stop, Diana. It's okay. It's goin' to Goodwill anyhow." A loud squeal of tires grinding against hydraulic brakes filters its way into the upstairs window. "Truck's here," Wally adds. Diana is already kneeling below the bed, pulling out several small plastic items and a second flyer for Naughty Nelly's. This time the question cannot be swatted away with the dreck of the afternoon. It cannot be packed in the Zoom bag and ignored until the never-never land of peace and quiet allows her to sort the chaos into order.

She doesn't need to put it into words, Wally can see it written across her features. In the battle between comforting Diana on the one hand, or letting her see the true nature of Ted's character on the other, Wally doesn't even blink. "These flyers are all over the city. They plaster 'em on people's windshields. The place is way the hell down in Tempe."

"Near the campus, then?" asks Diana, folding the second flyer and folding it again.

"Tempe's a big place."

"Yes, but it says right here, 'Only one block from campus.' How convenient."

Wally is deterred from trying to convince her further of Ted's innocence by the sound of the doorbell.

Two large men with Rasta braids make quick work of carrying out the bed and various nightstands and bureaus from the guest room.

Wally sweeps the tile floor with a broom, waving away Diana's protests. "Why don't you get rid of the stuff in the bathroom? I thought we'd store your supplies under the sink."

Diana gathers Ted's things and carries them into the master bedroom. The logo on the credit card catches the glint of dying sunlight as she passes the window, but Diana isn't interested in holograms. She is concentrating instead on the name of the bank. Switzerland is awfully far away, and this card is shiny and new. Why and when had Ted decided to open an account? Was it before or after last week's lecture on how little he will make after taxes, appreciably less than he did in Oxford? Ted had somberly requested her Barclay's charge card, paired it with his own, and placed them in a bowl of water. "This way, if we need them," he said, setting the bowl in the recesses of the freezer, "we can thaw the ice. Until then, we'll avoid temptation."

This very morning, before she got the call about Eleanor, Diana had been standing at the door of the freezer, trying to remember on which shelf Ted had placed that bowl, rehearsing the script for why a trip to the art supply store was something she needed, rather than wanted, though there was that, too.

She'd nearly jumped out of her skin with the sudden ring out of nowhere, the call from Eleanor's school saying that she'd wet her pants and needed to be picked up. It had brought Diana back to Earth, the teacher's voice asking gently if there was something going on at home that might be "stressing Eleanor out." Even as she was telling the teacher that no, everything was fine, Diana was already blaming herself.

How had she let herself get swept up in wanting; had she forgotten her own feelings as a child? Diana's father, a diplomat, had been overseas for months at a time, often taking Diana's mother along for company. The children had been shipped off to boarding schools and summer camps. "It's not as though he does this out of greed," Charlotte would tell Diana and Blair. "He travels for the good of the country, and I travel because, without me, he can't maintain his equilibrium. You children, by being so good about all this, you're contributing as well."

Diana had found these chats less than convincing, and she always suspected that her father traveled not because of the greater good, but because of the sheer adrenaline and pleasure of knowing he was influencing History. So how did that differ from Evelyn's father, who spent his nights at the factory because of the sheer pleasure of accumulating all that wealth? And how could the desire of a child for the company of a parent compete with that? How could a seven-year-old's tears, as she boarded a plane to England, persuade him of anything? Diana had sworn, when she grew up, that she would never fool herself about her reasons for doing something, and more to the point, she would not consign her children to the care of nannies and boarding schools so that she could sacrifice them upon the altar of accomplishment, all the while thinking that was somehow morally superior to the altar of greed. After all, emotional neglect was just that, no matter how you cut it.

Diana puts Ted's Montblanc and new credit card on his dresser.

"Diana?" Wally asks from the hall. "Can you come to my car for a minute? I got some stuff, but if it's wrong, there's no point in unloading it. I got, like, architects' drawing pads and stuff."

"Wally, I can't accept—it's very sweet of—"

"Stop. I'll write it all off. So just come down and help me look through it all."

"Wally, I can't. I don't have time."

"It'll just take a minute."

"No, not to look at the boot of your car. I mean, I don't have the time to be an architect."

"Make the time."

"It's complicated. The children, I never know when they'll need me. And if I get caught up—"

"Look, I know what you're saying. I wish I could take back those years I worked twenty-four/seven and didn't spend time with Audrey. But I—you're a good mother. That doesn't mean you can't take time for yourself, too."

"Wally, I haven't practiced in years. And with Ted working so much, I can't see how—"

"What's he working on? Until we make the announcement, he won't have to do jack."

"But he's got academic commitments to keep."

"So? Why does he get to keep those and you don't get to do anything? That's not fair. Marriage is a partnership."

"This from an admitted workaholic? Did you and your wife manage to split the day down the middle then?"

"No, but Mary Kate—she never found anything she felt really good at. I guess part of my reason for pushing you is that I think she felt this emptiness, like she didn't think what she did was ever good enough, no matter what I told her. Hell, I could never have built the business without her. I couldn't work like I did unless I knew Audrey was taken care of. And Mary Kate nursed my mom when she was sick; she entertained clients. Still, no matter what I said, she—her self-esteem was like a bottomless pit. No matter how great I told her she was, she didn't believe it."

Diana notes that this is the first time she has ever heard Wally say anything about his wife that isn't glowing with nostalgia. She is thinking of this when she hears her name called from below.

"Diana!" shouts Ted. "Why are there Africans in the driveway?" He catches sight of Wally, standing behind his wife as they descend the stairs, and for one moment all three are aware of the possible misinterpretations a jealous spouse could place on such a scene. Diana recovers first, for she has years of experience in anticipating and deflecting Ted's moods. "Wally's just redone the guest room, Ted."

She leaves it to Wally to explain why.

Wally fishes for the words, then shrugs and says, "If Diana's going to work for me, she needs an office."

Ted turns his open mouth to Diana, who turns her open mouth to Wally. "But I haven't even submitted anything yet."

"You don't need to. You're the one. I trust my hunches."

"For God's sakes, man, do you have any idea how insulting condescension can be? Diana will feel you've simply chosen her for her looks."

Wally turns his full gaze to meet Ted's eyes. He radiates such dislike that even Ted realizes he's overstepped the bounds. "Look, buddy. I didn't read your work before I hired you. It never occurred to you that my hiring *you* was condescending, did it? I saw Diana's drawing yesterday, and I know she won the national architecture prize and I've seen her dollhouses, and I can see she's got the patience of a saint. The fact that her beauty takes my friggin' breath away, that's beside the point."

Seven

For a man who's cut his teeth on the razor's-edge of callow, Ted has an unerring instinct about when to stop behaving badly. It is as though each time Diana has seen enough to know, just when Evelyn and Humphrey are holding their separate, unconspiring, yet cross-continentally connected breath to see what it is she will do, this is the moment when Ted will find a way to redeem himself.

The delivery van is long gone. Diana sits in the elevated chair in her new office, her elbows pressed against the pine drafting table which Wally has ordered. Her head is in her hands and she is staring out the window. She is speechless. The mountains in the distance are blue-grey, ringed by a halo of smog that captures the colors of the desert: coral, magenta, copper, ochre.

The door is open, but Ted knocks anyway. His posture is head-to-toe deference. "Diana. I've been a hopeless cad. I hope you can forgive me. I hope you know that it's not that I'm not supportive of your talents. I believe in you fully and completely. It's just, I don't trust this man. I don't trust his motives. Bad enough I have to work for him, but to pull you into his web—I care about you. I don't want you hurt."

Diana cannot seem to open her mouth.

"The more I see him in action, the less I think of our Mr. Gold. He's notorious for going off on tangents and then, when it's time to go forward, he abandons those he's taken down the garden path and forgets they've ever been inconvenienced. I just don't trust his emotionalism, the way he impulsively decides to hire you and then delivers new furniture, without so much as a by-your-leave. I mean, do you not wonder just a bit about his mental balance? Can you really trust him with your future? Especially after so many disappointments?" Ted pauses long enough to stare pleadingly into his wife's unseeing eyes. "I just don't want to see you hurt. After all, I should know how it feels when your dream comes close and is snatched away repeatedly. The Fletcher Prize Committee hasn't called, and as it's past their decision time, I know that once again, I'm out of the running."

Diana forces herself to look his way. She doesn't speak, but he believes he can spot a glint of sympathy in her eyes.

Ted waits for her to say something soothing. When she remains silent, he reminds her of all that they share, of all she holds dear. "Where're the children off to, then?"

Diana clears her throat. She shakes her head, ridding it of her unreasonable desire to never again utter a single word. She forces her voice to be emotionless and steady. She is still angry, but Ted can see she's turned a corner. "Eleanor's napping and William's at a mate's."

"William's got a friend?"

Diana nods. "Adam, a boy from school."

"And?"

"I met his mum. They're playing football."

"Well, that's a wonderful development!" says Ted, his voice rising interrogatively. "Don't you think, Diana? You've wanted him to have a mate."

"Ted, I've signed him up for the American soccer team," lies Diana. "It's what he needs." She still looks out the window.

"Look, there's no need to scold. We'll agree to let it go this time. Let's have a kiss and try not to squabble."

Diana turns her cheek for a quick peck, but Ted turns her mouth to his and kisses her hungrily. Diana wiggles out of his embrace and places his hands out in midair, away from her body. "I've got dinner to get started," she says, backstepping out of the room.

Ted follows her downstairs. He hums while he mixes a vodka martini. He sits at the table, slurping his drink and watching his wife as she clears the tea plates and begins washing lettuce at the sink. "So, you naughty creature: How did you pay? For William's trainer."

"They told me I could bring a cheque tomorrow," Diana says woodenly, the invention coming to her without much forethought. "One hundred and eighty dollars. Will you make it out for me, please, before you forget."

"Yes, I remember the amount, Diana. I do have one question, however, before we sign off for a hundred pounds just like that. If you take Gold's Faustian offer, how will William get to the practice field?"

For Diana, the promise of making a real building, even if it will be in a theme park, the promise of that: It is a cloud in her brain that swells with rain, eclipsing all that went before it. Diana cannot remember herself before this hope began to grow, she cannot see the person she was just a few hours before. She can only feel an overwhelming desire, and while she tells herself it is more like greed, the observation makes no real difference to the blinding sense of fullness that blurs the edges of her priorities. The possibility that she might have it all, that her children will not only survive, they might even prosper: This is a glimmer on the horizon that she's unwilling to press for the truth. She'll work out the details later; just now she will allow herself to enjoy the experience.

In this state of punch-drunk obstinacy, Diana flicks away the bait that Ted has dangled before her. "Oh, don't worry about that. I'm sure Mephistopholes will help me find a way. Do let me mix you another drink."

* * *

AUDREY and Humphrey are sitting in Audrey's van, which is parked in front of the Lively household. They've already sent in Eleanor and William, but Humphrey can't seem to make himself budge. He is gathering his nerve. "It's so stuffy!" he shouts, startling Audrey, who has been trying to calm him with some quick lessons in meditation.

"It's time to go in and face it, Hump. Just remember. You're eighteen."

"Could you please, please pop on the air?"

"Humphrey, do you see that beautiful sunset? Let me tell you about particulates. They capture the color of the desert and cause cancer in children—"

"Audrey, not now. Just pop it on."

"No. I won't. Just get out of the car and tell your prick of a stepfather you're going to the Blue Goose and he can stuff it up his skinny little ass."

"Easy for you to say."

"I'll go with you. Now, chip-chop, last one in is a beastly fundamentalist."

When they arrive in the kitchen, Diana is surrounded by the debris of dinner preparation. The tea plates are stacked in the kitchen sink, underneath a colander of dew-covered lettuce. Spread across the counter are a jam jar, its lid askew, vegetable carcasses, crumpled paper wrappers, a jumble of papers from school, and a tea strainer bleeding grit onto the granite counter.

Humphrey looks at his watch. It cannot have been only eight

hours since he last saw his kitchen. The floor is littered with crumbs, unidentified black bits, and at least two stickers in spitting distance that will shortly be nearly impossible to scrape without leaving a permanent smudge of adhesive against the shiny gleam of the burnished tile.

"Humphrey! Darling!" glows Diana. "How are you?" There is a light in her eyes, a high bit of colour in her nose and cheekbones, despite her proximity to unattractive carrot heads sprouting on unwiped surfaces, that would, Humphrey thinks, cause profound desolation and despair in most Homo sapiens. If this is how the house looks, after one day of his absence, how on earth will his mother manage once he's taking full tuition at the Blue Goose?

"I'm well, Mummy. And you?" he asks, bending to kiss her forehead while simultaneously swiping a handful of vegetable peels from the counter towards the sink. "Where's Ted?" he asks. Audrey and he have agreed: best to break this news to both of them at once. That way Mum won't be indicted as a coconspirator in Humphrey's defection to the Great Unwashed.

"Checking his study. He's not quite convinced the Jamaican deliverymen didn't duck into his room and nick something."

"Deliverymen?"

Diana looks up from her chopping and tries for nonchalance as she tells Humphrey of the new studio and Wally's job offer. Her eyes have an almost glassy quality to them, her color is high. In another context, one might diagnose a fever.

For Humphrey, her words are on one track, his regrets on another. He is outside himself, watching to see what he will do. When he realizes that she's stopped talking, he forces himself to take the reins.

"Oh, Mum, that's glorious. I'm so happy for you," Humphrey mumbles and he embraces his mother so she cannot see his expression.

Audrey, though, has a perfect view of Humphrey's troubled face; his eyes that circle the messy kitchen and meet her own. With a brief but nonetheless ferocious squint of his eyes and an outward flick of his hand from his mother's back, comes his demand for silence.

Audrey plays deaf. "Humphrey has news, too. He wanted to tell you and Mr. Lively together, but maybe—"

"Audrey," warns Humphrey. "You promised you'd let me tell!"

"Oh, come on then, what is it, darling?"

By now Humphrey has crossed the room. He swoops Audrey into a fierce embrace, kissing her lips into quiet. When he emerges, and separates himself from Audrey's astonished open mouth, it is with a flushed grin. "We're going steady, Audrey and I. We wanted you to be the first to know."

* * *

TED falls into bed a happy man. His wife has been pouring him drinks all night, with uncharacteristic generosity. She's been drinking with him, an uncharacteristic camaraderie. She's looking lovely. With the mist of the nightlight, and a little imagination, Ted can see her wearing a thong and chaps and a little sheriff's badge that pins the latch to the gates of Heaven. "Come over here," he mumbles.

It is all Diana can do not to groan aloud. Sex is the last thing she wants, and in her tipsy state, she admits to herself that she is truly repulsed by her husband. She pretends to be asleep, but Ted worms his way over to her, and he swipes at her breast before taking her hand and bringing it down to his erection.

Ahem, correction of fact. There is no erection, there is instead this bafflingly loose assortment of skin and cording that wraps around her hand and refuses to stiffen. It is all Diana can do not to scream.

"Sorry," she whispers as she pulls her hand back and swipes it on the outside of her pajamas. "I'm not . . ."

"Normal. You're not normal."

"Look, Ted, it's the vodka. It happens to most men when they've had too much to—"

"Right. It's my fault for drinking too much. Right. Has nothing to do with the fact my wife doesn't want me."

"I'm sorry. I'm just tired, Ted."

"You're never *not* tired. I can't remember the last time we made love, Diana. I'm tired of it. I want you to get help."

"Help." Diana repeats the word slowly. "But can we afford a maid? You just were saying how—"

"Not a cleaning woman, for God's sake! A psychiatric consultant."

"I don't know—"

"Diana, listen to me. I think you may be depressed. Your indecision, your inability to stick to your guns with the children, the fact that you barely go outdoors for fear of stepping on an insect, this whole intense need to prove yourself with architecture when you know it's not practical. P'raps it's a midlife crisis, or who knows, an early childhood trauma coming back to haunt you. Whatever the problem, don't you think it's time we faced it head-on? June Smithson went on Prozac last year, you know. It's nothing to be ashamed of."

"June Smithson?"

"Harold's wife. She's much better now. Quit smoking, lost twenty pounds, got her hair blonded."

"I don't think I know her, Ted."

"Well, that's not the point! The point is that their marriage improved immensely when she got the help she needed."

"Help," Diana repeats, trying the word on for size.

"Look, if it's making the appointment that's stopping you, I'll find you someone with credentials."

"No Ted, I don't need—I don't need your help."

"Look, don't be ridiculous. Don't cry, Diana."

* * *

AUDREY is perched on the marble countertop, leaning into her bathroom mirror, trying to see what Humphrey saw just before they kissed. She giggles involuntarily. Jesus!

Her eyes have these hazy brown lakes in them, like the stuff old mirrors get around the edges. Like a lost island in the forest. Like the settlers of Roanoke. Found really, not lost. Audrey has been writing her history paper on the Lost Colony of Roanoke, left by the English. Well, they never returned/no, they never returned/ and their fate is still unlearned. Audrey's theory is that the colonists were forced to admit that her Native people had it down when it came to living in paradise. She could see the women starting to come round to it when they realized those pinafores weren't gonna stay too white if you had no roof over your head. Even the men. Hell, you get hungry enough and you start to learn there might be better ways of hunting. The scholars label it "assimilation" theory. Audrey liked that explanation better than its evil twin: what her history teacher calls annihilation.

By the time the ships returned to look for them, the colonists were gone, all right, but maybe they were there, too. Let's see, did they want to be forced to dress like pilgrims and live in the stinky hold of the ship, or did they want to run free through the woods and share the natural wonders of the New World with strong braves and beautiful sisters? I'd have hidden, too, but good, thinks Audrey. England was already polluted and feudal as all Hell, so it wasn't even really a choice, not when America was the new Eden, before the streams and rivers got so polluted. She could imagine the colonists lying in wait behind the bushes. Trying not to sneeze when the men came tromping through with muskets, smelling of beer and stale sweat. By then the women would be fit and tan and wearing Indian garb. No wonder they'd hidden. Otherwise they'd be taken for squaws and raped before getting shipped back to England to be deprogrammed from their "savage" ways. I'd get lost but fast, thinks Audrey, wondering if those lakes in her eyes are the pigments of her lost tribe, folding into the green as protection against the twenty-first century.

Humphrey's kiss is still with her: It's still on her lips in a tingly kind of way that she doesn't want to let go. At the very same time she is telling herself to *get real*. It's like an order she's repeating, trying to burn it into her thick, thick skull. *He was just keeping your mouth shut. He's gay, for God's sake, Audrey. Get it into your dim bulb of a brain.*

He doesn't know what he's fooling with, using me as camouflage. I can't just stay still like the forest, I might have to wrap myself around him like a vine. I might have to hold on to him for a long, long time.

* * *

HUMPHREY lies in bed, clutching his pillow over his face, wracked with indecision. Should he get up now and start the housework or try to get some sleep in the next ten minutes before the alarm begins its infernal beeping? Should he change now or shower after he tidies up and makes the lunches? Will Eleanor eat celery if he spreads it with peanut butter and raisins or will it come home smeared all over her Postman Pat lunch tin? And William: Why isn't William eating anything? Boys didn't get anorexia, did they? But then it's not exactly true he doesn't eat, is it? After school he's off the bus, running towards the kitchen, moaning "Starving!"

Poor William. When Humphrey asked him about Adam, William

had blurted out "Brilliant!" Humphrey realized it may have been the first happy sound from his younger brother since they'd left England.

Happy. Humphrey thinks of how he felt yesterday, jubilant at the thought of having done it, signed up for the Blue Goose, borrowed the money, said no to Ted. But he'd not thought it through, had he now? Of course not. He'd gone ahead and jumped off his own private cliff, grasping at his own selfish plans without glancing back to see who else might need saving.

If Mum took the job, who'd take care of Eleanor? Who'd meet William each day after school? Who'd cook and clean and shop and keep chaos at bay? Eleanor's preschool was only to eleven-thirty and only four days a week.

The point was, he had his whole life in front of him and plenty of time to do anything he fancied. Mum had given up so much already, passed on the Winston Fellowship when she'd gotten pregnant with him. Humphrey had overheard Evelyn and Mum talking about it one night, and Mum dismissed it as "nothing," but Humphrey could hear the wistfulness in her voice. She tried to pretend it didn't matter, but all one had to do was sleep in her childhood room at Meemaw's, with its models of buildings, its quotations from Frank Lloyd Wright. This was something she'd always wanted.

The trouble was, would the school refund his money? And if they didn't, how would he pay it back? His plan had seemed so solid yesterday, a year of school, a year at a local restaurant, living with Audrey and her father once his family returned to Oxford, just until he'd paid them back. Of course, there was MeeMaw's money coming, but now that Humphrey wasn't going to school, Ted would have his pincers in it. Ted would never let found money go to waste on his children, not when there were wine cellars to plunder and stocks to buy.

Just move, Humphrey tells himself. *Get out of bed and put one foot before the next until you get to the Admissions Office and politely ask may you please have the money back that you borrowed from your New Best Friend.*

At the thought of Audrey, Humphrey groans into his pillow and rolls over to hide his eyes. The look on her face when he'd pulled away. The kiss had come from nowhere. He'd been desperate to keep her from talking but also desperate to feel her mouth against his. Another cliff he'd jumped off without thinking.

Last year a boy at Humphrey's school had approached him about joining a club for Gay, Lesbian, Bisexual, and Transgendered Youth. Humphrey had asked, "What about a club for people who don't know what they are?"

"You're in denial," Spencer had said, and turned on his heel, so certain he'd not even waited for a response. Humphrey had stood there and wondered how Spencer could know something about him that he himself didn't. Was it all written in stone?

He had taken to watching *Will and Grace* as though it could reveal to him the deep dark secrets of his soul. Was there no way around this? he wondered, scrutinizing Will and Jack, ticking off the attributes that seemed to cluster around the gene for male homosexuality: the gene for window treatments and flower arranging and pastry cooking and neatly folding and drinks with fruit in them. If Humphrey lived for Martha Stewart's Holiday Entertainment special, mustn't he also want to fuck men? But that made no sense to Humphrey because men were hairy and ugly and frankly disgusting while women were soft and smooth and pleasing and smelled so much better. It seemed to Humphrey if you were at all sensitive to aesthetics, you'd choose a woman over a man any day. Still, all that had been somewhat theoretical until Audrey came barreling in with her Laura Ashley doppelgänger sheets. Her cat-eyes that changed colours like the sea, her angel-bright flaxen hair, her skin the colour of perfect *crème brûlée*, dappled with caramel freckles—each of these was imprinted on Humphrey's longing to hold her and keep her as she was, to hold her and protect her like the mother she had lost.

* * *

"WAIT, let me see if I've got this right?" asks Evelyn. Her voice sounds clear as a bell, as though she were right next door, not at her country house in the Lake District, several time zones away. "He's the bloke whose wanker's wilted, due no doubt to his love affair with that Russian slut, Madame Stolichnaya, and *you're* the one who needs help?"

"I didn't say he was impotent, Evelyn."

"I'm not an imbecile, Diana. If you were arguing about sex, it stands to reason that he's finally having trouble with his equip-ment. The way he drinks, I'm only surprised it's taken so long. But why is that your problem?"

"Evelyn, the point is that—it struck a nerve. What is wrong with me that I absolutely dread sex?"

"Oh, Diana, I don't relish sex and I happen to adore Gordon. I don't know a single woman who's as hot for it as the ladies' mags pretend. Except Harriet. But of course she's also fond of *children* as a general category, so you can't call her normal. Besides, it's not your sex life you're worried about: It's your love life. Or lack thereof."

"I don't know. It just all makes sense suddenly that I might be de-pressed. I'm so forgetful lately and I really don't enjoy much of any-thing, except the times I do, and then I'm horribly guilty over it."

"But of course you do. You're defying your husband's whole purpose in life when you enjoy yourself. You must see someone straight away or Ted will go quite mad. The great man is too busy to see his own doctor, so he persuades his ever-willing wife to save him the trouble. Brilliant, bloody brilliant."

"I'm serious, Evelyn."

"That's what frightens me, Diana. You consult a therapist over this and you *are* truly mad. Where's your self-respect?"

"It's complicated."

"No it's not. You get a job offer and Ted gets flaccidopholous. Simple as that."

"I never said—"

"Diana, you didn't need to."

"Look, I thought you loved going to see your consultant."

"I do, darling, but it was my idea, not Gordon's. Ted's got a bloody nerve convincing you that you're the one with the problem. Look, go if you want. It'll be good for you. But promise me one thing. Don't let Ted tell you it's you. It's not. It's just the idea of you being happy, or worse, *successful*, that's causing Willie to fly south."

"Evelyn. Stop it. I know you always see the best in me, but I do feel guilty, and properly so, for not being interested in making love with the man I've promised to love, honor, and—all that. I'm denying him someone who reciprocates—"

"Hah! Look, if Ted married someone who reciprocated, they'd have eaten each other alive by now. But, Diana, that reminds me! I saw Glenda Cheswitt in Sainsbury's last week. She thinks her daughter's having an affair with one of her tutors at St. Mark's! Do ask Ted if he knows who it is."

"Glenda Cheswitt?"

"You know. She was on the Children's Hospital board with me.

Married to Ronald and soaking in department-store money. Fiona had lunch with you and Humphrey when she came up for her interview?"

"Oh, that girl. Lovely child. I'd completely forgotten about her. I'm not sure Ted even knows her, but I'll ask. What makes her mum think she's sleeping with a don?"

"She read some of Fiona's e-mails. I guess it's pretty clear."

"What? Can she not just read the last name on the account? The Fellows all use their last names."

"Oh, she tried that. No, this is from—I can barely say it—Hotman@hotmail.com."

"Ick!"

"I know. It's embarrassing, really, when you think about it: Countless years of higher education and God knows how many thousand pounds in grants, and all the man can think of to ensnare a young female is the linguistic equivalent of a cheap hairpiece."

* * *

WALLY sits entranced, watching his computer screen. If Ted could see him now, it would only confirm his stereotypes of greedy capitalists, for Wally is mesmerized by the stock symbol his Internet search has unveiled. MaryKnoll Technologies, a company that's patented several building products without formaldehyde and other "sick-building" ingredients, has also announced the discovery of a rare mineral that will allow batteries to operate up to ten times longer. The implications of this for solar power and fuel cells are exponential. This promise would cause great jubilation among his daughter's EARTHCARE ARIZONA friends if they were privy to Wally's investments. It's not every day that one of the state's biggest ordinance dealers takes his money out of death and puts it into a technology that could reduce dependence on fossil fuels by forty percent. It is only a slight technicality that, because the

Huntington sale has not yet gone through, Wally's money is still locked up in the gun business and he is borrowing against it to buy a stock which already doubled in the past week, for some unknown reason. Audrey has put him onto this search after her friend Baby Face sold his patent for garden misters to the company, but she had thought her father might put fifty thousand or so into this fund. She never expected such a wholesale response to her constant chatter about the possibilities of green technologies. However, it is not the environmental benefits that drive her father to call his broker. Nor is it greed that propels him, as Ted might assume.

It's bigger than that and it fills him with wonder: the ticker symbol, MRYKT is calling him to place his trust in a future so uncertain it cannot be grasped. The sensation of believing pulls him into the air at the same time as it knocks the wind from his lungs.

In a matter of seconds Wally has authorized the use of his margin account to take a flyer on a stock that he expects to go sky-high. It's all there in capital letters, the ticker symbol is right there, plain as day, and it has been waiting for him to discover it, waiting patiently through the benevolent coincidence of Audrey's suggestion, for this exact moment. He gives the buy order for MRYKT, at eight bucks a share, half a million shares, his heart gladdened by the exhilarating risk of believing in something beyond his own experience.

* * *

HUMPHREY pulls into the only spot available in the Blue Goose parking lot, marked Deliveries. He jogs up through the arched entrance and strides down the dark hall of the mission-style building. The smell of lemon and garlic is enough to make him cry, but Humphrey bites his lip and opens a door marked Admissions. He stands there waiting at the counter for a hugely overweight secretary to look up from her magnifying glass. "You all right?" she asks, in an accent he can't make out.

"No, actually, I've had a spot of bad news. My stepfather's ill. Atrophic carcinoma of the heart. Inoperable. So sorry, but I'm afraid I'm going to have to withdraw."

* * *

"Diana, do you know what your daughter's done now?" asks Ted, poking his head into his wife's studio. "She's wet the bed. If we don't get in there to clean, we won't be in need of a goat to achieve medieval verisimilitude."

Diana is only too glad to leave her drafting table, where she's been staring at a piece of empty paper for what seems like hours. The notion that everything is falling into place, that she might actually be able to accept Wally's offer, all this is well and good, except there's still the slight technical problem of putting pen to paper and proving herself worth the trouble.

Diana strips the bed and collects a pair of damp knickers from the floor while Ted stands in the doorway watching. "Poor Elly," she says, bundling the linens into a ball. "I've noticed she's slipped back into baby talk, as well as this problem with wetting herself. Well, she is only four and she *has* moved continents."

"Ah, p'raps that's what they mean by incontinent."

"Ha! I hope she's all right."

"Of course she is!" Ted snorts. "She's just too lazy to get up and use the W.C."

"You don't know that."

"What's bitten you?"

"Nothing. Well, everything. Elly wetting the bed and Humphrey's had such a disappointment with that cookery school being full."

"Oh stop."

"P'raps if we went and spoke to the Admittance department, Ted. P'raps they could make a spot for him."

"Are you truly mad? The last thing he needs is to get into that line of work. They're all gay, chefs are, you know."

"Why in the world would you say such a thing?"

"Because Humphrey's a very nice-looking chap. He doesn't need to be in a school where all the instructors want to sleep with him."

"Ted, you've never even seen the place! But that reminds me, do you remember a girl named Fiona Cheswitt, at St. Mark's? Her mum's a friend of Evelyn's."

"Can't say that I do."

"Her mum thinks she's sleeping with one of the dons."

"I highly doubt that, Diana."

"Well, if you don't know her, you wouldn't know, would you, Ted? It so happens that the child is absolutely gorgeous on top of being rather appallingly rich. Her great-grandfather started the department stores."

"She's one of those Cheswitts!"

"I thought you didn't know her."

"No, of course I don't. But the thing is, you know Paul is always after donors. I think he's got no clue that there's an heiress in his midst."

"Better not tell him. Let the poor girl alone. She's got enough on her plate if she's sleeping with a don. Who in the world could it be?"

Ted shakes his head very convincingly, expressing the perfect blend of consternation and astonishment that someone might betray his professional trust by sleeping with a student.

* * *

THE silky pastel ribbons are Humphrey's gifts to himself, a condolence prize to the disappointed chef. Humphrey uses pinking shears to fray-proof the ends. The linens are laid out on the oversized dining room table, which he has protected with table pad and towels.

One by one, Humphrey irons the sheets, dousing them with lavender water, then bringing the heavy iron across the furrows in an uprising of heavenly steam. Bringing the ends to each other reverently, crisping the fold that marks their divide, Humphrey steadily creates a perfectly stacked tower of squared edges and binds them together with the graceful embrace of the ribbon. By the time Audrey knocks at the front door, the table boasts soft yellow kings wrapped in blue, Elly's pinks in innocent white, William's blues in butter yellow, and the dual set of Laura Ashley's roses in blushing pink.

Humphrey takes a deep whiff of calming lavender and walks towards the door, casting backwards glances at his handiwork, telling himself that he will somehow explain himself, make things right.

"Audrey!" he cries, administering European air kisses as a way of avoiding her eyes. Lovely cat-eyes that he wants to kiss, softly closed. "I'm reengineering the linen closet. Wait till you see."

Audrey strides into the room and hardly even glances at her friend's handiwork. She's got something to say, having thought about it all night. Humphrey cannot quit school. "Look, Humphrey, can we talk?"

"We may," he says.

Audrey is so bent on saving him that she doesn't even notice his reflexive correction of her grammar. "Look, I won't participate in this scam. You need to come clean with your mom."

"What are you talking about?"

"Pretending that we're going together—" she says, blushing. She giggles, hating herself for losing her cool. It's just that she's suddenly been blindsided by the memory of how she'd been totally flayed when he'd come out of nowhere and kissed her.

This was not what she's planned at all: this giggling girl crap.

Humphrey, who has almost but not quite successfully chased his tormented attraction to Audrey into hiding with the contemplative ritual of ironing, is faint with embarrassment. "Sorry," he says, laughing, too, which is a stretch, because this is a very painful conversation and he knows that her next words will be something to the effect that she doesn't like him in "that way," at which point he will lay down on the floor and quietly expire. "You know I was just covering," he stammers, saving her the embarrassment of having to say another awkward word.

"Of course," Audrey replies quickly, the words tripping out over themselves. "Don't worry. I understand and I didn't want you to feel like you—like I might be, uh, wanting—you know."

Humphrey nods knowingly. Every muscle in his beautifully sculpted body has abandoned him; a weight pulls him into the floor. What a mistake he's made! And besides, how does he know he's not just seeking a refuge in Audrey? With this last enquiry, something inside Humphrey begins digging in the sand, a spot just large enough to bury his head.

"The thing is," starts Audrey. "For your own happiness, well, I know you want to make your mom happy, but sometimes its better to be honest because later you'll just—oh hi, Elly!" cries Audrey, her voice rising giddily at the child's interruption of her lecture about not quitting the cooking school on his mother's account. Audrey sweeps Eleanor into her arms and closes her eyes for a moment, savoring the uncomplicated child she is hugging

Her relief and pleasure are palpable: their origin is not. Humphrey assumes that Audrey has just dodged a relationship bullet. Nasty graze it would have been, had he not admitted he'd been "covering." But for that, she'd have had to tell him she didn't like him "*that* way," wasn't attracted at all. Whew! for both parties and their friendship. Better he's gay than hopelessly in love with a girl who doesn't return his affections. The fact that he'd meant something entirely different by covering, that was beside the point. Besides, for all he knows, he *is* gay and just seeking relief in an unavailable girl so he won't have to spend his life in Ponce Purgatory. For all he knows, his attraction to her might be based on the fact that she is so like a boy in so many ways. Clumsy and athletic and controversial, Audrey says exactly what she thinks. Moreover, she's domestically challenged.

"I'm so stupid," moans Humphrey. "Please forgive me, Audrey. Off-putting, wasn't it?" he laughs, trying to bring her out, so that they can set all their cards on the table. Audrey looks up and the hurt in her eyes is unmistakable, but Humphrey cannot see it. He has turned to the newly ironed linens, seeking solace in their unmistakable geometry.

Eight

To: FionaC@StMarks.edu.uk
From: hotman@hotmail.com
Re: missing you

Dear Feefee,
Can't stop thinking of you. Am on plane to Florida next week to meet with some consultants from the "themed entertainment industry," which should be amusing. Won't you meet me there?

* * *

BECAUSE Guy was with Wally in Vietnam, all the employees at Gold Ammunition say they're like brothers, but worse. First off, you can't even accuse them of nepotism. Wally doesn't play favorites, says the office scuttlebutt, but he lets his best friend ride his ass all the way into town and back again.

"You take up weed again?" Guy is asking his boss. "What the Hell were you thinking?"

"What's eatin' you? The stock's up from when I bought it."

"And you are a complete moron! How many times did I tell you, you can't sell your company stock right now? How many times?"

"Stop nagging, Guy. I wasn't planning on it."

"I don't get how you can be so rich and so stupid at the same time. Buying on margin against the stock is the same thing. With that interest, four million adds up. And when you buy that many shares of any company, you've just bought a strip search from the SEC. They're gonna be all over your butt about how you knew to buy right before that company got bought by TechGreen. Newsflash! Insider trading's the prosecutor's New Best Thing."

"I'm telling you, Guy. I didn't! Audrey's buddy—you remember Baby Face—this company bought his patent for garden misters. Then when I saw the ticker symbol—" Here Wally holds up his hands, as if to say, no further explanation is necessary.

"Oh, that'll go a long way. You spend a truckload of money, money you don't presently have, to buy a stock you never heard of, because it spells your wife's name in the sky. *And* you just happen to make twenty-five grand over the weekend?"

"Hey, I didn't make anything yet. It's just on paper till I sell it."

"And guess what, Sherlock? You can't sell it now, or the SEC will be even further up your intestinal tract. When you buy that many shares, idiot, you gotta go through a whole notification process. Which, Mr. Gold, you neglected to do. And by the way, why didn't you just take the money and burn it? Nobody's gonna make money on do-gooder gadgets."

"How do you know that? I'd pay more to build a house that's not poisoning me."

"Look, let me tell you something, contractors gotta make a living. They can't afford to worry about long-term effects when they gotta make payroll every Friday."

"Look, those chemicals leach into the water. I told you about Roger, Baby Face's uncle."

"Look, I'm sorry for the guy. I was happy to bend the rules to have the company pay for his chemo. But listen, there's a million Rogers out there competing for customers, and as long as everyone else is using cheaper materials, their bids'll come in lower and drive Mr. Careful out of business. You can't compete with cheap. Cost drives the American Dreamboat, and if you can't compete with price, you're dead in the water. Speaking of dead in the water, you might want to figure our how you're paying for all these impulses of yours, buddy."

"Look, it's not that long till the buyout."

"Stop changing the subject. This isn't a condo in Glendale we're trying to sell. We got so many hoops to jump through, the guys in Legal are wearing Air Jordans to the office. And by the way, you got any idea what the hourly is on those consultants meeting Professor Pinhead back East? Or how much we're paying for the Dreamy Draw land? We are so screwed."

"Hey, we'll do a "lot loan" if we have to. Or cash in one of my other accounts. Calm down."

"I won't. All your stocks are for shit right now. Even the mutual funds. And by the way, Personnel ran your hiring request by me. Forget it."

"Take the money out of my salary. I don't care."

"You can't do it, Wally."

"What do you mean, can't? It's done. Figure it out."

"No, you can't. You gotta put this job out to bid. We get federal contracts. We signed an agreement saying that any contract over twenty grand goes out to bid."

"I can't hire who I want?"

"Within reason, you can. But she's not a citizen and she's not even entitled to be here except with her husband. If she wins the bid, we can at least make the case for a B1-H1 visa, where someone has a skill you need that you can't get in the local population. Legal's still calling her husband the 'Green Card from Hell.' I am not putting 'em through that again, not while they're here twenty-four/seven

tryin' to get the acquisition papers right, after which they're gonna
do the same with building permits up north. Oh, and hey, now we
got your stock buy to defend; on top of it. I am not asking them to
stop what they're doing, and neither are you, right now. Just do me a
favor. Tell the lady to put in a bid and we'll get the committee to approve it. Tell her it's a formality. Handpick your committee, Wally.
Right now's not the time to break any more laws. To say nothin' of
my balls, you turkey."

"Come on, Guy."

"No, you come on. Listen, you know Justice is gonna hear from
Antitrust over the sale of the company, as it is. Huntington owns too
much to avoid that. We don't want to give 'em any more ammunition."

"So to speak."

"How can you joke at a time like this? I mean it. You want this
deal to work, you gotta help out a little. So tell What's-her-name to
put in a bid."

"Diana. Her name's Diana."

"Whatever. Let's just make sure we know her vendor number
when the drawings come in so we can be sure and pick her."

"She's good, you know."

"Yeah, buddy. Good and married."

"It's not like that. Just . . . she's got a lot of talent and she oughta
have a chance to show it."

"Like I said, Wally, just get the vendor number. Or, hey, I got a
strange idea. You really believe in this chick like you say you do,
why not let her compete, fair and square? You're the one said she
was good."

*   *   *

THE EARTHCARE ARIZONA community garden, planted in the
no-man's-land of the south side of Phoenix, is cradled by the

Calderesque wings of the junction between I-10 and I-17, the state's major east-west and north-south highways. The area is like one of Georgia O'Keefe's skulls, stripped clean of anything breathing, white on white with sun-bleached grit, grime, and garbage. Just two blocks from the garden are corrugated tin buildings pocked with bullet holes where junkies shoot up and wait longingly for better days to come back by again.

This ZIP code is always in the crime report of the paper, and the incidents—unlike the missing bikes in Audrey's neighborhood— most often have an accompanying paragraph in the Obituaries. Audrey has promised Wally she won't go past the parking lot of the clubhouse, where little kids come to hear cautionary tales against gangs and drugs, and memorials in the form of wreaths around prom photos, blue bandannas stained red forever, the waste insensible after a while. Inside the hurricane fence, though, a riot of color says No! to drugs, to gangs, to overpriced convenience stores selling cigarettes and Sunny Delight.

It has taken Sophia and the other organizers four years to clear the land of its manmade dreck, weapons against the poor in the Best-Run City on Earth: hypodermic needles, bullet casings, plastic flasks, aerosol cans, rusting metal barrels filled with toxic angst. The local community college science department and volunteers from EARTHCARE ARIZONA have helped with the removal of the dirt: five feet down, plastic gloves, full bodysuits and face masks on the days of the dig, a truck that had carried it away. An organic farmer in Prescott donated the new topsoil, and still, it was two years of composting and worming and nitrogen-fixing legumes before they'd harvested the first crop: five acres of jalapeños, cilantro, onions, and tomatoes. It is five acres of salsa named Abuelitas, honoring the matriarchs of the clans of lost boys, sold out in the specialty stores even before the News

Channel Three is on Your Side reporter had featured the garden project.

Audrey lifts a bag of ash from the back of her van, squatting to heft the weight, monkey butt out like her dad had taught her in the gym with the "dead lift."

The organic ash was expensive, but why would you use anything but? It was the least she could do. Sometimes Audrey even pretended it was her mother's ashes, from the body they never found, rising out of the flames like the bird that gave the city its name.

Her mom would've liked this garden. She'd have liked Sophia and the other ladies, the way they would wag their palms through the air dismissively or shrug and raise their eyes to Heaven when a volunteer would say something stupid.

Like how her mom was. She can almost hear her saying "You *po-quito loco*, mister, but I love you anyway," the way she did when she couldn't believe Dad would do something, like when he came home with that circus tent when she'd sent him out for milk. "They were raising money for kids," he'd say. "On the radio," he'd add, like that explained anything.

Dad was a sucker for charities, which was how Audrey could live with the fact that he made so much money off the gun business. He stole from the violent and gave to the poor. Something like that.

"Hey, Baby Face, open the gate, will you?" she yells, carefully pulling at the bougainvillea to peek over the fence. It's too bad, she thinks, that she can't go for Baby Face instead of Humphrey. Here he is, a real T'ohono Odum Indian from Guadalupe, and instead she can't stop thinking about Humphrey, whose ancestors colonized most of the Third World. Audrey's shame expands her smile, her perfect teeth flashing at the slightly pudgy handsome young man wearing chains around his huge overalls.

"W'sup?" she asks Baby Face.

"You coming to the Green Forum?" he asks, taking the bag of ash and carrying it over to the potting shed. "This speaker'll blow your socks off, Audrey."

"I don't know," Audrey hedges, but Baby Face is insistent.

Baby Face is majoring in industrial design at ASU and is—in this land of libertarians—a one-man band for green technologies. Ever since his uncle had got sick, he's gotten ever more passionate in his need to change the world.

"Look, put your money where your mouth is. And bring your dad."

Baby Face is extremely savvy and only mildly manipulative. Last year, when Baby Face invented an organic filtering system for the garden's misters, Wally had given him the money to go to a lawyer and get it patented. Whenever Baby Face needed the last two hundred bucks in books, Wally has always been ready to help. Between Audrey's hard and Baby Face's soft cop routine, Wally has almost single-handedly funded EARTHCARE ARIZONA for the last five years.

"Don't hit him up right now, okay? He's totally not liquid, and it'll just make him feel guilty."

"Yeah, right. Cash-flow traumas of the Camelback Mountain set."

"No, seriously. I overheard his CFO reading him the riot act."

"Yah, you'll have to cut back on the Kate Spades, darling."

"I'm serious. I guess he put a lot of money into that company you told me about."

"That's excellent."

"Yeah, except he might be in trouble for insider trading."

"Why?"

"I don't know. Something about a company called TechGreen buying them and Dad bought right before—"

"TechGreen? No shit! I've heard of them. Maybe I'll finally make some money on my stock options."

"Talk about the Camelback Mountain set, you fat cat you."

"Hah! Honey, I am still wearing these overalls from 2002. So far I've not seen dime one."

Audrey shakes her head. "Why is that?"

"No market yet. I guess people would rather buy cheap and worry later."

"But how can people just dismiss what they're putting into the earth?"

"Well, for one, the poisons are mostly invisible. And two, for hundreds of years, businesses haven't been asked to clean up after they've made a mess. Why would they start now?"

"But then the taxpayers pay for the cleanup, or we have to pay for medical care for people who get sick from what's been dumped into—"

Baby Face's cheeks flush and he says quickly, "Audrey, my family's so thankful."

Audrey waves her hand, embarrassed. "I didn't mean Roger. My dad was glad to do it. I just wish . . . I wish there was more the doctors could do for him."

Now it's Baby Face's turn to look away, to ignore the awkwardness of discussing something so painful as watching his virile uncle Roger decline into a skeletal wraith in a wheelchair.

"Look, bring your dad to this lecture next week. This guy is a total visionary. He basically invented Green Architecture. It'll make him feel better about where he put his money, at least. I'll send you three tickets and you can bring that English kid, too."

Audrey looks sideways at Baby Face, wondering if she's totally gotten her signals mixed. Between the Kate Spade comment and the way that Baby Face was looking way too nonchalantly at the back of the Organic Ash bag, she wonders which side of wild he came down on.

* * *

TED is crouched down, rooting around in the honor bar. The expense-account concept has come to him rather naturally. *A quick study I am*, he tells himself, twisting off the top of a miniature Kettle One. "Fiona!" he shouts. "What'll it be? Dom Perignon or Veuve Cliquot for dinner?"

"You choose," she trills from the bathroom. "I'm so jet-lagged, I could drink Ribena and fall down drunk."

Ted orders two lobster tails, two filet mignons, a Caesar salad for two, and six strawberries dipped in chocolate. "I'll have a bottle of Dom and one of Veuve Cliquot. It's not the Grande Dame by any chance?" he asks, preening at his reflection in the mirror. He is wearing one of the hotel's robes and it's fallen open enough to reveal his chest. He sucks in his almost invisible paunch and throws out his chest just enough to delineate the smooth crest of his pectoral muscles. *A quick study*, he thinks again, before he thanks the room-service captain and hangs up the phone.

The session today couldn't have gone better if Ted had written the script himself. Here in the land of Disney, the consultants had been confused by Wally's original hiring instructions, more of a caveat really, that his daughter was "into the environment" and he wanted a theme park that didn't "mess things up." This confusion among consultants is exactly what Ted has relied upon, for if this park were to be created—as Wally's thick-witted locution would have it—without "messing things up," then Ted's hopes of returning prematurely to England, check in hand, were down the drain along with the next ten months of indentured servitude. While Ted might yet try to stir up protest among a Native American tribe, Fiona has already pointed out that the fastest way to a redskin's heart is through his sacred waters, or whatever it was his primitive mind attached to the concept of holiness.

Best to kill two birds with one stone by getting the environmentalists *and* the Indians to work together against a common enemy. The challenge was to get Gold to drop his free-lunch attitudes about ecology and embrace a plan that even Americans would find objectionable. That was the challenge to which Ted brought his superior intellect, a challenge to which he would—as he discovered once the meeting was underway—all too easily rise. As Franz Bibfeldt, the consultant, explained at lunch, after a martini, these highly skilled entertainment contractors were in the business of Wow!ing kids, of bowling them over with sights and sounds, of making sure they had fun in an all-encompassing way. It was one thing to do that, another to be limited by environmental-impact worries. In fact, as the avuncular consultant finally admitted, this mandate from Gold was so vague, so naive, it was playing havoc with their creative process.

Ted had nodded knowingly, sympathetically. It took him less than thirty minutes of discussion—into which he wove flattery, conceit, and no small deception as to the nature of his relationship to Wally Gold—to assure Bibfeldt that no matter what his misguided client thought he wanted, what he needed was something else. Technicolor, movement, noise, and commerce. After all, Ted reminded them, Wally was in the ammunition business: He'd hired them for their entertainment expertise. It was up to Franz to steer their client in the right direction. Between Ted's knowledge of Arthurian legend and their avant-garde place at the edge of the entertainment envelope, they owed it to Wally to create the most spectacular theme park ever. After all, didn't Aristotle say that all entertainment was spectacle? Now, he'd pressed on, as I'm sure you know, in the legend of King Arthur, water is absolutely paramount. Lots and lots of water. Don't you agree?

There had been the one rough patch, when the team leader had suggested they get Wally on the phone, to discuss their ideas, but Ted had been able to avert that with some quick thinking. "And oh, I might warn you," Ted had confided, "whatever you give Mr. Gold, it must be first rate. No rough drafts, no sketches. Take it through to the final product before you pitch it. Otherwise he'll find the T you didn't cross and kill your contract right then and there."

Not only had the meeting gone well, but the lovely Fiona is more beautiful than ever, her complexion pale after the long plane flight. She's promised him a surprise. Knowing this girl and her capacity for sexual play, it will be all he can do to stay standing.

* * *

DIANA opens her FedEx from Gold Industries, expecting the contract Wally has told her to return. "Just sign it and we'll fly up to Dreamy Draw to look at the land," he'd said last week. As she reads the terms of the Request for Proposals, Diana becomes more and more puzzled. She dials Wally's private line at work.

"Wally?"

"This is his secretary. What can I do for you?"

"Oh, hello. I'm Diana Lively. The architect?"

"The what?"

"The architect for the project?"

"Hey, honey, you're gettin' ahead of yourself. You gotta apply for that job. Bids close in two weeks."

"I think there's some sort of mistake. Wah-Mr. Gold is my neighbor?"

"Yeah?"

"Yes. And my husband, Ted, is already the technical expert on the project."

Beverly, Wally's assistant, takes a deep breath. Ted Lively is—without question—the biggest rectum she has met in her fifteen years of working for Wally.

"Okay?" Bev continues, leading the woman on.

"Well, Mr. Gold had told me to expect a contract in the mail?"

"Oh, he did, eh? Look, I think you might a' misunderstood. On this side a' the pond, a contract means you're hired. It's what you do *after* the bid."

"No, I understand. But I understood—perhaps I misunderstood, but—"

"Look, instead of us spending time trying to straighten this out, why don't I give you the Web site with the RFP on it?"

Diana hears the call-waiting beep. Instead of arguing with this woman any longer, she decides to wait until she can speak with Wally, who may, at this very moment, be trying to get through. "Thanks much, I've got it," says Diana. She hangs up quickly so as not to miss Wally's call.

When Ted's voice breaks through instead, Diana cannot keep frustration from seeping into hers, a frustration which, once it's infected her greeting, causes Ted to let off a quick offended intake of breath.

"Look, I don't relish spending my life with cretins. You needn't treat me like one when I ring."

"Sorry, Ted. Honestly. I'm sorry I sounded cross. It's just—never mind."

"No, what?" asks Ted, his ability to pick up a certain tone of vulnerability in his wife's voice unobstructed by fiber-optic telephone wires. "Tell me."

"Well, *you* thought he'd offered me the job, and *I* did as well, but I just got off the line with his secretary—"

"Slag."

"It sounds—well—she didn't know who I was. I feel foolish, because she mentioned a bidding competition. I don't remember us talking about bidding for this contract. Do you?"

"Oh, Diana," clucks Ted. "He's not to be trusted. I told you that. Reminds me of my dad as a matter of fact. Very generous he could be, too. He'd give you the shirt off his back. Just don't quibble when you find out the shirt actually belonged to someone else. Do not trust Mr. Gold. Promise me you'll extricate yourself from any professional relationship with him."

"Ted, I—I haven't actually spoken to him."

"Yes, well, I can tell you, experienced victim of confidence men that I am, no matter what he tells you today, you cannot count on it for tomorrow. Just gracefully extricate yourself. We've already discussed your exhaustion and how it affects our marriage and— Oh shite, someone's at the door, Lady Di. Let me ring you back."

With that, Ted hangs up before Diana can express her sympathy for her husband, having spent the day in meetings, stranded now in a hotel room without benefit of human companionship, doomed to watch cable on telly and eat the overcooked fare available through room service.

"Poor Ted," she says aloud, feeling disposed to sympathy now that he's mentioned his father. Of course, that would explain his antipathy for Wally. After years of relying on an unreliable parent, Ted would be apprehensive about trusting anyone, especially someone who spent money the way Wally Gold did. Of all his father's characteristics, it was what Ted called his father's "faux generosity" that he most reviled, spilling over into the son's skepticism of largesse in general. Wally's giving nature could easily be misinterpreted. Further-more, Wally's plan had, from Ted's point of view, forced the professor out on the edge of precipice, putting his career at risk. Years ago, in the early part of her marriage, Diana might have tried to bring the two men together and mediate some sort of mutual understanding. Now, though, thanks to her dear Evelyn's intransigence and Ted's inexhaustible hubris, she's learned her limitations as diplomat.

Diana decides she will call Wally, straight away. She even presses the first nine of the ten numbers required to reach him at home, but by the time she is poised over the final digit, she has convinced herself that Wally would not have misled her. Even posing the question will put him in the uncomfortable position of having to reassure her, when he must be in need of reassurance of his own. After all, he's the one risking his fortune with a park that he's hinged on her untested abilities. If he's said she's got the job, then this bid business must be about something else. Diana chides herself for having doubted him and vows to let him be the one to bring up the subject, should he need to, in his own good time.

* * *

ELEANOR locks her bedroom door and tiptoes into the closet. Humphrey has sorted through her toys and created shelves labeled with pictures so she'll know where things go. The Barbie car is not on the Barbie shelf. It's mixed up with Ken and Midge, and Kelli but it doesn't belong to them, mutters Eleanor: It's for Barbie. Humphrey has insisted that Ken might drive the pink minivan because he might be the house daddy. He might take care of the children, might collect them at school, and take them to the park while Barbie works in Finance and gets money at the bank. But Barbie must be the mummy, Eleanor has insisted. Ken can't answer the doorbell with his halter top backwards, like Barbie can, when Postman Pat rings.

Ken has no boobies. As far is Eleanor is concerned, daddies aren't acceptable for naked door-answering, nor do they know how to make her a snack like Humphrey and Mommy. They never read her stories, and they only talk when they're being mean at their children, or worse, when they are trying to say how brilliant and smashing their children would be, if only they didn't fidget, if only they wouldn't leave their Wellies on the floor, if only they wouldn't chew on fingers, or talk like babies. And on and on and on.

Mummy says a pest is an annoying thing, a nuisance. Something that won't leave you alone. But then Humphrey had said "like Ted," and Mummy had got cross, and then Humphrey said he was only "winding her up," but Mummy said, "You really ought to consider who might be listening." Mum shouldn't have scolded Humphrey because Daddy was on a plane to Business and couldn't hear a thing.

What Eleanor doesn't understand is what Audrey has told her about pests. Why would Daddy eat sugar leafs in Africa? He doesn't even eat sugar at home. As she considers this, Eleanor is visited with an epiphany of understanding. The sugar bowl. Is the sugar bowl sprayed with Audrey's magic potion? Maybe that's why Daddy doesn't eat sugar. Maybe it's already sprayed. Having arrived at this conclusion, Eleanor nods her small perfectly shaped head. She carefully picks up the Lalique mister and tentatively sprays her father's favorite martini glass, just enough to scent the rim with a faint aroma of tequila, jalapeños, and that infinitely comforting smell of wet knickers. Then, just so she can spray it again, Eleanor uses Ted's College tie—the one with two swords crossing—to wipe the inside. She holds her nose and gives the glass one last shot of preventive prophylaxis.

* * *

WHEN Diana and Wally emerge from Gate 2 at the Lake Havasu airport, Wally waves to a man feeding quarters into the vending machine. Brenner is a muscular, very bald man wearing cowboy boots, jeans, and a plain white T-shirt. Near him, a statuesque redhead—her braid wrapped round her head like a crown—has abandoned her queenly aura for hand-to-hand combat with the screw top of her Diet Coke. Wally takes the bottle in one hand and hugs the woman with the other. He hands it back to her, opened, then swats her companion. "Where's your manners, Brenner!"

"I'm not helping Ravenna kill herself with Aspartame. She can do that all by herself," Brenner says, opening a package of peanuts and offering them to the new arrivals.

"Diana, I'd like you to meet one of my oldest friends," Wally says. "AKA Yul Brenner, the mayor of Dreamy Draw. And Ravenna, his better half."

Brenner shakes Diana's hand and introduces her to his wife, who smiles and wipes her chin with the back of her hand before extending it. Brenner guides them outdoors, where two large Harleys lean in toward the curb. Ravenna extracts two helmets from the saddlebags and hands them to Wally. This is the first that Diana has heard of their mode of transportation.

"I've never done this," she stammers. No wonder Wally has suggested she wear pants and walking shoes.

"You'll be fine. You just hold on to me," Wally murmurs soothingly. "Here, maybe we should take your hair out of that bun so you can get the helmet on." Diana doesn't have time to object. One minute Wally is easing her hair out of its knot, the next she is straddling on the back of the bike, her arms around Wally's waist in a wonderfully acceptable and perfectly justifiable embrace. They drive for what seems like minutes but is actually forty, and Diana's mood flickers in and out of terror and hilarity with each passing car. She has rarely felt so exposed to danger, yet somehow she is also convinced of Wally's sturdiness in a way she'd never before noticed. Her arms grip his torso. Every now and again, with the slightest movement of his head, he checks to see if she's all right.

Brenner and Ravenna beep and wave as they take the turnoff into town. Wally continues straight ahead, weaving round a small mountain road until it turns to sand and then to ruts. Wally abruptly stops the bike and lets her dismount. "We'll have to walk the rest of the hill," he says. "You okay?" He takes a folded blanket and an insulated bag in one hand, and grasps her hand in the other. "Come on. I can't wait to see what you think."

They climb the foothills, moving quickly up through the trails that ascend through clumps of fragrant sage and rosemary. Here and there, a palo verde tree tops a cluster of other plants that Diana doesn't recognize, some cactuses, golden-topped flowers, and a curious otherworldly deep-green, spike-leafed collection of right angles turned in upon the earth. The trail grows steeper, and then they are abruptly at the summit: a long flat plateau studded with plants and rimmed by shade trees. The west side of the overlook dips precipitously down to the lake, and Diana stops herself short to take in the view. The water, a shimmering plane of deep green, is vast, spreading out to fill the bottomless thirst of desert. She can spot Lake Havasu City across the water, the graceful spans of its imported London Bridge strung along the banks. The surface of the water is pocked with marks of the storm that will soon blow in from California. Already the black hedge of clouds presses itself over the horizon. The wind is up, carrying with it a scent of rust and smoke.

Diana makes her way towards the east end of the plateau, where the rocks look like geometric faces of Eve, checkered down the mountain likes steps to the Garden. A thin ribbon of bright turquoise water slips into gullies crowned with lush desert plants. Rising pediments are varnished by sunlight, shadowed by clouds, the edge between the two states razored in the electricity of the coming rain. It is familiar, it is beautiful, it is terrifying. Where has she seen this before?

Diana is assaulted by a sudden panic, like the wind coming over the water. God help her, she is completely unprepared for this. What does she know about fun parks, for Heaven's sake? She's a housewife who makes dollhouses when she's not taking care of her children. She's undone by this terrain, has never been to Disneyland, and has only recently been able to draw anything, much less create a plan for a site that deserves no less than the Hanging Gardens of Tivoli. Suddenly all the hideous buildings she has ever hated come rushing up to taunt Diana. They each had architects behind them with egos profoundly larger than their vision and skill.

She can't do this. Has no business. This land deserves better. Diana can imagine an oasis here, with terraced beds of jubilant flowers, crowned with arches and angles that frame God's masterpiece in each direction. What in the world is Wally thinking, using someone as inexperienced as she? Diana closes her eyes. How can she have been such a fool? It is in this moment of weakness, her defenses down, that Ted's voice enters, uninvited. *Promise me you'll extricate yourself from any professional relationship with him.* When she hears a rustling behind her, she clenches her fists against her sides, struggling for words to explain to Wally her sudden change of heart.

It is an indication of just how troubled she is that Diana is almost relieved by the sight of the snake. At least it's not Wally, with a tuppence for her thoughts. Cold sweat drips down Diana's armpits, into the folds of her white cotton T-shirt, down into the gullies of her waist. Before she's had time to reflect, the snake has moved on, into the underbrush, staying just long enough to fix her with its glittering grin.

Though it's too late for action, it's never too soon for hysteria. Diana's feet are off the ground, one, two, three jumps, a startled arpeggio. She releases a muffled whimper from the high-pitched roof of her mouth, her lips still frozen shut. Wally is next to her in seconds, and somehow wordlessly understands—through her emphatic stabs towards the vanishing snake—what it is that she has seen.

"You okay?" he asks, putting his arm around her shoulder and walking her towards the blanket, where he's been busy setting out a picnic on a large flat rock.

"No," Diana murmurs, just as her knees give way and she collapses on the picnic rock. For some reason, she is absolutely starving.

Wally unwraps baguettes filled with Brenner's humus, halved cherry tomatoes, and homemade banana peppers. There is raspberry iced tea to drink and a container of fruit for dessert.

"Hey, you're holding out on me," says Wally.

"Pardon?" asks Diana blankly. Seeing the snake appears to have erased all cognitive function from her jumble of a brain.

"Humphrey told me you wrote a kid's book on King Arthur. It won a big award?"

"Well, I just did the drawings. And I wasn't trying to keep it from you. It's just a sore point with Ted. Because Johnny wrote it."

"Your first husband."

Diana nods. "He was an Arthurian scholar, too. He wrote the story for Humphrey. As a lark really, one afternoon when he was restless with his real work. Somehow, he got me involved. We planned it as our own private book for Humphrey. Anyway, few months later Johnny's adviser came to visit and saw the pictures. Three weeks later he'd sent it to an agent who'd been in one of his classes, and the next we knew, it won the Newbery Award. Ted hates that, of course."

"But why?"

"Because he and Johnny came at the legends so differently. Johnny never stopped being enchanted by them. And Ted, he saw John's enthusiasm as a frailty, a loss of scientific objectivity."

"What do you think?"

"I think it's impossible to choose between one's living partner who may very well neglect to take out the wastebin from time to time and the love of one's . . . well, you know what I mean."

"But I don't mean that way, Diana. I mean, do you really think Ted's right? That you can only know something if your heart's not in it?"

"Well, that's not it, exactly. It's just, I think—Ted thinks that a scholar has to guard against letting his emotions get in the way of seeing things for what they are."

"Ted thinks or you think?"

"I don't have time to think."

"I'm serious. Take something else. Take your kids. You think you can know them without loving them? Or that your love stops you from being able to see them?"

"No," says Diana. "But with the Tales, there's so much debate about them, about what they mean. And Ted's point of view is that it's not his job to tell people what they want to hear, it's his job to tell them what the evidence of history shows."

"But the meaning of the King Arthur legend, it's all—I don't know how to say this. Where's the meaning *without* what people want from it? Know what I mean? It's like, only important in that all these people, generation after generation, all found something in these stories that they wanted. So to separate that out, it just seems,

I don't know. Like throwing the baby out with the bathwater. Anyway, all that to say, you ought to be really proud of that book."

"Oh, well, I am. Johnny had a wonderful way of telling a story."

"Hey, it's you I'm talking about here," Wally reminds her intently. He is caught up in this woman's problems, cannot see why she's so hard on herself.

The whole plane ride up here, Wally has rehearsed his script: The moment where he tells Diana about the bidding process, explains how it's just a technicality. The trouble is, Wally can see how uncertain Diana is. How will it sound if he tells her she'll have to put in a bid? Cursing Guy for talking him into this ridiculous bid requirement, Wally kneels up to look over the ledge that juts out over the east side of the butte, peering down at the ribbon of water disappearing into a gorge. Diana sits beside him, mute, staring at a huge boulder across the crevasse.

"Diana?" starts Wally, thinking that maybe he will get the bad news over and done with.

Diana turns towards him. Her nose has blotched red and her slate blue eyes are pooled with tears.

"What's wrong?" he whispers, taken back to that awful dream where he'd made Mary Kate cry.

"Johnny," she explains. "When I see something this beautiful, I want to turn to him and say, 'Look! Isn't it brilliant?'"

"Yeah." Wally nods. He wants to reach out and pat her shoulder, but she's too far away. He shakes his head. "Twelve years and you still miss him." It is almost a question. At the same time it's a plea for contradiction.

"I do. Sometimes, even now, twelve years later, I'll be walking along and it will just hit me, this realization that he's *still* gone. It's as though I've expected someone to pull away the curtain and say,

'Right. Time's up. Enough suffering. It's over.' As though once the crisis is past, you're done. And it's rather a kick in the stomach to understand that he's gone forever."

"Do you really feel that way?" Wally asks, sitting up straight. "That he is?"

Diana looks around them, as though eavesdroppers might be crawling through the rocky terrain. She turns her face towards Wally. "Not always. I dream about him. And in my dreams he's quite real. Sometimes he's even annoying me, pinching or teasing me. I once read that the Maori people, in Australia, believe that spirits do actually travel to be together in one's dreams. I liked that concept."

"Past tense?"

"I don't know. Ted brought home the most depressing piece in one of his colleagues' science monthlies, about how dreams are really just neurons refiring in the brain and the patterns are completely random."

Wally shakes his head. "Why would he do that to you?"

"He's not trying to hurt me," objects Diana. "Ted's—I don't know—the original anti-mystic. Thinks anything spiritual is a lot of claptrap."

"I used to be like that. Before Mary Kate died."

"Truly?" asks Diana. "You don't strike me as someone—"

Wally laughs. "I came home on the plane from Vietnam next to a chaplain who kept trying to counsel me, and I remember saying to him, 'Hey, buddy, you're wasting your time. I don't have a spiritual bone in my body.' And I didn't, either."

"So what changed?"

Wally exhales loudly. "Mary Kate. I mean, suddenly, these questions of what happens afterwards, they're really pretty interesting."

"But don't you find—?" interrupts Diana. "I'll tell you what worries me. What if we're just making it up because we can't bear to think it's not true? What if it's just a way of denying that they're really gone?"

Wally nods. "I know. But—things happened to me I didn't make up. Times when I was hurting and suddenly out of the blue—" He stops, appraises Diana, and continues. "Did I ever tell you why I came to England in the first place?"

"Well, to dedicate the library."

"Yeah, but, how I got that idea, it all started with—" Wally squints off into the distance; his brow is furrowed, as though the words might fly up out of the landscape and present themselves. He clears his throat.

After Mary Kate's accident, he'd had trouble sleeping. It wasn't the sleeping, so much, as the dreaming. So he was short on sleep, working twenty-four/seven just to keep from thinking. One night, a few months before he'd gone to England, he'd been downloading a file from the office that was taking forever. He'd been restless and turned on the TV. There on the screen had been one of those nature shows that Audrey was addicted to. Two grasshoppers or praying mantises, maybe. Something green and skinny-legged and cute. Wally had been half paying attention, thinking the bigger bug who was heading down the branch to the little one, maybe it was the mommy, bringing a snack to the baby. Out of the corner of his eye, with one hand on the mouse button, Wally watches the bigger bug take the little one, and then he sees that the snack *is* baby. The camera is watching this and the voice is narrating it calmly. Nobody is stopping it. Suddenly it had hit Wally like a load of bricks. This baby bug was out there alone. There was no cavalry coming in to stop it from getting eaten. And if it was the case with nature, what made people different? Were they on the planet, just like the bug, without anyone watching? The awful emptiness of that vision, for some reason, it hit him in a way he'd never felt it before, not even in Vietnam.

Wally speaks hesitantly. He holds up his hands to express his inability to articulate what he feels, but Diana is nodding like she gets it, gets everything he is trying to tell her in his clumsy way. "I had it bad," he murmurs. "I just said, 'God help me.' Out loud."

Wally looks away, then back at Diana, who is sitting quietly, watching him with the look of sympathy, or maybe it's empathy, because she is lost in a kind of reverie, even as she is listening so fiercely. "I was that desperate."

"And?"

"My computer crashed."

Diana chokes back a laugh.

"Yeah, I know." Wally shakes his head, remembering how he'd fallen into bed and held a pillow over his face for what seemed like the whole night. "The next morning I got a call from Guy, with a question about the file I'd been trying to download. So, anyway, I had to reboot and when I did, my screen opened on this completely different file, not anything I'd seen in years. What's weird, Diana: It was a something Mary Kate had sent me right before her accident. She really wanted to go on this England-Scotland trip and had sent me the itinerary that stopped in Oxford to see the cups and books in the St. Mark's library."

"How odd!"

"Yeah. But the really strange part, Diana, is that I still don't know how that file got there."

"Well, isn't it possible your program pulled up an old one, from the recesses of its memory?" muses Diana.

"No, because I'd had a completely different computer before."

"Unbelievable," whispers Diana. The skin on the back of her arms has gone cold.

"I guess it sounds that way," says Wally abruptly. "But I was there. It happened."

"Oh, sorry. I didn't mean it literally. I just—it was just a manner of speaking." She sighs. "Do you know how happy I would be if such a thing were true?"

Wally softens, recognizing the hope and fear playing themselves out in equal parts in Diana's eyes. "Yeah. I don't want to analyze it too much, and I definitely don't want to give it to people to look at. It's too—it's like barely there and if you look too hard you'll make it disappear."

The sentiment that Wally expresses is so like what Diana feels about Johnny, that she cannot help but smile and nod her head. Despite her habitual reserve, she cannot help but describe the dreams she has had of flying through the night sky to save her lost husband. Wally is silent as she talks, but she can see that for the first time since Johnny died, she has been listened to and understood.

Somehow, the act of trusting Wally with something so private, telling him causes her to feel a lift in spirits, a wonder not unlike how she feels when she rediscovers the art of flying. It is at this moment that she recognizes the view from the east side of Wally's prospective site for what it is. She recognizes it for the very first time.

But it's not the first time, of course. It is the desert in her recurrent dream, right down to the boulder where Johnny crouches, digging, with William. It's a place she's seen countless times in her sleep. Diana blinks, stunned by her recognition. This land, now real, appears unreal, or surreal. She nods to herself, understanding now that: This dream, this land, it's hers to own if she'll have it.

So entranced is she by this possibility that she barely hears Wally tell her that her flying in her dreams, that's the exact feeling she should aim for if she ever decides to take William's advice and learn how to swim.

Nine

When Valeen smells the pot, it's enough to make her heave, the last in a series of clues that Dolores is hiding the truth from her. Nothing she can say will make it go away, this news that speaks itself in seasickness bands, in taking off from work, in the new wig catalog hidden under the bed.

"Damn it, Dolores, why can't you confide in me?" Valeen whispers, knowing she won't have the courage to say it out loud.

She knows Dolores feels bad enough as it is. Besides, with the marijuana, their conversation will start to feel like a labyrinth of alternatives. "He said, She said." Or in this case "She said, She said."

Valeen never knew anyone so secretive before she fell in love with Mystery Girl. First there's the money. Dolores's always got cash: It's like never-ending. Second, there's the plastic surgeries. Not that Dolores'd own up, but Valeen can feel the scars during lovemaking. Third, there's like Dolores's whole lifetime before Valeen knew her. When Dolores was married and lived the whole suburban life. Kristen, who works with them and knew Dolores back in the day, acts like she knows something Valeen doesn't. She'll dangle hints out there from time to time, but Valeen is damned if she'll suck up to some slut that's in a different customer's bed every week and then acts like she's got something over on Valeen because she and Dolores used to party together. That fact alone tells you what kind of friend Kristen was, thinks Valeen, knocking at Dolores's door. What a piece of work that Kristen is, Valeen thinks as she opens the door and crosses the room to lay her palm on Dolores's fevered brow. "Oh, sweetie," is all she whimpers, before she hurries from the room and calls the doctor.

* * *

"So, Adam, your aunt's in hospital, then?" Humphrey asks, driving the boys home from their first soccer practice. He can see Adam's face in the rearview mirror, nodding, his eyes flickering self-consciously.

"She's got cancer," Adam murmurs, glancing down at his knees.

"Oh, that's awful," murmurs Humphrey.

"No, it's not the bad kind," insists Adam. "It's, like, totally curable. My mom says it's just a pain 'cause they got to keep on top of it."

"Well, that's comforting," says Humphrey.

"The only really bad part is that when my aunt Dolores is in the hospital, my mom cooks. We get, like, frozen dinners and junk. Aunt Dolores—she's, like, this really awesome cook."

"Why don't you eat with us tonight? I'll ring your mum on the cell and ask. That way she can stay later at hospital."

"Humphrey's awesome at cookery, too," ventures William.

After Humphrey's arranged with a grateful Valeen to bring Adam home at nine, the phone sounds abruptly, this time with Diana's frantic voice at the other end.

"Don't worry, Mum," asks Humphrey. "All right. All right. Yes, we'll call right back. Don't worry. We'll suss it out, Mum. No, that's ridiculous. Besides, with four different terminals, how'll you know which flight? Never mind, just hang on." Humphrey sets down the phone and changes lanes. "William, did you move the orange notepad from Mum's room? She wrote Ted's flight information on it last night and it's gone. Now she doesn't even remember which airline."

William shakes his head and winces at Humphrey in the mirror. "She should try Elly's room."

Humphrey shakes his head. "Been there, done that." He sighs. He picks up the phone and looks at it apologetically before putting it to his ear. "Mum, he hasn't. Look, Ted'll understand. And if he doesn't, too bad. Are you not allowed to make mistakes?"

"Hey!" interrupts William. "He flew on e-tickets. I can find them."

"Mum, William can get onto Ted's computer and find what you're looking for. We're driving into the neighborhood right now. Oh, come now. That's standing on ceremony, don't you think?" Humphrey hangs up the phone and shakes his head. "She doesn't want to invade his privacy."

"Bugger that," snorts William. "I'll look."

Adam watches all this with a puzzled distraction, wondering why the uproar over a lost piece of paper.

When they arrive home, Diana is upstairs, turning the house upside down in search of Ted's flight information. Her rhythmic footfalls provide a strange accompaniment to Eleanor's muted Teletubbies video, in front of which she stands, two fingers in her mouth, rapt.

"I'll just lay the table, William, while you look for that piece of paper," says Humphrey, steering his younger brother towards Ted's office with a meaningful look.

"How will you get in?" asks Adam, after William has booted up.

"I know his password. Unless he's changed it," whispers William. "Close the door."

Though William hasn't used this password since he was four years old, when his father asked him to enter it, he remembers it perfectly, for he'd recognized the pattern. The first letter of each of his family's Christian names, transferred to their numeric order in the alphabet. William enters the password, then waits for the server to deliver him to Ted's post box. It takes several minutes, for the shortcut to Hotmail boots up automatically. William resists the temptation to hit Cancel and start over, for he knows this will just slow him down. Besides, he reminds himself, his dad might be getting his e-mails at Hotmail instead of his college address. Just as he's ready to shut down and start over, William's patience and perfect numeracy are rewarded. He is able to click on Old Mail and see an orderly listing of Ted's last one hundred posts, including one entitled, "Travel Plans and Pictures." Here, William clicks again, with a triumphant flick of the wrist. Now he'll just have to create a fib about how he remembered seeing the notepad after all, and remembered the time, airline, and gate. Mum will believe him, she's accustomed to his photographic memory.

"See, I've found it already," he exults. Adam looks over his shoulder.

When the pixels on the screen form into the shape of a beautiful blond woman wearing nothing but an airline cap and hip boots, William's first emotion is a blinding sense of shame. Quickly he exits the mail and is about to shut down completely when he sees a post from Gold Industries entitled "Your E Ticket." From this point forward, until he writes down the numbers and hands them to his older brother, William is on automatic pilot. William is grateful for Adam's silence, for pretending that neither of them saw the text scrolling across the young woman's ringed belly button, promising to meet his father at his Florida hotel, "with bells on."

By the time dinner is cleared and his mum has rushed to the airport, William is still not himself. Or perhaps, he thinks, he's more himself than he ever has been before, carving his initials into the huge dining room table. His hand shakes with the power of indignation as he digs a large W for *William*, then an S for *Sennett*. The S is a tribute to Johnny's valiance, a rebellion against Ted Lively and all that he stands for. It is not until William's brushed the wood shavings into his hand, planning to distribute them evenly in the nether spaces of his father's keyboard, that it occurs to him: This table he's defaced, it's not his father's to begin with. Second, he'll likely never notice his son's vandalism. No, it will be Mum who does, and how will he explain himself? William places his geography book over the offending letters and races into his father's office to scatter the scraped bits of WS across the computer keyboard, taking particular care to spit on the T and the L as an added measure of patricidal contempt.

* * *

DIANA is waiting in front of Terminal 3 when Ted exits the automatic doors, holding up two fingers towards the Le Sabre. His expression is debonair, as in urbane-young-prince-hailing-taxi. Diana hops out and pops the trunk, grateful that William remembered seeing the flight numbers. By the circles under Ted's eyes, Diana can see it's been a tiring flight. The last thing he'd have stood for would be an endless wait while Diana circled the various terminals, hoping to chance finding him. *What is wrong with me*, Diana wonders, lifting Ted's valise into the trunk, *that I can't remember the simplest thing?*

"Rough trip?" she asks, once they're settled into their seat belts and she is pulling out into the left lane of faster traffic.

"Hmmn." Ted nods, wiping a fleck of spit from the corner of his mouth. "I'm knackered. Chap next to me snored the whole way home, and the imbecile they had waiting on first class broke the only bottle of good vodka. The swill they serve in coach tastes distinctly like cat piss."

Diana accelerates up the Squaw Peak Parkway, reflexively cluck-clucking at the obligatory pauses in Ted's tale of woe.

"So, how was your appointment?" Ted asks, when he's exhausted his critique of American standards in food, wine, hoteliering, and air travel.

"Appointment?"

"Look, you didn't forget, did you?"

"Forget what?"

"I told you I'd arrange things, Lady Di. All you had to do was remember to attend. The consultant?"

Diana is shaking her head as she turns off the freeway onto Indian School Road.

"The psychiatrist? The one in the Yellow Pages?" Ted asks patiently.

"Ted, I never agreed—"

"Remember, Diana. I mentioned that her area was midlife crises?"

"Honestly, I thought you were joking, Ted."

"Look, if you're fearful about seeing someone, Diana, I could go with you."

"That's not the point, Ted. I will see someone when, and *if,* I decide I'd like some help."

"Dammit, I'm sure we'll be billed now, Diana. At seventy quid an hour!"

"Whose fault is that, Ted? If you're looking to cast blame—"

"You're scolding me for daring to be concerned about your mental health? Can you not take an hour out of your pressing schedule to see a woman who might help our marriage—?"

"Ted, as a matter of fact, I was working."

"Look, we've discussed this already. There's no real point to doing dollhouses here. You won't have time to build up any sort of client list."

"No. I was up looking at the site for the park, Ted. I told you I was going."

Ted rears back in his seat and looks sideways at his wife, who has pulled over on the side of a quiet street near their house. "Why would you do that? Did I imagine our phone conversation, then?" he asks quietly. "When we agreed that Gold couldn't be trusted."

"I never said that!"

"Diana. I remember our conversation verbatim. You'd just gotten off the line with Gold's secretary, who informed you that he had neglected to mention the bidding process when he offered you the moon?"

"I remember talking about her. But the thing is—"

"No. What matters is that Gold is winding you up. And you're letting him."

"He's not."

"Yes, he is. First off, he mentions a competition, then he arrives one afternoon with an architect's practice full of furniture and tells you you've got the job, won't need to bid. Just a few days later you discover he's misled you and hasn't had the decency to spare you being made a fool of in front of a clerical worker!"

"I think I misunderstood his secretary, Ted. I really do. We went up to the site yesterday and, he, I'm sure— If I weren't on already, Wally wouldn't have taken me there."

"Did you actually confront him about it?"

"I'm sure she just had it wrong, that's all."

Ted lets out a huge storm of breath. "You're being played for a fool here."

"No, I'm not. I can trust—"

"So, where is this site? And who went with you?"

"No one. Remember, the location is under wraps."

"Oh, aren't we impressive? Have you forgotten that I'm the technical expert, having been paid a very handsome sum to be treated as your inferior?"

"I thought the compensation was less than your salary at home, Ted?"

"Look, might we just please stay on the subject at hand for more than a nanosecond, Diana? Look, the point is, of course Gold wants you to keep the location secret. From strangers, you silly git, not insiders! It's only to prevent investors from driving the stock price too high for the sale of his company to go through, or land speculators from buying properties before he gets to them."

"Oh really?" asks Diana, in mock surprise, her hand over her heart.

"Yes, really."

"Well," Diana says, switching on the engine and pulling back into traffic. "I would tell you—"

"And the land, Diana, you do know that's a separate issue from the stock."

"But if word were to get out—"

"To whom exactly do you expect I'll leak this information, Diana?"

"No, it's not that. I keep trying to tell you, I don't even remember where the land is. We went there on motorbike, and I had my eyes closed most of the way. So I couldn't tell you even if I wanted."

"You must remember how near it is to the lake, and what the elevation is."

"These questions aren't like you." Diana turns to look at Ted out of the corner of her eye. "Why are you interested?"

"Well, despite myself, I'm curious as to where and how this project will be sited. It's not as though I can take my millions and scoop up the land from underneath him, is it now?"

Diana laughs, relaxing her shoulders for the first time since seeing Ted. "You know, even if I wanted to invest in cutthroat economics,

I'd make a hopeless corporate spy, given my sense of direction. Wally could better explain to you where it is."

"I'm sure he could. Must ring him, first thing tomorrow," says Ted. "Though I've noticed he's a lot more likely to answer your calls than mine. Funny thing, that. I'm sure it's that prize you won at University, Diana, that's got him hanging on your every word. Oh, but that's right, he didn't really ask much about that, when he told you he had to have you aboard his ship of fools. Did he now?"

* * *

WALLY filters into the Al-Anon meeting just after they've read the Serenity Prayer. The regulars give him a surprised little wave. It's been months since his last meeting, but it's like he never left. The repetition of the familiar words—very much like those read out loud in the AA meetings down the hall, but aimed at the family and friends of the drinker—calm him down. When the readings are through, and the circle makes its way around to him, he finds himself ready to talk, despite his plan to "pass."

"It's funny how you can find stuff in every reading," marvels Wally. "The whole idea of rescuing: That's a big one for me. My wife, she ate up these medieval stories, like where the knight rides up and rescues the damsel, but man, it was a whole different story towards the end of our marriage. She'd get so mad at me for 'putting her on a pedestal just so she could fall off.' She kept saying she couldn't stand on her own two feet because I'd always come along and pick her up, sometimes before she'd even tripped. I know I probably—no, not *probably*. Make that *without a shadow of a doubt*— I enabled the Hell out of her. Coming to Al-Anon, seeing how I was being controlling when I thought I was just taking care of her, I think I came a long way. Trouble is, now I feel like, with my kid and with—"

Here Wally pauses. He is searching for the right word. He hesitates, then continues. This is an audience he can trust. "With this new friend, I find myself doing it again. So I thought maybe I'd better get back in here where no one lets you lie to yourself. It's been too long since I took any kind of inventory, much less a fearless one."

After the meeting, several members of the group approach Wally and give him a hug, telling him it's been too long, at which he nods his head like a backseat Chihuahua. The odd thing is, that even as he agrees with the principle of *letting go and letting God*, he is already mentally saddling his horse and shining his armor, just in case a plundering villain should appear down the trail.

EARTHGYRL: Where the Hell have you been?

SKYGYRL: Been right here, all along. Just throwing up. I can chat, though.

EARTHGYRL: Tell me you're not preggers.

SKYGYRL: LOL. Not unless the Immaculate Conception's back in town for a reunion gig. Just a flu. How about you? What's up?

EARTHGYRL: I've been in my own little Hell. That's where the Hell I been.

SKYGYRL: Por que, mi hija?

EARTHGYRL: Whoa. That's something my mom used to say.

SKYGYRL: You and every other Mexican in town.

EARTHGYRL: You know I'm not Mexican.

SKYGYRL: Hey, I love Mexicans! So sue me. So what's the matter, anyhow?

* * *

DIANA sits cross-legged in the middle of the living room, a box cutter in one hand. She has just opened a parcel from her mother, and the very smell brings tears to her eyes.

It had been spring when Johnny brought home that patchouli to cover up the musty smell in his parents' cottage. He'd sprinkled it everywhere as a surprise, and by then it was too late to tell him that she associated the scent with an awful upper-form prig from boarding school, the one who'd tormented poor Evelyn for wearing makeup when the prevailing fashion dictated facial nudity. No matter how Diana'd worked, she couldn't wash the smell out of their things, couldn't rid the cottage of it, and each time it greeted her, on return from a day away, she'd had the conflicting images of a holier-than-thou-hippie-bully and her heart-stoppingly-handsome young man whose inept acts of kindness were part of his charm.

After the funeral Diana had packed up her architecture texts, her portfolio, her Winston Prize certificate and stored them in her mum's summer house, thinking perhaps she'd work in some practice during Humphrey's school breaks. Trouble was, there was always something else to occupy her, something that saved her from noticing how much time had gone by, never to be recovered again. She'd had an awful dread of seeing her work again, because then she'd have to face the fact that she'd fooled herself, fooled the Winston committee, fooled them all. What she'd completely forgotten was the smell, the scent of patchouli over jasmine and chocolate. She sits, seeing dust motes in the cool light of the late afternoon, seeing Johnny lying on the shabby chaise, reading. Humphrey would have been sprawled on the sofa, a toddling miniature of his father except for the look of consternation on his forehead, the flickers of his eyelids, a dream causing concern. Diana remembers exactly how she'd felt watching them, utterly guilty for what she had: a beautiful husband and child, a prestigious prize, a future. She'd been gripped by a sudden fear, clutching at the skin on her forearm, pinching it hard, as though to inoculate herself against Fate's punishment of those whom luck has favored too much. Distracted by this memory, Diana reaches out for the card-board and yanks her past forward into her lap. She opens the box and retrieves a large portfolio envelope, the contents of which she slowly reviews.

It is not at all as she has feared all these years.

Her work is unmistakably good, recognizably so. What Diana can-not fathom is how she'd done it, drawn those beautiful shapes, had the vision to create such a lovely set of images. It is as though some other hands have set angle to angle, not the ones that presently turn the pages. Not these hands, the ones that scrub potatoes and are bitten down to the raw nailbeds with the constant alertness that living in her present life seems to demand. In a flash of insight that flings Diana's eyes shut with longing, it occurs to her that the miss-ing ingredient, the magic of her former glory, it may have de-pended on being happy in ways she has only recently been able to remember.

* * *

VALEEN has volunteered cheesecake for the Mesquite Elementary School bake sale, much to her regret, since she'd counted on Do-lores to help her. If she is perfectly honest, Valeen would admit she's counted on Dolores to do more than help. Typically, when Valeen tries to make anything, Dolores will get so impatient watching her flounder that she'll ask her to please just get the Hell out of the kitchen and come back when the cooking is done. But now Dolores is lying down with an IV bag, and Valeen is trying to figure out whether the springform pan is supposed to be greased with oil or butter, all the while picturing the Sara Lee cheesecakes in the frozen section and wondering if anyone would know if she was to put one of those in a plate of her own.

Before leaving for the grocery, Valeen checks on Dolores to see if she wants anything.

"A gun," moans Dolores.

"Oh, honey, I'm so sorry. You'll feel better tomorrow."

"Come here, sweetie. Sit down."

Something in Dolores's tone of voice scares Valeen. "Look, I'll be back before you know it."

"Valeen."

Valeen is already crying by the time she kneels next to Dolores and kisses her cheek.

"Sweetie, you know this isn't working. Right?"

"No, I don't."

"So why are you crying then?"

"I'm trying to make cheesecake!" blurts Valeen, her nose and eyes collapsing into themselves, overpouring, a Niagra Falls of the sinuses. "I can't even make cheesecake without you!"

"Sweetie, buy cheesecake," whispers Dolores. "It's not important. What's important is telling Adam the truth. Take it from me, you don't want to lie to your kid."

With that, Dolores gently pulls the IV shunt from the crook of her elbow and curls up into her lover's embrace.

* * *

A seven-foot stuffed brown bear greets customers at the Superstition Saloon in Dreamy Draw. The bear's matted coat is thick with decades of cigarette smoke, beer fog, and peanut shell dust. The saloon clamors with the hoots of cowboys pounding motorcycle helmets on their tables, the waves of boilermakers sloshing and waitresses quietly tucking joints behind their ears as a gratuity they won't kick out of bed. Not yet.

A waitress carries three Buds (the bikers), three Anchor Steams (the hippies), and one hot water with lemon verbena (Crazy Martha) to the booth in the back, where the Dreamy Draw city council meets every Thursday, right as rain, or maybe even better than rain.

"Hey, cheers, all," Brenner says, opening the meeting with a toast, as is customary in Dreamy Draw. All the city council members except one—Crazy Martha—clink their glasses. So the meeting begins.

Brenner takes five minutes to summarize their deficit spending situation, their storm water runoff problem, their inability to interest investors in any sort of bond issue, and their impending head-on collision with flooding, septic failures, water-borne parasites, and a fire truck that needs a new engine.

Then Brenner sits back in his seat and takes a long sip of his beer. Nothing like silence and the whooshing bullet of insolvency to concentrate the brain. When it comes to Wally's offer, he figures, hunger makes the best cook. Brenner sits and waits for the council members to think of a solution.

"Now, listen," Crazy Martha, the tea drinker, interjects. "People have been drinking water from the earth for centuries. I don't see why we need to get all caught up with this anal-retentive bullshit when everyone knows you need bacteria in your system or you're dead."

"It's not that simple, Martha," Brenner says, keeping his tone level. "The earth's not like it was centuries ago, and the septic systems ain't gonna be pretty when they start to back up down the mountain into the town square. The cachement's off right now 'cause of the road the logging company put in."

"Don't patronize me, Brenner. This is just another way to consolidate your empire."

Brenner shakes his head, wipes his chin, and appraises the bitter expression of this woman whose sole mission in life appears to be giving him shit. Martha's husband had run away with a biker chick, and for this, she holds Brenner and his Harley distributorship personally responsible. She even picketed his store one time. Friends had urged Brenner to kick the sign-wielding Martha off his property, but Brenner had ignored her and so had his customers. In fact, just like he said, she may have done more for business than an ad in the paper, the Dreamy Draw constituency being about as contrary a consumer population as you could imagine.

Crazy Martha yanks the hemp tie around her herbal teabag and a nearby spoon, strangling it. She watches as small teardrops of tea are shed into her waiting cup. "I still think we should let nature take its course."

"Anyone want to second that motion?" asks Brenner rhetorically. This is a common tactic they've developed to deal with Martha's off-the-wall, take-no-prisoners devotion to the reconstruction of life as it never was, back in the imaginary day, before motorcycles, and husbands that disappeared ass-backwards on the end of one.

The beer drinkers answer by taking particularly long swigs of their beer. The waitress returns with their next round, by which time Brenner has introduced Wally's offer, and his confederates are nodding and grinning. The two bikers are thinking they'll maybe set up a Jet Ski and motorboat ferry business to take tourists back and forth to Lake Havasu City. The coffee shop lady is trying not to count her lattes before they're hatched, and the earth mama thinks maybe she will get a job now that her daughter's in high school. The group asks some questions, mostly about the mysterious buyer. The fact that Brenner's known the man since the seventies, that he's a donor for EARTHCARE ARIZONA, and that he has never developed any real estate before this, all this stands in his favor, but when Brenner mentions that he's the father of the girl who planted lantana in the town square and that his dead wife has been sending him signs from the afterlife, that's enough to clinch the deal.

At least this is what Brenner thinks, when the vote's been held and it's five-to-one to draft a sales agreement. It's only then he spots the gleam in Martha's eye.

"First off," she gloats, "you aren't too fresh on our constitution, are you, Brenner? All land sales have to get a unanimous vote from the city council or they're tabled for three months."

"Martha, what do you want?" he groans, as though he didn't know. Martha owns the natural foods market. By the time the bar closes that night, the booth in the back is filled with amber bottles and its three ashtrays are heaped with green teabags surrounded by hills of ash. It's only through the hippies' intercession that they make any progress at all, though Brenner's not sure that's how Wally will see this document, the one that is being set into calligraphy at this very moment. As Martha crosses the T in *nontoxic*, curlicues the O in *organic*, and levels off the W in *whole foods*, Brenner is trying to remember Audrey's cell phone number. If they're gonna sell Wally on Crazy Martha's stipulations, it's time to get a look at Mary Kate's old recipes, the ones from her vegetarian days. Maybe they can cobble something together that will be a true tribute to their long-lost lady fair, who'd brought more than one famished soul back from the brink.

* * *

DIANA is hard at work in her studio. The vision she'd had at the site—an inverted pyramid of terraced gardens that overhangs the apex of the hill—is taking shape on the page. It's almost as though someone else is doing the work; she's just providing the hand that holds the pencil. The main building will look like an inverted medieval castle and house a maze, she thinks, one watered by a system of interior misters and plants. The walls will be thick stone, double-paned concrete to save on energy, and if she is remembering correctly from her reading during the early eighties, an envelope-like effect will do wonders for air flow. She has just toured the courthouse in Phoenix, where the newest form of water conservation entails a self-contained, almost rain-forest effect within the building. Could this not somehow be used in Dreamy Draw, where water from the lake might be filtered within the "plant" of the building? And could the roof not be planted with succulents that hold moisture to reduce the water lost to runoff during storms?

So intent is she on this vision that she does not hear the phone. She is flipping the pages and making quick sketches. Her fingers and forearms are aching. They aren't accustomed to this pace, but she's afraid she'll lose her train of thought if she doesn't put this all down on paper. When Humphrey taps her on the shoulder with the portable phone, she howls out loud. It takes a second or two for her to recognize her son, even longer for phone to take shape in her brain.

"It's Wally," whispers Humphrey.

"You okay?" Wally asks.

"Better than you, I expect," Diana murmurs. "Your poor ears. I was lost in my work. I've been drawing all morning and I'm so happy! I can't even—"

"Well, Diana, there's something I need to tell you," Wally interrupts. The words come out in a rush, carrying with them Wally's frustration at not being able to circumvent the bid requirement. "Guy says there's some legal trouble with hiring you. We have to go through a bidding process, after all. Something about equal opportunity—"

"You don't have to explain yourself," blurts Diana, wishing he would do exactly that. And soon.

Diana is already working out the permutations. It's clear enough. Only one explanation fits the facts. Diana has gone too far, gushed too much on that mountaintop, revealed her weaknesses. Now that he's gotten to know her, Wally understands that she's completely unsuited to be at the helm of a multimillion-dollar project. The bid facade will allow him to withdraw his offer gracefully.

"You know, you *may* tell me if you're having second thoughts," she says quietly.

"Jesus, Diana! I promise, that's not it! This is just a hoop you gotta jump through, is all. I'm on the selection committee with Guy and Audrey. You're not allowed to put your name on your proposal, but nothing's to keep me from looking at it ahead of time. Or you could give me your vendor number once the computer assigns you it."

"Is that how much confidence you have in me?"

"I do. But—"

"I absolutely will not cheat to get this job. Absolutely not."

"It's not cheating."

"Yes, it is! I'm sorry you thought I would need to, but if I can't win the bid fairly, I won't take the position."

"Damn it, Diana, that's ridiculous."

"No, it's not. Actually, I'm rather insulted."

"I didn't mean to—"

Diana shakes her head. "Look, never you mind. I'll look over the packet and I'll sit at the lovely drafting table you bought and it will come to me. If it doesn't, I'll know I have no business trading up from the miniatures. After all, if you really believe in signs from God, it's time to leave the decision up to Him."

* * *

WALLY hangs up the phone and glowers across the table at Guy. "Any more shit you need me to eat?"

"Well, as a matter of fact, yeah. Did you forget about the licensing part? How she has to work under the supervision of someone certified in the U.S.?"

"That's just technical. We'll pay somebody to do that once this is done. I'm not throwing that in her face yet."

"You know, orchids don't do too good in the desert."

"What's that supposed to mean?"

"You know. She hasn't worked in fifteen years, she's got little kids, and she's under the thumb of a guy I wouldn't hire to wipe my windshield. I wouldn't even hire him to wipe my butt."

"Look, Guy, don't sugarcoat it."

"Well why'd you hire him? You should see his expense report. On top of everything, I think he had some hooker join him in the hotel. We got charged for a double, and get this, they took the bathrobes in the room. One ninety a crack."

"You serious?"

"As a heart attack."

Wally shakes his head. "He oughta be shot."

"See, just what I'm telling you. You're selling the company just when we could use the ammo."

"Oh, so who's got a sense of humor now?" asks Wally. "Does humiliating me cheer you up?"

"More than you could ever know."

Ten

"Adam, sweetie? Don't you ever wish you had normal parents?" asks Valeen. She and Dolores and Adam have just played their third set of cribbage and Adam's won the pot of plastic swizzle sticks shaped like bikini-clad ladies.

"What?"

"You know, like a normal family, a mom and a dad," Valeen asks, figuring it's just a matter of time before her son realizes Dolores is not her first cousin, nor do they share a room solely to conserve on space. "Like William's mom and dad."

Adam snorts. "If that's normal—just shoot me. His dad's got a girlfriend."

"How would you know that?"

"We saw this stuff on his computer."

"Adam, you aren't allowed to go on the Internet! You promised."

"I didn't, Mom. I swear. See, we had to get into his dad's e-mails to see when his plane was coming. And this lady, she sent a picture of herself to Will's dad, naked."

"Maybe it was just one of those pop-ups you can't control, Adam," murmurs Dolores, the family's resident expert in all things digital.

"No. It had this whole message about how she'd meet him at his hotel in Florida."

Valeen's jaw drops. She shakes her head. "William's mom is gorgeous."

"And really nice too," Adam adds. "Whenever his dad's home, it's like, there's a funeral going on. Everyone's like, you gotta be quiet, 'cause Ted's working. They all mock him out behind his back, but you can see they're kind a' scared, too."

"What a crappy way to feel about your father," muses Dolores. Yesterday, when dropping William at home, Dolores had seen Ted checking the mailbox in front of the house. She'd ducked her head, hoping he wouldn't remember having seen her at Naughty Nelly's, not gauging the slim odds of Ted remembering a waitress who'd once served him breakfast, much less her partner who'd been inspecting him from the safety of the next station. Besides, behind the wheel of her car, Dolores was just another invisible woman driving car pool. Still, she had decided there and then not to risk being seen again, and to warn Valeen that the Customer-from-Hell was none other than William's dad.

Now, though, hearing just what a liar this man is, she begins to think more creatively. Maybe exposure of an entirely different sort is just what the doctor ordered. Dolores resolves to speak with her old friend Kristen, then turns her attention back to Valeen and Adam, who are waiting for her to say something. "Sorry, I meant *crabby*, not *crappy*."

"Aunt Dolores, it's okay. I've heard the word before."

"I know, I know. Just trying to give you a little *Ozzie and Harriet*."

"Who?"

"Just this TV show from when we were kids."

"Give it up," laughs Adam. "More like Ozzy Osbourne."

* * *

THE doorbell rings before ten-thirty, just like Brenner promised. The FedEx man stands there with his clipboard. "Come on in," Wally says, already turning towards his desk. "It'll just be a minute," he continues, tearing off the strip of the package. Scanning the document quickly, Wally dials Brenner's number. "Hey," he says, flipping through the pages. "It's here. I'm signing and sending as we speak."

"Look, don't rush into it, buddy. Take your time."

"It's the price we agreed on, Brenner. What's not to like?"

"Did you read it, Wally?"

"I'll have Legal go over it next week. They're really busy right now."

"There's no fire, Wally. Slow down. It makes me nervous if you don't read it through. Guy tells me you're mortgaging your house for this money."

"No biggie. Our new corporation papers haven't cleared the state yet, so it was easier to take out a personal loan on such a small amount."

"Small? It's over a million bucks, Wally. Look, read it before you sign. There's a chick named Martha. Crazy Martha. It's a long story, but she only wants organic food on the menu—"

"Hey, look, don't sweat the small stuff."

"Look, there's another hurdle I just found out about called the River Board. They have to approve new construction on account of Lake Havasu feeds into the Colorado. There's a risk they'll nix this, or regulate you to death."

"It's okay. We're gonna do this project right, anyhow, Brenner. That land is beautiful. I want to keep it that way."

"I know, but still, I worry about you. What do you know from theme parks?"

"Not much," Wally admits to Brenner, though he's recently

denied the same deficit to Guy. "Other than I always wished I could go with my friend Mikey, when he got to go to Sandusky. I used to fantasize about my mom winning the lottery so we could build one in our own backyard. This'll be my chance."

"Okay," Brenner says. "I just want you to go in with your eyes open."

"Hey, I'm excited. So don't worry. I already got Guy on that job, for half the planet, at least."

* * *

WHEN Ted arrives home from work that evening, he makes himself a martini, locks himself into the study and opens an envelope marked PERSONAL AND CONFIDENTIAL. Such directions are unnecessary in the Lively household. Diana would never dream of invading her husband's privacy. Moreover, she is also singularly disinterested in the flood of papers that define her husband's professional life: student essays, tenure deliberations, upcoming administrivia regarding offices and assistantships and other hard-fought academic prizes. Of course, Ted's new solicitor, whom Fiona has recommended, has no way of knowing this detail, and it's not in Ted's character to ruminate on Diana's finer points, not when this letter carries with it a betrayal of sorts, which he'd rather not face at present. So it is that Ted reads the lawyer's letter, composes his reply and hunts for postage. By the time he has sealed the return envelope, Ted's mind is on Fiona, and their recent weekend, not on covering his tracks. The lawyer's words, printed in Times New Roman on creamy thick stationery, are crumpled in a ball and flung into a tasteful hemp recycling bin on the very first try. For the deftness of his toss, which lands like a pebble in the exact center of a pond, Ted can be nothing but proud. In two flicks of his wrist, he has opened his e-mails and thus does not have time to consider the ways in

which a stone, once thrown, can create its own widening circle
within the deep.

To: FionaCheswitt@St.Marks.edu.uk
From: Hotman@hotmail.com
Re: missing you too

Dear Feefee,
Delighted that you're home safe and snug. I am shattered to
be back in this desert, away from you and my first editions,
but will, with any luck, return home soon. In the meantime,
I'm lining up all my ducks. No sense in not making hay while
the sun shines with its bloody intermininable brightness.

After sending this message to Fiona, Ted turns to the creation of
what he considers to be several minor masterpieces of innuendo
and clicks Send. It is just as he is in the process of signing off that
he receives a most intriguing solicitation:

From: naughtynice.com
To: Hotman@hotmail.com
Re: Congratulations!!!

As our seven hundredth customer this month, you've won a
free Bloody Mary, served nearly naked at Naughty Nelly's.
Please come on a Monday or Wednesday night and ask for
Kristen. You'll be glad you did.

* * *

TED wanders into the Stocktraders' Limited branch at eleven-
thirty. Behind the counter a fashionably dressed young man with a
Polish surname on his nameplate talks on the phone while Ted taps

his envelope on the counter and looks at his watch. When the man's done, Ted explains what it is he wants.

"Sure," Lech Kowalski says, pulling his hand back through bangs that won't stay in place. "I'll have to check the ins and outs of what papers you gotta file, but sure, you can do it. We got lots of foreign money in the market and tons of 'em use that same bank in the Bahamas."

Ted signs the paperwork and moves on to his next transaction.

The young man listens closely, then pulls out another form for Ted to sign. He is surprised at Ted's choice, being English and that. He doesn't look like he knows his way around a peashooter, much less one of the biggest names in the ordinance trade.

"A good choice," Lech says, his rote response for first-timers. "This is a good one for the long haul."

Ted shakes his head impatiently. "Thanks ever so much for your exquisite advice. But in case you haven't been paying attention to a word I've said, I'm buying today and selling two days from now. This is a quick 'in and out.' Rather like everything else in this fast-food nation. Now, please, do tell me where to sign this bloody order form as we need to get this in before the market closes."

* * *

THE next morning, in the *Arizona Republic*, a short article about the stock Ted has acquired leads the business section, just as he'd been hoping it might.

ARIZONA'S AMMO KING STEPPING DOWN?

By Terrance Pierce
KNIGHT RIDDER NEWS SERVICE
Wallace Gold, CEO of Gold Industries, has allegedly made a deal to sell his Ammunitions division to the nation's largest gun

manufacturer, Huntington Incorporated, according to an anonymous e-mail sent to our Business Editor early this morning. Unnamed sources have confirmed that Huntington declared interest in the company last month and that a deal may indeed be in the works. News of this acquisition—which was also posted on the message boards of several well-known investment Web sites—sparked a jump in Gold Ammunitions stock from its opening price of 35 and 3/8 to 42 and 1/8 as of this printing.

Not all Gold shareholders were happy to hear the news, however. Glenn Nestor, of Nestor's Guns and Ammo, with stores across Arizona, Nevada, Wyoming, and Utah, said, "Looks like he's selling the chicken coop directly to the wolf, if you ask me. How's the little guy gonna have any leverage with a company like that?" Similarly, Stephan Birnbaum, of Birnbaum's Bait and Tackle, in Yuma, asks, "We're basically a union of buyers who've just been sold out to our biggest vendor. Who's gonna represent us now?"

Huntington spokesman, Moira McKelvey, dismissed the conflict of interest by saying, "Huntington's ammunitions holdings are small. This allows us to join forces with Gold, but we're in the business of making high-quality hunting weapons and to that end, would offer a unique advantage to smaller stores by expanding their discount opportunities on a whole range of supplies. If you look at what's happened in other parts of the country, you'll see that network members continue to enjoy price parity with other large concerns."

Wallace Gold could not be reached for comment.

* * *

"DIANA! Where's my College tie?" Ted is shouting from the master bath, pointing at the area between the two sinks. "I had it right here last week and now it's gone!"

Diana, making the bed in the adjoining bedroom, shakes her head. "I haven't worn it recently."

"All I ask is that you leave my things where I keep them and not where you've decided—in some sort of *haus frau blitzkrieg*—they should go."

Diana bangs the feather pillow against the headboard. She swallows and forces out a breath, then tries to clear her cerebral cortex, which at this moment is blocked with the collision of sentences that can't be finished or even started. "Ted, I didn't touch your tie. Have no interest in your tie."

Ted has been at home long enough now for his mind to clear of any guilt he might have suffered over his interlude in Florida. Indeed, after three days of researching Colorado River water rights and the laborious complex of interagency relationships governing them, he is feeling somewhat entitled to moan. About something, anything. Impatiently he dumps a basket of handkerchiefs onto the dresser top. "Dammit, if Eleanor's taken it, I'm going to punish her, Diana. I'm sure it's either she or Humphrey—and incidentally, would you just please restrain your son from straightening in here? He doesn't put things where a sane man would find them. Between the two of them, I'm losing the last bits of what's left of my mind."

Here, Diana is torn between refusing to speak to her husband, as would any self-respecting wife, or taking preemptive action to shield the children, as would any self-respecting mother. Mother wins out, as always. "I'll look," she mutters. "But it's probably in your closet. You have looked?"

"Do you really think I'm an imbecile, Diana?"

From the next room Diana treats herself to a satisfyingly vigorous nod of the head before striding quickly towards Eleanor's room. Truth is, the child probably *has* taken it.

"Oof," Diana says as she opens her daughter's closet. Not only is the navy-and-white tie wrapped around the pink Barbie minivan, but there must be at least one pair of wet knickers kicking around on the floor, because the air is foul. Smells like the Tube after a particularly prolonged and suspenseful World Cup.

Poor Elly. She's regressed.

Diana breathes through her mouth and frees the tie. Dashing downstairs she turns on the iron and waits impatiently for the heat to register against quick taps of her palm.

"He could just wear another," Diana mutters to herself. "But no, the others haven't the heraldry of swords and shield." Since she's known him, Ted's insisted on this tie for special occasions: weddings, funerals, his thesis defense, hairsbreadth tenure denials in the College.

"What's he got today?" she asks, without real interest, giving the material a quick sweep of the hot iron before running back upstairs and handing him the warm tie.

"Look, please don't reprimand Eleanor," Diana warns. "She's wet the bed again, if I'm not mistaken."

"And your reasoning? Eleanor wets herself repeatedly, wringing ever more sympathy from an overindulgent parent. How's she going to learn? My mum would've had me scrubbing the linens eons ago, I can tell you that. It's a wonder she bothers to use the W.C. at all." Ted takes the tie and quickly wraps it around his neck. "Ugh. You'd better do something, and soon. I can smell her room all the way in here!"

* * *

WHEN Ted arrives at his office that morning, he finds the door blocked by reporters. "What do you think of the boss selling out?" yells one of the reporters, running towards Ted's Caprice with his cords trailing behind him.

Ted ducks his head and marches past, forcing his smile into a frown.

By the time he gets settled at his desk, however, the smile is genuinely in retreat. Ted mashes his intercom. "Beverly? Beverly? Report to my desk, please."

Wally's secretary is ready to lose her mind with the phone that won't quit ringing, the questions that she can't answer, including where her boss has gone off to. For this reason and this reason alone, she heads towards the Rectum's office, spoiling for a fight.

"You rang?" she asks, but this moron doesn't even get her sarcasm.

"Look here, is the cleaning service doing my room? Because I'd like you to take a whiff. How am I expected to produce anything of merit in this refuse bin."

"Look, janitorial's been through twice since Tuesday. And who the Hell do you think I am? The White Tornado?"

"Do you not smell it?" demands Ted, standing over his desk and leaning towards the middle as though trying to locate the exact location of the odor with his nose.

"No, I don't. It smells fine in here," Wally's secretary lies.

Beverly can smell it, all right. Reeks like Tijuana. Like jalapeño peppers maybe, like margaritas, or maybe margaritas that you spilled on a pair of really ripe tennis shoes. Maybe a lot like the back of the bus. Deep inside her belly, a hearty chortle silently rings Beverly's bell.

"Look, I gotta go, but if you don't like your office, I can find you a cubicle in the main lobby."

Ted shakes his head, not bothering to respond. "Do you have any idea who I—?" he starts to ask. "Do you have any idea what I'm being paid to be here?"

"Oh yeah. Sure do, Mr. Lively. Sure do," says Bev. "Hey, by the way, you better get that smell thing checked out. I saw a special last week said psychomatic smells are the first sign a' cancer a' the privates—" She waves a hand dismissively towards Ted's crotch.

"Naw, that can't be. Don't you worry 'bout it, Mr. Lively. Just breathe through your mouth till it goes away."

* * *

WALLACE Gold cannot be reached for comment. Wallace Gold is at his favorite dive in North Phoenix. His waitress keeps coming back to take his order, but she doesn't get that Wally's not in any hurry to eat, pay, and get to work. His phone's turned off and he has no interest in leaving. No interest at all.

Interest is the problem, Guy would say, but money is not what's holding Wally up here. The problem is his customers, who've been e-mailing him since six a.m. In all his thinking about this, which, granted, hasn't been too deliberate, Wally hadn't considered how his longtime customers were gonna feel when he handed 'em over to a big corporation like Huntington. Nestor was right, in the paper. It was like handing the wolf the key to the chicken coop. "I'll just have coffee for now," Wally says, turning towards the door, just in time to see Guy, who is marching towards him, pumping his arms, his head tucked in to one side.

"What's up?"

"Turn your phone back on!"

"How'd you find me?"

"I had a GPS chip inserted in your butt last week. And since your head's been up there the last few days, it was pretty friggin' secure."

Wally turns apologetically to the waitress, who has already turned tail and moved back to the front of the restaurant. He shakes his head. "What's up?"

"Oh, not much. This and that. You know. Buyout's goin' south, SEC's on the horn about how you knew to buy MaryKnoll Technologies right before it got bought by TechGreen, your margin got called this morning. Nothin' really. Oh, well, there is one thing. TechGreen took a swandive based on the fuel standards not goin' through Congress. But hey, my goldfish Marvin's still alive, so thank God for that."

* * *

"HUMPHREY?" asks Audrey, when her friend picks up his phone and says absolutely nothing.

"Um, hello, Audrey," Humphrey whispers, his tone warm despite its nearly undetectable volume. "Elly's seeking and I'm hiding. What's up?"

"I've gotta go to Wickenburg to meet a friend of my dad's for lunch. Want to come with? I could use your advice."

"We'd have to bring Elly," says Humphrey, folding a pair of tiny hot-pink Capri pants with white pom-pom trim. No matter how many times they play this game, Elly forgets to look in the laundry room, which works out nicely for catching up with a load of clothes here and there.

"S'okay with me. Why don't you let yourself be found?" suggests Audrey, ransacking her father's desk for office supplies. "I'll bring some stuff of my dad's to keep her busy. Just get her car seat."

Humphrey loudly pounds the top of the dryer with his fists until he's sure his sister's heard him. He crouches down, as in praying not to be detected, hiding his head. By the time Eleanor pounces, he is able to give off convincing squeals of alarm. "Oh, you wretched child! Now you've beaten me! Very unsporting of you. Now listen. I'm going to get some snacks from the kitchen. You go to the loo and wash your hands afterwards. We're going for a ride with Audrey."

Humphrey forages in the fridge for something to hold his sister on the car trip. She has just had a snack, so she is unlikely to need it, but there is absolutely no predicting her. Humphrey extracts a bunch of grapes and is off to the garage. After pulling Eleanor's spare car seat from its shelf, he raises the garage door and is leaning back into the house to shout for Elly to hurry when Audrey's car appears in the driveway. She honks hello, startling Humphrey.

"Hey, Humphrey, can you get some scrap paper?" Audrey asks, jumping out of the front seat. She reaches down and picks up Eleanor, who has ducked around Humphrey, aiming straight for the older girl's arms. "It's the one thing I forgot."

After installing the car seat, Humphrey returns to the hallway outside Ted's office, where a bin of handwoven hemp holds the recycling. He fingers a stack of white twenty percent bond and nearly dismisses the cream-colored crumpled ball on top. At second glance, though, Humphrey reasons that this last discard will do as a makeshift juggling game, in case the backseat *artiste* becomes jaded. Humphrey uses the pile of straight paper as a tray for the cream-colored paper ball, which he bounces jauntily on the way out to the waiting car.

Eleanor stays absorbed during the long ride to Wickenburg, so struck is she with the possibility of the things Audrey's brought her: a miniature stapler and hole puncher and Post-its, a new, bright red binder. Humphrey is too caught up in his conversation with Audrey to notice that the cream-colored ball will not be needed as a juggling device. Good thing, too, because of all the surfaces in Audrey's hastily assembled art kit, the topographical feel of the crumpled paper is what most excites Eleanor's creative impulse. And so it is that she carefully traces over the words her father and his new solicitor have exchanged. She highlights their phrases with yellows and reds, the colours of leaves in those parts of the world that have seasons, the colors of the sun, salsa, and indigenous corn in those that do not.

* * *

THREE hours later they are leaving the Wickenburg Diner. Miss Eleanor is clutching her folder against her chest while Humphrey holds the door for Audrey. Brenner and Ravenna stand at attention next to their bikes. Ravenna kneels down to give Eleanor a candy bar she's found in her jacket pocket. Eleanor, charmed, takes her two favorite pictures from her folder and hands them over. Ravenna holds the papers out in front of her, as far as her arm will reach. She is farsighted, too farsighted to read the print that's been obscured with the Magic Marker, its ink spread into the rough tributaries of the fancy cream-colored paper. Remarkably, the texture of paper that has been crushed and restraightened resembles nothing more than the rugged topography of the high desert. Even the brilliant colors are appropriate. The reds, yellows and oranges, these are the hues of mirage, of fading moisture and dust particles suspended vastly in the frame of the setting sun.

"It's really nice. I'm gonna put it in my studio," says Ravenna. Her voice, deep and noninflected, is so different from that phony lift most grown-ups adopt when speaking to children that Eleanor is prompted to believe her. She can tell by watching Ravenna, noting the way she carefully places the picture in between her leather jacket and generous chest, that these drawings will be given the pride of place they deserve.

On the way home Audrey plays the Talking Heads. Elly and Humphrey sing along, this particular album being one their mother puts on whenever she feels melancholy seeping in. "Letting the days go by and the water flowing down, into the blue again, after the money's gone, once in a lifetime, water flowing underground. Letting the days go by!" they croon, the words so familiar that their possible relevance is, by this time, more than a little beside the point.

* * *

From: ComputerSleuth.com
To: Guy.Stringer@GoldIndustries.com
Re: Monitoring Services

It has come to our attention that your company recently suffered leaks of confidential information through e-mails to the media. A colleague has recommended we contact you regarding discreet investigations of unauthorized computer activities by employees. Attached is our client and price list and references. We look forward to your call.

SKYGYRL: Hey, gyrl. I found those online cooking classes I was telling you about. Why don't you give me your boyfriend's e-mail address and I'll get him signed up?

EARTHGYRL: He's not my boyfriend. I'll give you his address, but don't tell him it came from me.

SKYGYRL: Your wish is my command.

* * *

As luck would have it, when Humphrey receives Skygyrl's solicitation, he is on the phone with Audrey. "Look at this," he murmurs.

"Are you doing e-mails?" Audrey scolds, though she, too, is checking her mail as they speak.

"Just deleting junk."

"I'm not scintillating enough?"

"Listen to this. Three months' free tuition in the culinary arts. Taught online by a certified instructor."

"Cool! What do you have to lose?"

"My sanity, for one. I told Brenner I'd have a skeleton menu within the month."

"Hey, don't derail your education because of my dad's park. It's not your fault these Dreamy Draw people went off the deep end."

"But I want to help. It's a challenge."

"I'll say. My mom always said vegetarian cooking was the hardest of all. Did I ever tell you about the time she decided we were giving up meat?"

"You?" Humphrey asks, having witnessed the gusto with which Audrey could tuck into her steak au poivre.

"At home at least. Except when Dad and I would sneak to Wendy's."

"You flesh-eating magpie, how did you stand it?"

"My mom could make anything taste good, even tofu. Besides, with her, nothing ever lasted too long. You just had to wait it out and she'd find her next New Best Thing."

" Look, you don't happen to have any of her recipes I could look at? It would be so much easier."

"I wish. I already looked, because Brenner wanted me to bring them to Wickenburg. I don't know if my dad threw them away or what."

"Announcement. Having major anxiety attack, NOW."

"Relax. You can do this. Hey, you never answered me. You gonna take the lessons, or what?"

* * *

EARTHGYRL: Hey, did Humphrey sign up or what? Maybe you should have said you knew me.

SKYGYRL: Well, technically, I don't know you. We've never actually met.

EARTHGYRL: What, three years of chatting don't count? By the way, you know whether this school does vegetarian, organic stuff? Humphrey's helping with a menu for my dad's park.

SKYGYRL: Has your pop gone off the deep end again?

EARTHGYRL: No, for once, it's not him. Just a long story.

SKYGYRL: So, don't keep me in the dark. Tell! I'm dying to hear.

* * *

"ADAM, I've been meaning to ask, how's your mum's cousin?" asks Humphrey. "The one in hospital last week?"

"Excellent," says Adam. "All better now. She's always like cooking cookies or like, sewing stuff or like, going online."

"That's brilliant."

"Yeah. You know she's gotta be better when she doesn't even have to finish all her medicine. She says she's gonna make a pie for you guys."

"Oh, that's not necessary!"

"Well, she thinks it is, and like my mom says, when my aunt Dolores gets something in her head, just grab your hat and get out of the way. We used to live over in Sunnyslope and my aunt *made* us move here on account of the schools. There was, like, no saying no to her. I had to go to Mesquite and I had to do it, like, right away. So you're getting a pie. Count on it."

* * *

MARSHALL Swindle is the lead accountant for SEC investigations in the state attorney's office. His team hasn't had anything big since the Keating years, and Marshall's boss has been on him about punching up the department's profile with the press. The letter—written on Crane stationery by somebody named Lance Gawain—alleges that the tender offer by Huntington for Gold Ammunitions would violate antitrust laws by eliminating free competition in the marketplace. While this is an issue for Justice, not the SEC, and would normally wind up in the wastebasket next to his desk, Marshall is intrigued by the timing of the accusation. Not only is Gold the kind of guy that Marshall loves to hate, but he's just been dealt a get-out-of-jail card on insider trading for MaryKnoll Technologies. Last week Marshall had stayed late every night to try and find some link between Gold and the principals at MaryKnoll and TechGreen, but they claimed never to have met. Marshall's boss, who speaks out of both sides of his mouth, has squelched any further digging, claiming the department doesn't want to be accused of CEO witch hunts. More like Gold knew whose pockets to line, if you asked Marshall. These CEOs thought nothing of playing God; or doing deals with the Devil, which ever came first. Marshall makes a note and double-clicks on the previous file as he calls his friend in Antitrust to tell him he's sending a courier over with the file. "Hey, and who would I talk to about violations of the drug-free workplace act?" asks Marshall. "This source also says Gold's got a soft heart for drug addicts and refuses to do random drug testing."

"I don't think a refusal to test is actionable. But I'll see what I can do on the monopoly question," says Marshall's contact in Antitrust. "Maybe I'll slip a heads-up to my friend on the Corporation Commission."

"Thanks, my friend," Marshall says somberly. "I'll owe you one."

* * *

"Look, you sure you don't mind doing this?" Dolores asks.

"Are you kidding? At least he's cute."

At this Dolores pulls back and shoots Kristen a skeptical wince. She can't repress her distaste, not after the online research she's found herself drawn into doing, despite the fact that this man's philandering is really not any of her business. She's learned more than she ever wanted to know about the British professor. On the other hand, if William's mom is as nice as everyone says she is, and her husband's cheating on her, it's time he got caught with his pants down. Or knickers, as they might say in Jolly Olde England.

"I put some extra in the envelope, sweetie, 'cause he's not gonna tip for shit."

"You didn't have to do that," says Kristen unconvincingly.

Kristen needs the money and Dolores knows why. Dolores might try and get Kristen to go get treatment, but on the other hand, once Kristen's said she isn't ready, Dolores's not judging anybody. She's been where Kristen is: She knows. Besides, you might as well shoot yourself in the head as go cold turkey on downers.

"So, remember what we talked about. If it goes anywhere, you gotta use a condom. And don't get messed up—"

"I won't! You know I never use before work."

"Okay. Listen, thanks. And remember, this is just between us. Don't tell Valeen."

"Hah, like I'd talk to Miss Priss about anything anyway."

After Dolores leaves, Kristen leans forward in the mirror and lines her lips with the Scarlett Fire pencil. It's the exact color of her bra and thong, but by the time she gets that far, the guys don't really seem to notice her attention to detail. They're too busy tucking their peckers back in their pants and wishing real nurses could deliver Kristen's brand of rest and relaxation. The outfit cost her a mint but it's like the goose that keeps on laying its golden egg. The mesh is silk and shows just the right amount of flesh. Enough to get 'em goin' without giving too much away. It has a million snaps and they open at the press of a finger. Ten dollar bill by ten dollar bill, Kristen always says. This English John has no clue how lucky he is, getting comped by Dolores for what other guys might have to pool their money to see. It's not just seeing, though. She knows how to make a guy feel pampered, using her long red fingernails to set their napkins on their lap in a lingering sort of way. Knows how to table-dance within an eyelash of contact, how to shimmy when dancing so they get crotch-kissed with each thrust of her hips, how to stop by the table for a drink on the way out.

To tell the truth, she's kinda looking forward to this. It's not for nothing she took all those acting classes, and if Dolores's got a good reason for leading this turkey down the garden trail, Kristen's only too happy to stroke his tail feathers all the way there.

* * *

FOR once, Ted is grateful for the heavy cigarette fog at Naughty Nelly's. Ever since that slag suggested it, he can't get out of his head the notion that the odor he is continually smelling today is possibly a symptom of sorts. Normally it wouldn't provoke a blink, except Ted could vow that he has, in fact, read a monograph, perhaps a piece by one of the medical fellows at St. Mark's, that traced a relationship between psychosomatic sensory response and related dormant disease. The paper had discussed a man with a "tinnitus" of the nose, a "ghost" smell that hung about without any verifiable stimulus. Was it prostate cancer? Or perhaps a rare carcinoma of the scent glands? Each time Ted succeeds in repressing this trail of inquiry, back comes the smell of urine to haunt him.

It's enough to drive a man to drink, Ted muses as he waves down a cocktail waitress and hands her his coupon for a free Bloody Mary. "Look," she says, after squinting up and down the printout of his e-mailed coupon. "I'm new here. But I'll get Kristen."

Ted is just vowing to himself that he'll make an appointment with a doctor, when out of the blue, out of the fog of cigarette smoke, Florence Nightingale comes to call. Sheets of silky red hair draped across white nurse's tunic buttoned ever so precariously across the suggestion of fire beneath the pale. Red hot lips pout dismissively as she takes his hand and leads him back to a private room. Her willing subject follows the sashay that moves from the base of the spiked red heel to the crisp white hem of her uniform.

She closes the door behind them and seats Ted in a modern

leather chair with tufted buttons. "Shall I dance for you, big boy?" she asks.

"In a minute," says Ted. "Come here first."

Kristen leans in, a mock victim, while Ted undoes her top three buttons and nuzzles his nose in her cleavage. Freeing her breasts from their crimson lace traps, he licks each nipple and murmurs, "I think you know what I want."

Kristen, homing in and smelling the distinctive scent of Audrey's homemade pesticide clinging to her client's tie, finds herself surprised. "You kinky boy," she laughs. "If that's what you want, perfect timing. I'll serve it right up. Let's take your clothes off and get you into the tub."

* * *

An hour later Ted aims a blow dryer at his temple. He uses it to resculpt his Prince Valiant into a semblance of royal chic, inhaling the mixture of bath soaps, of which he's availed himself in huge foamy splurges, compliments of the house. What a divine force of nature this has been, this serendipitous timing: he the seven hundredth customer, brought here initially by the flyer placed upon his car two days in a row! The flyer itself had been revealed by Nature, opening the sky to drop rain upon the desert.

Much to his surprise, the Golden Showers, rather than inciting the disgust he'd always imagined, had lit fires within that he hadn't known were there. Not only that, but the surprise had offered him an explanation right off for the smell he'd noticed all day, the one that Beverly AKA Slag couldn't detect. No, it had *not* been the sign of a nervous disorder, nor an incipient illness. Only a blessing to come, an event that he was prescient enough to intuit before the fact. Yes, yes, yes, he'd have to make an appointment to return to Kristen, sexy chit. After all, soon he'd be heading back to England and the cares of a family man. For now, he might as well enjoy his stay.

"Kristen, I say!" he shouts. "Let's make plans for another rendezvous."

"Just a second," replies Kristen, who has just ejected the recorded portion of the day's events from the video camera. She tucks the videotape into her Prada bag and hurries into the bathroom as if Mr. Lively was offering a handful of Qualudes instead of a muzzle full of hot air.

Eleven

Guy is seated in the chair across from Wally's desk, typing into his laptop. Every now and then he will reconfigure his spreadsheet, looking for a different outcome, but no matter how he sets up the categories, he ends up with the same conclusion. When Wally finally hangs up from his phone interview with a reporter, Guy clears his throat, but Wally beats him to the punch. "What the Hell did I do with my time before the *Republic* broke this story? Which reminds me. What'd they say at that computer place?"

"They finished the research, but I been playing phone tag with some kid named Sigmund. Anyway, I'll try right now." Guy punches some numbers into his cell and hits the Call button. "This is Guy Stringer from Gold Industries." He listens and writes, shaking his head. "Okay. Thanks."

"What?"

"Three guesses."

"Gotta be someone at Huntington trying to make some money on their options."

"Nope. The tracers led back to a computer on our network. Address came from a computer on Gelding Drive."

"Ted! But why? Why would he do that?"

"The little prick knew he was gettin' paid, no matter what. Remember that guaranteed-payment clause I told you not to sign?"

"He's out of here."

"Well, hey, at least we can prove he violated the confidentiality agreement. We'll ship him back with nothing."

"What a son of a bitch!"

"Well, we knew that. Now we got him. We'd have to go to court to get back what we already paid him, but at least we'll save a hundred thou on the rest of his pay."

Wally clears his throat, already seeing repercussions. "The thing is, though, if he goes, what'll happen to his wife and kids?"

"They're here on his visa. They'll have to go back, too."

"But I need Diana."

"She's married, buddy."

"For the project, Guy ."

"Yeah. Right."

"So how do we get around this? Can we fire him but keep him here?"

"No. Once his employment's terminated, so's his visa. And hers and the kids' visas derive from his."

"Wait, can't we get her a work visa?"

"Theoretically, yes. But only after she's won the bid. And let me tell you, the backlog at INS is ridiculous. Plus, it means pulling someone off Legal to put it together when none of them have had more than three hours' sleep in the last two weeks."

"Let me think about this."

"What's to think? He's gotta go. He's poison, Wally. Besides, not to depress you, but we could really use the money."

"Look, Guy, just give me some time. I'll figure it out. Just don't say a word till I do."

Guy nods, rolls his eyes, and shakes his head. He opens his mouth, shuts it, and shrugs. "You're the boss."

"Yeah," says Wally, as though trying to convince himself of that.

"So call Sigmund Freud back and have him do a constant feed on Theodoric of York's e-mails. From this day forward. We'll go from there. Then let's talk about what we're gonna say to the next reporter that calls."

* * *

SIGI hangs up the phone and absently takes a bite of the hamburger that's been sitting on his desk since lunch. He spits it out with a loud "blechh" and glares at the plug of food as if it owes him an apology.

His friend Raz twirls a dreadlock at the desk behind him and winces. "You pig."

"You want me to get food poisoning? I completely forgot how long it was sitting there. Hey, listen, I got a weird scene here with this client and I don't know if I should tell her or what."

"Talk to the hand, man. I'm hung over."

"No, seriously, Raz. You know Skygyrl from the EARTHCARE chat room? She's been our client since we were still working outta your mom's den. Anyway, this guy she's been tracking for—like— ever, man, this Gold dude, *he's* just hired me to watch somebody else."

"So?"

"The new guy he's tracked down, it's this same Hotman that Skygyrl called about, like four days ago. They're both watching the same address.'"

"Duh. So why'd you take the new trick if she's your bread and butter, man?"

"My mistake. See, the guy she was watching, like he's a big hoohaa CEO and the name I had was for another guy who works under him. I didn't catch it."

"How'd you get the gig, anyway?"

"Came in on one of our customer referral forms."

"Which customer?"

"They didn't say. Sometimes they'll do that, even if they miss the ten percent discount."

"Still, I don't see the big deal. They all want to watch this Hotman dude, you just keep 'em each in their own little cubbies."

"But that's the thing. Skygyrl's been getting a feed of the CEO hoohaa's e-mails. Now she's gonna see messages from him to me."

"So tell her the truth. She's the one you gotta be loyal to, she's been with us so long. And since he's not watching *her,* he'll be outta the loop, right?"

* * *

HUMPHREY is having one of his very good days. His days are like the little girls in the nursery rhyme. When they are good, they are very, very good and when they are bad, they are horrid. Today Elly ate her Cheerios without any complaints and was actually humming as she dressed for playgroup. William had been able to find his soccer togs without assistance and had actually been waiting when the bus pulled up instead of lumbering out to the sound of its honk. Mum was upstairs working quietly. Humphrey'd spent the whole weekend getting Elly and William's Halloween costumes together, sewing, tidying, puttering. The fact that Ted seemed to be at the office more than was normal—that was icing on the cake.

The house is especially immaculate today, having been shifted into a new arrangement, the better to reflect domestic Heaven in all its glory.

The peace Humphrey felt when staring out the kitchen window, savoring the sight of a bowl of brilliant peonies against the burnished wood of the table, framed by the aqua of the pool and the wall of Bougainvillea: It had been enough to get him past his jitters. Humphrey had forced himself to push the first button on the keyboard, then another. When he reached the bookmarked site, he'd found the Yes box, brought the mouse to position, and clicked in his answer.

Now hours have passed, as well as a voluminous volley of mail exchanged. Now that he's officially enrolled, he has difficulty remembering why he'd been so hesitant. The name Skygyrl, with its punky spelling, p'raps that had put him off, but when she'd written back, she'd been perfectly approachable.

As was the wonderful Desmond Le Maitre, who'd been teaching cooking for twenty years. "Not to drop names," Desmond had written,

> but it's a household name, my restaurant, and to tell you the truth, the celebs bore me to tears, but I love to talk shop with people like you, Humphrey, people who understand the creativity that goes into making such a small but nevertheless marvelous gift of Self to the Universe. Our food lasts not only in the memories of our tasters, not just the dish in its final presentation, but also the warmth in the belly and the song of the soul. Oh, and Humphrey, it goes without saying that we use only organic products, only fresh and wholesome foods. Our cows are happy, our pigs, our chickens, all raised on a farm out of Mother Goose, fed only organic produce. The last three weeks of their life they get only cream and apples and hazelnuts and walnuts. Oh, and by the way, this project of yours sounds extraordinary. I'll think of it as a chance to influence the palate of the West's next generation. Let's work on the starters, as you Brits call them. You'll find the recipes at my home page, just click on hors d'oeuvres until you find something that rings your bell.

The *ding!* of the oven shakes Humphrey out of his reverie and he checks the cheese straws, which, exactly as promised in the instructions, are just slightly bronze, brushed by the heat, and lined up like golden—that's it!—why, these could be shaped into small swords! And perhaps served with bruschetta sculpted into shields, or better yet, those wonderful Thai sweet potato cakes with a piquant mango dipping sauce. Desmond's site is a dream come true, thinks Humphrey, and he vows he will write Skygyrl this very moment to give her thanks and praise.

* * *

"HERE's the deal," Audrey says, sliding her science notebook across the table towards Alison Meadows. "Imagine you're holding a watering can over a pot of soil and pouring it. The water seeps in slowly, and, if there are plants in it, they drink the water. Or it goes slowly into the soil, until later. That's Mother Nature's filtering system. Deeper down there's this humongous bowl underground called an aquifer. That holds on to the water and sends it back into lakes and streams and such. Anyway, now. Imagine pouring the same amount of water over a sheet of plastic. What's gonna happen?"

"It won't soak in."

"Right. So think of all these cities, all over the country, with all this pavement everywhere. Not only does it look like shit, but that pavement is your big ol' piece of plastic that prevents the water from soaking in. You with me?"

"Uh-huh."

"So what happens when all this water has no place to go?"

"It gets all over the table."

"Yeah, Alison. Except there isn't really a table with a sheet of plastic. Anyway, what happens is flooding. The water finds the course of least resistance, downhill, and it gathers force and becomes this raging river and then what happens?"

"Um. It soaks in?"

"Yeah, kind of. Except it's moving so fast and running so hard that it doesn't just gently soak in and seep down through the filter, into the water table, like it's supposed to. Instead it's going so fast with so much force from having been pushed together into too small of a space and it rushes along the ground and carries away plants and kicks up the dirt and rocks and brings them along, too. This is erosion, which causes an even worse problem because any toxic waste that's sitting in that earth gets stirred into the mix like some holocaust tea. All this water, it all flows downhill, but there's less and less earth for it to dissipate into, so it funnels, causing more erosion and flooding and even more pollution in the water."

"Gross."

"Exactly."

"Okay, I get it. I don't know why Sister Margaret didn't explain it like that. Thanks, Audrey."

"You're welcome. Listen, you should come to the EARTH-CARE meeting next Sunday. You know that treated wood they make playgrounds out of? It's saturated with chemicals. Little kids are climbing all over these things, and the particulates get ground into their hands, or into dust they breathe, until it's washed into the canals during the monsoons."

"I don't know, Audrey. That's the Brophy crew carwash. I told Taylor I'd help."

"Great. Just tell Taylor and his friends if they want a river to crew on they might want to stop hosing gas guzzlers' grit down the drain and come help us harass the idiots who want to hose the Clean Water Act instead. There's only this one planet and we gotta preserve what's left of it. Or like they say in the bumper sticker, LOVE YOUR MOTHER."

* * *

THE themed entertainment consulting team is headed up by a man by the name of Franz Bibfeldt. Bibfeldt got into the business as an engineer, though his demeanor is more that of a very thoughtful monk. Franz has an overly avuncular and somewhat fastidious side to him. He speaks with a soft Southern accent, his shiny head is sparsely covered with tumbleweed clumps of red frizz. His skin has a clammy look. Of course, he's about fifty pounds too heavy for his five-ten frame, and he breathes with the peckish rhythm of a man forever plagued by an asthmatic reaction to the compulsive overuse of hygiene products, but nevertheless, Franz trudges through life with an untroubled air, doting on his wife and grandchildren.

Despite these trappings of domesticity, Bibfeldt's assistant, Forsythia, is convinced he's gay. Her first week on the job, she found a nipple-piercing kit in his desk, and no self-respecting grandma's gonna let him near her with that. Franz gives Forsythia the creeps, not because he hits on her, God forbid, but because he's always so kind to her, a saint almost, with his courtly, concerned syllables asking after the health of her family and their cats. The way Bibfeldt tells it, he was right up there with Martin Luther King and Malcolm X when it came to marching for Negroes in the 1970s. Sometimes, when Forsythia's having a shitty day, she imagines both men having actually assassinated themselves just to get away from the sound of his voice, which never stops.

The man was vaccinated with a phonograph needle. Sarcasm like this, and the image of that nipple-piercing kit, they're like Forsythia's force field, helping her hang on, because whatever else Franz might do, he is also the best independent amusement park consultant in the business. Syth plans to stick it out until she's learned enough to start her own company or until she gets hired away from him, whichever comes first.

Where does he get these outfits? she wonders. *I ain't seen Ban Lon pants and polyester shirts like that since our trip to South Beach with the old Cuban guys. He's so out of style, he's back in style*, she thinks, giving her braids a flick with her long painted nails. When the client comes in, Franz wants Forsythia to hop up and offer him coffee while he boots her PowerPoint presentation. Not that she'll get any credit for it in front of the client, but that's okay. Franz'll be all gooey later telling her how phat she is. Besides, Forsythia's not working for anybody's pat on the hand. She knows she's good, and once that English dude told her what the client wanted, everything else had just dropped into place.

Shoot 'em up, that's what kids like. Look at all the video games nowadays, all the movies. They're all about kill or be killed.

"Hey, that English dude comin' with?" asks Forsythia.

"No, I think Gold's bringing his little girl. If they ever get here."

A knock sounds at the door and Bibfeldt blinks rapidly, wiping away at his forehead, before he stands and works his way towards Mr. Gold and his little girl, who's not so little. Audrey is wearing brown bell-bottoms and a peasant shirt. She's carrying a notebook and a pencil.

Franz scrapes and bows and sits them down. He launches into his reverent unveiling of the video they've edited night and day for the past two weeks. Bibfeldt is so caught up in his pride and joy, he fails to notice his audience is silent through the initial viewing of this lush green woods at the tip of a small mountain in the desert, a wonderland of sights and sounds and thrills and chills. *Whoosh!* sounds the monitor when the virtual passenger on his armored horse barrels down a gully, topsy-turvy, and is righted at the very last minute. "They'll get splashed and cooled off at the end," says Franz. "But not too wet, because the air-conditioning would be too cold for that."

"AC?" squeaks Audrey. This girl seems intensely focused.

Bibfeldt mistakes her pitch. He smiles triumphantly.

"Yes. You see, in order to replicate Medieval England, we need to cool the ambient temperature down to about 60 degrees. Otherwise the plants Dr. Lively told us to use won't survive. He says they're essential, really, and I must say, though we often do fake foliage, there's nothing like the real smell of pine to lift you right out of your life and into the past," exults Franz.

"But it can't be feasible to cool that much space," Wally says, shaking his head.

"It's not as hard as you think. Plus, you can easily figure the electricity into the cost of the ticket. I figure we can go to fifty per head, easy. And people will pay it, my friend, because their children will be chomping at the bit to get in. Sythia's suggestion is brilliant, by the way. She created mock-ups for a video game based on swordplay that will introduce young ones to the park. You might have a whole series of games. But I'm getting ahead of myself. Miss Forsythia, will you please start the next clip?"

Wally and Audrey are inanimate objects, glued to their leather rockers while Franz narrates an exodus through giant tubes of concrete and PVC, over vinyl-lined reflecting pools, within oversized metallic armor. There is even AstroTurf surrounding the Christmas trees planted sparsely throughout to represent woods. "Oh my God," says Audrey. "They even got the decimation of the forest right."

"Well, we've been doing this for years," chortles Franz, proud of his young apprentice.

"Look, you know this'll be in the high desert? Along the Colorado River?" asks Audrey. "Where California and Nevada are already fighting Arizona over who gets how much of the water? Although, with the runoff from this project, maybe they'll be begging to give it back!"

Bibfeldt's head turns as if on a swivel. Audrey's ejaculation has reminded him of something. Wally's initial instruction, to not "mess up" the environment, it must have come from this young lady. Bibfeldt puts out his hand, absolving a nonexistent penitent. He understands perfectly the girl's point of view.

If there's anything Franz is good at, it's talking clients like her down, out of the redwood tree, and onto the backhoe.

"Actually, the way Colorado River water rights work is that the Upper Basin states band together against the Lower Basin states and each party's allocation is based on how much they used the year before. It's like a government bureaucrat's budget. The less you use now, the less you'll be able to request next year. So believe it or not, no matter what the state's paying lip service to, they've got every reason to encourage people to use more. Plus, you know, tourism's been down since nine-eleven. No one's going to suggest you take your money and abscond to Florida, Mr. and Miss Developer. Those days are past. You'll find the locals receptive, I think. Presently, all they have going is a big Indian resort farther downstream and a few rinky-dink hotels on either side of the bridge."

"What, and they aren't gonna put up a fight with a competitor coming in?" asks Wally, stalling for time. He can feel hives breaking out on his forearms.

"Not in my opinion, no. The local business community, environmentalists, and Indians are too busy fighting each other to mount any kind of mutual resistance to a newcomer. I have a client in Nevada who just got a Permit Four approved without a peep from the usual constituencies. I'm telling you, the time is ripe, right now, while everyone's worked up about the stock market, to get this through."

Wally coughs. "Speaking of the market, what kind a money we talking here?"

* * *

AUDREY keeps quiet all the way across the parking lot, but Wally knows it's just a matter of time. She's got that look about her, the blotches on her neck, the lips spasming into brackets at the corners.

Wally opens the passenger door for her and strides around the back of the Jaguar. He opens the driver door, ready to head her off at the pass. "Listen, before you get started," he says.

"*Moi?*" asks Audrey. "*Moi?*"

"There's not a chance in Hell of that place getting built."

"I don't know, Dad. Mr. Bibfeldt seemed to think he had the courts in his pocket."

Wally pulls out of the lot, edges around the block slowly, and heads west towards home. "Look, I want you to know. When I hired that group, I specifically said I wanted something that didn't add to the mess we've already made of the planet. But I'm not even talking about that right now. The cost is out of sight. No way I could come up with that, even if I did want to build that monstrosity. Which I don't."

"Look, Dad, if that's the case, why didn't you just tell them that? Why'd you take their DVDs like you're gonna run them by your people at the office? And shake their hands like they're golden?"

"Sometimes it's better to let your adversaries think they're winning, babe."

"Hey, Marshmallow Man, they aren't your adversaries, they're your employees. You got a right to complain."

Just ahead on Frank Lloyd Wright Boulevard, a truck whizzes around them and cuts off Wally's access to Stetson Way. Wally pounds on the horn and the brakes at the same exact time. He looks over at his daughter as if to say "See?"

The fact is, as he watched the video, Wally was beating himself up over having dropped the ball. He'd been too vague, assumed these high-powered consultants would come up with a plan that would knock his socks off. He'd assumed Ted would do his job, helping them get the details right. Sending Ted, who Wally had thought would care enough about his own subject that he'd keep this team on track: That had been Wally's big mistake. So, even if Audrey's right, that these folks are working for him, Wally's right, too, in recognizing an enemy who just happens to work for him, who must continue to work for him until Wally can think of a way around the deportation of his chosen architect. Though he can't put into words the idea that's begun to take shape in his subconscious, his instinct is to play along for now, and cloak his reaction to the proposed park. "Look, trust me. I've got my reasons. And don't call me that, okay?"

"Sorry." Audrey looks over at her dad, who is staring at the road ahead like it's a map he's trying to read. He looks very young and very old at the exact same time. "Dad? You all right? I heard Guy on the phone the other day. Are you, like, having money trouble?"

Wally gives Audrey a quick sideways glance. "Nah. Not really. Just I'm not real liquid until the sale goes through."

"Dad, have you thought of doing something different with the money?"

"Audrey, we've been through this sixty million times. What's it gonna take before you get it?"

"Get it?" whispers Audrey. She shakes her head, mouthing the words again before turning to her father and damning the torpedoes. "Dad, you better pull over. It's time you hear about Mom and me at Disneyland. How much fun we really had."

Even as Audrey is saying the words, she is hating herself for giving in to the temptation. She knows she is letting herself off the hook but only by nailing her father to the wall. Still, at that moment, confronted with her father's *blindness*, Audrey has no way of stopping herself. She cannot tolerate another minute of his not knowing. That last trip, when she was twelve, how it ended, with her mom insisting they return to the park to ride the roller coaster. The problem was, who needs a roller coaster when you've got Mary Katherine Gold on a tear? Audrey is screaming, all right, and they haven't even had to stand in line. They are on the wrong side of the freeway headed to the park, and the horns are blaring and her mother is lost. She is simply lost.

Did she back up and turn around? How did they get home? Wally is choking on the words. Audrey wants to tell him, but she cannot remember. All she can see is her mother's head cradled in the steering wheel by the side of the road, trying to pull herself together. *Oh baby,* she'd vowed the next morning, *we aren't coming back here. I promise you that.*

* * *

DIANA carries her daughter's plastic craft bin downstairs and places it at the kitchen island, where Eleanor is sitting. Keeping her at bay is rather like making sure the lions have enough to eat so the Christians can last until the crowds arrive. Stacks of scrap paper are to one side of the child; at the other, a long-suffering watercolour set of uncertain provenance and now the stamp set that Humphrey's painstakingly collected over the past year, composed of children's characters throughout the ages. "Elly, don't lose these, awright? Keep them all together. And only on paper, right?"

"Elly want Mummy's desk."

"No, Elly. You need to stay downstairs so Daddy can hear you while I'm out. Just knock on his door if you need him. Are you quite certain you won't come?"

Eleanor wrinkles her forehead and gives her mother a withering frown, which Diana takes to heart in her vulnerable mood. She shakes her head and hurries into the hall to knock on Ted's door.

"What!" shouts Ted. "I'm working!"

Diana takes a deep breath. "I know, Ted. But I've got to run to ArtDepot and Elly's happy with her crayons in the kitchen. I'll be right back."

"You spoil her," Ted scolds, opening his door. "She shouldn't be making the decision about whether she goes or stays."

"Actually, I'll be much faster if she's not with me. And my deadline's today. Please? Humphrey should be back soon. He's just run to the market. Please. I'm running behind."

"Well, I hope this won't be the normal course of events," mutters Ted. "I'll take an early lunch then, while you're gone."

Diana steps back and towards the front door. "She might be hungry, too, Ted." Ted frowns and Diana is quick to retract the hint that he might feed his daughter something of what he was planning to eat. "Or, never mind, Humphrey can do that when he gets home from the market. Thanks so much."

The drive across town takes Diana longer than she expected. By the time she returns, Humphrey's Le Sabre has replaced Ted's Caprice in the driveway. "Hullo?" she calls, opening the front door. The house is silent. "Shhh!" Humphrey whispers, poking his head up from the couch where he and Audrey are examining a *Bon Appetit*. "I've just gotten her to sleep."

Diana tiptoes up the stairs, whistling softly and looking forward to the easy pleasure of putting the finishing touches of colour on her drawings. She envisions her drafting table, her new pens, rods of colour at the pencil ledge, poised to soften the sharply drawn angles of the terraced museum building she has drawn. Adding colour is one of her favorite tasks, rather like placing fresh flowers round the house after a day of heavy cleaning.

"Mummy!" Eleanor calls from her room. "Mummy!"

Diana lays down her pencils by the door to her studio and hurries to calm Eleanor.

"Mummy! Help!" Eleanor is thrashing about in her covers.

Diana swoops up her daughter, still wrapped in a comforter, and carries her into her studio. She kisses Eleanor's forehead and sets her down on the daybed. "There, there. Lie here in Mummy's bed and I'll rub your back."

"Mummy, do you love all of me?"

"I love one hundred percent of you."

"What about the naughty bits?" asks Eleanor, with the stern face of an inquisitor.

"Even the naughty bits."

"But you don't love my boogers!" says Eleanor, a look of mock indignation on her face.

"Well, maybe not those, but they're technically not part of you."

"Daddy says if I'm not a good girl, you won't love me anymore."

"That is so untrue, Eleanor. I love you even when you're naughty. Daddy gets mixed up sometimes, when it comes to Mummy's feelings."

"Daddy says I'm not a hopeful little girl."

"Oh? I don't know what he means by that."

"He means I don't hope around the house like Humphrey does."

"Oh. Help, darling." Diana sounds out the word. "You're only four. And I think you're wonderful."

"Not when I'm naughty you don't."

"What is all this nonsense about being naughty, darling? You're perfect. Now why don't we get your craft box and then you can sit at your desk and I'll sit at mine and we'll both colour. How's that?"

"But I've already done that, Mum. My fingers don't want to colour."

"Well, let's find something they want to do. Because if Mummy doesn't get her work finished soon, she'll be very sad."

"Don't worry, Mum. I hoped you already."

"What do you mean, Eleanor?" asks Diana, feeling the first prickle of unease in her belly as she turns towards the drafting table and sees what Eleanor has accomplished with her hopefulness. For several moments, Diana cannot move. All she can do is stare at the jungle of imaginary beasts that have been stamped on the careful geometry of her work. They are hot pink and Granny Smith green and neon yellow. They are the three little pigs, the three bears, the three blind mice, three billy goats gruff. They are dinosaurs, unicorns, knights, Robin Hood, Prince Charming. A king in an ermine cape, a crown of gold. Peacock-blue stars hang from the terraces, blooming side by side with black big bad wolves and purple Teletubbies.

"Oh, darling!" is what she says, finally. Her voice is carried back to her ears as though it has come from far, far away, ragged with the remnants of conflicting emotions: frustration, love, anger, astonishment, fear, and a shatteringly real bereavement.

* * *

WALLY wants nothing more than to bury himself at the bottom of a bottle of Jack Daniel's. Given the circumstances, though, alcohol is out of the question, so he is running through the *arroyo* that backs up to the bottom of the mountain. The sweat is a river he is swimming. It stings his eyes, blearing the boundary between what he can see and what's been sitting there right in front of him all these years. He doesn't know what to do with this need to punish. Mary Kate is gone and it's a good thing, because if she wasn't, he would have to kill her. Her own child. How could she do it? How could she do it?

A memory hits Wally like a sudden block of concrete in his path, tripping him up. It is almost real, this somersault he is in, almost real. A month before the rafting trip, she'd been up late, packing for Europe, and he'd gotten out of bed to get a glass of water. There she was in the kitchen, folding clothes on the table, but there was a deliberation in her movements that he associated with the old Mary Kate. Her lips had tightened around her words in that dainty way they did when she was high. She'd insisted she was just cleaning up, and Wally had forced himself to believe her. How could he think otherwise of this woman he loved? He'd forced himself back to bed, chiding himself for not trusting her, instead of pushing through, coming close enough to her face, to her eyes, to see if she was drunk. Truth was, he'd been terrified that night. Afraid to confront her because all he wanted to do was get *away* from her as fast as he possibly could. He'd just wanted to go to bed and cover his face and not have to see the damage.

That paralyzing love and hate he had felt, just like with his own mom, who'd worked night and day to put food on the table, who'd pass out on the couch, night after night, erasing her past so she could be sure of going to sleep without dreaming. The nightmares came anyway, but she was too drunk to remember. Wally would bury himself under his pillow, hiding from the terror in his mother's voice, remnants of the night his father had been killed and she'd been raped. Even at five Wally would go to sleep with a plastic knife, planning to protect her. At ten he'd saved enough from his after-school job to buy a cheap Browning, and he'd kept it under his bed, with the bullets in his school bag, so she couldn't hurt herself. The gun had made him feel better, though he'd never had to use it. The gun had made his mom feel better, too, though she'd kept right on drinking and he kept right on clenching his chest shut against the pity he felt and the deadening anger he didn't know where to put. It had no place in his heart. No place in a heart that owed its beat to a mother who scrubbed floors for a living and made him read and do his work. She drank only when she thought he was safely asleep. He owed her everything and this treacherous anger had no place to go. It chipped away at him, creating only a vacuum that could never be put into words. If he loved his mother, he loved her. Loved her as he put his pillow to his ears against the cries and sought blind escape.

From his mother, from his wife. That look in Mary Kate's eyes, the chaotic loss weaving back and forth, all he'd wanted was to get away. If he had to do it through working hard, through going to bed early, through coaxing himself through silent nights, it was so much a reflex, he'd never thought of it as a choice. But of course, now he realizes, tripping down the wash, through runoff that has nowhere else to go, it was a choice. And an unconscionable one. He'd neglected to comprehend that he'd consigned his only daughter, the center of his being, to the care of a liar who'd convinced him she was trustworthy. How many times had she promised it would never happen again? How could he have believed her? How could he? He knew she loved her daughter more than life. He had relied on that love, without giving a thought to the refuge he'd been seeking when he sent them off to Disneyland each year. Pebbles fly out from Wally's soles, scattering in his path, and he can feel the sweat dropping in great clots to one side, then the other, wherever he hangs his head, casting a shadow on the fool's journey he's undertaken. "How could you?" he cries out loud, and a jackrabbit skitters across his path before running to ground in its hidey-hole.

* * *

BEVERLY can tell by the sound of Wally's message on her voice mail that he's not doin' so good. He hasn't sounded this bad in ages. Bevery adores her boss, and it's been for his sake that she puts up with Ted Lively's shit, because for some reason, ever since Wally went across the pond, he's been different. Hopeful like, the way he used to sound when Audrey was little and Mary Kate was alive.

Until now. "Cancel my appointments," the message had said. No explanation. Not even any breath left in the man, it sounded like. Just this dead flat voice that folded miserably into itself. The next message had been from that Mrs. Lively, who sounded like she was choking back some sort of hissy fit, needing an extension on the bid deadline. While Wally's mood was bad enough, this lady's frantic sentences would have put him right over the edge. No, Wally would not be calling her back. Beverly wouldn't be writing any While You Were Outs, not today. Instead, Beverly dials the Rectum's home phone, keeping her fingers crossed that she'll talk to an answering machine.

"Lively Towers! Three Floors of Fun and Frolic!" a young man's voice trumpets. In the background a marching band is playing a John Philip Sousa tune.

"Diana Lively, please!" shouts Beverly.

"She's not in. May I ask who's ringing?" asks Humphrey, reaching for the remote to turn off the sound.

"Beverly from Gold Industries."

"Well, I'm not sure where she's gone off to," murmurs Humphrey. "May I take a message?"

Beverly clears her throat. "Look, tell her Mr. Gold can't grant extensions."

"Extensions?"

"For the Request for Proposals. Some kind a disaster, she said."

"She did?" asks Humphrey.

"Look, I've got another call coming in. Just tell her she's gotta get her stuff postmarked today."

Humphrey takes the stairs two at a time to his mother's studio, where he finds her portfolio box neatly addressed, but empty. Scattered across the daybed are typed responses to the Request for Proposal. It is in Humphrey's nature to tidy these pages, and as he sweeps them up, the better to sort them, he sees what is underneath. He sees what it is that Eleanor has accomplished with her hopefulness.

His sister has brought about in minutes what her father manages only by dint of persistent and painstaking effort. Diana's passion for line, her vision that so perfectly twins the old and the new in a fetching geometry of pure form, these gifts are barely discernible against the loudly colorful and slapdash dance of characters that play across each page, crowing for the viewers' attention. "Oh my God," whispers Humphrey. His heart goes out to his mother, whose abrupt departure without explanation is now understandable. He even has time to feel a bit sorry for himself, having sacrificed the Blue Goose for nothing. However, such emotions flee quickly in the face of urgent need. Humphrey quickly glances at his watch, calls the Federal Express office, and selects a medium-width teal marker from his mother's cache. Using a ruler and his most serene deep breathing, Humphrey follows his mother's steps from base to apex and back again, highlighting her buildings in a colour that holds its own against the noisome rainbow of kings, queens, unicorns, and knights, timeworn icons from the cluttered hierarchy of happily ever after.

Twelve

Pointe Tapatio is a mountaintop resort on the north side of Phoenix. From the bar at the summit, the city is far enough below to appear manageable, its flaws vanishing in the blur of distance. At the outdoor cocktail bar, Wally and Guy are each ordering another drink. Scented flowers in rectilinear planters surround the wrought-iron tables, classical music is piped in at just the right volume, and the smells of cedar, dust, and smoke haunt the dry desert wind. At neighboring tables golfers shift tanned calves atop sculpted knees and laugh about the trivia of failed swings while the sun recedes into Lookout Mountain. The lights of the city wink on, one by one, in gladdening randomness.

This resort—like so many others in the Valley of the Sun—is kept in pristine condition by hordes of black-trousered, white-shirted personnel. This clean-cut army shoos away jackrabbits, lizards, rattlesnakes, and the occasional born-again itinerant preacher. They water the lush flower beds, pressure-wash the patios, and polish the square granite surround for the pyrrhic fire bed that is set out on the precipice of the canyon, at the edge of the patio terrace.

To the north, Moon Valley stretches out between Lookout and Moon mountains, its lawn-to-rock ratio increasing near Karsten Solhiem's country club and golf course of the same name. To the south, the city extends all the way to Awautukee before the Pointe at South Mountain offers anything close to a similar view.

The cocktail waitresses here wear tight black skirts, sheer black nylons, and high-heeled pumps. Watching his server disappear with another drink order, Wally is put to mind of 1960s stewardesses, whose legs had been enough to tie his tongue for whole flights. Now, though, instead of the nostalgia he usually feels, this image provokes an automatic contrast of the way he'd felt then—an awestruck young man on his first flight—with now, a middle-aged penitent sipping a tasteless beer and looking backwards through shit-colored glasses.

Guy—who has just about had it with Wally's moping—tilts his glass to the sky and opens his mouth like a baby bird to catch the last remnant of Bloody Mary–tinged ice clinging to the upturned base. "Hey, Wally, don't you have a buddy in the Justice department? Or ATF, maybe?"

"John Mink?"

"Yeah. Look, you need to give him a call and pull the dogs off this Antitrust investigation. Huntington's getting nervous."

"That's idiotic."

"No, it's not. They got vertical arrangements all over the country. This could be a clusterfuck, if Justice wants to go there."

"I haven't talked to John in like, two years."

"So what. Call him and suck up."

"You know what? I'm tired."

"Well, wake up, Wally. Smell the friggin' coffee. I mean it. This whole thing could go south any second."

"I really, I just, Guy, I don't know. Maybe I—"

"Look, don't you go gettin' cold feet on me. I spent the whole weekend without sleep. Just hang in there, buddy."

"I don't know."

"Look, Wally. It's me, Guy What the fuck's wrong with you?" Guy's gentle tone contradicts the harshness of his words. He takes Wally by the elbow, puts an arm around his friend's shoulder, and walks him to the edge of the patio, overlooking the glittering snake of Seventh Street as it slithers south, into the foothills. "What's wrong?"

"Guy? You know what? I think you were right from the start. This is all a stupid, stupid idea. Like you said, I'm selling my bread and butter for a merry-go-round in the middle of nowhere."

* * *

AUDREY and Baby Face are sitting at an outside table at the Coffee Plantation. A folk singer is belting out Peter, Paul, and Mary songs. Audrey has just substituted espresso for decaf and Baby Face is drawing on a napkin made of unbleached recycled paper. Audrey's chair is pushed back; her face is almost at table height, and she appears to be fighting a fierce impulse to levitate.

"They can do that now? You're sure, Baby Face?" she demands as the singer is crooning "California Dreamin'." "Don't shit me."

"Look, you shouldn't have bailed on the lecture. You'd have seen for yourself. See, it costs more to plant the garden on the roof, but then you save so much on the storm-water reclamation; it's worth it. Hell, you could even grow arugula or fresh flowers for the park's restaurant. And the internal plant would filter water for the town and even return a net amount to the lake."

"Are you serious?"

"Totally."

"I love it. But I still don't get what the kids would do. I mean, who'd go?"

"Who'd go? Who'd not go? Look around you, girl. Go to any of the places the kids like in town. Rock-climbing walls, reverse bungee jumping, water slides, laser tag, and the trampoline park. They aren't high-tech applications, honey. It'd cost a Hell of a lot less than that mass-culture, passive-spectator crap from the White Man on the DVD."

"You are wicked smart, Baby Face. Too bad you didn't enter a bid."

Baby Face is no shrinking violet, but it is clear he is suddenly embarrassed. He purses his lips and winces at Audrey. "Look, I'm not supposed to tell you this, but I cannot tell a lie. See, I'd never have thought of this stuff without looking at the drawings."

"Drawings?"

"Humphrey's mom's drawings. I can't say more, 'cause you're on the Selection Committee."

"That's—Humphrey called you?"

"What's that supposed to mean? I can be attractive to some people, you know."

"Oh, I—" Audrey swallows her question. *So. Baby Face is gay. Fair enough. Guess that tears it for Humphrey, too.* She swallows again and nods brusquely, chasing down the lump in her throat. "Sorry. I just, I didn't think you knew Humphrey."

"Audrey, think about it. You're the one gave his mom the tickets when you bailed last week. They sat right next to me. And by the way, don't think I don't know about your little white lie."

"What lie?"

"It seems a certain person forgot to tell her neighbor she had the stomach flu. And that neighbor just happened to tell me, when I asked, that you were looking fine when they stopped to pick up the tickets."

"Baby Face. I don't broadcast my stomachaches to everyone."

"Audrey. Your nose just grew so fast it hit me in the face! Humphrey said you were eating lettuce wraps from P.F. Chang's!"

Audrey takes a deep breath. "Why are we getting off the subject? If you must know, my dad and I had a blowout and I didn't want to leave him. So Humphrey took his mom."

"I knew there was something you weren't telling me. You cannot tell a lie to save your life."

Audrey shakes her head dismissively. "So don't try getting me off track here. You and Humphrey, you, uh, hit it off?" she asks lightly. *It is of no concern to me. No concern to me.*

"Well, to tell you the truth, I spent the whole time talking with his mom. She took the seat next to me. Did you know she's read everything William McDonough's ever written?"

"Who?"

"The lecturer, idiot. You know, the father of Green Architecture? The deity I worship?"

"Oh, duh. My bad. So, back to you and Humphrey."

"Oh. Like I said, I didn't really pick up any kind of signals from him. And I can usually tell. Even with closet queers. But then he called me, like, I don't know, two days later."

"He must have been pretty interested to track down your number." Audrey forces the words out, though there is a building pressure behind her eyes that makes each syllable painful.

"Well, he found my business card with his mom's drawings."

"He hasn't mentioned a word of this to me!" Audrey says.

"Audrey, you're on the committee that reviews the bids. How would it look if he calls you, crying. Don't be hurt, honey. He just, well, you know the story already, how his little sister coloured all over Mrs. Lively's sketches."

"No, I don't. He hasn't said a word! But, I still don't see what you were doing with the drawings."

"Humphrey was trying to rescue her blueprints. But when he got to some of the internal systems, he wasn't sure what to do. So he asked me to help. He called at, like, two, and I had to book to meet him at the FedEx on Scottsdale Road."

"I just can't believe he didn't tell me! I didn't know any of this."

"Honey, he didn't have time to do anything but get the damn things in the mail. Besides, don't feel bad. As of yesterday, when I called to see if he'd heard anything yet, he hadn't even told his mom about it! I think he's not sure which end is up, right now."

"He and me both."

"Well, girlfriend, I hope for my sake, that it's Humphrey's. End, that is. I just love his accent."

* * *

WHEN the conversation happens, Guy is as gentle as he can be in explaining to Wally their financial position: Essentially, they are butt-cheek flat against the canyon wall, holding on for dear life, to the slippery handhold of a mile-high ledge, between a rock and a very hard place. First, to review, Wally has bet four million he doesn't presently have, on the purchase of a stock called MRYKT, since having become TechGreen and having lost forty percent of its value in the weeks following the failure of Congress to pass CAFE standards, the drop in oil prices, and the rollback of clean air and water laws. This loss is more than a little upsetting given the recent creation of a three-million-dollar trust to endow the Mary Katherine Gold Chair of Arthurian Studies at St. Mark's College, Oxford University. Worse still, Hal, Wally's Merrill Lynch broker from way back, has chosen this year to use Wally's retirement account as a blank check for every Piece of Shit (POS) stock that analysts have bandied about in house by its scatological acronym while praising it to clients as a Buy. Thus, the cash reserves in the retirement account are gone, and its value has declined from ten million to two million within the space of a year.

Furthermore, for some reason Guy cannot explain, or understand, but has verified with three separate tax attorneys, there are taxes due on this account in excess of the two million dollars remaining. If the sale of Wally's company goes through, he will clear about five million dollars, meaning he can pay off the four he owes to the margin account and pay off the lot he's bought in the middle of nowhere. Then, based on a plan put together by the consultants, he can probably get some venture capital to fund the rest of the park, which he needs to do, because otherwise he'll have to empty his retirement account, selling when the stocks are low, rather than waiting for them to go back up. All this, though, is contingent on the sale to Huntington, which relies on the company stock not going too far above the tender offer price of forty bucks, the Corporation Commission approving the change in ownership, and the Justice Department's not raising any red flags over Huntington's concentration of yet another market under its corporate logo.

Wally sits for a minute, staring at his drink, before countering Guy's analysis with a suggestion. "What if I back out of the deal with Huntington? Maybe the vendor network can buy me out."

"The little guys don't have that kind of money. And besides, they're so ticked off at you, I can't see 'em doing it. Besides, we *can't* back out of the contract with Huntington after we've signed in good faith."

"Okay, so what if I just take the money and do something else with it? Not the theme park but something else?"

"What else you gonna do with that million-dollar lot you just bought? And the consultants you paid your left nut to."

"I don't know. Maybe we'll just put a cabin up there and use it as a vacation house."

"Wally, you've put too much money into the planning to back out now. And you don't have the cash to spend a million on vacation property. You owe two million in taxes."

"Look, building a theme park—I just don't think I've got the stomach for it. I want out. I'll sell my houses here and move into something smaller. Manage my money better. Figure a way out of the deal with Huntington."

Guy, whose brain is automatically firing off logical responses to Wally's financial self-immolation, refrains from saying anything out loud. He has to clamp his teeth tight. *You can't sell your houses right now. The luxury market's tanked with everything else. And didn't I just finish explaining to you that you got no other options but to sell to Huntington to pay off your margin account? Plus, the Dreamy Draw city council has you down—in writing—as planning to build a theme park up there. They sold the land for that purpose and you won't get out of your commitment to contribute to the local economy without exploiting the land or its inhabitants, to say nothing of the organic produce you signed on for. Besides, who do you think is giving you a brain transplant and wallet-hand amputation so you can manage your money for once in your life?* Guy says none of this out loud, though his jaw is killing him. He holds his hand up in the sky and points it towards the approaching waitress, twirling once like a halo over their two chairs to signify another round. Wally holds up one hand, forefingers V'd in a peace sign, otherwise interpreted as a double, and the two friends are off and running towards the hangovers of a lifetime.

* * *

WHEN the cab drops Wally at the house on Gelding Drive, it takes a minute for him to remember where he is. Even when he remembers, he doesn't. His key, a SCUD that repeatedly misses its target, is scraping the veneer on the front door. That last Stinger was a mistake, thinks Wally.

It's as if his liver finally reaches out and rewards him for this insight, however tardy. He hits the hole. Metal scrapes metal but Wally is too drunk to master the turning of the lock. This leaves him in a quandary.

Or is the word *conundrum?* he asks himself, sitting on the stoop and leaning against the door. He's stayed out this late and got this drunk so Audrey wouldn't see him high. Better to wait till she was safely asleep, he'd reasoned. Of course, his thinking was faulty, 'cause the longer he stayed out, the more he drank. Now he is too shitfaced to get at the door. Maybe he'll sit and admire the sky. Or better yet, maybe he'll toddle next door and give Ted a knuckle sandwich. Knock at the door and just plough him down before he had a chance to say "old man" or whatever condescending term he used to make Wally feel like an idiot.

On their way home, Guy had been drunk enough to mention the worst thing of all about this whole mess: If Wally didn't do the park, it would make Ted's day. He'd go back to England early, take his wife and kids with him, occupy the chair created with the last of Wally's wealth, and even get to keep his consulting salary, since his violation of the confidentiality clause would be old news, and pretty minor compared to Wally's clear intent to abandon the project.

Wally leans back against a door he has confused with his own. In point of fact, it's not that he doesn't own it. He does, in fact, own the whole damn house, but it is not where he presently lives. In his drunken abandon, he has guided the cab driver to Gelding Drive. It is a tribute to said drunkenness that Wally is still not aware that he's confused his dead wife's dream house with his own. Wally leans back against the door that is in the process of moving and stares up into a pair of flour-covered hands reaching out to help him.

"Wally?" asks Humphrey, lifting his neighbor in a graceful,

seemingly effortless twist of the wrist. It is not for nothing that Humphrey's grandmother has purchased fencing lessons all these years. "You all right?"

"Shhh. Where's Audrey?" whispers Wally, looking around him in a bewildered scan of the hallway.

"Asleep, I would guess," says Humphrey. "I should be, as well, but this recipe for Navajo fry bread took several years of my oh-so-young life. Will you try it? Everyone here's tucked in and I'm too knackered to eat."

Wally totters after Humphrey with the look of a man who is trying to remember something important. "God, I haven't had fry bread since Mary Kate was alive. Bring it on."

Humphrey settles Wally with a big glass of water at the end of the dining room table. "Just sit here and I'll be right back."

Wally drinks his water and sticks his chin into his palm, elbow smacking on the table. Only the thrum of his funny bone keeps him from falling right to sleep. Since Wally does not want Audrey to find him there in the morning, he tiptoes over to the far end of the table, where Humphrey has, as part of his evening ritual, straightened William's school books into a perfect tower and set out a pad of new blank paper for his little sister, weighted down by a pretty basket filled with crayons.

Wally sits at William's spot and opens the boy's mathematics book, only to close it quickly when the tilted numbers and angles cause the room to swirl.

"Crayons are more my speed," he mumbles, absentmindedly taking one from the basket and pulling a blank piece of paper from the tablet.

Wally scrapes the blue crayon against the middle of the paper, first tentatively, then with greater confidence. He has not coloured since he was a boy, or maybe he did it when Audrey was little. *This is really good*, he thinks. *I feel really good. Maybe when they put me out to pasture, I can colour all day long.*

When Humphrey marches in with the tray, Wally is just coming to terms with the fact that he has made his pasture blue instead of green. The horse he has drawn is standing in a field of Martian grass. With the quick thinking for which he'd become famous in CEO circles, Wally quickly reckons that he can convert his pasture to a pond by covering his minuscule vertical blades of grass with a uniform horizontal stroke and an elliptical border. By the time he has finished the fry bread, he has also finished the picture.

When Humphrey tactfully suggests it's time to go home, Wally leans his head quizzically to one side like a stupid black lab. He starts to laugh. He laughs and laughs. He laughs until he appears to be crying, but even with Humphrey's shushing, Wally cannot stop. He has realized where he is and it is not home.

Nevertheless, all this was meant to be. Humphrey's fry bread may be the best thing he's ever eaten. Besides, he has a new pasttime, the conversion of pastureland into ponds. Wally is still chuckling as Humphrey opens the back door and guides him by the elbow towards the rear gate. Wally allows himself to be tucked into bed, clutching his drawing, which, by virtue of his vehement rubbing of blue from east to west, has revealed William's sin against the dining room table, the replacement of his father's surname with Johnny's.

The W for *William* and the S for *Sennett* are centered in the blue pond, their carved furrows resisting the dark blue press of Wally's crayon against the wood. Were William to see this primitive etching, it would have caused him no small alarm, but he needn't have worried. As they stand, the incandescent letters are not detected, for Humphrey is too tired to look and Wally is too drunk to see.

As for Wally, to whom the WS will soon enough be revealed, he will sleep a deep and Technicolored sleep. When he wakes, he will not have a hangover, a minor miracle among several, the most no-table one being the hazy glow that has somehow reattached itself to his late wife's memory. Indeed, when the sun comes in through his window at ten o'clock, Wally's brain feels different. It's like he's gotten a tune-up. A new filter, gasket, spark plugs. It feels like he's been scraped clean.

Wally will not overanalyze this benign feeling, but it has some-thing to do with the fry bread, he thinks. Mary Kate used to make him fry bread on Saturday afternoons during the playoffs, and Au-drey'd march it in with a bowl of that special sweet sauce with jalapeño jelly in it. Just like the sauce Humphrey had brought in last night.

Wally reaches for his phone, which he's left under the covers all night, and it is there he finds his picture of the pond. Maybe it's the sunlight, or maybe his sobriety, but whatever it is, he can see clearly now. There, in that stupid picture he's colored, is one letter, then another, that he'd completely missed last night. *WS*, it says, just as clear as day. Wally Sell. Wally Sell.

* * *

MARK Stevens has been married to two different alcoholics and is the father of a drug-addicted daughter, a fact that doesn't seem to have detracted from his day job as a successful psychotherapist. Mark—Wally's Al Anon sponsor—has guided Wally through the first three Steps. This morning, already back from a hike on Squaw Peak and drinking iced coffee on his patio, Mark holds the cordless phone and listens while Wally catches him up on recent develop-ments. Mark motions his wife into the kitchen, apologizing with his eyes for the call he knows will occupy the next half hour. Forty minutes later Mark has uttered thirteen *Uh-huhs*, two *I hear yous* and one *I'm sorry, Wally*, before he asks Wally to explain what the roller coaster in the dream looked like. He listens for a minute before asking, "Magic Mountain? That's what the sign said? And she was kneeling and praying at the bottom? I guess I think you can probably interpret that for yourself, Wally but it sounds like a resurrection fantasy to me."

* * *

SINCE the Ammo King is always up and off to work early, and the garage is empty, Audrey doesn't even think of looking for him in his bedroom, where he is, at this very minute, reading something he had written down in September, on his trip to England. He is lying against his pillows, his brows pulled together in concentration, and mouthing the words he can read only if he holds the index card out at arm's length. In a scrawl he barely remembers, he has written: "Fencing is as much a game of the mind as the body. The bout consists of bluff and counterbluff, feeding false information to one's opponent while trying to anticipate his next move."

Her father thus occupied with philosophical perambulations, Audrey drives to the office. She pulls her van into the company parking lot and lets herself into the back entrance that leads directly to the executive suite. Wally and Guy share a bathroom, kitchen, and a small two-storied library complete with fireplace and laddered shelves. Audrey peeks in at Wally's empty desk, then heads for the library, where Guy is knee-deep in huge thick legal texts spread across a conference table. "Seen my dad?" she asks.

Guy looks up and shakes his head. "Not yet."

"I wanted to get a head start on the architects' proposals. Just to see what's come in," Audrey explains. "Know where they are?"

"Beverly's got them stashed somewhere and she's not in yet. Besides, you might want to save yourself the trouble. We might be dropping the whole thing."

"What?"

"Your dad didn't talk to you?"

"No."

"Well, he's gonna, I'm sure. He, we, were out last night and he's decided—I should let him tell you."

"Tell me what?"

Guy pulls off his reading glasses and looks up at Audrey. He points to the chair nearby, but Audrey remains standing. "He told me about Disneyland, honey. He may just drop the whole thing. See, it seems stupid now to create a theme park as a tribute to your mom. It's like, the last thing, right? Especially since, she, well, you know . . . it can't be a place of happy memories. He just didn't know, Audrey! I wish you'd told me."

"Guy, you two are blowing things way out of proportion."

"You could have been killed."

"So. I wasn't. And Mom, she felt really bad. She didn't do it on purpose."

"Still, it had to be hard on you. And your dad feels—he can't stand that he sent you there, over and over."

"You know, my mom and I, we worked this out, Guy. She even took me to a therapist. I never should have told Dad. I just lost my temper. Now I've ruined everything."

"Honey, you are still a kid. You aren't responsible for any of this."

"Jesus," groans Audrey, hugging her elbows into her body and looking up at the ceiling as if pleading with the Almighty. "I gotta talk to him. I heard these great ideas last night. That's why I wanted to see Humphrey's mom's drawings. I think they'll give us a way to make a place that's way cool up there."

Audrey stops, looking at the pained expression on Guy's face, the one that feels sorry for her, that doesn't see her as anything but a kid. She needs to talk to her dad. "Where is he, anyhow?"

"If his head feels anything like mine, I don't think he's feelin' so good." Guy is saved from further elaboration by the soft buzz of his cell phone. "Hi," he says guardedly. "No, I didn't call yet. The stock's a tick lower than Huntington's offer, but I wanted to see what the contract said— Oh. Okay. You sure this time? No, that's okay. If Captain Kirk says to turn the mother ship around another fucking time, who the Hell am I to bitch?"

Audrey mouths "My dad?" at Guy. He nods and turns around towards the bookshelves in the corner. "Look, let's talk about this when you come in. But listen, guess who's right here in the library with me?" Guy says.

His voice is suddenly unconvincingly hearty. "Yeah, sure I will."

Guy hands the phone to Audrey, mutters to himself, and proceeds to close and stack his law books. Guy turns and watches Audrey, who is listening to her father's news that he's decided to go ahead with the park after all.

She is nodding, and shaking her head, and finally, a signal she and Guy have exchanged thousands of times in the past, she points her forefinger at her temple and cranks it in a circle. "Thanks, Dad, but I didn't give Humphrey the fry bread recipe. No, Dad. I was looking for her cooking notebooks last week, and I thought maybe you'd thrown them away." Audrey listens a minute, shaking her head.

"Dad, no offense, but how could you forget? She didn't use cookbooks and she never, ever, gave away her secrets. Brenner was the only one who might have had them, but he doesn't. That's why I was looking. For Brenner. He wanted to see 'em. I'm serious."

Audrey nods and says softly, "Hey, you know what? It doesn't really matter. What matters is that she loved you and she loved me and food was definitely a big way she let us in on that."

Thirteen

When the Lively children set out for their first Halloween in America, they are understandably excited. In England, trick or treat is not a verb. Candy does not magically get showered into one's waiting plastic pumpkin by aggressively friendly strangers. Parents aren't party to a charming but nevertheless insulin-cresting pilgrimage for more sweets. In England there isn't much more than a perfunctory nod at the American custom, most notably from the greeting card manufacturers and candy purveyors.

William is dressed as the Grim Reaper, the cloak for which Humphrey has fashioned out of black serge, on sale at the Fabric Barn. Death's scythe has been acquired ready-made at the Party Store, for, despite Humphrey's best efforts with papier-mâché, *his* crescent blade had resembled nothing more like an overused Miracle Mop, frozen before its time.

Eleanor is a pirate who looks more like a gypsy, because she has refused to wear pants. Humphrey has slapped together a charming layered skirt out of lace napkins and silk scarves, after the carefully scissored black beachcombers he'd made had inspired a veritable storm of foot stamping, hip-holding, and wailing to the Gods of Fashion. Despite her contempt for the pirate's trousers, Eleanor insists on wearing the eye patch. Both Humphrey and Diana have tried to talk her out of it, but she will not be remonstrated with, not in the name of safety, aesthetics, mixed metaphors, or even the fear of spiders she might not see, crawling up the right-most portion of her bag of candy. In Elly's mind the patch is every bit as essential as the plastic hoop earrings and purple kerchief. They all came together in a molded plastic package that had silently but no less meaningfully shouted her name in Walgreen's over a month before. If the makers of such an enchanting fantasy prescribe a triumvirate of headgear, nothing short of the holy trinity will do for this larcenous child.

Halloween is the holiday which Diana and Humphrey have marketed to William and Elly as a definitive bonus of living across the Atlantic. But if the children are suitably enthusiastic as they march towards Wally's front door on their virgin run, their mother, and truth be told, Humphrey, are not. Humphrey has read at least twelve domestic magazines in search of the proper Halloween protocol, but still, he feels unschooled and anxious. It may have more to do with the stress of having submitted his mother's drawings without her permission, or worse, of having impulsively altered them in an irrevocable set of strokes. The longer he puts off his confession, the worse things seem, and yet, if he tells his mother, he may feel unburdened, but then *she* will have to endure the waiting for the committee to review sketches to which she may very well have been be ashamed to sign her name. Oh, and there is that, too, Humphrey thinks, wincing as he reminds himself that he's added forgery to his list of crimes.

Diana, who has resigned herself to the loss of a job she wasn't at all sure she could manage, is nevertheless nervous about nothing in particular and everything in general. With so much time on her hands, and a restless sense of anticlimax, she has resorted to watching hours and hours of television. Rather than the bland, mind-numbing effect she's sought, she has found herself drawn irresistibly to adrenalinizing "news magazines" about the disasters lurking in everyday life: child drownings, asphyxiating Hanta Viruses, old women walking into sheds and unleashing killer bees, a man who reached into his linen closet for a towel but came out with a black widow. Everywhere she looks, jeopardy is the dominant fact of existence. Today, for example, seeking escape in the fictional, Diana has watched three films: *The Birds*, *Tsunami: The Last Tidal Wave*, and that Australian movie about a dingo who ate someone's baby. So reactive is Diana to her free-floating anxiety that she doesn't connect the broadcasts with the convention of Halloween: that jolly good stateside sport of terrifying viewers with a wink and a nod, as though Death and Catastrophe are as approachably artificial as plastic Santas or a synthetic Easter Bunny.

Audrey opens the Gold's front door, lifts Elly in a quick embrace, and cries, "I just knew you wouldn't be a pink princess! I just knew it! Does she know about Grace O'Malley?" exults Audrey. "Elly, she was a princess and a pirate! Braver than any man!"

William's face is unreadable behind his netting, but his body language spells discomfort and disappointment with this much ballyhooed Halloween. Thus far, it's been nothing but Eleanor getting all the attention, per usual.

Diana smiles uncomfortably, hoping Eleanor doesn't repeat Ted's tired rant on Grace O'Malley, or *Graniulle*, as she's sometimes called. "Legend," Ted will snort, whenever the name is brought up by guests eager to show off a favorite tidbit of Irish history. "No historical evidence for most of it; just a bunch of Irish feminists embroidering their own revisionist tapestry. It's the gender equivalent of America's *Roots*, as far as I'm concerned. Besides, even if it were true, that was English blood she shed, so I'd be doubly a fool to revere the bitch."

William pulls off his hood and appears ready to speak, only too happy to shed rain on any parade of Eleanor's. "My father says she's a myth," he starts.

"Your father," says Diana sharply, and for an instant, Humphrey fears his mother may begin to cry. Her mouth turns in upon itself in a puckered O, her eyebrows crinkle into her brow. She shakes her head and smiles brightly at Audrey. "Oh, yes, we know all about Grace O'Malley. A fierce and independent spirit who scared the wits out of generations of English men. They're still denying she ever existed, as though that would allow them to salvage their pride at being outfought and outthought by a mere woman. Worthless, spineless creatures, the lot of them."

Humphrey has wondered for years when his mother might face facts about Ted, but his satisfaction, when the long-awaited moment finally appears to have arrived, is destroyed by the recognition that knowing something and doing something are still miles apart. This is true whether the distance is measured as the crow flies, or the fish swims, or even as the Halloween stragglers proceed, towards the next orange glow in their own particular patch of dark.

* * *

WALLY is standing at the edge of the property in Dreamy Draw, looking down. Across the lake he sees the lights come on as the darkness falls. A string of incandescent pearls drape the span of the bridge, diamonds glitter in the cosy village, and off to the far left, an island castle is illuminated by warm pink flames that rise from golden sconces.

Wally narrows his eyes, seeing the place he'd dreamt about going when he was a kid. Mike Costanzo had sent him a postcard from Sandusky once, with a Ferris wheel and an oversized hot dog. Wally's mom had kept it on the fridge, and she talked about how they'd go someday, but the longer it took to save up the money, the less Wally thought about the Ferris wheel. Instead, when he closed his eyes to fall asleep, he'd create something grander: a castle, exploding fireworks in the sky, a troupe of characters suspiciously like the ones in the movies made by Disney. The castle, of course, was always shown at the end of those movies, the emblem of Walt Disney's empire. Wally's dreamworld was even grander than television's, though, unlimited by reality or the mechanics of special effects. Here, the boy and his mother walked hand in hand with their heroes. Here, the dark could grow bright with celebration all night long, the fortress was secure, and Cinderella, toiling away, was given her reward at the end.

Wally has come here to think. He can't get his sponsor's idea of resurrection out of his mind. The thought of selling to Huntington and possibly hurting his vendors, it's not something he set out to do. However, the notion he's taken hold of, the idea of undoing what happened to Audrey so many years before, or at least of making it up to her, that's got a certain irresistible appeal.

* * *

TED is working late at the office. Wally is still out of town, and everyone else, even the slag, Beverly, has left to attend to Halloween festivities. When the cat's away, Ted whispers, delighted with himself. He is in the conference room, slowly sifting through a pile of architectural proposals. Though not an official member of the selection committee, Ted hopes to be solicited for his opinion. Best to be prepared.

Ted sifts through the bids: rifling a stack of huge envelopes. One of them, surprise, surprise, contains Diana's drawings. His first reflex is to be hurt that his own wife has lied to him. But then Ted stretches his sympathies and admits that were these his work, he'd deny them as well. They were amateurish and childlike. They didn't conform to any of the conventions a proper architect would employ if trying to impress a selection committee. Small comfort no one else would witness the humiliating spectacle of her submission, in which the teal-colored triangle of inverted terraces was peppered with imaginary characters, as though Mother Goose had chartered a plane and dropped the whole lot for one last ride on the wind. Ted finds himself cringing at his wife's pathetic efforts to redeem her work.

In a fit of generosity that forwards large doses of serotonin to the correct neuralgia, Ted saves his wife further humiliation. Careful to remove the drawings and envelope stamped with proof of submission, he quickly scans the room until he sights a crevice behind the filing cabinet, filled with rolls of clearly ancient paper, some held by rubber bands, others by cardboard tubes. He opens the end of one tube marked GELDING DRIVE, PLANS, rolls his wife's work into a neat scroll, and forces it into the empty dark well enclosed by faded blueprint. Judging from the dust that lines the tube's edges, the GELDING DRIVE blueprints haven't been touched in years and are thus unlikely to be disturbed any time in the near future.

Closing the top and placing the tube behind several others, Ted feels an almost overwhelming burst of sympathy for Diana. He has warned her not to make a fool of herself, and though she hadn't taken his counsel, he couldn't, in good conscience, allow anyone else to scrutinize her *haus frau* efforts. Better to think the drawings were lost than to suffer such humiliation.

The other submissions are almost anticlimactic. One workman-like firm suggests a set of cottages with crosshatching, surrounded by primitive wooden walls and connected by rough wooden walkways. It has the right look of artificiality about it. Indeed, these buildings look suspiciously like a well-known restaurant chain that sells fried fish. A few minutes of combing through the résumés yields the fact that yes, this firm has indeed put itself on the nation's ever expanding map of culinary rapidity. They'll lend just the right aspect of banality to the project, thinks Ted, and he carefully places them at the top of the pile. Then, with the painstaking attention to detail for which he is justifiably famed in academia, Ted performs minor surgeries on each of the other competitors. On one, he spatters a minuscule amount of cold coffee he's found in a paper cup in the trash. On another, a pencil eraser smudged here and there erases most of one wall, creating a deconstructionist look. A third is fair prey to crumpling and folding, as its lines are in such fine point that they disappear into the crevices created by Ted's adjustments. By the time he turns out the light to the conference room, Ted has stacked and sorted all the altered applications into a neat pile that closely resembles the one Beverly had created, on the open shelf of a carved wooden console. For everything, there is a season, Ted tells himself, as he masks all detectible evidence of his very own Halloween mischief.

* * *

"Humphrey?"

"Audrey?"

"Hey! Long time no see."

"I'm so sorry!" Humphrey's rushed apology tumbles over itself. He's so missed Audrey, but truthfully, he's been afraid to completely trust himself around her. "By the time I get off the computer and over the stove to finish each day's homework, I'm exhausted. I'm trying to come up with Brenner's menu—"

"Hey, did you get something in the mail from him, by the way?" Audrey asks. "He called for your address last week."

"No. Not yet. Did he find your mum's recipes?"

"I wish. I—I'm not sure what he was sending. But that's not why I'm calling. It's just—look: I saw Baby Face the other night. He told me you'd submitted your mom's drawings."

Humphrey lowers his voice to reply. Diana is in the living room with Eleanor, and though the television is on, one cannot be too careful. "I asked him not to say anything," he whispers, troubled still by the fact that he's not told his mother she'd been entered in the competition.

Audrey mistakes his tone. "Look, you don't have to keep it a secret," she says, trying not to care what it is that Humphrey feels for Baby Face.

"The thing is," Humphrey confides, "my mum doesn't know. I can't think of a way to tell her."

Audrey has prepared herself for this revelation, but still, when it arrives, she feels like she's been kicked. Still, she loves this boy. If Baby Face makes him happy, she's got to toughen up. "Yeah, I can see how it would be hard," she stammers.

"So, about the drawings?" Humphrey enquires, staying on the subject at hand, though to his new best friend, it appears that he's moved on.

"Just, they sound so awesome. The selection committee's meeting tomorrow and the thing is, I sort of snuck in to peek, but I didn't find anything that sounded like what Baby Face described. So I was wondering if you had another copy."

"There wasn't time. By the time Baby Face finished tracing in the systems, we had to send them off. The delivery man was standing there, waiting for it."

"Do you have the tracking slip number?" Audrey asks, and while Humphrey moves to an upstairs phone, Audrey explains the selection process.

The Architecture committee is made up of eight appointees. Audrey, Guy, Wally, and Beverly, her dad's secretary, plus four people she doesn't know. These recent additions to the committee are investors, or venture capitalists, as her father calls them, whose participation has caused Guy to follow the Request for Proposal Procedures Handbook to the letter of the law.

"I'm not supposed to be looking at any of the bids until we all sit down together," Audrey admits. "But it's a good thing I did."

"I'll call FedEx and call you back," Humphrey offers. "You're an angel for doing this," he adds, lifting Audrey's spirits despite her fiercely held and longstanding denials of the existence of any and all Heavenly intercessors.

* * *

AT what point the Selection Committee meeting slips out of Audrey's control is not apparent. One minute she's ahead of the game, with Beverly remembering having signed off on the FedEx from Humphrey's mom, and the next she is powerless as the group shrugs about the missing drawings and plows ahead with the task of picking from among the remaining submissions. Worse, Wally disappears for what seems like an hour, dragging Beverly with him. By the time they return, empty-handed, Audrey's been forced to agree that there is only one acceptable museum submission, a boring set of buildings that look like fake Tudor pubs, connected by walkways made of rough wooden planks.

What ties Audrey's tongue is the presence of these four money men, whose "buy-in," she's been told, is essential. She can see by the embarrassed look on Guy's face, and her father's, as well as on the impassive expressions across the table, that things aren't going well at all. It doesn't look good when the only bids you've got have a second-hand aura, like they've been driven over or spit up on or have maybe served as bedding in a cage for someone's hamster. Audrey can see that Beverly is shaking her head at the condition of the documents, but if the secretary says it out loud, that she doesn't know how they came to get ruined, it will just make this whole operation of Wally's look even more sloppy. If the investors aren't impressed, what will it mean to her father? Finances are one thing, but his sense of himself, how will it suffer if he fails at this enterprise, after he's been punishing himself for what Audrey's been reckless enough to reveal about her mother?

When Guy brings out the videodisc from the consultants, Audrey is almost relieved. "Guy," her father is warning, his eyes fastened on his daughter, but Audrey gives her father a quick imperceptible shake of the head.

"Oh yeah, you'll like this," Audrey finds herself saying, surprising herself. After all, she tells herself, maybe they can use this videodisc to play for time until the lost drawings are found. The truth is simpler than that, and it involves protecting what she perceives as her father's most immediate interests, even if they appear to betray everything she stands for.

And so it is that the venture capitalists are wooed to provide the funding for Wally's newest enterprise, though whether there will be any resemblance between his original vision and this garish tacky dream they've signed on for, that is a question Audrey would just as soon leave unanswered.

* * *

WALLY's voice, when Diana picks up the phone, sounds like it is being transmitted from far away. It is the first she's heard from him since the phone call in which he'd finally told her the truth about the architect's competition. That had been their last conversation, unless of course one were to count as conversation her highly panicked message the day of the deadline, the day he hadn't called back, the day she'd cursed herself for having believed him.

"Speaking" is all she can utter, for "Yes" would be too affirmative, "Hello" too friendly, and "Damn you" an understatement.

"Look, about the bid," Wally begins. "I—Baby Face told Audrey your drawings were great. I wanted to get you to—"

"Oh please! Don't pretend!"

"I'm not. See—Well, to make a long story short, they've gotten lost, and I'd really like to take a look. As soon as possible. We're kind of under a deadline here."

"Wally?" Diana asks, her voice so quiet it scares him. "May I ask why you're doing this? I missed the deadline."

"How did you know?" Wally says, wondering if Audrey text-messaged Humphrey during the meeting. "The thing is, I'm hoping to find a way around that."

"Look," Diana says, the tears rising in her throat despite herself. "You had no obligation to choose me. But I do wish you'd paid me the courtesy of ringing me back."

"When?"

"The message I left, in which I made a complete fool of myself whining about the disaster with the drawings. I know it was unprofessional, but I'd had no sleep."

"Diana, what are you talking about? I didn't get a message."

"Right." Diana shakes her head and considers pounding the phone back on its cradle. "May I ask why you've rung?"

"When did you leave a message? Did you talk to Beverly? You know I'd have called back if I'd known about it. You know that, right?"

"Right. Now. If you don't mind, I've got beds to make and toilets to scrub, to say nothing of hunting for a calculator your property appraiser managed to lose last week, so if you're ringing for Ted, you might have saved yourself some awkwardness. He's left already."

"No. I'm calling to ask you—Well, see, I was hoping you might have a copy of your bid. We can't find it."

"Oh really? How surprising!"

"Don't be sarcastic. I feel terrible."

"Mr. Gold, had it occurred to you that when you didn't ring me back, when I made the dreadful mistake of humiliating myself on your machine, that I might miss your deadline altogether?"

"Diana, I swear. I never got any message from you."

"Well, that's a huge relief. No harm done then. I'm going to hang up now."

"Diana, look, the bid is just a technical thing we can get around. We can say they were lost."

"Wally. We cannot. I did not submit them."

"Are you sure? Because FedEx says they delivered something."

"Look, I do think I'd know if I'd sent them."

"Listen, can I come over?"

"Why are you doing this? Please, just tell me that."

"Doing what?"

"Torturing me?"

"Look, unless Audrey's lost her marbles—"

"No, please, stop. I'm standing at my studio closet now. Humphrey would have put them away in here. Just a moment, please. Just to prove to you. Yes, here they—no, well. Look, I can't put my hands on them right now, but that just means my overprotective son put them somewhere to avoid reminding me of this whole chapter of spectacular failure on my part. If he's had any sense, he's thrown them away."

"You aren't a failure! You didn't have copies, Diana? Could I just come by and—Diana? Did you hang up? Diana?"

Diana shuts the closet door and sinks on the floor. She braces a hand against her crossed legs, collecting herself. "You know, Mr. Gold," she says, her voice steadier than her trembling knees. "If you don't mind, I think I'll decline to put myself back on staff of your ship of— I think I've had all the fun I can muster for this go-round. Must be off now, but I wish you all the luck you deserve."

* * *

EARTHGYRL: I so totally sold out yesterday.

SKYGYRL: What do you mean?

EARTHGYRL: I can't even tell you, it's that bad.

SKYGYRL: Nothing's that bad.

EARTHGYRL: My dad was in trouble at this meeting with the investors. Instead of sticking to my guns and standing up for Humphrey's mom, I just caved. Big time.

SKYGYRL: Humphrey's mom?

EARTHGYRL: Baby Face says she had these awesome plans for the park. Totally green in every way, roof gardens and mazes, with trapezes and slides and trampolines and rock climbing and bungee jumping. Well, somehow, when it came time to review the bids, her stuff was nowhere to be found.

SKYGYRL: So why is that your fault? You are way too hard on yourself.

EARTHGYRL: I could have stuck up for her more. Instead, I actually pretended like I liked the Florida consultants' ideas.

SKYGYRL: The ones you hate?

EARTHGYRL: Exactly.

SKYGYRL: Bet you had a reason.

EARTHGYRL: I thought the investors would bail and leave my dad with no money.

SKYGYRL: Why?

EARTHGYRL: I could tell they were not enthused. And my dad is, he's just not like he used to be.

SKYGYRL: How so?

EARTHGYRL: Just not so sure of himself. I'm kind of worried about him.

SKYGYRL: :(Is there anything I can do?

EARTHGYRL: Forgive me for selling out, maybe?

SKYGYRL: Sweetie, when it's a choice between the people you
    love and a principle, you always choose people.
EARTHYGYRL: Sometimes you remind me of my mom.
SKYGYRL: Is that good or bad?
EARTHGYRL: Good! My mom was great.
SKYGYRL: Sorry. You don't talk too much about her. I wasn't sure.
EARTHGYRL: It's just hard for me to go there. I miss her so much.

Skygyrl's natural instinct is to comfort Earthgyrl, to say something like she bets her mom misses her back. However, Skygyrl has
built their relationship on caution. She knows better than to foist
her own recently found spiritual optimism on a teen who's made
her rejection of "fairy tales about Heaven" all too clear. Instead,
Skygyrl treasures the compliment that Earthgyrl has given her and
wishes, as she stamps the colon and then the parenthesis on her
keyboard, that she could give this child the no-holds-barred hug
she deserves, instead of this stupid sad face she must settle for sending instead.

* * *

WALLY is speeding down Scottsdale Road, trying to get to the bank
on time, when he realizes he's forgotten the house plans.
"Dammit!" he says, wincing in the mirror at the cop who's just
pulled into traffic behind him. Pressing number three on his speed
dial, he launches into an apology before Beverly can even finish
saying "Gold Industries."

"Stop already, it's my job," she murmurs. "But I didn't see anything about plans on the checklist for the closing."

"I know. There's some kind of screw-up with the appraisal. They
did the calculation on the Gelding Drive house at four thousand
square feet instead of six."

"How do you make that kind of mistake?"

"The appraiser claims he lost his calculator when he was taking measurements. He was doing the stuff in his head and he messed up. The temp sent the file out before he looked at it. Anyway, he's all over it, apologizing, and he's sending the correction, but the title company still wants the plans, just in case there's a question later."

"Okay. I'll get a courier there in ten minutes."

"The thing is, I'm not sure where they are, the plans—"

"Where they've always been, behind the laterals in the conference room. I'm on it."

"Bless you," says Wally.

The title company manager keeps Wally and Guy waiting while he checks with the lender one last time. "These guys change the requirements more often than my son changes majors." He shrugs, while all three stare at the receiver he dangles against his neck. "Uh-huh," he says. "Okay. I'll tell him. Back in two."

As the mortgage guy is detailing the lender's last-minute queries about Wally's four-million-dollar margin on his TechGreen stock, now worth two-point-four, the courier arrives with a large cardboard tube marked GELDING DRIVE, PLANS. Wally screws off the lid and tries to slide out the contents, but his hand is too big. He struggles to pincer his thick fingers into the small dark hole while Guy explains how the tender offer makes Wally's company's shares a lot more bankable than anyone else's stock holdings.

Just seeing Mary Kate's writing on the tube is enough to cause Wally all kinds of grief, not the least of which is the knowledge that the last time he looked at these plans, she was alive and well and spitting mad over the changes he'd made while she was in Europe.

It's not until he sees the expectant look on the title manager's face that he realizes all conversation has stopped and they are waiting for him.

"Here," barks Guy, reaching for the tube, turning it upside down and pounding its upended bottom to knock the tightly rolled papers out onto the mahogany conference table. He separates out the spec sheet and hands it across the man's desk.

The rest of the blueprints begin their curl back to oblivion before Wally pounces. He presses his swarthy forearms onto the rising edges of the lost drawings and adjusts his glasses, poring over the perimeter and back to the center, as if to convince himself they're really there.

Even as the title guy is droning that he'll need a statement from Huntington Incorporated confirming its plans to buy Wally's shares of Gold Ammunitions, the Ammo King is lost to the outside world. He is caught up in a cluster of inverted teal pyramids peopled with imaginary creatures. Even without the neatly scrawled signature at the bottom, Wally understands that these are his neighbor's missing drawings. What he cannot grasp, though, is how Diana could have known about his childhood park, the one where he'd never once been, unless you counted the hazy twilight of falling asleep. His fortress of light, built and rebuilt, night after night, had been similarly overrun with storybook heroes. In his fantasy, the kings and queens and unicorns and knights and wizards, there'd been so many of them, it was like Times Square on New Year's Eve, all of them crazy, dancing, mixing it up, to cheer them on, Wally Gold and his mom, when they finally arrived for their day in the sun.

The rest of the closing is a blur for Wally, who is caught up in trying to read the blueprints and find a natural explanation for how they'd ended up in a storage tube instead of the conference table where Beverly swears she'd put them.

It is this last item that snags Wally's attention. If Beverly had put Diana's drawings with the others, then who'd have wanted to hide them? One person immediately comes to mind, for if his wife was chosen as the architect, Hotman's plans to sabotage the park's development would be complicated. That and the fact that he might have trouble convincing the rest of his family to follow him back to England prematurely. *That son of a bitch,* Wally thinks, but he is also realizing how lucky it is that Diana's husband has shown his true colors this way. Again, Wally thinks of the Scotsman's words, the ones that keep coming back to him. *The bout consists of bluff and counterbluff, feeding false information to one's opponent while trying to anticipate his next move.*

What made Ted pick this hiding place, among the many that were available, that question might never be answered, but Wally cannot help but be uplifted by the serendipity of this discovery. He decides to keep the drawings to himself, telling no one but Guy. He'll keep this from Diana, keep it from Audrey. No way will he put Diana in the no-man's-land between her husband's machinations and his own. He tells himself he'll go slow, be patient, keep up appearances, and placate the money guys until he's gotten all his ducks lined up. His daughter has undergone enough disappointments, and he cannot bear to have Diana get her hopes up again, either. Still, as he's reaching for uncharacteristic restraint, in a deeper part of himself, Wally cannot help but be assuaged. Surely, having found the plans now, just when he'd resigned himself to a compromise he couldn't really accept, the answer has turned up in a cardboard tube he hasn't opened in years, inside the plans for the house that Mary Kate built. He cannot help but find a larger meaning in this happy accident, another link between his dead wife and Diana Lively, the beam of coincidence illuminating his quest to reclaim what he might have otherwise lost forever.

* * *

FOR Ted, Monday is a bit over the top. First thing, at the office, Guy knocks on Ted's door, barrels his way in, grabs Ted's hand, and pumps it up and down in a frenzy, praising him for having done such a good job with the consultants.

"They're finished?" Ted stammers, trying to pull his hand out of the moving vise.

"Wally met with 'em a few days ago," Guy explains. "Boy, did you have an ace up your sleeve or what, you bird dog, you!" Guy is a wild card, a loose cannon, a bull in the china shop. He can't keep his admiration from spilling over into Ted's personal space. "Listen, Wally wants you to come see him, right now."

Ted walks down the hall, wary of an ambush. He'd known these people were stupid, but he'd granted them more intelligence than this. Instead, it's over before he knows it. Wally could not be more friendly, more effusive. For a moment, Ted can almost see the man's charm shine through his unpolished linguistic turns of phrase. "Come on in, Ted. Good work down in Florida! I want you to take a look at the video the consultants put together, and then I want you to look at the architects' proposal we've decided on. The money people are coming back next week, and I want to have some more specific suggestions by then."

They leave Ted standing there in the conference room, gob-smacked. He's not expected it to be this easy, enticing Wally to pull the hoist for his own petard. It is not until after he's reviewed the videodisc, though, that Ted sees how completely successful his manipulations have been, for this sort of park will be as expensive to build as it is to maintain, and the resource costs will be astronomical.

Hours later, feeling sorry for his wife, Ted stands outside her studio and knocks gently. He enters to find Diana asleep on the daybed that Wally has purchased and supplied with the best in eight-hundred-count cotton sheets. It doesn't take a Freudian analyst to see the repressed hopes in Wally's donation of a daybed to

Diana's studio, nor to feel the lash of *resentment* in Diana's pretense that Ted's snoring has made their conjugal bed uninhabitable. Diana lies on her back, one arm covering her eyes. She looks so innocent in her sleep that Ted has second thoughts about rousing her. Ted decides his news can wait. He is just turning to leave when Diana moves her arm and senses a darkness in the space above her. She opens her eyes, flinching when she sees her husband.

"Sorry, luv," says Ted, sitting on the side of the daybed.

"Uhm," moans Diana, and closes her eyes again.

Ted rubs her arm. "Di—I've got news."

"The Fletcher?" she asks, with such undisguised pleasure that Ted experiences a shudder of remorse. She's so supportive, this wife of his. Genuinely cares. Of course, on the other hand, she is clumsy with her hopefulness, reminding him now of what it is he has lost. Well, needn't scold her for that, not when she'd understand soon enough just how badly she'd made him feel.

"No. Not that. I told you already, they'd have rung by now. No, it's about the bid. The architectural committee made its decision."

"I thought you weren't on that," Diana says distractedly. "Besides, it doesn't matter to me who designs his park."

"But you worked so hard."

"Ted, are you *trying* to torture me? You know I didn't submit my drawings. You knew that the day that you let Eleanor ruin them. So it's moot."

"How can you accuse me of that? You know I would never, ever deliberately let her destroy something of yours. I can't believe you'd suggest such a thing."

"Look, it's over," sighs Diana. "May we please just let it go?"

"I just thought you'd be interested."

"Why on earth would you think that?" Diana mutters, rolling over and burying her head in the pillow.

* * *

SEVERAL afternoons later, outside William's school, a cluster of young blond mothers waits. The bell rings at 2:10 but Humphrey has noticed that these mums are always at least fifteen minutes early. Many of them wear tennis skirts, tennis bracelets, and improbably snowy tennis shoes. Others, sunlit hair glossily cascading over upturned streamlined sunglasses, are blossoms of the desert, in pastel Capris and tiny linen shells. Humphrey can't help but notice their perfection, right down to their beautifully pedicured toes arching on delicately sandaled feet.

Humphrey leans back against the door of the convertible Le Sabre, the better to catch William and Adam on their way to the bus.

What a brilliant day! The sun is inexhaustible, permeating every inch of space, and Humphrey wants to know why more of the fair-haired mothers don't move their glasses down over their eyes, to protect themselves from retinal damage. Humphrey is wearing a very chic pair of shades Audrey had given him the first week they'd met: an overly angular set of tortoiseshell rectangles that he slides up the bridge of his nose before using his thumb and forefinger to draw his flopping bangs back over his head, unconsciously imitating the ladies at the gate.

Humphrey sees Adam first, and he calls out: "Adam?" The boy keeps on walking and kicking at a stone in his path. Humphrey strides quickly into his path and puts a gentle hand on his shoulder, steering him towards the car. "Your mum wants you to go home with us today," he says, beckoning to William, who is exiting the double doors of the school.

Adam shakes his head. "She does?"

"She's got to take your aunt in for tests at the clinic," explains Humphrey.

"But is she all right?" asks Adam.

"I think so," murmurs Humphrey. Valeen has revealed enough of her sad, sad story, but it's not his place to discuss it with Adam.

"I know I have to tell him," Valeen had said, when she'd called that morning. She'd sobbed, unable to get the words out. "It's not fair," she'd choked, after a long pause, in place of any other explanation.

"No, it's bloody not," Humphrey had agreed. "You must let us know what we can do."

"Thanks," Valeen had said. "Just taking Adam is such a help."

"He's a good lad," Humphrey had replied awkwardly. He'd wanted to tell her that he'd lost his own father when he was a boy, that he knew about loss, but he couldn't think of how to say it without sounding pessimistic about her cousin's prognosis.

"Would you like him to spend the night?" he'd asked, knowing she'd refuse. No matter how late Valeen stayed at the hospital, she always picked Adam up on the way home. "I want things to be as normal as they can," she'd explained.

Today, though, Valeen has surprised him by accepting immediately. "That'd be great. It's going to be a long night." She had sighed, and it was then, more than when she'd wept into the phone, that Humphrey understood just how close things must be.

When they arrive home, the boys finish off what's left of Humphrey's third experiment in main courses: a salad of sesame noodles with a relish of lemongrass, mango, kohlrabi, and mint. Eleanor has already pronounced the item "disgusting," so it is heartening to see the boys shovel it in with groans of appreciation. "Where's Mum?" William asks, having come up for air and a cold glass of water. "Any more of that?"

"No. Did you like it?" asks Humphrey.

"Yes. Where's Mum?" answers William. Most unsatisfactory.

Humphrey shouts silently to the gods. *Will someone please notice my brilliant food?* Audrey's been tied up with her EARTHCARE petition drive and is not even returning calls, Mum's been in a tailspin, and for some unknown reason, he can't get any response from e-mails to Desmond, his cooking mentor, or from Skygyrl, with whom he's been—up until yesterday—exchanging wonderful volleys of chat. Where has everyone gone? Furthermore, who is he if no one knows he's there? A tree falling in the woods, wailing silently? *My self-concept has fallen and I can't get it up*, mugs Humphrey, turning back to the boys, who are staring at him, with a look of expectation on their faces.

"Oh. Mum. She's on her way back from the doctor's, having Elly's forehead looked at, *again*."

"Humphrey," William warns. "Scorpions are dangerous."

"William, I'm as much in Mum's advancement camp as you. Still, it's a bit much to believe a scorpion's landed on Elly's brow and has taken a bite without her noticing. It's a mosquito sting."

"We don't have mosquitoes here," offers Adam.

"There she is," says William, cocking his head towards the garage at the sound of a low rumbling hum. "Or Ted."

"Look, you'll get me in trouble if you don't stop that."

"Why should he shout at you because I call him Ted?"

"Why should he ever shout at anyone? He doesn't need a reason. Bad enough I made the mistake of being someone else's birth child, God forbid you neglect his starring role in your conception."

"It's not your fault, Humphrey. It's nothing to do with you."

"I know, but try and remember anyway," says Humphrey. He turns to Adam as the back door is opened and Diana and Eleanor spill in, carrying a bag of products from the pharmacy. "You must think we're quite mad," he says to Adam.

"Crazy," explains William at Adam's confused tilt of the head.

Adam shakes his head and sinks his chin down towards the counter to rest on his fist, the better to survey William's "mad" family in all its distracting glory.

"Oh, hullo, Adam! How nice to see you!" Diana smiles, depositing Eleanor and several boxes on the counter.

"Well?" asks Humphrey.

"Mad. They think I'm completely mad. It's contact dermatitis."

"And what's the offending agent, then?" asks Humphrey.

"They don't know. The nurse practitioner said she was mystified. She asked if we were using one of those sunblocks you spray, because the rash almost has a dripping shape to it."

"Mummy!" complains Eleanor. "Milk!"

"Of course, darling," replies Diana. "What a bad mummy you have!" Diana busies herself pouring Elly's milk, Humphrey wipes the counter, and William licks his fingers, wishing he could lick the plate, as he would do if his mother and brother weren't within eyeshot. Only Adam notices that Eleanor drinks not even one sip of her milk, but looks pleased with herself for having changed the subject of spray bottles to something far less dangerous, invoking her mother's predictable self-flagellation at having gotten distracted by something outside her children's immediate needs.

* * *

WHEN the post arrives that afternoon, it contains two items that would have caused Diana no end of distraction, had her darling daughter not pocketed them both and scurried upstairs to her closet. The first, addressed to Ted, is more of a parcel than a letter. It contains a videodisc copy of Kristen's recording and a brief, curt note of warning. The second, addressed to Humphrey, is from Brenner, a brief recapitulation of the menu requirements. Stapled to it is the drawing Eleanor had given to Ravenna, with a hastily scrawled Post-it on top.

Dear Humphrey,

Please don't let your little sister know I'm returning this. I wouldn't want to hurt her feelings, but it looks like she drew on some legal document, and I didn't know if your dad would need it back or not.

Sincerely,
Ravenna

Underneath Audrey's colorful rendition of a spider on a mountain lurks the letter from Ted's solicitor.

Dear Mr. Lively,

Your case was referred to me by Mr. Salisbury. Because he works for Mr. Cheswitt, he cannot advise you on a prenuptial agreement with Fiona. However, I would be happy to answer the questions you raised in your letter and to act as your solicitor in the divorce and custody issues that will need to be settled before your marriage.

Firstly, it is advisable for you to be remarried well before your son's birth, if you plan to exercise your full legal and fiduciary rights. (BTW, the lab tests confirm paternity.) Your fiancée did read the late Mr. Cheswitt's will correctly: Her son must be legitimate to benefit from his great-grandfather's will.

Secondly, as regards custody of children from your present marriage, I cannot advise you as to the disposition of such matters should they be settled in the United States courts. It would be best if you could persuade your wife to return to England, so that the children would be nearby, and, as you point out, able to develop a relationship with their half brother. Should your wife refuse, you might consider bringing your children back with you on "holiday," and then, once they are on British soil, file for the right to keep them. Given that Ms. Cheswitt can afford to put them in the very top boarding schools, there is no reason to think they'd be any better off in the United States, given that nation's subpar educational reputation.

Should you be unable to do either of the above, then at the very least you might return to London, where we could petition the court for custody. While I cannot predict the outcome of what would be a very complex case, I will say that the American judicial authority has often honoured the British courts' decisions in prior custody battles.

Meanwhile, might I remind you that your behaviour will also be considered important to said courts? While I am certain that a man of your eminent stature would have no trouble assuring the courts of suitability, I must remind you to please avoid situations which might cast doubt upon your fitness as a parent.

Respectfully yours,

The Honourable William Merrifield III
Seaton Manor
London, U.K.

P.S.: Yes, your wife's mental balance, or lack thereof, would certainly be relevant to determination of custody.

While this letter, on the one hand, and the videodisc, on the other, would have created a stir in the Lively household, their contents are not immediately discovered. The unsealing of envelopes is not within the scientific protocol established by the household's resident kleptomaniac. After Eleanor has dowsed the outside of both stamped envelopes with Audrey's urine-and-tequila mixture, she hangs them up to dry in the area she's cordoned off in the storage attic behind her closet, the area that opens out behind her clothes and shoes.

This is a place that Humphrey doesn't think to check each time he opens her closet door and smells the whiff of something indefinably foul. He has removed and washed all the toys, sniffed and pawed at each individual dress and shirt and pair of trousers, but he has not taken down the tightly packed hangers with their lavender-scented, perfectly clean cargo. Nor has he pushed back the neat wall of plastic storage boxes that hide from view his sister's version of her mother's studio and her brother's kitchen. Here, a drying rack is flagged with clothespins—both nicked from the laundry room. On the floor, a Stonehenge of miniature plastic bottles containing shampoo and conditioner and mouthwash, having been liberated from Daddy's suitcase after his trip to Florida, stand at the ready, primed to contribute to the Lalique mister's diminishing supply of more powerfully fetid liquids.

* * *

EVERY time she talks to Humphrey about the bid catastrophe, Audrey feels truly awful. Worse, she knows she has only herself to blame. True to her standard operating procedure, Audrey castigates herself for not having done something, anything, to prevent disaster from occurring. Her father's happiness notwithstanding, she shouldn't have capitulated so readily. She should have stuck up for an earth-friendly plan. She should have left no stone unturned to find Diana's drawings And why hadn't she thought of bringing Baby Face in, to explain Diana's ideas to the committee?

The answer to this last question, occurring to her the afternoon Humphrey drops by to chat, is the most incriminating of all. Calling Baby Face to the rescue would have provided just one more arrow in Cupid's quiver. Much as she has tried to be unselfish, Audrey's subconscious appears to have refused to go with the program, and now there is nothing much she can say to explain such betrayal other than to apologize to Humphrey yet again.

"It's such a mess," she stutters. "I feel so bad."

"Is it true what Ted said then?" Humphrey asks. "That the architect your committee picked had designed fast-food restaurants? Because he took great pleasure in telling us that. You should have heard him. You'd have thought he'd been Mum's biggest supporter, telling her it was just as well she hadn't entered a bid, that the other competitors were beneath her."

"But she did! Enter a bid."

"Well, she doesn't know that. And I certainly don't have the heart to tell her, seeing as we've lost her only copy. Better to think she didn't submit, than to know she might have had a chance, or worse, might have been rejected for the architectural equivalent of Wonder Bread."

"Humphrey, are you sure you shouldn't just own up? Maybe she and Baby Face could recreate the plans." For this last improvisation, Audrey is momentarily proud, but Humphrey is shaking his head.

"She's too fragile; I won't risk it. Unless you could tell me for certain her plans would be accepted. Can your committee change its mind?"

"I don't know! The thing is, I don't have a lot of control anymore. Even my dad doesn't. He's got to please the people who are putting up the money."

"Well, it sounds rather hopeless then," Humphrey says diffidently. He is trying not to be angry at Audrey, who'd gotten his hopes up, just as Wally has gotten his mother's hopes up. Truly, he cannot bear to imagine how his mother would suffer if she knew he'd sent off her best effort, only to lose it in the bowels of corporate America. "Look, the reason I've come to chat: I've—I'm getting rather busy at home. Elly's been regressing and Mum's hopeless right now, and I—don't think I can work on your menu anymore. I'm sorry, but when I agreed, I thought things would be different." Humphrey leaves off explaining further his desire to be divested of all activity having anything at all to do with her father's enterprise, one that increasingly appears to be selling its soul to the Prince of Darkness, lock, stock, and barrel.

Humphrey hands Audrey a scroll of thick creamy paper, tied with a piece of raffia, for even in abandonment, Humphrey cannot help but be stylishly elegant. "I brought what I've already done, starters for the most part, but I just don't think I can do more."

* * *

WALLY has learned from Guy the unwelcome truth about his new investors: They truly care about one thing and one thing only, making money. Well, maybe two things. These men, real-estate tycoons who have amassed millions in the previous two decades of astonishing growth of metropolitan Phoenix, see environmentalists as tantamount to Communists, with a capital C. Their self-image, as the last defenders of the free market, is strongly, even vehemently held, despite the fact that developers in Phoenix have enjoyed a government-business climate so friendly, it borders on corporate welfare. Unlike "back East," where contractors must bear the initial development costs of putting in sewers and streets and water pipes and electrical lines, the Valley of the Sun is a paradise indeed, for all of these costs are borne by taxpayers, even on unincorporated desert land. Minimal risk, maximal profit, an incentive to build farther and farther out, until the Valley approaches Los Angeles, not only in acreage, but in air pollution, to say nothing of epidemic levels of lung cancers, unexplained childhood asthma, and other respiratory distress. The worse the air gets, the higher the price of gas, the more heated the debate, with insults hurled on both sides. The result of this battle has been an increasingly defensive attitude on the part of the builders, who quite reasonably argue that they are not forcing people to buy their houses, nor are they convincing them to buy the biggest gas guzzlers on the market to drive across town. Besides, the fact that the builders have allowed thousands of tradespeople to put food on the table should not go unnoticed. Bottom line, as Guy puts it, these men will not be receptive to a park the main selling point of which is its environmental benefits. In their view, such talk has only ever been associated with people whose presence in the state has become a constant thorn in the builders' increasingly thin-skinned sides.

After talking it over with Guy, Wally is forced to admit that he cannot execute the most straightforward of his plans, that of getting Diana's bid retro-approved and dumping the ideas from the Florida consultants. Instead, he is forced to think creatively. After mulling things over, Wally emerges from solitude with what appears to be a case of tunnel vision. To all appearances, he is carrying out the practical plan and forcing himself to accept the loss of Diana's and Audrey's hopes along with his own. His strategy, if one could call it that, has not been, cannot be, completely spelled out, even to Guy. Wally Gold cannot explain where he is headed and each step comes to him only as he picks up his foot and begins to set it down. It is easy for him to maintain appearances: He's got lots to do. There are dinners with the minions from Huntington, to keep them happy. There are lunches with the two biggest players on the Corporation Commission, who must be placated if the sale is to be approved. There is research to do about the constitution of the River Board, whose approval of the proposed River Protection Accord would be a serious impediment to the construction of the project his committee has chosen. To this end, Wally must have many sessions with Elizabeth Stanton and her people, to find out what exactly they would need from him to vote the right way. To complicate things, the venture capitalists have vociferously opposed any cooperation with the pain-in-the-ass tree-hugging hippies from Phoenix and Tucson, and so Wally's aforesaid negotiations had to be done in secret. Another faction represented on the River Board are the outdoor outfitters, who include some of the hunting and fishing stores Wally's done business with in the past, and he can't be quite sure they won't vote against him out of spite, since they're still ticked off about him selling out to Huntington. Then there are the mining and ranching and logging interests, whose votes are predictable, and the tourist industry representatives, whose opinions are harder to read than the Dead Sea Scrolls. The Native Americans appear to be reasonable, except when it comes to trusting federal, state, or local agencies, having borne the endless legacy of too many years of broken promises. This River Board, with its hornet's nest of acrimony, is crucial to the success of Wally's endeavors, and thus a veritable minefield of opportunities and catastrophes. It takes all of his concentration to keep moving as if he knew exactly what he was doing. These maneuvers he must constantly choreograph on the spot. They bring him into a state of almost spiritual ecstasy: The closer he gets to knowing what his dead wife has been trying to show him, the farther he gets from anything he could spell out to anybody.

To Audrey, for whom all of this is ostensibly being done, it appears that her father is losing his mind. She is truly spooked by the way he's been looking: haunted, she'd have to describe it, staring off into the distance over the patio, like he could see someone, talk to someone whom no one else sees. This fear for her father's fragile state of mind has translated itself into an uncharacteristic reticence in her approach to him, as if the slightest dissent might throw him right over the edge. Wally, not about to look a gift horse in the mouth, tells himself that when this is all over, he and his sweet girl, they'll be closer than ever.

And Guy, who has seen Wally throw himself off the cliff before, is deeply worried. Wally appears to be going along with the plan they've gotten funding for, to build a quick "in and out" theme park they can sell as soon as possible, before the plastic starts to fade from too much sun, or the equipment breaks or the government jacks up the price of water to reflect the real costs of wasting it. However, Guy has never known Wally to give in this easily. It's more like he's just going through the motions, and barely "present." Plus, Guy keeps finding his best friend at his desk, staring at Diana's blueprints, despite the fact that there is no way they can use them, not and keep the venture capitalists onboard. Guy and Wally have discussed it from here to eternity—the idea of bringing Diana's bid to the committee—but changing horses at this late date, it's not practical. Guy, who loves Wally like a brother, and wants to hear him out, even Guy finds this alternate plan too "pie-in-the-sky" for his comfort. No way the lenders on the committee are going to risk their money funding Wally's version of the Taj Mahal, substitute girlfriend as architect, the recipient of all this generosity. Guy loves Wally, but he also remembers way back when he'd fallen in love with Mary Kate and let her serve salmon aspic and Kir cocktails at that first vendor party. Guy had come to him, then, and told him he might as well kiss his ass goodbye as insult the gun guys with fish Jell-O and faggot drinks.

"Mary Kate, she needs a boost," Wally had insisted. "I'm not gonna bust her chops right now. Not when it's been one thing after another going wrong." Saving Mary Kate, that was more important to Wally than his own skin, and the richer he got, the more he seemed willing to give it away, like nothing mattered as much as wearing your heart on your sleeve. You could let the rest of your clothes go to shit, but keeping your eyes on the prize of complete self-sacrifice, that's what mattered, even if the person he was trying to help had long gone, or never even existed in the first place.

Fourteen

Elizabeth Stanton is tall, thin, rich, and well-spoken. A fifth-generation Arizonan whose parents have often regretted sending her to a Seven Sisters school back East, Elizabeth has spent her whole adult life and much of her trust fund income bucking the Old Boy network of ranchers, miners, and loggers and protecting what she can of what little natural beauty Arizona has left. "And they dare to call themselves conservatives when conserving is the last thing they care about. The only thing they're holding on to is their longstanding license to pillage the land. Which—by the way—they lease at rock-bottom rates, subsidized by the taxpayers. It's corporate welfare at its finest," she is fond of telling reporters.

Elizabeth refuses to dye her once-black hair, now streaked with bolts of white and gray. This look just happens to work wonders for her dark skin, her blinding white teeth and her neutral palette of Eileen Fisher outfits. Elizabeth is the Mother Teresa of the Save the Earth set, except she looks a hell of a lot better without lipstick.

Audrey's known Elizabeth Stanton for three years, and has been a youth representative on EARTHCARE's board for the last two, but still, after all this time, she has a difficult time overcoming the awe she feels in the older woman's presence. Nevertheless, despite her intimidation, despite a fierce loyalty to her father, Audrey has forced herself to schedule an emergency appointment with the EARTHCARE director.

"Sorry," Stanton's administrative assistant had said, when he showed Audrey into the conference room. "She's on the phone. She'll be down in a minute."

Audrey contents herself with reviewing her notes and drumming on the table, practicing her speech. When Liz arrives, her hair and linen jacket flowing in unison behind her, she apologizes again for keeping Audrey waiting. "A cup of tea, Audrey?"

"No, thanks, I'm okay."

"Everything all right with you? I got your memo about the petitions you've collected. And getting Baby Face's uncle to talk to reporters, that's great. You've really pulled so much together in such a short time."

"Thanks, but actually, that's not what I wanted to talk to you about," Audrey starts. "It's just, I think I need to resign."

"Why, sweetie?"

"It's a long story," Audrey starts to say, but then she cannot help but tell the long story, confessing what she's done, and how badly she feels about betraying the cause she's so devoted herself to. To her surprise, Elizabeth's face remains sympathetic. From the way she's acting, it's almost like she is already aware of everything Audrey thinks she's betraying her father by revealing. When Audrey's done, Elizabeth shakes her head and says, "Sweetie, don't quit over that. You can't help what your dad does."

"I could have voiced my opposition. He'd have followed my lead. Anyway, what's done is done, but I think you guys ought to raise Hell up north before the meeting of the River Board. Get them to vote the right way, for once."

Elizabeth, who hates to see Audrey so upset, is tempted to tell her about the phone call she's just taken, in which a very influential state politician has offered a trade, passage of the SafePlay campaign in Phoenix in return for EARTHCARE not endorsing the River Protection Accord, as it has in years past. Elizabeth, a member of the River Board, will still be allowed to cast her vote with her conscience, but if she doesn't make a public fuss, she can be guaranteed a win on the playground campaign. For Elizabeth, it's a no-brainer. First, she's been swayed by the strategic arguments of the caller, and second, she hasn't gotten as far as she has by biting the hand that feeds her. It would be fund-raising suicide for Elizabeth to publicly advocate passage of a law that would so deeply affect the fates of their biggest donor. However, explaining all this to Audrey, it would require too much time and shock Audrey's idealistic sensibilities, to say nothing of revealing secrets Elizabeth's agreed to keep to herself.

Still, Elizabeth can see the worry and guilt in her protégé's eyes. She decides to throw her a bone, one she can afford to release since this tidbit is already a matter of public record. "I don't know if you know about this, Audrey, but somebody sent a videodisc to every member on the River Board, with a cover letter suggesting they see for themselves what the Ammo King of Arizona was proposing for the Lake Havasu watershed. He's also been visiting select members I know, because two of them mentioned it."

"My dad did that!" Audrey says, her spirits lifting at the thought of her dad fighting back, even if it meant cutting off his nose to spite his face.

"No," Elizabeth murmurs, struck by sympathy for Audrey. "But maybe he sent the guy. He's British."

"Oh, Ted. How do you know this?"

"I'm on the River Board."

"You are? That's excellent!"

"That's a matter of some debate. However, given the paucity of activists in the state, I get a lot of appointments to boards, the token environmentalist."

"So, you can speak from within, convince them why they need to pass it?"

Elizabeth, who has already had several discussions with Audrey's father on this very subject, and has agreed to keep these conversations to herself, is unable to offer Audrey much in the way of comfort, knowing, as she does, how getting the board to vote on anything is a lot like trying to herd cats into an icy sewer. "I can only try," Elizabeth says.

"We should get together a bunch of kids to protest, don't you think?" Audrey asks, forgetting her earlier despondence.

"No, sweetie, I truly don't think that will get us where you want to go," murmurs Elizabeth, with a sincerity borne of the near-perfect twinning of both her tactical and strategic interests.

* * *

"Diana? Am I waking you? I can never sort out what time it is in the Land of Large Servings."

"No. Just let me turn off the sound here, Evelyn."

"I just called to congratulate you, darling."

"What?" Diana asks distractedly, still focusing on the large TV screen, where a crew of emergency personnel huddles over a badly injured motorcyclist. She has clicked on closed-captioning.

"I did wake you, didn't I! I'm so sorry."

"No, it's just teatime here, for God's sake. I'm just— How are you?"

"Excited for you."

"That's cruel."

"What?"

"Did Ted tell you about the bid, then?"

"Tell me what, Diana."

"That architect's job. The one I didn't get. Did he tell you why?"

"Why, what? When would I have voluntarily spoken to Ted?"

Diana watches as the paramedics pull a cloth over the injured boy's face and lift him onto the ambulance. The credits begin to play and she terminates her connection to the real-life drama with the click of the remote.

"Well, Humphrey, then," she explains.

"Diana, what on earth are you talking about?"

"Look, I know you're trying to cheer me up, but I'm fine, really."

"Diana. Have you finally contracted Mad Cow? I'm talking about the *Tattler* piece."

"Evelyn, I'm not subscribing anymore, you know."

"You don't know, do you?"

"Know?"

"You don't know that you don't know?"

"Is this a dream?"

"I should think that it were, if I were you, Diana. The *Tattler* is doing a piece on your dollhouses."

"What!"

"The reporter called me to set up an appointment. She wants to see Simon's and take snaps."

"What?"

"Yes. And the Hewitts are going to be in, too, because I talked to Sylvia. I cannot understand why they've not contacted you, though."

"I've not been checking my messages. But this is mad! Out of nowhere! I've not even been home in weeks."

"Well, absence makes the heart grow fonder. The reporter called and said that one of Ted's students at St. Mark's had mentioned the houses to her. Raved about how talented you were."

"I don't know any of his students, Evelyn."

"Well, they appear to know you, darling. You may be the next It Girl."

"Is this a prank? Because, truly, Evelyn, I'm a bit punk right now."

"No, it's not. I called the reporter back. They really are doing a feature on you."

"That's amazing. How—"

"Maybe Ted's been singing your praises. It's about time he supported you."

"Ted?"

"Just speculation. I know the reporter said that she'd been doing a piece on Sloan Rangers at Oxford, how they're a throwback to the fifties. All they want to do is get married and have children. Anyway, one of the girls from St. Mark's mentioned seeing photos of your miniatures. Said you're Ted's proudest boast."

"Now I know you're mad."

"I know, it doesn't square with the man's history, but perhaps he's had a conversion."

"More like guilt. When he let Eleanor ruin my drawings for the bid, he claimed he'd make it up to me, but I had no idea he'd— No, it can't be Ted, he wouldn't have."

"Well, whatever the source, take the money and run. It's time you finally get some appreciation for your gifts."

"I'm stunned."

"Gathered that, Diana. I wonder if they've gotten your phone there or if they're ringing your mum's house in Dover."

"I can't believe this."

"Well, I can. I've only been telling you for years."

"Mum's in Scotland. I doubt she's checked her calls."

"I'd ring her if I were you. They must be trying to reach you."

* * *

WALLY has been putting off calling Brenner, so thus, when Guy suggests it, Wally is all the more irritated. "Would you stop nagging me? I've been busy."

"Don't you think he'd like to know we've run into some snags?"

"He's fine. What are they gonna do? Back out over a couple of weeks' delay?"

"It might take longer. You gotta get through the Corporation Commission meeting and get the financing approved, which means making a silk purse out of a sow's ear, buddy."

"It's not like everyone else isn't in the same boat."

"Yeah, except they're not trying to switch boats in the middle of a goddamn tsunami."

"Look, Brenner'll be fine."

"The point is, Wally, you know as well as I do, if the River Protection Accord goes through, you're screwed. Don't you think you should give him a heads-up?"

"Look, I've got the money to buy the land. No matter what happens, I'm not leaving Brenner hanging."

"It's not Brenner's land. It belongs to the town. Anybody ever tell you, you have a self-destructive tendency?"

"Anyone ever tell you you're a pain in the ass?"

"Only Mary Kate in her cups. God, I miss that gal," Guy retorts, his voice breaking, belying his irreverent facade.

* * *

WHEN Ted returns home that evening, he's bearing a single pink rose. "Hullo, Diana!" he shouts, bending at the waist and saluting her with a diagonal swipe of the rose. "I've brought the most incredible news! The *Tattler* is trying to reach you for a piece on your houses. Humphrey, William, Elly. Come! Let's celebrate. Your mum's going to be in a Glossy!"

"What do you know about this?" asks Diana, scrutinizing her

husband's face to see if it's really the man she's been living with all these years.

"A reporter from the *Tattler* e-mailed me through St. Mark's. Said a student had seen your photos hanging in my office. She wondered if she might have a look."

"Photos in your office? What photos?"

"Diana, last spring when you were trying to find work and you asked me to post them on my reminder board? Do you not you remember?"

"But I thought you said it wasn't done to mix my business into your work at the College?"

"I never said anything of the kind. And the proof is in the pudding, Diana, because how else did the reporter hear about you? Come on now, let's not look a gift horse in the mouth, shall we?"

"Should I ring them, Ted? I don't know what's expected."

"Yes, of course you're to ring! But there's no hurry. The writer is working on another piece right now and can interview you when we're back in England on holiday."

"Holiday!" asks William.

In reply Ted retrieves a sheaf of airplane tickets from his jacket pocket and lays them gracefully on the counter.

Suddenly everyone is talking at once. Even Eleanor is disposed towards a hug for her father, who has also brought home Cadbury bars in celebration of his wife's good fortune.

"To your achievements in the world of the miniature!" Ted cries, ruffling his wife's hair and pulling her in for a quick peck on the cheek.

So contagious is the children's excitement at this surprise that Diana finds herself swept along on the wave. She does not examine her own motives, much less Ted's. Even Humphrey, who has been so worried about his role in his mum's loss of the bid for Wally's project,

swallows his reflexive critique of Ted, who is, even now, constitution-
ally unable to praise his wife without slipping in the knife of double
entendre. Instead, Humphrey convinces himself to let go his worries
and to enjoy the moment. Suddenly he feels a rush of homesickness
that he hadn't even known existed until the possibility of assuaging
it has been raised. He swings his baby sister into a holiday jig and
wonders aloud if they'll need to buy sweaters for the journey home.

* * *

SEVERAL evenings later Ted, in the grip of a restless joy, has finished his third vodka martini. He has sucked the juice of the olives
and licked the rim of his favorite glass. "William, my boy!" he sings
as William and Adam jostle over the controls to the video game
they're playing. "How would you like to see a video game in the
making? I've brought home some mock-ups from the consultant."

William looks at Adam, who shrugs, and they both sit quietly
while Ted loads the DVD into the player. "Now, here," instructs Ted,
warming to his subject. "Never mind that these knights would have
traveled on foot or that they hadn't bathed in decades. Historical accuracy has been pitched out the window along with such niceties as
taste and logic. I want you boys to see what Hollywood's done to
Britain's sacred literary treasures. Now, who'd like to try it first?"

After dinner the boys continue to play while Ted continues to
drink, though he's switched to red wine, which, Adam can't help
noticing, has stained his teeth pink and his tongue an almost black
color.

"All right, William. Enough," Ted snaps irritably, at ten o'clock.
"Take the disk and put it in on my desk. Now, William! Not tomorrow!"

William quickly removes the disk and motions to Adam to follow.
He intends to obey his father's instructions, but first, there are warm
biscuits Humphrey's left on the cooling rack in the kitchen. One

biscuit leads to another and before long, the boys have embarked on a first-class, postwar sack of the pantry. Somehow, as is wont to happen in the final moments of Adam's visits, both boys find themselves shocked by the abrupt demise of their time together. In their keening for moments lost, Ted's disk goes by the wayside.

At least by William, at least until the next morning, when he is sorted out in no uncertain terms, starting with a rough pinch of his shoulder. "William! Wake up. Where's my videodisc?"

William, pulled from a dream in which Johnny has been teaching him to dig in the sand, stumbles for speech. "I, uh, in the kitchen, I think."

"And why, may I ask, did you leave it there when I specifically instructed you to put it on my desk? Is there some defect in your hearing that translated it into 'Lose it, please, so your father will be made a fool of when Gold asks for it back?' "

"I'll call Adam," William offers, still groggy. "P'raps he took it home on accident. I left it right on the counter!"

"By accident, not on. The sooner we're back on British soil the better, before my children turn into subliterate imbeciles. Bad enough you've shown no respect for property. Twenty quid, those copies cost to make, and now this one's wasted. Now get out of bed and give your mate a ring. You're not to do another thing until you've reached him. Make sure he brings it to school."

An hour later, William is still in his pajamas when Diana comes down for breakfast. "Darling! Hurry! You'll miss the bus!"

"Ted says I'm not allowed to do anything before I reach Adam. And I'm only getting the machine."

"What's so important that you must do it before you're dressed for school? Have you eaten? Did he not even give you breakfast? Honestly." Diana is so annoyed with her husband that she neglects to correct William for calling his father by his Christian name, rather than giving him his proper patriarchal due. Indeed, somewhere in Diana's heart of hearts, she understands all too well the way in which small rebellions and slips of the tongue can soothe one's pride and straighten one's spine in the face of otherwise impossible circumstance.

* * *

When Brenner calls Wally to tell him that Ted Lively has been poking around Dreamy Draw, wearing a pair of brand-new cowboy boots, he is surprised to hear Wally laugh. "He's a real piece of work, isn't he?"

"What are you thinking, sending him up here, buddy? He's managed to piss off a bunch of the locals and run up a huge tab at the Superstition Saloon. You might want to make sure he stays down in Phoenix from now on."

"I didn't send him. The guy appears to be quite the self-starter, if you know what I mean. Really takes initiative."

"Really takes the *cake*," Brenner says. "Ravenna says he came in her store and started hitting on her."

"Like I said, he really takes initiative."

"Well, pull his leash and yank him downstate, buddy. He's not doing you any good up here. Trust me."

Wally apologizes to Brenner for any offense his employee might have caused. This leaves Brenner wondering. What if Guy and Audrey are right, that Wally is losing his grip on reality? All Brenner can conclude is that no one in his right mind would ever think Ted Lively's insults were anything but intended, for no one, not even this Englishman wearing brand-new cowboy boots, could ever be that obnoxious without trying.

* * *

WILLIAM is lying in his sister's bed, holding a Nerf Blaster. He is waiting for Eleanor to emerge from behind her closet door, having been reduced to this, playing with a four-year-old for lack of anything better to do.

It's been three days that Adam's been absent from school. Ms. Marsh had said he was "sick," but no one's answering the Johnsons' phone.

Meanwhile, Ted has placed William under house arrest until he can find the missing disc, which holds all of Ted's edits and historical suggestions, painstaking efforts to push the envelope of bad taste past its own national borders. To have it gone missing like this would mean explaining what he'd done with the office's other copies, which, being the frugal chap that he is, Ted has mailed hither and yon without making backups. Who'd have thought his son could be so careless, or that his mate would suddenly cease attending school?

At least three times a day Professor Lively has towered over William while he punched in Adam's phone number and left yet another message. All this despite the common sense question William hasn't dared utter, but which pounds its drum constantly in his head, in the silent battle he carries on with his father. Surely, if they were home, they'd be ringing back. Leaving more voice mails would only be irritating, to say nothing of embarrassing. Now, at least, the voice mailbox is full, so William can't pester Adam's family further. Even this, Ted refuses to accept, chiding his son night and day about his irresponsibility.

It has been the most boring weekend ever, and the only entertainment has involved loading up the Nerf Blaster with balls and waiting for Eleanor to cross the line.

The closet door squeaks open and Elly runs out screaming while William pelts her with a splatter of small ping-pong–shaped bullets.

His sister has conveniently reached "base" in Humphrey's room when William shouts for her to help him retrieve the spent ammunition from the back of her closet. "Ack! It stinks like wet knickers!" he shouts, pulling away the plastic boxes over which his ammo has flown, his eye caught by the glint of gold letters spelling Knight Appraisals.

"I'm going to murder you, Elly!" he shouts, meaning it now. He kneels, appalled, for he's discovered her laboratory, and most important, center stage, sitting on the drying rack, tied to the bars with leopard shoelaces and counterweighted by a calculator from Knight Appraisals, is the missing videodisc. The Rewritable CD, over which his father has tortured him night and day. To say nothing of having forced William to make a complete and total fool of himself on Adam's answer machine.

William unloops the shoelaces from the rack, collecting the looted objects and blurry papers into his arms. He runs downstairs and hands his mother the calculator and stiffened papers. "She's gotten into your post, Mum! And remember the man looking at the house the other day, who lost his calculator? She nicked it, just like I said. Where's Ted? Elly's the one what had his DVD disc the whole time."

"*That*, not *what*, William. And please don't call your father Ted. It hurts his feelings."

"Mum! Where is he, anyway? Maybe now he'll stay off my back."

Diana shakes her head. "What a sponge for vernacular you are. He's in his study."

Diana sorts through the pieces of mail that William's presented her. Both envelopes, long since separated from their contents, are completely illegible, having received the brunt of Elly's prophylaxis. All that remains are faded amoebic shapes of blue and black ink, respectively. Behind them, badly crumpled, is a Post-it in blue ink from someone who signs his name with an R. The only words Diana can make out are *legal* and *hurt her feelings*.

The next letter, written in a smooth Italic script, a different handwriting, says,

> *Hey Pinhead. Cease and desist with your sabotage of the project, or we'll send a copy of this to your fair lady.*

It is unsigned. Diana is trying to think who her fair lady might be as she turns the page and sees a large red spider crouched atop a bright orange hill under a pale yellow sun. She can see that it's Eleanor's work, but its relationship to the previous notes makes no sense. She is still puzzling over the warning as Eleanor spots her drawing.

"Mine!" she demands, and so her mother surrenders the picture without seeing the typewritten words that are submerged beneath its colorful mélange.

Eleanor, for her part, tapes the picture to the bottom of the Sub-Zero, at the height of her waist, where she will be able to add stickers at will, but where adults, who will be looking at it from at least four feet away, will have a hard time detecting anything more meaningful than the innocent caricature of a venomous creature.

William carries the disk into his father's study. "Daddy?" he asks. "I found the videodisc in Elly's closet!"

"It's about time, William."

"Wait, are you even going to punish her?"

"No. You're the git who left it in the kitchen for her to nick," says Ted, ruffling his hand through William's dark hair. This gesture of affection is all William's likely to get in the way of apology from his father.

"May I watch it again?" William asks. "If you don't need it right now?"

"No, I hardly think so. Not now. You ought to consider something a little more active. You're getting a bit pudgy round the middle, I've noticed." With this statement and a poke at William's waist, Ted takes the disk and places it inside the plastic box labeled Video Game Mock-ups. With this last bit of fatherly counsel, Ted straightens his spine and returns to his work.

William leaves the room without speaking and runs up to his bedroom, where he locks his door, removes his shirt, and pinches the dimpled skin above the waist of his trousers. Like most prepubescent boys, William has recently developed a thickened waist, a small amount of which can be seen as cellulite, and most of which happens to be necessary for the serious growing he will do once his body shifts into hormonal overdrive. If Ted were half as knowledgeable about developmental staging as he is about King Arthur, he'd know that this baby fat of William's is not anything to fret about. Instead, Ted is the worst sort of ignoramus, for he extends the arrogance of his academic specialty into all fields of knowledge, and believes there is nothing under the sun about which he might need to learn. His confidence in his own wisdom is impervious to doubt, and thus all the more damaging to its hapless victims.

William stands in front of the mirror and tries to suck in his abdomen, wincing as he notes how little such measures accomplish. Soon, the entire fourth grade will be attending a Harvest Fest pool party at Austin Wilken's house. William is certain there will be no one who looks worse than he does in bathing togs. Not only is he pudgy, as his father puts it, but he's also extremely pale. Unlike his classmates, he'd spent the preceding summer in rainy England and even now that he's in sun-drenched Arizona, with a backyard pool, he's been too sensitive to his mum's feelings to insist on using it much.

William avoids looking in the mirror as he changes into his swimming trunks and runs downstairs.

"Mum!" he cries. "May I please, please sit out by the pool. I promise I won't go in the water."

"No, darling. You may not. Daddy's working and Humphrey's gone to the market."

"You could watch me," William complains. "I won't go near the pool. I'm just—" It is here that William veers away from the truth. He cannot bear to expose himself to Diana's sympathy. He cannot say it. He will not even admit to himself how he dreads the party. It will help if Adam attends, so that William will have someone to pal around with in the water, but Adam is one of the few fourth grade boys who've been spared Male Baby Fat Syndrome. Moreover Adam has a deep coppery skin tone, with not a single mole or freckle. William will look like a ghostly Telletubby next to Adam.

If William would only tell his mother how he feels, he would find her eager to help, but instead, he simply pulls his arms into his chest and says "I'm—cold. I want to sit in the sun."

"Well, put some clothes on, for Heaven's sake. It's November, William. I can't watch you. You know that."

"Why do you have to be such a Fraidy Cat!" he asks, hating himself once the words are out but unable to stop himself from expanding on this particular theme. "You won't even try to be normal! You won't even try!"

The words hit their mark, dead in Diana's breastbone, next to that muscle otherwise known as the heart. She is already well fed up with her timidity. Each morning she rises, planning to ring the *Tattler* reporter. Every time she thinks of actually placing the call, however, she cannot locate the number that Ted had brought

Diana Lively Is Falling Down 319

home. She'll search ineffectually among papers she hasn't touched in months, knowing she won't find it. She'll tell herself that she'll ring tomorrow, that she'll ring as soon as she can.

None of her worry takes place on the surface, where she might attack it with logic, but instead, it's buried within a cloudy set of scenarios. The images vary: Diana will dial the number and discover that all of this is a huge hoax, or a case of mistaken identity, or she will actually have to compete for the reporter's attention. Perhaps the writer is busy, working on another story, perhaps she'll be irritated at the ring from America. Or perhaps this reporter, having viewed photos of Diana's work, has decided not to do it after all. Diana does not think she could bear another awkward rejection. Better to pretend she's too busy to call, or has been out of town, or some other excuse.

"Daddy says I'm to be more active!" William says, his eyes filmed with hot tears. "But how can I? And now you won't even let me sunbathe. I'm not a complete baby, you know!"

"I know, William," murmurs Diana, pulling him into her arms for a quick hug. "Look, I'll come and sit by the pool and you may do some swimming. If you start to drown, I suppose I can always shout for your father."

"I can give you a lesson," urges William, already feeling remorse for his outburst. "Just put on your suit."

"Ha!" chokes Diana, and both of them laugh, because the sound she has made is so little like a laugh, so much like a yowl. Diana will not put on her suit, she will not go near the edge of the pool, but she will at least keep him company, in her own white-knuckled, self-hating way. She points at Eleanor, who is watching the telly, then brings her forefinger to her mouth in a bid for silence as they tiptoe outside and open the wrought-iron gate.

Thus Diana comes to be seated by her swimming pool in the middle of the afternoon, pondering the merits of Prozac, or another drug perhaps, something that will help her overcome her many anxieties. She will not do it because of Ted, no. She will do it for her children, do it for herself. It's just a matter of finding a doctor, she tells herself, wondering how long it will take before the happy pills kick her life back into anything resembling a smoother gear.

When William finishes swimming, he puts his elbows out on the edge and begins his coaxing. "It's not that hard, Mum. I promise. Just come and put your feet in the water. Give it a try. Trust me."

His mother would so much like to please him, but this desire is nothing in the face of a her inability to move from the chaise longue. She cannot let go of the warm metal arms that need no cuffs to hold her prisoner.

"Come on, Mum. I'm not asking you to bloody walk on water," coaxes William.

"Don't use that language, William. Honestly, what's gotten into you today?"

"I just wish you'd trust me," he says, and there is something in his eyes, some hurt, some deficit of confidence, that makes Diana feel the stakes are higher than she'd known. She lifts her arms and stands up, forcing herself to move one foot in front of the other. Slowly—as if her feet were glued down—she makes her way towards William and the edge of the pool. *Pretend there is no water*, she tells herself. *You can do it*, she tells herself, and she is breathing deeply and lifting her enormously resistant feet when the French doors slam shut and Eleanor accusingly screeches, "Mummy!"

Hell hath no fury like a child scorned, or in this case, having discovered she's been cheated on in the swimming department. The unexpected shriek from behind brings Diana to sink instantly into a terrified crouch, scraping her knees and scratching palms in her rush to safety.

It is comical, this sudden panic, at least to those not in possession of minor injuries.

"Silly Mummy!" cries Elly, stripping down to her underpants and skipping forward towards the water.

"Come back, Mum!" William laughs. "It's all right. You can do it."

Diana crawls back to the chaise and pulls herself into it, grimacing at William but shaking her head, as well. "No, I can't, William. Not today," she says, her tone brusque with the adrenaline that's flooded her system.

William slowly pulls himself out of the water and eases his body onto the warm cement. "You are such a silly mummy," he mutters, sliding his head onto one splayed elbow, turning away from her and towards his sister, who is holding on to the stair rail and gracefully dipping her toes in the water. Though William is simply trying to keep an eye on his sister, Diana takes his about-face as a further rebuff.

Now she sits and stares at her son's pale back, reinforced in her realization that she does, indeed, have a psychiatric problem. *Find a doctor*, she tells herself. *Get yourself some pills, and then you can learn to swim, you can ring that reporter. Take back the life that's somehow managed to get bloody well lost in your morass of insecurities.*

Fifteen

Early Wednesday morning, a meeting in Wally's office brings Ted to the round table, eyes bleary, hands shaking. After the obligatory how-do-you-dos, Wally straightens his back and slaps himself in the face. "Hey, Ted, where's my manners? You want Beverly to bring you tea or coffee, and some of her special date-bran muffins?"

If not for one word in that sentence, Ted would have refused, for his stomach is still raw from last night's binge. But the idea of Beverly being forced to serve him pleases him too much to decline.

"If it's not too much trouble, I'd love that. And perhaps a glass of juice?"

When Beverly brings in the tray, she is properly sullen. She sets a plate in front of Ted and he thanks her in his most patronizing fashion.

Ah, when he took this position, he didn't foresee how much satisfaction he'd have, once he'd stopped taking it so seriously. Ted daintily does away with two date-bran muffins, which, even he must admit, are excellent. He drinks two cups of coffee and is listening to Wally complain about the cost of assuaging the EPA, DEP, DIA, and SEC as well as several other acronymic bodies when a knob in his intestines turns sharply, suddenly, forcing him to rise without even waiting for Wally to finish his sentence. "Excuse me," says Ted. "I need to duck out to the loo."

"Use the executive washroom," Wally offers. "It's that door over there."

Ted has barely closed the door and pulled down his pants when Beverly's date muffins wreak their revenge. He clenches his gut and counts to twenty, waiting for the next wave, which is already announcing itself in whimpers from his sternum.

It's not until this sudden onslaught has cycled to its end that Ted can pay attention to the sound of Wally's oversized voice in the next room.

"So, the venture capitalists are getting cold feet?"

"Wally! Shhhh."

"He can't hear."

Ted cocks his head towards the wall and busies himself dispensing air freshener. He leans into the vent to improve his reception.

"All I know is that if they put two and two together and see how much money you put into EARTHCARE, or how Audrey's been taking a stand on the treated-wood issue, they're not gonna like it one bit."

"Why would they care about treated wood?"

"Think about it. We've talked about how they think the ecoterrorists are conspiring to overthrow the world. Plus, these guys have built thousands of decks and hot-tub surrounds. The last thing they want is homeowners getting lawsuit-happy. Besides, I hate to tell you, but one of them has some treated wood he wants to dump cheap. Since he's not a vendor, he's not prohibited from disposing of what he already owns."

"No way we're putting that poison up in the Draw."

"Yeah, well, you can try to talk them out of it, but they've got four votes to your four, when it comes to the construction phase of the project. If Beverly turns, which she just might since her pension is tied up in this, you're out of luck."

"Christ."

"No, more like Antichrist, which is what we'll look like if the money guys find out you're the deep pocket for EARTHCARE."

Ted washes his hands and whistles as he considers what he's overheard. The men they're discussing should be listed on the minutes of the selection committee meeting. And Audrey, he'd have to think of a way to innocently introduce the subject of treated wood. Perhaps she'd like to come out in public support of the Protection Accord. If that didn't sway the River Board, it would at least suffice to alarm the lenders, perhaps to the point of jumping ship.

Had Ted believed in God, he might attribute this streak of good fortune to be some sort of approval on the Almighty's part, but more's the pity that Ted believes only in himself and so can only delight in his infinite intelligence and quick wit.

Ted gives himself a grin and a tip of the head in the mirror before hurrying out to express his concern. "Is something wrong?" he asks, "It sounded as though someone were shouting."

Guy and Wally look at each other, and then at Ted. Their faces are wiped clean of emotion as Wally shakes his head and mutters, "It wasn't anything important. Let's get back to work. Oh, and Ted, did you bring me that disk of the mock-ups for the video games?"

* * *

"ANXIETY can mean many things," the therapist is telling Diana. Dr. Morales is a handsome, chubby, thirty-five-year-old with dark skin and a trimmed goatee. His advert in the Yellow Pages has emphasized his skill with phobias. "For some people it's a symptom of depression, but not always. Remember, in some ways, anxiety is a good thing. It keeps us alert, and moves us out of the way when danger approaches. Back in the days of primitive peoples, this was essential, right? Now let me ask you something. Besides your fear of swimming, which is easily understood given the trauma of nearly drowning, are there other fears that interfere with your enjoyment of life?"

"Oh yes. Insects—I hate them."

"And how does that hatred affect your life?"

"Well, I'm not keen on the outdoors. And I'm always worried for my children, for one thing. Occasionally, I'll wake up in the middle of the night and have to check their rooms to make sure they've not been bitten by a black widow. Or scorpion. And when they go out to play, I worry incessantly about Africanized killer bees."

"And why do you think you fear them so much, Mrs. Lively?"

"Because they're attacking people! Is it such lunacy to think it might happen to someone else? You must have seen the bit in the news a few weeks ago, the woman who was working in her garden and died a horrendous—! Is it really so wrong to fear something that can kill or cripple a child?"

"Tell me, do you think that fear might have been helpful in the jungle, among early man?"

"Well, yes, I do."

"Well, maybe it's not so crazy to have an aversion to an insect that can really hurt you. Maybe that fear is a kind of legacy in your brain chemistry, Mrs. Lively. Lots of people feel like you do about spiders, for instance. But has it ever occurred to you that your anxiety may have to do with something larger than these tiny creatures, something they represent to you that's affecting your life in a much bigger way?"

"Such as?" Diana asks.

"Well, that's what we'll try and figure out in the next few weeks. It might not be that realistic to eradicate your fear of insects, not completely, though you might feel better if you could temper it with your intellect. Statistically, the chances of getting stung by a—"

"That's the thing!" Diana interrupts. "I know all that. I repeat it to myself several times a day, but I still wake up screaming in the middle of the night."

"And what's happening in your dream?"

"A spider has bitten my daughter and I can't wake her up. Or we're being chased by a swarm of bees and no matter how fast we run, they're on us, all over the children. I should never have watched the coverage of that poor woman's death. Just when I think I'm better, I'll go into a complete tailspin worrying that William will be attacked on the football green."

"William's your son?"

"Yes."

"Mrs. Lively, when you have these episodes of intense anxiety, you've mentioned your children. How about your husband?"

"Hmmm. It's the children mostly, though sometimes it's me. I."

"And with the swimming, does that feature in your nightmares as well?"

"Strangely enough, no, not really. It's odd, actually, since it nearly killed me, but when I dream, I'm often flying or swimming, and it's not frightening at all. But once I'm near a real swimming pool, it's as if I'm a paralytic."

"You know, it might just be a matter for you of trying to slowly get used to it," Dr. Morales says. "You could try dipping your toes in at first, then maybe just try wading in the shallow end. Try holding your breath underwater in the bathtub, with your face submerged. You've got to allow yourself to slowly disconnect the experience of water from your association with trauma. Slowly you accustom yourself, so that instead of clenching up, it starts to feel safe to you. Have you ever heard of a technique called visualization?"

* * *

HAVING got caught in traffic on I-17 on their way back from Sedona, Valeen, Dolores, and Adam have come straight to Dolores's doctor's appointment. No time to drop Adam at school, nor change out of wrinkled clothes, nor prepare themselves for the other patients in the waiting room.

"Do I look that bad?" Dolores whispers, knowing she doesn't. Still, Valeen can see that Dolores is pretty much unhinged by the wasted faces and bodies shoved into clothes that peak around missing shoulders and rise over bloated waists.

"No, honey. You look beautiful."

They are still recovering from last week's trip to the oncologist. At the last minute Dolores had gotten it into her head to ask him for "one more round of chemo," and if that wasn't surprising enough, the tears in Dr. Rifkin's eyes when he told her he couldn't give it to her, that sent Valeen right over the edge.

"I want you to call my wife," Rifkin had said, handing Dolores a card. "She specializes in pain management."

"I never got why they had to make you so sick to get you well, hon. Maybe it's better this way," says Valeen, trying to cheer Dolores up, while she surreptitiously checks out Adam's impassive expression. Ever since they'd told him Dolores was dying, at the top of the mountain overlooking Sedona, Adam has been acting like nothing was said. Like everything is the same as it's always been. Valeen knows this isn't right, but she can't make him cry, either, especially when Dolores's acting like this is no big deal, with her jokes about the Grim Reaper.

Valeen, the saddest of them all, in her book, is not above counting on a miracle. She is a font of information on visioning and imaging and tumors that shrink from the size of a melon to the size of a pea all through nutrition, prayer, what have you. She believes that the Pink Jeep tour they took to the Natural Vortices may have just started the turnaround deep inside Dolores's energy fields.

For the sake of harmony, Dolores lets Valeen dream on, but she knows better.

She's known since August, when she went in for a scheduled CT scan. The way the technician wouldn't meet her eyes after she came out of the tunnel, the same guy she'd been joking with for months. That's when she'd known, or thought she did, but now she's learning there's different ways of knowing. What she'd been coasting along with, that had been the "Oh, isn't it weird?" *head* kind of knowing. Way different from the panic she felt in the middle of the night, the *gut* bludgeoning "I can't do it" dread.

Dolores leans over and whispers in Valeen's ear, "Some scam. Think Dr. Rifkin pays her husband a kickback for the patients he's been able to knock off?"

This black humor: It's all she has when she's blue. Valeen doesn't like it one bit, but Dolores is off the hook, because Valeen is busy. She's raising her left palm, hushing Dolores, as she bends her ear towards the tiny phone in her right.

"Sorry, hon. I was getting the voice mail," Valeen murmurs, when she's folded the phone shut and is handing it out toward her son. "Adam, honey, you need to give William a call. Something must be really wrong at his house. He left, like, a million messages. Something about a disk?"

"Oh, that. I'll bring it in to school tomorrow. It came home in my backpack."

"What's that?" Dolores asks. "Something's wrong at William's?"

"Nah, I doubt it. Just his dad, being a dick."

"Adam."

"He is. It's just this stupid video game thing. It's not like it's the cure for cancer or anything. Oh, shit. Sorry!" he yelps, and for a second, it looks like he will start to cry.

Dolores, who's always been so good with Adam, reaches out and salutes him with a high-five. "Atta boy, sweetie," she laughs. "Tell it like it is."

* * *

Forsythia, the themed-entertainment consultant, throws a videodisc across Wally's desk and tells him in no uncertain terms: "Look, I'm not getting paid to put up with this crap."

"Come again?" Wally says. "Have you forgotten who put this thing together in the first place?"

"That, I don't wanna know. I gotta tell you. I don't think that kind of thing is funny."

"Okay," murmurs Wally, reaching forward to push Beverly's Call button twice, their signal that he needs to be interrupted. "You do know our technical expert spent the whole weekend watching your show and making suggestions."

"What are you saying?"

"Miss, no offense, but your company put this thing together."

Sythia's braids whip back and her eyes narrow regally. "You better be ignorant, mister, 'cause otherwise, I'd have to shoot you with some of your own damn ammo. You better sit down and watch what you just accused me of 'putting together.'"

With that, Franz Bibfeldt's assistant exits Wally's office, giving the swinging door a vehement slam of her palm on the way out.

Wally shakes his head and presses the button to open his computer's DVD player. He then leans back into his chair and clicks the remote to unscroll the large screen that descends from the ceiling.

Wally has already forced himself to view the video mock-ups once, all the better to wax enthusiastic at the meeting with the consultants, but he isn't looking forward to having to watch it again. From what he can tell, it's just more of the same: two guys in armor trying to kill each other. *Look alive*, he tells himself as the screen explodes with light. *Let's see how Ted's managed to completely piss this girl off.*

Wally waits for the heraldry of rising music, the riffed hooves of stamping horses that introduces each section of the consultants' videos. Instead, Wally is brought up short by the sudden rough cut of Ted sitting on a leather chair while a sultry voice asks him if he'd like her to dance. Wally knows then and there he's stumbled on something private, but he can't make himself press the requisite buttons. Instead, he puts his feet on the floor, clasps the arms of his chair and is glued to the screen. Wally winces at the sight of Ted stripping off his clothes, but he can't stop watching. Ted crawls into a bathtub wearing only black nylon socks and holds himself, groaning out loud while he's sprinkled with what appears to be— what is that? Wally has to rewind the tape and replay several times before he figures it out. From the position of the red spike heels, and the angle of the legs, it sure looks like Ted's on the receiving end of a practice that up till now, Wally had thought limited to sad sacks at the tassel end of the sexual fringe.

"Oh my God!" chokes Wally, grateful for such a completely un-expected but nevertheless perfectly conceived answer to his prayers. His low gravelly chortle opens up into itself and blossoms into an infinite and breathless ladder of startled yelps until he finally stops and regains enough control of his faculties to push Eject and get Guy on the phone.

* * *

ELEANOR's laboratory has been decommissioned. The drying rack and clothespins have been wiped down with disinfectant and left in the sun to dry, the tiny bottles of hotel potions returned to the guest room, the calculator mailed back to Knight Appraisals. Audrey's missing Lalique mister has been soaked in hot water and bleach. It is now drying upside down on the granite counter, perched in the exact middle of a pretty blue-and-white dish towel.

"Don't touch," Humphrey warns Eleanor, who is snaking her way across the counter, admiring the way the sun lights a purple flower in the precise peaks of leaded glass. "Audrey's on her way to collect it."

"Elly fix," she pouts, reaching a tiny hand for the mister, which, if Humphrey would only stop bossing her, she knows how to attach to the spray bulb. Humphrey vaults across the floor, and in the sudden melee—the agency of which will remain forever unclear—the fetching blue-and-white towel is swept up. Mary Kate's treasured Paris souvenir topples to the floor. "Ow!" shouts Humphrey as the lead crystal shatters onto the tile.

"Stay!" he commands, setting his sister on the counter and tiptoeing round for the broom. Eleanor is already keening forward; a firm believer in the preemptive tantrum as a means of averting punishment. Humphrey, too softhearted for his own good, puts his hands to his ears and wants to cry himself. Instead he pats his sister's knee and uses his softest voice to assure her that if she'll just stay still until he's swept up the mess, he'll let her watch Teletubbies. In several deft movements, Humphrey bends broom to dustpan to dustbin and gets down on all fours with a wet paper towel.

"The owl and the pussycat went to sea, in a beautiful pea-green boat," he prompts, delicately wiping the floor in front of the Sub-Zero to attract any treacherous splinters that remain. "What's next, luv: Do you remember?"

"They took some honey and plenty of Mummy wrapped up in a five-pound note," chants Elly.

"*Money.* Not *Mummy.*"

"No, Humphrey! That's not right! Mummy told me!" demands

Eleanor, as threateningly zealous in her misinterpretation of sacred text as any Crusader.

"All right. You win. Mummy, wrapped up in a five-pound note. That would be clever. We'll have to wrap more than Mummy to pay Audrey for the Lalique you've managed to break. Oh, that rhymes. Now stay there while I do one more round with the wet . . ." Humphrey's sentence trails off. He is suddenly caught up in the more prosaic wording that has—until now—been subsumed in the noisy colors of Elly's drawing.

Atop the mountain, between the setting sun and the prominent egg sac of a bright red spider, Humphrey finds himself absorbing the words that explain his stepfather's unexpected extravagance in the purchase of trans-Atlantic tickets. So rapt is he by the possibilities that suggest themselves in the nouns *blood work,* custody, present wife, *fiancée,* and *mental balance* that he has nothing left for verbs that would ordinarily occur to him, action words like *stand up* or *take charge.* Eleanor, usually so demanding, understands that something heavy is pushing on her brother, forcing him to stay on the floor, to drop his wet paper towel, to read the same words over and over with open mouth. She remains silent, allowing him some peace to absorb the incomprehensible.

Audrey taps at the French door, opens it, and walks in without a word. Eleanor is quietly perched on the counter and Humphrey's on the floor, scrutinizing a drawing. "W'sup?" Audrey asks, kissing Eleanor's neck and gathering the child into her arms.

"We've managed to break your mister," drones Humphrey. His inflection is off, as though he'd said the words already and is now repeating them to a particularly *thick* taker of dictation.

"Humphrey?" Audrey asks. "You okay?"

"I'm not sure," he answers, handing her the letter to read and taking Eleanor. "Here, Elly. Let's put on Laa-Laa."

When he returns to the kitchen, Audrey asks, "Who the hell is this Cheswitt chick?"

"I haven't any idea."

"Jesus. Where'd you find this?"

"On the door of the—it's been right here for days and no one, apparently, has read it."

"Don't you think you'd better show your mom?"

At this Humphrey sighs and drops his head to his chest. "I don't know what to do, Audrey. She's already so demoralized."

"What a loser that prick is! If you only knew the things he's been— Wait a minute. Humphrey! Wait a minute!" Audrey's face glows with the power of her idea, an idea so breathtaking, she can barely risk saying it out loud. "Where is he?" she whispers, crouching down on the floor.

"At work. And Mum's at market."

"Listen," she says, still crouching, still whispering. "Guy told my dad that Ted was claiming expenses at some titty bar down in Tempe."

"Titty bar?"

"You know. With strippers and such. I didn't say anything because I wasn't supposed to be listening, but see, I was trying to find out what they're up to with the Dreamy Draw project." Audrey stops and wipes the blond hair from her brow.

She lays her hand on Humphrey's knee and interrupts herself, saying softly, "I feel really terrible about everything. All the work you put in. And your mom."

Humphrey holds up his palm, stopping traffic at the intersection of her father's project and his mother's predicament. "Back to Ted," he reminds her.

"Oh! Well, here's my idea. See this part, where it says he's supposed to avoid behavior—to get custody, the wicked stepfather's gotta look like Mr. Perfect. Let's borrow my dad's video camera and try and catch him in action down at the titty bar. Then if he tries to take away the kids, she can show a judge what kind of perv he really is."

"You're brilliant!" groans Humphrey, pinching Audrey's shoulder blade.

"Stop it!" she yelps, throwing herself across his taut lap and circling his waist with her arms. "I know where to tickle you, too!" Audrey shouts, illustrating her point with a sweet jab of her fist. Humphrey collapses into helpless strangled sounds that join her own sweet peals, and they fishtail across the floor, united again, in their own blue Heaven.

* * *

EVERY time Guy and Wally look at each other, it is all they can do not to fall screaming to the floor, especially when Ted drones on about the ubiquity of water in Arthurian text, about its symbolic and metaphoric weight.

"It's essential really," Ted is saying to Guy, whose eyes are widened beyond the capacity of their sockets, whose eyebrows are frozen in what Ted can only interpret as amazement. Ted turns to Wally, who is staring furiously at Guy's elbow, and suggests, "These water parks are quite popular in Florida, I've noticed. Of course, in Lake Havasu City, one would need to heat the water since the park will be air-conditioned."

"Didn't you investigate some natural delivery system for warm water?" asks Guy with a completely straight face.

At this Wally has to run to the bathroom, where he struggles with the same coughing fit that's already interrupted their brainstorming session two times. Guy and Ted wait awkwardly while the sound of the hand dryer and shower muffle all but the repeated *thud* of Wally forearms pounding against the wall. "Sounds like he needs help," Guy says, and he is coughing, too, as he motions Ted out the door. Ted scurries away, and Guy leans against the closed door, gasping for air. It sounds to workers passing by like their CFO is weeping.

"Look," says Guy when Wally pushes open the bathroom door. "What are you waiting for? It's time to grab him by the short and curlies, before he gets a chance to cause any more trouble up north."

Wally wipes his eyes with the back of his hand and says, "Guy, think."

Guy settles back into his chair, pulls at his earring, and purses his lips. This is a posture he's learned for the rare occasions he can't read Wally's mind. A moment of silence is followed by the sixty-four-thousand-dollar question. "You want him to cause trouble? I don't get it."

* * *

TED has long since planted the seeds of betrayal among the members of the River Board. Now, however, having been dismissed early, he takes the time to try his solicitor's cell. It may be time for the pubs to close in England, but Ted isn't drinking yet. It's time Merrifield earned his damn money.

"Tallyho, Yank!" shouts the Honourable William Merrifield III.

"Very funny, Merrifield. I'm not disturbing you, am I?"

"I've just lost me dart game, so you might as well have at it."

"I'm certain you can clear this up quickly, it's just a matter of interpretation of this contract from the Cheswitt Trust. It says in-laws are to reside in the family house in Portsmouth for at least forty weeks of the year. I understand they want their grandson nearby, but as I read it, it appears that *I'm* required to be there for that time, too. I imagine it's something standard, for the females who marry in, to assure that mothers remain with their children, but, of course, my work is in Oxford. I can't possibly take this newly endowed chair if I'm out of the country shooting skeet in Bloody Fucking Wales with Fiona's father." Ted pauses, waiting for the solicitor to laugh or tell him he's right, but all he hears is the sinusy breathing of a man who's eager to get back to his next pint. "So anyhoo," Ted continues. "I just thought I'd clear it up rather than wait the weekend."

"Did you think you were getting sixty thousand pounds a year for bloody naught?" asks the solicitor.

"Of course not. But surely they understand any man worth his salt, he must have his own profession."

"I don't think they care about salt, man. They want their daughter nearby. End of story."

"But why would they demand my presence? Surely I could fly up on weekends, with that sort of money."

"Why would they demand your presence, man? Well, I could think of a reason or two, not the first of which is that some unscrupulous sorts might find it hard to honor the marriage vows when they're off the bloody premises."

"That's insane!"

"No one ever said the rich were anything but. But look at it this way, there's a sizable grammar school in Portsmouth. You might be able to get on there as a lecturer just to keep your hand in."

* * *

TED is standing at the counter of StockTraders Limited. The money he has made on Gold Industries' price surge, after leaking news of the buyout, has long since been placed in the Bahamian bank account, but now it's time to up the ante. The poetic justice of Ted's being able to make money again when the stock falls, it's too perfect for words. It would almost be enough to make the trip worthwhile. And so, impatient as always, Ted is placing another order.

"Now, you sure you know what selling short means?" Lech asks Ted. "You borrow the shares and sell at today's price, before you buy them. Then you hope the stock goes down and you can buy it at a price lower than you sold so you can repay the bank. The problem is, this stock's been pretty stable. If you look at this chart on share price, it shows a steady upward progression."

"Well, the bigger they are, the saying goes," Ted mutters, copying his address into the written form.

"It goes down, you're in like Flynn, but that's a huge *if*."

Ted shakes his head. "Thank you, young man, but I'm not in need of instruction at your hands. Now if you don't mind, place the order. I've got miles to go before I sleep."

Sixteen

Dolores sticks hot-pink Naughty Nelly's flyers under the wipers of parked cars at the Superstition Mall. Though she can't wait tables any longer, Mike, her boss, has insisted she stay on the payroll so she can keep her health insurance. Mike doesn't expect anything for this kindness, but Dolores needs to do something to repay him. Besides, when she has episodes of feeling okay, it's better to stay busy. Working a rhythm, Dolores breathes deep and tries to use the monotony as a means of escape.

Today at the AA meeting, the one in Mesa, far from her old stomping grounds, Dolores almost came apart with a longing to rewrite the past, to have gotten sober years before she actually did. Here she is, finally clean, after so many years of failing at it, and then cancer takes away her future, well, such is life, which no one ever promised would be fair. This she knows. Most days, she'd have made a joke about it, using her black humor and pessimism to ward off disappointment, but today Dolores has been ambushed by the windswept sadness of saying goodbye. For so long she has worked to keep her feelings under wraps, protective, or so she has hoped. To-day, though, at that meeting, when that young father told about his little boy drowning in the slip of time it took to fetch a beer, Dolores was faced with the memory of her own failures. After locking her-self up so tight, something had snuck in, just for a second. Long enough for Dolores to be sucker-punched, crippled by regret that she'd not been strong enough to quit drinking, even as she knew she'd had to do what she'd done instead, remove herself from a place where she might—in making promises she couldn't keep— obliterate all that she held dear in the world. Better to say goodbye than end up like that young man, who may not be drinking right now, but who will never, ever erase the scars that alcohol has made, not for him, not for his poor wife, and for the child that loved them. *There, for but the grace of God, go I,* Dolores tells herself, but even then, knowing she has dodged a bullet, she cannot begin to forgive herself for all the things she has so recklessly thrown away.

* * *

EVERY Tuesday, as long as Audrey's known him, Guy has gone to the shooting range. What started out as a public relations move had turned into something else, not that Guy'd ever admit it. Teaching kids from the *barrio* gun safety was a no-brainer, he'd say, dismissing the work it had taken to get Know Your Firearm accredited with the local schools. With free transportation provided by the NRA, and free ammunition from Gold Industries, the course was a bestseller in the homeboy crowd. Maybe it had saved a life or two, over the years, he'd say, when pressed by Wally to take credit for his volunteerism.

Audrey pulls into the parking lot just as Guy's leaving his five-thirty class. He's covered with sweat, which drips down from his forehead in little rivulets, landing on the hood of his car as he bends to open the trunk. "Hey!" he shouts, spotting Audrey. "Change your mind after all this time?"

Audrey shakes her head. "Not in this lifetime. Can I talk to you?"

"Can you talk to me!" he laughs. "Not without giving me a kiss. You wanna go inside where it's cooler?"

"No, I just want to get legal advice on something."

"Sweetie, you in trouble?" he asks, leaning against the door of his car.

Audrey sits down on the curb in front of him and looks up at him, her chin on her fists. "No. Just, see, it's kind of a long story."

Guy wipes his brow with the towel he's extracted from the trunk and squats down to settle next to her on the curb. Their heads swim back at them in the shiny blue metal door of the Mustang. Audrey shows her godfather the letter from Ted's solicitor.

Guy's lips appear to retract into his teeth as he reads, then reads again. "Does your dad know about this?" he asks, avoiding Audrey's puzzled expression. "Did you show it to him?" presses Guy, knowing the last thing Wally needs is a damsel in distress when he is already up a tree and the dogs are nipping at his heels.

"No."

Audrey finds herself unaccountably irritated by Guy's question. Of all he could have said to her, she didn't expect him to jump off the subject and ask about her dad. Does he not *get* what's being done to Diana and her kids? "I can't count on my dad for any-thing."

"Audrey, don't let me hear you talk like that."

"Look!" Audrey says, her eyes welling up as she digs her chin into her knees. "My dad promised me things. This park, it's just gonna heap more crap onto to the synthetic shithole we've already made of the planet and why? So he can tell himself he's building a monument to my mom? That's what makes no sense! How can he do this in her name? She'd have hated that place he's planning."

"Sweetie. Listen. Your dad doesn't have control over this any-more. He's got to do what's workable, what the money men will loan him money for. He lost a lot in the market this year and every-thing he's got is sunk into that land. He owes taxes and all kinds of stuff. Unless you want to see him lose his shirt, you gotta under-stand. No one's gonna lend him the money to finish the project without it making a profit. They're not gonna invest in a pipe dream."

"It's not a pipe dream! It could work."

"Sweetie. You gotta listen to me here. Your dad loves you. You think he's trying to disappoint you?"

"Feels like it to me."

Guy shakes his head. He takes Audrey's chin and pulls it to look at him, like he used to when she was five and not listening. "Let me tell you something. A few days ago he spent three hours with his company's board of directors, trying to talk them into not selling the business, but instead letting him use the company's assets to build a place up in Dreamy Draw that you'd have felt better about. He brought in that friend of yours, Boy Face, and that lady with the grey hair, the one I can't stand."

"He had Elizabeth there? And Baby Face?"

"He'd clock me for telling you. Especially since the board turned him down. For the first time since he's been in business. He made a fool of himself for nothing, all because he cares so much about you."

At the look on Audrey's face, Guy winces. "Oh, shit, honey, I didn't mean that way. But see, he's spent his credibility now. Even his own board members think he's gone off the deep end. They think it's better for the company to sell, and even if they didn't, they can't drop their fiduciary responsibility by letting him use pub-licly held assets to build the next Shangri-la. Not when the alterna-tive is a tried-and-true, out-of-the-box, themed entertainment park with proven profit margins and a quick turnover. Once it's built, he can flip it, pay off the debt, and figure out what to do with his life. Really, sweetie, he's between a rock and a hard place on this one."

"But this makes no sense at all. He—they—wait, I just thought of something." Despite herself, Audrey is lifted by her excitement. She turns around and squats to face Guy, grabbing him by the knees. "Listen! If the Colorado River Protection Accord passed, no way can he build the tried-and-true, out-of-the-box AstroTurf nightmare. Just the water use alone! His committee would have to change their mind."

Guy's pitying look is more than Audrey can bear. "What?" she asks, though her inflection doesn't rise to the interrogative. It's not really a question, not with the look on Guy's face.

"Sweetie, that vote—it's never gonna go anyplace. Never has. Never will."

"I wouldn't be so sure of that. I hear there's new support for it up north," Audrey says. "I wish my dad could use his influence with these people."

Guy knows more than he wants about Wally's influence, but he will not say so to Audrey. He will not tell her that her father's just spent two nights in the past week taking a bunch of Indians out on the town. Guy would bet his left nut, it's not on account of them being Audrey's long-lost ancestors. Hell, Wally's hasn't even told Guy why he's spending so much time talking to the tribes' representatives on the River Board. When he heard about the meetings, Guy had volunteered to go instead of Wally, do the dirty work of persuading the Indians to play ball, but Wally had insisted he be the one, and that he go alone. No way he's gonna want his daughter in on that little tidbit. The tribal council has four votes on the board, and if they play along, like Guy's pretty certain they will, having been cultivated up the wazoo, then the proposition is dead in the water. So to speak. He's never known Wally to pull this political crap before, but then again, he's never seen Wally in this kind of trouble, either.

Well, at least not since Vietnam, which had been a different kind of trouble. Come to think of it, that duty had inspired the same kind of hunched and haunted look that Wally'd been wearing the past few weeks. At least back then, though, Guy's best friend had had the satisfaction of knowing his strategies came to something in the end, keeping his friends alive. To say nothing of making fools of those idiots at the Officers' Club. They never did know who'd pulled the wool over their eyes, and Wally was the last guy they'd suspect. Mr. Marshmallow would play the fool as long as it took, as long as it worked, knowing that in the end, success was the best revenge.

* * *

By the time Ted arrives at Naughty Nelly's, Kristen's into her third Harvey Wallbanger. It's her day off, but she's come in for a drink with her favorite regular, who just happens to rep for a drug company. Nick is long gone now, having dashed off to coach his son's Little League team after a quick blow job in the screening room, for which Kristen had been tipped three Xanax and a Percoset, thank you very much.

"Mhah" is all she can say when her neck is nuzzled by none other than the overly handsome Englishman that Dolores comped her for.

"We meet again," Ted whispers, licking the tickle spot on her collarbone.

"Mhah."

"Any chance of a rendezvous? *Avec vous?*"

"How about a ride home?" asks Kristen. "The smell of a cab right now would not work for me. How you doin'?"

"Very well, thanks. And you, my minx?"

"Three sheets, baby. Three sheets."

Ted nods knowledgeably, though he hasn't understood a word

she's said. Kristen's wearing a demure white peasant top, a short red skirt, and a pair of red mules. Her red hair is plaited in a loose braid that dangles past the edge of her barstool. "Shall we?" he asks, tugging playfully on the braid.

"Mhah," Kristen murmurs, for the Xanax is kicking in. The Englishman's looking better and better. "Only if you promise not to tie me up," she pouts, jumping onto her shoes and prancing out the door, where Ted's convertible Caprice awaits in the stark sunlight.

*   *   *

HUMPHREY, parked a safe distance away, presses the zoom lens and watches as they get into the car.

"What did I tell you?" Audrey whispers. "He's a trip, is he not?"

"Rhymes with," mutters Humphrey, pressing the camera's Stop button as he puts the Le Sabre into gear and folds into traffic behind his stepfather's car.

Audrey pulls the camera from Humphrey's lap. "Look, maybe they'll play kissy-face while they're on the road." She aims the lens at the back of Ted's head, which remains remarkably steady, despite the gyrations of his passenger, who has changed the radio station to rap and is writhing to the sound of the bass while her beautiful white shoulders rise out of her drawstring neckline.

"I don't know. Looks like 'unsuitable behavior' to me," says Audrey as Ted drives into the private entrance for McClintock Ranch Luxury Apartments. The Caprice is stopped at the gate, music off, until the guard spots Kristin and waves the car through.

Audrey continues to film while Ted turns over the engine and nods back at the guard before jolting forward. "We got him."

Humphrey shakes his head. "No, he can just say he's a Good Samaritan, giving the poor stranger a ride home. P'raps we should head back to that bar and take a look at what's happening inside, though."

* * *

Now it is Ted's turn to say "Mhah." Kristen has stripped to her thong and bra and is reaching her hand into his pants pockets.

"Hey, sweetie, let's just get the payment out of the way and then we can take you where you want to go."

"Payment?" asks Ted. "I thought you cared about me?"

"Hon, you're a total fox. But a girl needs shoes, if you know what I mean."

"But last time?" moans Ted, who's been carrying the same hundred-dollar bill in his pocket for the last three weeks without breaking it.

"Last time Dolores comped you, but—shit!" Kristen winces at the look of surprise on Ted's face.

Kristen may have the mores of a cat, but her affection for Dolores, whom she's known for years, is genuine.

"Who's that?"

"Nobody."

"No. Tell me," murmurs Ted, pincering Kristen's arms and pinning her against the bed.

"Look, it's nobody."

"If it's nobody, why does it matter if you tell me?"

Kristen, in her chemically enriched state, cannot see her way around the logic of Ted's question. "Just a friend."

"And why would she give me such a generous gift?"

"She didn't say."

"Come now, think," says Ted, reaching down with his pointed tongue to palpate Kristen's nipple through her red lace cup.

"Look, she's rich. She just works at Nelly's for fun. So it's not a lot of money to her."

"And have I had the pleasure of making her acquaintance?"

"How should I know?"

Ted pulls Kristen's arms up above her head, where he holds both hands in one fist and uses the other to unclasp the front of her bra. "What does she look like, this Dolores?"

"You mean, now? Or before?"

"Ah, naughty Kristen, riddle wench. Speak the King's English, won't you?"

"Dolores's had some nips and tucks since I first met her. She's like, a whole different person now."

"Attractive?"

"Let's put it this way. She lost about twenty years and twenty pounds since she started seeing a certain surgeon in Scottsdale."

"Does she dance at the club then?" asks Ted.

"Up to a while ago."

"Oh, how have I missed her? I'll have to return and thank her for her generosity."

"Don't you dare! Please don't tell her."

"Now, Kristen, if a man hasn't his manners, he's lost."

"Look! I'll do you free. Dolores's—I promised I wouldn't say nothing. Please? Please?"

"It's a start. But let's do this as well, my sweet. Tell me everything you know about the enchanting Dolores, both before and after her metamorphosis. And which Scottsdale surgeon did you say did the work?"

* * *

KRISTEN can feel the regret in her mouth when she wakes.

Spilling her friend's guts faster than a three-dollar beer, Kristen had suddenly realized the Englishman's threat to tell Dolores, it didn't hold water. The boss had already said Dolores wasn't coming back to work, so how was he gonna find her, anyway? Oh why had she been so fucked up? She hadn't mentioned Valeen, or told him where she and Dolores lived, but she'd said too much. Years ago

Kristen had sworn up and down, after a shared bottle of Jose Cuervo, that she'd never tell a soul what Dolores had confessed, about the deals you could make with a million bucks in offshore bank accounts. Course, maybe Dolores would forgive her. Hell, she knew better than anybody: Nothing unlocks the vault like a fix your whole body craves, day and night. The hunger and relief, it turns you into someone you'd rather not be, but know you are hurtling towards, at the speed of slow-fucking-motion.

Those were the days, highflying days, before Valeen started at Nelly's and got Dolores to AA. Now Dolores swears up and down about those meetings: *You have to give them a chance, Kristen. I only wish I knew then what I know now, but it's water under the bridge, or a river of vodka, maybe, ha! But it's never too late to try, sweetie-pie. Never. Look at me, taking it easy, a day at a time, for almost eighteen months and counting, and if only I'd known then what I know now, I'd have changed everything.*

Kristen rolls over and digs her hand inside her pillow, where a Baggie holds the last remaining Xanax. She uses her nails to pincer it out and drop it on her tongue, closing her eyes with the same sweet sorrow as a communicant who's neglected to make her required confession but seeks the grace of a forgiving God, who's she's hoping like hell isn't as nitpicky as everyone's cracked Him up to be.

* * *

PRESSING down on the intercom button, Wally clears his throat. "I'm back, Bev. Send Lively in, will you?"

"He's just stepped out for lunch. Can't wait to see the expense form on that one."

"Bring him in when he gets back, will you?"

"With pleasure. Listen, that reporter from the *New York Times*, he's called you three times. I'm running out of excuses."

"Refresh my memory."

"Guy by the name of Tom Peterson. Seemed to know a lot about your plans."

"Like what?"

"Like fast-food architects might be doin' the work."

"Ow. Maybe he talked to Guy?"

"He talked to somebody," Bev says darkly. "But Guy never heard a' him."

"Look. Google him for me."

"Printed out and on your desk."

"You're amazing."

"Don't I know it? Listen. You might want to think twice about talking to this guy."

"Because?"

"You'll see when you read some of the articles he's written. Not exactly a friend to developers. Let's just put it this way: When he was asking about this idea of an air-conditioned water park, he didn't sound like he was ready to get in on the ground floor a' investors."

"Okay. Thanks for the heads-up. That's the kind you *want* to talk to. Maybe I can change his mind."

"Yeah. And maybe pigs will fly and your Englishman will decide to pull that pencil out a' his butt and join the human race."

* * *

ON his way back to the office, Ted rings his lovely Fiona, who rings her father, who recommends an information broker capable of discreet investigations in the United States. Within twenty minutes Ted has the broker on the phone, defining his parameters: all patients named Dolores treated at the Scottsdale Plastic Surgery Clinic, aged thirty-eight or older.

An hour later Ted's mobile phone rings at his desk.

"We've found five women named Dolores who had work done.

One, a woman with the last name of Johnson, had several operations, beginning, let's see, just about three years ago."

"How old is she?"

"Well, from the date of birth, let me see. She'd be forty-three or so."

"How delightful. You've got my e-mail, don't you?"

"The Hotman one?"

"That's it. I'm booting up now."

"Listen, I can send you a summary on my cell phone text messager. I'm on my way to Vegas for a conference. Or I can have one of the other consultants go in and pull the records, but that'll cost you their hourly, too."

"Oh come now. At what I'm paying, I'd have thought—"

"Look, mister, I did the rush job for free, and I got you the information you wanted."

"Still."

"Look, I'll give you ten percent off the price we agreed on, if you just wait until Friday for the actual records. In the meantime, you'll have my text message summary."

"Make it fifteen percent," Ted pushes, never one to pass up a bargain.

* * *

When Beverly ushers Ted into Wally's office, round three o'clock, he's looking every bit the cat that ate the golden canary, though Beverly notes with pleasure his slow, tentative descent into the chair across from Wally. Maybe not a pencil, she thinks, but something is definitely orbiting Uranus.

"To what do I owe the honour?" asks Ted.

"Look. Cut the shit. I just talked to a reporter from the *New York Times*. Seems someone here sent him a copy of the videodisc from the consultants and other confidential documents."

Ted coughs and starts to speak.

Throwing a purple videodisc across the table, Wally cuts him off. "Look, I'm gonna make this simple. You'll do what you're told from now on."

"What's this?" asks Ted.

"Footage of you and a lady with red spike heels, though it's mostly you. And more of you than I ever wanted to see."

"What?"

"Peterson's not the only person in possession of incriminating video. Let's just say that the next time you get naked, dump the black socks. It's not a good look."

"I—don't know what you're talking about."

"Let's put it this way. You're in a tub, getting a Golden Shower. Memory refreshed?"

"What!"

"Look, I'd rather not go into it. But see for yourself. I made extra copies. You can keep this one."

"You wouldn't—" Ted swallows. "You wouldn't expose Diana to this, would you?"

Wally's eyes narrow. He shakes his head and can barely think, blind to everything except his disgust. "Oh, it's your wife you care about!"

"Of course I do."

Wally nods, dipping his head towards his neck in that over-played credulity that accompanies disbelief. "Look. I don't believe a word you say. Basically, if your lips are moving, you're lying. But you're in luck. I'm not going to let Diana find out about it. She's got enough heartbreak living with you on a daily basis. But let me tell you something. In two weeks, if I don't have a doctor's report that you're clear of VD, *and* my investigator's report that you've stopped cheating on her, then your brush with water sports is getting overnighted to President Bernard, with a retraction of the Gold Industries endowment. Guy checked the paperwork. There's a clause where gross moral turpitude is sufficient reason to revoke the gift."

It's Ted's turn to blink. He has squirmed to the edge of his chair. "Is that it, then? You might want to know, before you cast the first stone, that Diana has—that we haven't—I haven't enjoyed my conjugal rights in months. I hardly think I can be blamed for seeking solace—"

"Whatever you say, buddy: Your lips are moving. And no, by the way, that's not 'it' at all. I also want you to stop standing in your wife's way. I want you to support her for once."

"You're pathetic, you know. I think the last thing Diana would want—"

"Look. I can't even sit and listen to you say her name. But know this. I've hired the best private eye in the state and he's watching you. You do one thing to hurt her, or this project, and I'll send the disk on to President Bernard."

"How am I to know you won't send it later?"

"You don't. But look at it this way. If you don't do what I say, you're definitely out of luck. As long as Diana and your kids are happy, I'm happy, too. The only reason you're staying here at all is that they're on a derivative visa. So straighten up and fly right. Your first assignment is to go home and tell your wife how grateful you are for all she's sacrificed for you, when you didn't even deserve it."

"Look. Diana will not believe—"

"Hey buddy. This isn't negotiable. You want this endowed chair, you're gonna stop being such a prick and start treating her like a queen. If I see any sign you haven't, then the whole faculty and Board of Trustees or whatever you have over there, they'll get a FedEx of this performance of yours faster'n you can say 'pink slip.' Now get out of here before I have to hurt you."

* * *

SKYGYRL: You on, Sigi?

COMPUTERSLEUTH: W'sup?

SKYGYRL: That last e-mail to Hotman, I can't open it. What's he doing now?

COMPUTERSLEUTH: Pulling some chick's medical records.

SKYGYRL: Is that possible?

COMPUTERSLEUTH: Anything's possible, you pay enough. It's just a summary he's got right now.

SKYGYRL: Summary.

COMPUTERSLEUTH: Yeah. I'll cut and paste it for you.

Summary of search for Ted Lively
Dolores Johnson, 43, five procedures in last 41 months.
Will run complete scan Friday a.m. for hard copy of records.

COMPUTERSLEUTH: Skygyrl? You there?

SKYGYRL: Sigi, I need you to do something for me NOW.

COMPUTERSLEUTH: Look, I'm leaving in like three minutes.

SKYGYRL: I've never asked you a favor like this, Sigi, but I'm on my way over right now. Whatever your hourly is, I'll triple it. I need you to get into those computers and fix the records.

COMPUTERSLEUTH: I don't think that's legal. Besides, you'd need a special scanner and such.

SKYGYRL: Call Office Supply on Thunderbird and order all the equipment you need. I'll pick it up on my way. And don't worry about legal: These records are ancient history. All we're gonna do is set the record straight.

Seventeen

William's class trip to the Desert Botanical Gardens will be followed by a Harvest Fest pool party at Austin Wilken's house. Despite their excitement about the party, the trip to the gardens is a cruel disappointment to most of the fourth-grade boys, who've lobbied Ms. Marsh unceasingly and unsuccessfully to switch the trip to the zoo. The Desert Dwellers exhibit alone—described in all its delicious glory by the plaintiffs—provides the imagination with a multitude of slow and painful ways to die. Besides, the nocturnal dusk of the caves in which the scorpions and rattlers are displayed provides the proper ambience to see who's chicken and who's brave enough to step up and look death in the eye. Adam has shared with William his strategy for not flinching when the inevitable sharp pinch arrives out of nowhere, but it doesn't matter now, because the buses have landed in the garden's parking lot and the doom of being forced to walk around and look at a bunch of stupid plants has settled in over the entire lot of stone-shuffling, downcast warriors.

William is careful to pretend he shares his mates' disengagement, but the truth is, he doesn't mind at all. For one thing, the Desert Dweller proponents have been such powerful witnesses that he's secretly relieved not to be forced to test his manhood in front of Austin and his cronies. For another, these desert plants he is seeing, they might as well be grown on the moon. They're nothing like what he's used to. William slows his steps a couple of feet behind Ms. Marsh, who's reading aloud from her guidebook. He feigns boredom but listens carefully, imagining he's an astronaut, seeking extraterrestrial understanding.

* * *

The century plant—which can be kept alive for decades—blooms only once in its lifetime, shortly before death. The plant, also known as an *Agave*, expends all of its resources in the creation of a flowering stalk, growing at a rate of a foot each day, culminating in a magnificent bloom that can rise to ten yards, or the height of a three-story building.

* * *

IN the shadow of the mountains known as the Superstition, in a bowl created by the face of a steep mountain and the band of expressway around it, a row of pink buildings provides shelter from the sun. In apartment 24B, the shades are drawn, the lights low.

Perched against the pillows, balancing a laptop against her raised knees and inhaling the scent of lavender candles with a deep breath that would do Valeen proud, Skygyrl is staring at the empty screen. After the long hours she'd spent with Sigi, Dolores knows she has done all she can. Finally her work is finished, just in time, for the pain has gotten severe. She will start the pain meds tomorrow, and after that, she'll be unable to trust herself to say the right thing. And she can't just disappear. Not again.

Her hands sit out over the keyboard, ready to tap out her thoughts, but her fingers are stuck in time, stuck in place.

Skygyrl loves Earthgyrl. That's all she wants to say. However, she cannot say it without falling apart. Worse she cannot say it because such sentiments are just not appropriate to a chat room buddy, even after three years and counting.

Dolores has taken pains to set a certain tone with Earthgyrl. Fond but distant. Stepping over that boundary would have dragged them into forbidden territory. Impulsive as she had once been known to be, she'd held steady on that pledge.

For this, if nothing else, she could take credit, for the will it had taken *not* to play surrogate mother had been harder than quitting drinking, harder than the painful surgeries, harder even than chemo.

Guess what! types Skygyrl, wiping her chin, drenched with tears and snot, with the back of her left hand. *You won't believe what's happened! I'm leaving for El Salvador tomorrow to work in an orphanage. The thing is, they won't have e-mail and I don't even know if they have snail mail. Maybe I'm just being sappy or maybe it's the Valium I took for the excitement, but I gotta tell you, in case I don't have another chance, Earthgyrl: You are something special. Your mom would have been so proud of you and I would bet your dad is so grateful over how super a gyrl you turned out to be. I never knew a kid as great as you, ever.*

Dolores wants to go on, she wants to touch her child with her letters, but she is afraid to get going, afraid to let herself relax. All of her suffering, and more important, all of her daughter's, it will be for nothing if she let's herself go now.

Audrey has bounced back. However bad it has been for her, Audrey's still alive. She's been spared some ugly scenes from the battle with booze, the one Mary Kate had completely given up hope of winning. By the time she really got with the program, she had already disappeared, winning the battle, losing the war. Everyone knew it was "a day at a time" and no guarantees.

Now, though, the day-at-a-time thing was starting to look iffy. *At least*, she had comforted herself, when she heard her bleak prognosis, *at least Audrey and Wally won't have to go through this*. For that truth, Mary Kate is glad. Even as she will never forgive herself for the death she engineered in the midst of despair, she cannot help but be grateful. At least their suffering's mostly done.

For all of these reasons, it has never been right for Mary Kate to return, despite her constant battle with the painful, shameful longing to hold her daughter again, and more important, to be forgiven. She knew Wally wouldn't have cared about the money she'd taken, he would have gotten over the surgeries he'd not wanted her to have, but had she returned, he'd have done the very worst thing. He'd have believed her again, welcomed her back, trusted her to be reliable, and that was something she'd proven wrong time and again. And if she'd gone back, even if she'd stayed sober, they'd be suffering now through this diagnosis with her instead of already being a good ways through their loss.

Mary Kate knows it's too late to change the past. But more and more, something has told her to try and set things right, at least as much as she can. Part of her awakening flicker of belief has come from seeing how everything has fallen into place, the things she'd never planned, but which have helped her feel she is leaving her daughter in good hands. What had started out as the impulse to help Wally come to terms with his grief, suggesting that trip to England, it had turned into so much more than she'd ever expected. His visit to Oxford had blossomed into something else, the possibility of marriage, a mother for Audrey, siblings, too. Now, this jerk of a professor, brought into the club by the flyers she'd placed on his car, was all that stood in her way. However, with a little luck, and Kristen's video footage, Ted Lively would be hurried back to Britain. Then Wally would have somebody he deserved, and Audrey, too. Something to distract them from the problems they'd run into with the park up north. For that disappointment, it looks like there's nothing Skygyrl can do, but at least they'd have people who care about them, who'll care of them.

Take care of yourself, types Dolores. The name she has gone by; it derives from *dolor*. It is Spanish for *pain* and *tears* and *loss*, and all that she has wreaked, not just for herself but for her beautiful daughter, her steadfast husband. *I'm sorry I'll be out of touch, but I'll think of you every day. Well, gotta go. Luv ya, Skygyrl.* Before she can take anything back, before she can worry whether the casual spelling of *love* and *you*, will save her from coming too close, Dolores mashes Send. She shuts down the computer, blows out the candle, and closes her eyes to rest.

* * *

Small cacti such as *Mammillaria* and *Coryphanta* burrow into the earth during drought or extreme cold and/or heat. This protective mechanism—with its inversion—reemergence once conditions improve—is thought to be an adaptive trait that allows for the tiny plants' survival.

* * *

"I don't want to leave you here," Humphrey whispers. Audrey sits next to him in the car, in the back of the Naughty Nelly's parking lot. She is looking particularly girlish in her Catholic school uniform, which they both agree isn't likely to admit them past the bouncer leaned against the sign that very clearly reads MUST BE OVER 21.

"I'll be fine. Why are you whispering?"

"Why not just run home and you can change? Then we can both go in."

"Nope. We both know if you don't go in there now, you won't do it."

"Is it that obvious?" asks Humphrey, blushing.

"Look. Don't be embarrassed. Let me mess your hair up a little. It looks too neat for a lowlife." Audrey reaches over and dives her hand into his heavy blond locks, savoring the excuse she has for touching any part of him, grazing his ear with her baby finger, caught up short by a sudden desire to pull him across the bucket seat and to kiss him hard, despite the pretty much constant internal yelling she is carrying on to Stop Wanting What You Cannot Have. His hair, she notices, is coarser than she'd have expected. Such is the level of her desperation that she takes this as a hopeful sign: like maybe soft equals gay, while coarse, hey, that's rougher. Maybe he's being transformed, her New Best Friend, pulsing with hormonal flux, a painless sex change of sorts, a metamorphosis that can continue over time. One day he'll abhor housework and take up wilderness marathons and cigar competitions. Of course, that would only mean that he'd no longer be the Humphrey she is so very much wanting to kiss, so what is the point? Audrey sighs, lost in her own little labyrinth of speculation.

Her sigh, the emotiveness of which its author is completely unaware, releases in Humphrey his own flurry of wishful thinking. Audrey's intake of breath and quick release, a mouth that opens like honeysuckle, closes like milkflower, is so close and still so very far. Impatience with this line of fantasy, a constant background noise in Humphrey's ever-expanding *mise-en-scène* of unrequited attraction, prompts him to firmly grasp the girl's hand, gently ungrip it from the knot of hair she's been clutching, and set it back into her lap of plaid and pleated wonder.

"Lock the doors," he warns, before loping through the parking lot as fast as he can towards the heavily scratched door, towards the heavily muscled and balding bouncer whose T-shirt reads MAKE MY DAY, and whose grotesque forearms are crossed like swords in defense of his rippled abdomen and the city's fairest babes.

Humphrey extracts his wallet and concentrates on fishing a twenty-dollar bill from its recesses, all the better to avoid meeting the man's eyes, but a hairy hand waves his money away and the bouncer opens the door. "No cover before five. You stay longer, you gotta pay on the way out. And keep your hands to yourself. Got it?"

Humphrey nods and slinks into the first seat he can find. He prays to be ignored until he can get his bearings in this dark cavern where shapes are slowly assuming human form. As his pupils adjust, a wood nymph appears to ask if he'd like one of the chocolate martini specials. "Certainly" says Humphrey, whose acquaintance with alcohol is limited to sips of his mother's wine during dinner and an occasional glass of champagne on holiday. It's not until the girl returns, bearing an oversized triangular chalice, that Humphrey can see well enough to note that certain leaf petals of her tunic are for the plucking, the price for which is stamped in $1's, $5's, $10's, and $20's.

Humphrey dips his mouth towards the pool of dark nectar, careful not to slurp or wince as he sips its bittersweet taste. On the stage a stripper is slowly removing her French maid's apron, her eyes downcast in a highly convincing parable of shyness. Humphrey's eyes are glued to the exquisitely dimpled white skin between the hem of her skirt and the black border of her fishnet stockings. When the maid looks up and meets his stare, he looks into his glass and brings it up to tip quickly down his throat. He'd expected the women here to be older, more Ted's age. Tawdry. He'd expected to be disgusted.

Instead he cannot take his eyes from the girl on stage as she fumbles with the buttons of her bodice, torturing the audience with her slow, slow dance. The wood nymph appears, bearing a second drink, and Humphrey slurps it down without waiting. He knows this quickening he feels, this sudden warmth and urgency when the stripper removes her bra, this hunger puts him in a category of men like Ted, whom he cannot admire. Even as he castigates himself for the erection he has not summoned, even as he pays the bill and leaves without finding (or even seeking) the information for which he'd come, Humphrey holds his head high and hobbles towards the waiting car. Two chocolate martinis and an inescapable awakening have forced upon him another sort of knowledge, a truth that drives him to a joyful distraction. He knocks on the glass, startling Audrey from sleep. When she opens the door, he slides in on her side of the car, arches his spine over her waking body, and covers her petal-soft mouth with his own.

* * *

A Lewis Carroll poem, "Hunting of the Snark" gave the Boojum tree its name. Indigenous to Mexico, the boojum is fuller at the bottom and sparser at the top, like a huge parsnip, causing people to call it an "upside-down tree."

* * *

WHEN Audrey walks into her father's office, Beverly rises from her chair and circles around her desk to greet her. "Well, look who the cat drug in! What happened to your face, honey? Is that windburn?"

Audrey raises her palm to her cheek. Her swollen mouth pulls into a sheepish and unconvincing frown. She giggles, caught up in the sensation of Humphrey's mouth on hers. "Is it really bad?"

"Nah," Beverly murmurs. "But you might want to put some Maybelline on those hickeys."

"I—Jesus!" blurts Audrey, fumbling in her purse. "I didn't—" She whips out a small hand mirror and takes a quick look. "I think I'm allergic to something!" she wails, somewhere between laughing and crying.

"Hey," murmurs Beverly, giving Audrey a fierce hug. Since the secretary is not quite five feet tall, she collides with Audrey's chin. This sets both of them off again. "You okay, honey?"

"Fine." Audrey brings her palm up to her cheek. "I need to talk to my dad."

"He's got someone in there right now."

"You know anything about this rumor he's using treated wood for the walkways in the park? I just got this weird phone call from Mr. Lively."

Beverly shakes her head. "You want to wait till his meeting's done?" Beverly says, lifting the lid off a large ceramic elephant. "Here, have a Moon Pie."

Audrey, suddenly starving, reaches out, but when her father's door swings open suddenly, it's Wally and Elizabeth Stanton who look like they've been caught stealing from the cookie jar. Audrey's chin whips into full outraged tilt. There is a check in Elizabeth Stanton's fingers, which might be explained away, if it weren't for the sheepish expression on the EARTHCARE director's face. Audrey's mouth falls open and she doesn't know who to be more disappointed in, her dad or her role model.

She nods, getting it, getting all of it. "Oh, sorry to interrupt," she swallows. "I should have known you'd find a way to get around doing the right thing," she says to Wally, who is standing there with his lips pulled back toward his ears and his eyes pleading with his daughter to understand.

Elizabeth winces. "Audrey, it's not what you think."

"Right."

"Honey, I'm getting trouble over costs. I can't—"

"But that's the thing. You can. You didn't even try talking to Humphrey's mom." Audrey can't help but notice her father and Elizabeth's quick exchange of guilty looks. She can't help but wonder how much her father has had to pay Stanton to back off on the River Board protests. Or was he already hedging his bets, banking on Liz's position as the token environmentalist? Would she help him find a loophole, just in case the legislation squeaked through after all?

"Honey," explains Wally. "I got a board to please. "They're not gonna accept—they want tried and true. I gotta have a plan that'll make sense to them."

"See, Audrey—" Elizabeth interrupts, who cannot bear the hurt in Audrey's eyes. "I'm working on something—"

"Oh, don't bother explaining. I get it. Loud and clear."

With that, Audrey runs out the back door, gets in her van, and peels out of the lot so fast that her father puts his hands together, makes one large fist and knocks himself in the forehead.

"Have you not bothered to tell her anything?" asks Beverly, swatting her boss on the side of his head.

Wally ducks out of his secretary's reach. "Look, she's had too many disappointments already. Look, Elizabeth, you need a ride to the airport? And are you sure I gave you enough—?"

"I'm sure. Don't worry. I've done all this before, believe it or not."

* * *

The *Ferrocactus* is shaped like a barrel. Named from the Latin word for "ferocious" for its treacherous spines, the barrel cactus shrinks and expands with the supply and demand of water. Although myth has it that this succulent can provide drinking water to a thirsty wanderer, beware of its bitter pulp, which is often toxic.

* * *

THE Stocktrader's Limited branch is a bit out of Ted's way, but if he rushes, he can just make it before closing. Today's e-mails alone would more than make up the cost of the BlackBerry, even if he'd had to buy it out of his own pocket, but of course that wouldn't be necessary. That slag, Beverly, forced to accept any and all expenses by her fool of an employer, has just confided the ominous news that Huntington Incorporated is unwilling to supply written confirmation of their prior tender offer. "What could it mean? You don't think they're backing out? I got all my retirement in the company's stock plan."

Ted had almost felt sorry for her, but not sorry enough to suggest she sell out but quick. That would have taken time. Besides, people like that, they didn't have expenses. From the photos on her desk, he knew she had grown children. She could move in with them and make herself useful, helping with the grandslags.

Ted's broker is rolling down his shirtsleeves when Ted presents him with the buy order to cover his short sale of Gold Industries. "Look, I'd appreciate it if you'd execute this before you leave tonight. In case you get hit by a lorry," Ted jokes.

Lech isn't laughing. "Mr. Lively, the market's closed already."

"Yes, but computer trading is still accepting orders. I just want to make sure the order's placed, one less thing to think about."

"You'll have to enter it for the market price. Otherwise, you can't be sure it'll hit what you're hoping to buy it at, " Lech says, scanning the order form and then punching buttons on his computer to get to the screen he needs. "In fact, right now it's still at thirty-nine and they've got a tender offer for forty. No way you'll get it for thirty-five."

Ted deliberates a moment. If he waits until tomorrow, there's a chance he could make even more, but on the other hand, he's got too much to do to leave a detail like this up in the air.

"Look, I'm going to be rather tied up tomorrow. Put a limit order in for thirty-five and then, if it hasn't dropped to that by noon, sell at market. Even if it stays at thirty-nine, since I sold at forty, I'll make a profit."

"Hey, why don't you wait till tomorrow and see?"

Ted, who has no patience with advice from the undereducated, shakes his head brusquely.

"No, I'm afraid that won't be possible. I'm leaving the country. I just want this *finit*. The bird in the hand and all that."

"Okay, just sign this here, showing I advised you of the risks." Lech sets up the screen with the required information. Ted signs, hands the paper to Lech with a flourish.

Two clicks later Lech has executed the order and planned his script for the next commission. "Well, listen, you want to make some quick money, I got a tip just now that's very hot."

"I doubt that."

"Look, I'm being nice telling you this. I just got off the phone. A group upstate votes tonight on a law that would mandate stricter construction standards for any new development on the Colorado River. Do you realize how much land that is? The thing is, no one's predicted this. This group's been deadlocked for years. Now, though, word is, they might have enough votes to pass the damn thing." Lech peers at Ted, waiting for the news to sink in, but Ted seems unimpressed.

"You don't get it, do you?" Lech urges, holding his hands apart as if to clap Ted's thin head between it. "That's like Princeton beating Florida State in football. Imagine you had that tidbit before the bets were placed."

"I did, young Lech," Ted says triumphantly. "Let's just say, I may have dribbled the ball for Princeton."

"That's basketball, not football." Lech laughs, unaware of soccer terminology and Ted's Anglocentric lens for conversation. "But listen, there's money to be made if you can get in on the ground floor. See, there's only one company that makes the new products they'll need—"

"Young Lech. I know that here in Arizona, such things as a river governance structure for a local province might seem momentous.

But I highly doubt the rest of your benighted countrymen will even notice."

"No, but they will. That's eight states who gotta comply with whatever they say. My uncle Fritz works for Bear-Stearns up in New York, and he just called me to say the *Wall Street Journal* and the *New York Times* both carried 'turning tide' stories this morning."

"And your point?"

"Even a chance this might pass, and it'll get serious ink in the financial pages. The company that makes these new products, their stock'll go sky high. Nobody's connected the dots on this yet but I'm telling you, the share price'll go from the China to Mars. My uncle just put in an order for a quarter million shares. So, you wanna roll your profits into a buy?"

"No, I'm afraid not. But let me ask you. Just a hypothetical. Let's say a certain CEO of a certain company, whose stock is already falling because his corporate suitor has jilted him at the altar, let's say his plans for expansion are adversely impacted by these new environmental rules. How might that affect his ability to borrow money against his company to embark on said expansion?"

"Is that a rhetorical question or what?"

"No, I'm serious."

"I'd say he's upstream without a paddle. Maybe without a boat. Hell, he's SOL. The whole river's gone dry!" laughs Lech, proud of his extended metaphor.

"You know, on second thought, maybe I'll sell short on more of Gold Industries, at today's price, and then I'll buy it back tomorrow. A setback like this should cut the market's confidence in his abilities enough to bring it down even more!"

"You don't have a margin account, do you?"

"No, but I have resources. Let me call my fiancée and you'll have all the surety you need. Never fear."

* * *

Desert plants are remarkably adaptive. Agaves, for example, can produce seeds, or plantlets, that fall to the ground, or they can create genetic clones of themselves, otherwise known as vegetative offsets. These "pups," having dropped off, usually grow in a circle around the parent. The "jumping cholla," on the other hand, will hitch a ride on a passing animal or appear to leap from the parent plant, forming a new root by which to grow.

* * *

WILLIAM and Adam are holding their own against Austin Wilken and three of his cronies. The boys are fighting for control of a large plastic raft positioned under the fake rock bridge that rises over the middle of the Wilkens' lagoon-shaped pool. William kicks from behind and holds on to the raft while Adam, at the other end, is clenching handholds and kicking in front of him.

Austin, William has observed with no small gratitude, has a generous dimpled belly that presses over his tight elasticized Ocean Pacific Jams. Better yet, the boy has obviously applied some sort of instant tanning bronzer, which is coming off in swaths, like shoe polish. "Come and get me, faggot!" shouts Austin, running around the peak of the bridge and throwing a hidden cache of water balloons at the boys.

"Sorry, Austin. You're just not my type," laughs Adam, flicking his hand up to catch a large purple blob. "Hideyho!" he cries, sending the balloon easily back over the top of the bridge before he and William cast off towards smoother waters.

Austin, annoyed at having so little effect, crawls up on top of the bridge and dives off to splash next to William in the water. Tugging at William's feet, Austin tries to pull him away, but

William holds steady. Austin's friends dive from the bridge and relieve their leader so he can clamber onto the raft. At the moment of his victory, Austin heaves one leg over the top and lets out a humongous water-logged fart.

All of the boys are so giddy, so stunned by nature's miracle, that when William begins to woof "Who let the dogs out?" all the boys—even Austin—cannot help but be disarmed. They shout with giddy laughter, rising out of the water to drown William's British tones with their own Western twang.

It is then that William experiences the hand of God on the small of his back, the same God that has saved him from Year Five at school. He cannot help but sing louder "Who let the Dogs Out? Woof, woof!" and all of the boys, even Austin, greet his witticism with delighted barks of laughter, pure and simple.

* * *

Caterpillar Cacti are also called *Creeping Devils*. As the stems of these plants creep forward, their tentacles take new root, crisscrossing with the stems of fellow creeping devils. Thus the colony—a dense network of interrelated stems—moves ahead. Such progress, however, comes at a price, since as the front of the plant gains ground, inch by inch over the course of a year, the living cells at the rear guard are left to die.

* * *

Ted drums his fingers on the steering wheel, waiting at the red light, a new enthusiast of Pooty Tang M.D. He is nodding his head and uttering affirmatives with ghetto inflection. Should one of his colleagues happen to catch sight of him, they would not recognize the Fellow they've learned to tolerate these many terms. Nor would he appear to them as hunted, haunted, or any of the other adjectives that might apply to a man who's just been served with such notice as Wally had so recently shown himself capable of giving.

Why? these venerable scholars might ask themselves, is Lively thrusting his chin towards the dash with such rhythmic vigor, when he's just been caught on screen with his knickers down and unfortunate black socks aloft?

After certain facts have had a chance to percolate, Ted has been visited by the realization that he, not Wally, is in possession of the keys to the kingdom. The beautiful Dolores, enchantress of the strip club, is she not a troubling reminder of all that Wallace Gold has tried so hard to forget? Ted hasn't yet laid eyes on the woman, but Kristen's rambles and the medical records have provided necessary if not sufficient evidence that all was not as it had seemed in the sad, sad demise of the former Mrs. Gold. Happily, it is the mysterious Dolores's abiding interest in all things Camelot—mentioned only in passing by Kristen—that has pointed Ted in the right direction. Unlike the Arthurian tales, however, which sought to transform the mundane into the sublime, this modern version he's arrived upon is a burlesque reversal of the Romance and all it stands for.

Addiction isn't pretty, no, it's not, thinks Ted as he softly shouts, in unison with Dr. Tang, "Gimme some blow! You ho! Give it up! The blow!"

While it would have been most satisfying to throw his knowledge in Gold's face at the meeting this afternoon, something deep in Ted's strategic reserves had said, "Hold back." While alcoholic *haus frau* turned downtown stripper has a pleasant ring to it—in and of itself—Ted is enough of a student of literature to understand that timing can enhance even the mildest text, increasing its impact on the audience.

The most important question is, of course, does Gold know? Is his grief, awakening such sympathy in Diana, a sham? Has Gold used this ludicrous theme park as a way of "smoking" his errant wife out of hiding? Ted almost quivers with the possibilities that arise from this new line of inquiry.

Either way, as Ted sees it, Ted wins.

If Wally had been aware of his wife's disappearing act, Ted would wager his whole portfolio that Gold would move Heaven and Earth to prevent his daughter's discovering such a painful truth. For starters, her father would have deceived her most hideously. And then, of course, there is her mother's willful abandonment of her only daughter at the formative teenage years. Icing on the *gateau* is the inevitable contempt that Diana will feel for her rescuer when she understands she's been used as part of a *grande charade*.

On the other hand, if Wally has truly believed his wife is gone, what will it do to his manhood to find out she's alive and well, serving topless cocktails rather than living in a mountaintop mansion with her chump of a husband and deluded daughter? To what lengths will Mr. Gold go to keep his daughter from suffering the same devastating blow as he?

Timing is such sweet sorrow, thinks Ted, hoping he can afford to hold back until the financial house of cards begins to tumble, with just the slightest push from Yours Truly, whose strategic inferences have been consistently uncanny, almost to the point of persuading Ted of the existence of God, or at least of the God within.

"You ho!" cries Ted, magnanimously, saluting the feckless Dolores for having appeared just when he needed her most.

* * *

Arizona's state tree is the Paloverde, *verde* being green, and *palo* being stick. When the desert gets too dry, hot or cold, the tree's leaves drop off and chlorophyl in the bark takes over photosynthesis. Paloverdes offer shelter to smaller plants in the desert, especially seedlings of the Saguaro cactus, preventing the nascent cacti from being eaten, trampled, or extinguished during temperature extremes. For this reason, the Paloverde is called a "nurse plant."

* * *

DIANA is determined to redeem herself. She edges out to the pool fence, reaches up for the key, lets herself in, and holds on to the wrought iron as she forces herself, step by step, towards the hook where the life preservers are stacked. They are in soft pastels, three of them, chosen by Humphrey for their colors, stacked on the L-shaped metal bracket, like so many Froot Loops.

Just do it, she mutters, *just make yourself do it. William will be so proud*, she reminds herself, *so proud*.

Diana's skin is twitching with what feels like a plague of exposed nerve cells shrieking their lack of combat readiness, but it is especially her underarms that are frozen solid and peeling back in sinkholes of despair and self-loathing.

Stop it! Diana scolds. She pounds the fence for emphasis, loosening the inhabitants of a dense cluster of Cat's Claw.

How many bees there are, streaming straight for her face, Diana cannot say, for she has already begun to move. Despite her research on the subject, Diana cannot do anything right. She does not cover her face and run to the house. She does not remain calm. Instead, she waves her hands about her face, maddening the bees that are not Africanized killer bees at all, but a small swarm of everyday yellow jackets.

She is waving them away and they are coming towards her, pushing her back from the fence towards the pool, which has momentarily escaped her radar of terror, having been replaced by a more pressing nightmare. When she falls, it happens in slow-motion. She has time to register *"I'm falling!"* If it were a cartoon, she would be able to command her molecular structure in such a way as to reverse the film and put herself back on the pool deck, but Diana can only observe herself with the incredulous awareness that she is indeed falling into the pool. Thanks to Dr. Morales, she has practiced holding her breath in the tub. She is able to blow out her cheeks and rue that lost opportunity, that endless stretch of time between losing her footing and being pulled by gravity into a hopeless and unnatural state of submersion.

Diana Lively is sinking fast, curled into a hunched fetal crouch, her hands in front of her face, a late response to the now unreal threat of asphyxiation by bees, who, even as she has given up looking, are dispersing. Hands in front of face, knees bent to chest, none of these positions provides a functional solution to the very real threat of asphyxiation by drowning.

Diana can see her hands in front of her, they are trembling and overly pink, it seems to her. Everything looks just as it did so many years ago. The water is bluer than the sky above it and everything is in slow motion. It is the same but different. Before, Diana had seen her fellow swimming pupils standing on the side. Here there are no humans. No one is home, not even Ted, who wouldn't hear her if he were. She can see the edge of the pool, she can see the palm fronds shimmering to the right.

Diana's brain fights the paralysis of her body and races through myriad simultaneous images as she faces the fact of her imminent death. She can already see herself, her lifeless white body at the side of the pool, and it is with this image that a logarithmic calculus is played out at the speed of light. The short answer, which arrives intuitively, within seconds, is that she must get a divorce. She is going to die, and it is only when she sees her children being raised by a man with no imagination, no heart, that she understands. Staying with him for their sake is ludicrous. She sees the children being worn down by Ted in the same tireless way he's worked his mischief on her, undoing her sense of who she was so profoundly that she felt unable to honor Johnny, who'd been so much a part of her that she'd never really let him go, just tucked him in her subconscious and sworn her fealty with what she would not let herself have, with the prison she'd made of her grief.

As Diana's red blood cells cry out for oxygen, they slow down her linear reasoning. The process of cognition is aborted. Mrs. Lively spins into a dreamy flashback of her life, the one she hasn't let herself have. Wally is there with her. He is listening to her flying dream, gently suggesting that if she wants to swim, it's the same downward pressure of hands against invisible resistance. She sees his mountaintop, the site for her first real building, and she remembers her momentary conviction that this life was hers if she were willing to take it.

Despite these inspirations, Diana's body is frozen. Her ears hurt, her head is huge. Her knees are clutched to her chest, a sodden ball of terror. She is losing her life at the bottom of this pool. Ted will raise her children. Nothing she can do to stop him now.

It's William she set out to impress here, and it's William whose soul will slowly be drained by life with Ted. That much she understands. Elly is tough, she'll survive, but William is too much like Diana, too willing to open his heart to repeated assaults, too willing to let Ted convince him of what his heart insists cannot be true.

In the nanosecond it takes for Diana to see forward into her son's life, she again hears Wally's voice and decides that she might as well die trying to fly as waiting to die. She pushes her arms out against the water, trying to force her body along the current, as in her dream, but instead, because she is curled into a ball, she is sucked down even farther.

It is so surprising to her, this realization that her ace in the hole, her decision to finally apply for help—to help herself through the application of will—this effort will not save her. Her children will be raised by an unsuitable man and all because she cannot do what she has always said she cannot do.

It's finally her rage at those awful people who insisted she try this stupid, stupid sport, and even more, at Ted, who has scoffed at what now appears to be a prescient fear of water, that prompts Diana to thrash out with her left foot, kicking in sheer fury. Her baby toe meets the abrasive bottom of the pool at its most fleshy, tender angle. The scrape is such a painful insult to her system that without even thinking about it, Diana forces her weight on her other foot, as would be natural to her in an unpanicked, unsubmerged state. Doing so straightens Diana's right knee which—like the left—has been clutched in surrender to her predicament. Foot, ankle, knee, thigh, all raise the newly released torso against the floor of the pool, fighting gravity, through the water, to the sky.

It is not even funny, this fact that she has very nearly drowned in four feet of water, but that is Diana's first response as she pushes through the surface and takes a huge gulp of air. A laugh can be many things to many people, but for Diana this is the purest form of celebration: Her gurgle is high and sweet and not unlike the sound of a newborn as it takes in breath to let out that first painful yowl for recognition.

* * *

The Ocotillo plant, also known as a flaming sword, produces a tough spiny stick that tapers up toward the heavens. This elegant, close-knit burst of candle-like spines that bloom in the spring, can, when planted together, be wired at the top and used to create an invincible, organic wall against intruders.

* * *

HUMPHREY has been pacing in the front hall for what seems like hours, though he knows it cannot have been more than thirty minutes. Mum's collecting Eleanor from preschool and William from his swim party, a round trip journey of twenty city miles, at most.

The letter is folded in the pocket of his white Gurkhas. Though he knows he mustn't cause more damage than Elly's uninhibited artistry has already imposed, in case the letter becomes a court document, Humphrey cannot stop fidgeting. His fingers won't keep to themselves. The brain-body connection's gone a bit wonky, having been short-circuited by a fierce desire he cannot quench, and a huge disinclination to impose suffering on anyone, much less his beloved mum, at a time when he is so bloody delirious.

His mother has sacrificed everything for his worthless stepfather, to be abandoned like this, it will kill her. She's lost her chance to practice architecture, lost contact with her dollhouse clients, given up—

"Oh my God!" wails Humphrey. Diana's one consolation, her enquiry from the *Tattler,* is this a ruse Ted's effected to woo her back to England?

P'raps he should call Evelyn, thinks Humphrey, but as he is picking up the phone, he hears the dull hum of the garage door. Rushing into the kitchen, Humphrey busies himself with pouring drinks for the children, needing something to do with his hands.

When Diana enters the house, a few beats behind William and Eleanor, she is lost in thought. That much he can see. Her brow is pulled together in that way it gets when she's working out a problem with one of her dollhouses, or more recently, an architectural challenge. "Tea?" he asks. Diana shakes her head, coming around the counter to absently pat his shoulder before marching up the stairs.

"Mum?" he adds, after she's left the kitchen and cannot hear him. "There's something I need to tell you."

When he arrives at the top of the stairs—having delayed his

ascent as long as possible by sitting at the table and reading the solicitor's letter for the twentieth time—his mother is lugging a suitcase down the hall from the storage closet. "Mum?" he says, taking
the suitcase from her and trailing her into the master suite. "What's
this?"

His mother takes the suitcase from him and lays it on the bed.
Only then does she turn to her eldest son, fixing him with searching eyes, clapping her palm across his heart. "Humphrey," she says.
Her mouth works, searching for a way to explain. Diana Lively
closes her eyes, opens them, and blinks. She takes a deep breath.
"Humphrey," she repeats emphatically, her gaze nearly searing in its
clarity. "I lost my footing today."

* * *

The *Desert Night-Blooming Cereus* appear fallow and lifeless during the day, but during the early summer, only at night, having
stored moisture in a huge root that can weigh up to one hundred
pounds, they bloom into gorgeous flowered trumpets.

* * *

WHEN the River Board votes fifteen to fourteen to ban all toxic
construction materials within a thousand feet of the Colorado
River watershed, Elizabeth Stanton is deluged with calls from colleagues. Suddenly she is the Go To Gal of the environmental set,
what with the SafePlay campaign passed in Phoenix and now this
amazing turnaround up north. How did you do it? her friends want
to know, as if she had personally seduced, or maybe engaged in
hand-to-hand combat, each Yay-Sayer. Useless are Elizabeth's repeated protests to the contrary. For Elizabeth, a practiced politician
who's played her fair share of insincere doublespeak, such humility
is—this go-round—completely genuine. The votes, coming in as
they did, have surprised Elizabeth nearly as much as anyone else.

The reporter for the largest newspaper in the Valley of the Sun, seeking quotes for the article that will run in the morning, with a headline of ECONOMIC GROWTH DEAD IN THE WATER: SPECIAL-INTEREST GROUPS RAM THROUGH ANTIBUSINESS DECREE, calls Wally Gold first thing. The Ammo King's refusal to comment is disappointing, if not downright confusing to the reporter, whose analysis of the impact on Wally's plans is sincere, if not fully informed.

In fact, this River Protection Accord is the jewel in Wally's crown. The pieces of his plan have come together, and it is only after they have fallen into place that he can articulate how and why they've worked.

The fact that Ted Lively has unwittingly aided his employer in this task, this fact is icing on the cake, or *gateau*, as Ted would have put it. The professor's sabotage in Lake Havasu City, Laughlin, and Dreamy Draw, his attempts to promote a park that "even Americans would find objectionable," this has accomplished what do-gooders alone could not: the forging of a united front of clashing local interests along a battle-line of common advantage. They have repelled the obnoxious Outsiders with whatever force they could muster. The Lake Havasu resort owners, fearing another competitor for the scraps of tourist dollars that have dwindled since 9/11, have joined hands with the Outdoor Outfitting Association as well as the dreaded Elizabeth Stanton and her Birkenstock-clomping crowd. The Indians downstream, with four critical votes on the board, have responded in turn, on a more spiritual level, understanding that the harmony of earth and sky and water is a sacred trust. Auxiliary in their motivation is the visceral impulse, locked deep in their collective bloodstream, to give that patronizing English egghead a lesson in cross-cultural politics. Furthermore, the elders of the council are secure in the knowledge—confirmed by briefings with three government agencies in D.C.—that tribal sovereignty will ensure loopholes by which new construction on Indian lands can sail through as it always has in the past.

The loan the Amitola Tribe has promised—the subject of recent dinners with Wally at fancy French restaurants—will allow the man formerly known as Arizona's Ammo King to construct an inverted pyramid of mystical proportions, showcasing the new construction materials within environmentally sustainable parameters, on the original property in Dreamy Draw. Two clauses have sealed that deal: first, an advantageous interest rate, and second, an employment and training agreement for Native youth. The new development, not coincidentally, has agreed to be legally enjoined from "duplicating or competing with the guest services offered within tribally owned resorts within a two-hundred-mile radius."

Why this historic Protection Accord by the Colorado River Water Commission, by whose authority eight states had agreed to be governed since the early twentieth century, should make the Ammo King happy, when to all intents and purposes, it seems to impede him, is a matter of some confusion to most observers, save Guy, who has arrived at nine p.m. with a bottle of Dom. Guy has long since figured it out, but, then again, he has had a unique perspective. Not for nothing has the CFO been taking daily sorties to the TechGreen stockholder Web forums. Not for nothing had Guy witnessed firsthand the resistance of the Gold Industries board to using the more expensive building materials. Aside from Wally's tactical error of having Baby Face present his ideas, the board members had echoed Guy's original concern: If Gold Industries was the only one to build "clean," how would they keep their admission price low enough to compete with other area attractions?

Now, though, the River Board turnabout would accomplish several things. Not only would it level the competitive playing field, it would also provide an excuse to float a new architectural Request for Proposal, with a short enough deadline that Diana's reentered bid would be a slam dunk. Now the Ammo King, with Elizabeth Stanton's help, has tracked down "green" engineers willing to work around the clock to produce a plan that would breeze through the River Board's environmental review process, would, in fact, be lauded by the same board as a beacon of sustainable design and sensitive building practices.

Though the venture capitalists would have gagged at such hooey, they were no longer associated with the King Arthur Theme Park and Museum, having called Guy yesterday, upon receipt from Ted of a faxed list of EARTHCARE's donors. Not to worry, Guy replied, when they started explaining why they weren't comfortable doing business with someone like Wally Gold. Not to worry, Guy had said, forcing a resignation into his voice when, instead, what he felt up to was a quick little Mexican hat dance. Extricating ties with these four investors, who'd never have liked Diana's plans, who'd have had the leverage to ruin everything, this had been a challenge for which Beverly's laxative-laced date-bran muffins had been deployed.

Ted's acute hearing had been every bit as predictable as his extreme cleverness and his penchant for detail. These were traits for which, in the end, ten thousand pounds a month, plus expenses, were starting to look like money well spent.

The unexpected and unprecedented Accord was a two-fer, at the very least, because a huge market has now been created for TechGreen, the company that swallowed up MaryKnoll Tech shortly after Wally had taken a flyer on MRYKT. The parent company just happened to have patents on a large number of revolutionary, nontoxic building products. With the money Wally would make on the stock he'd received at merger, they might even be able to dispense with the loan from the Amitola Tribes.

Of course, Wally's motives on that deal had been muddied from the get-go. Mostly, he just wanted to help his daughter's dream come true, accuracy regarding her lineage be damned. It might not be a kibbutz, but at least she'd finally get to know a people she admired so much, captivated by her image of a noble and innocent past, a nirvana of nature and human equality, before material greed and gunpowder had wiped it away. Maybe they were Mary Kate's kin, maybe not, but what mattered was that they'd banded together with her husband to pull off a bloodless *coup d'état*. That was something any red-blooded activist, or Red-blooded wannabe, could celebrate with gusto.

For Audrey, who'd raced home from EARTHCARE headquarters as soon as she heard the news, this meant drinking sparkling apple cider from her mother's Waterford champagne flute while Guy and her dad gulped Dom straight from the bottle and replayed the triumphs of the day.

Discovering that her father had been on the side of the Good Guys this whole time, it trumps the Protection Accord passing, it trumps the success of her SafePlay campaign. The only pleasure it could not approach was that of hearing Humphrey's gasp as he'd lost himself inside her for the very first time, and her answering cry, a sweet wordless singing to navigate by.

Eighteen

Ah, the sunsets of the West. Never has there been a beauty more poignant, a dying light more revered than that of the desert at dusk. For Diana and Humphrey, this has been all the more true, even as there were children to be soothed, meals to prepare, tables to lay, and a large suitcase to pack. Not a leisurely pace with which to absorb the way fading sun could cradle the jagged hills and pointed rocks, not the expected hush when everything has suddenly changed, just the same recurring glory, over and over, while the household carried on with its demands, refusing to provide the stillness one might expect to accompany a major life epiphany.

Ah, the letter from Ted's solicitor, obscured by his daughter's Magic Markers until such time as it was no longer necessary to shake Diana loose from her husband's clutches, such a letter has nevertheless had its uses. Rather than what Humphrey had feared, the crumbling of Diana's self-esteem, the letter has strengthened her resolve and dispensed with the thorny nature of how to break the news to Ted gently. It has dispensed with words, altogether. How much more satisfying to bid farewell to each silk shirt and reptilian shoe tossed into the valise without a care for creases, tossed not with joy perhaps but with a huge sense of relief, made all the more tangible when Ted's voice, well past dark, had announced to one and all from the speaker of the answer phone that he'd not be home for dinner. Ah the beauty of sunsets in the West.

The following morning, sitting at his computer and considering his next move, Ted Lively is brutally hung over. While last night's celebration of the River Accord's Passage had seemed only fitting, the two-for-one drinks special at Outback had enticed Ted to consume beyond his normal limits. Further, since tequila had been the spirit-du-jour, Ted had renounced his vodka fetish for countless margaritas, all of which are now coiling like Medusa's asps in his larynx, playing havoc with his concentration. Thus, the professor has yet to put two and two together. Indeed, with a dehydrated brain that is curling back from a swollen skull, Ted is not capable of simple arithmetic, much less the inverted calculus in which environmental gains can stoke economic engines by creating new markets. Thus, as far as Ted can see, Wally's ship has been stranded. At the moment, it is all Ted can do to scroll his way through pages of electronic posts until he finds the information broker's attachment, a boon for which he's been waiting.

As he watches the promised medical records emerge from the printer, he cannot help but wince at the way in which the illegible handwriting causes his head to spin. Ted, unaccustomed to medical abbreviations, cannot take the time to decode these surgical documents with their dense lines of squiggles and signatures, pages of mysterious acronyms, and a dizzying array of meaningless numbers. Besides, the broker has come highly recommended for his medical knowledge. Moreover, Ted would rather give up his teatime spirits than admit to ignorance, and so he does not ring the broker for translations. Thus, our Oxford don is prevented from comparing the records he's been sent today with Wednesday's summary.

No, Ted Lively is a busy bee, with much to do. He's simply glad to have the broker's summary, for it will save him time, to say nothing of the humiliation of having to be guided through the records. All the better that he'd not paid extra to get them two days earlier. Still, these charts will be helpful, as they'll lend a layer of veracity to Ted's presentation, a credibility that will be further bolstered by getting Kristen's signature on the affidavit he's prepared.

Ted makes a spare copy of everything, one for Wally and one to persuade Kristen that she might as well sign off on the truth, since Dolores Johnson's life is already exposed. Because he needs to stop at Kristen's on his way to the office, because he is running late, because he is phenomenally hung-over, Ted ignores the stock alerts in his mail box, nor does he have time to glimpse an e-mail that's sitting farther down the queue, from the same information broker, apologizing for the fact that somehow, his automatic scanner must have initially misread the records, for Dolores Johnson, as the charts show is far too young for her to have been included in these results.

At ten-thirty the gate to McClintock Ranch Luxury Apartments is up. Ted drives in and plans his script.

Kristen opens her door barely wide enough to expose her creamy right shoulder. Her hair is disheveled, but that, thinks Ted, is something that may just add to his desire, on this day of days. "I'm busy," she says, through the opening. The chain is still attached.

"Kristen. Are you alright?"

"I'm packing. What do you want?"

"I brought you a parting gift. I'm returning to England." Ted slides a small vial of pills through door. "Take it."

"No, thanks."

"Dear? Is there anything I can do for you?" Ted asks gently, continuing to offer the medicine.

"You've done enough."

"What's that supposed to mean?"

Kristen pushes his hand back through the crevice, pushing the door to shut it. Ted's narrow crocodile shoe quickly bridges the distance between Kristen's ill-conceived rebuff and her more realistic drug-craving self.

"It's Demerol."

"Get out or I'll call the police," Kristen says. "I'm going to treatment and I don't need any more help from you, douche bag."

"I'll be gone if you'll just grant me one last favor, darling. I've taken the liberty of typing up our conversation. If you'd just sign it—"

Kristen's eyes narrow. She has turned him down with every inch of willpower, and here he stands, still fucking with her. She unlocks the door, takes the vial. She tells him to make himself comfortable while she collects her reading glasses from her bedside table. When she returns, she is wearing the glasses and pointing her grandmother's pearl-handled Beretta at his crotch. "I've had it with you, pencil-dick. Get the fuck outta my life."

Ted is so surprised he almost wets himself. This is not at all what he has hoped for. Still, his ability to read women hasn't been honed all these years without at least trying to remedy matters. "Kristen, I meant no offense—not to a lady as fair as you."

Kristen takes her gun and pulls back the hammer. "Out."

With that she rattles the drug vial, throws it at the professor, and motions him up with her gun. "Don't think I won't do it. Get out!"

Ted rises from the couch, zippering his pants, which he'd loosened in anticipation of a very different reception. In his haste he neglects to take the papers he's left splayed open on the ottoman.

Once his car disappears from sight, Kristen lays her firearm on the table and reaches for the file. She reads it as fast as she can, her mouth moving as she does so, and then she forces herself to punch a number into the phone.

"Dolores," she says, once she hears the familiar voice. "I'm so sorry, honey, but there's something I gotta tell you."

* * *

WALLY, who has asked Audrey not to tell Humphrey the good news until he has a chance to talk to Diana, is in his office, talking on the phone to engineers. Diana's drawings have been copied and shrunk, and are being framed with a caption that says "Winning bid, King Arthur Quest Center and Museum, Dreamy Draw, Arizona." Last night Wally, Guy, and Audrey had phoned Beverly and held a quickie quorum of the revamped selection committee. Wally plans to surprise Diana tonight. The only fly in the ointment will be the inevitable presence of her husband, but then again, it will be almost worth having him there when Ted finally realizes his sabotage has enabled the resurrection of his wife's dream.

Not one to gloat, Wally is nevertheless sorely tempted when Ted marches into his office unannounced. No knock, just the door flying open. Ted, for his part, is grasping his remaining manilla folder with two hands, his excitement hastened by two Bloody Marys and an Extra Strength Excedrin.

"Have you seen the newspaper?" Ted tsks, shaking his head. "What a shock!"

"The River Board vote?" Wally stares at his hands, trying for a look of consternation.

"Yes," Ted murmurs sympathetically. "I just heard. What will it mean to your—our project?"

Wally brings his hands up to his cheeks. "Well, we're pretty much dead in the water for the plan we were working on. I just paid off Franz Bibfeldt and sent him back to Florida. What a waste," Wally murmurs, but there is something in his manner that belies defeat, some sort of eagerness that is inconsistent with the misery Ted has sought to impose.

If slightly annoyed by Wally's ignorance of his own defeat, Ted reminds himself to take pride in having put a stop to an enterprise which would simply have heaped insult upon his academic reputation. *Tant pis* this conversation couldn't wait just a few hours, when the announcement of Huntington's change of heart— leaked yesterday by the slag herself—would trigger a free fall of Gold's Ammunition division. That free fall, would, of course, be reflected soon enough in the Gold Industries share price. Then Ted would have the satisfaction of telling his wife's patron that he'd made a small fortune on the man's colossally bad judgment. Ted had so hoped to have that scenario in place before administering his final tactical parry, but he has errands to run, planes to catch. Most of all, Ted is hedging his bets against the slim chance that his role in passing the accord is discovered prematurely, unleashing Wally's fury and, with it, the threatened FedEx of certain video footage to President Bernard.

Unreconciled to forgoing the pleasure of a full-tilt joust, however, Ted tries one last time to extract news of the buyout.

"And what of Huntington?" Ted enquires sympathetically. "Is it true what Beverly mentioned, that they're backing away from buying your ordinance division?"

Wally pauses just a few seconds to savor this moment. Ted's short sale on his stock has not gone unnoticed, though news of yesterday's transaction, funded with Fiona's money, hasn't yet trickled in via ComputerSleuth's daily Hotman updates. If it weren't for Diana, Wally would delay telling Ted what was happening, let him wait until he lost his friggin' shirt. No way to do that, though, not without hurting Ted's immeasurably better half, to say nothing of the kids.

"Good news on that front." Wally shrugs. "We got a fax from Huntington confirming their tender offer late last night. And Justice and the Corporation Commission both approved the paperwork. In fact, the stock's at forty-one already. The only worry we have is whether it'll go too high for Huntington to get stockholders to part with their shares."

Ted drops his tightly grasped folder. He is speechless.

Worse, he is terrified, thrown back to his childhood poverty in an instant. As he kneels to retrieve the scattered papers, he groans, "I've just remembered an urgent phone call."

With that, Ted and his folder leave the room.

When he returns, five minutes later, Ted's cheeks are emblazoned with scarlet patches, a physiological response enjoined by four-point-eight minutes of screeching into the phone at Lech Kowalski, who insists Ted's market order has already been placed at noon as per his instructions.

At this point there's nothing Ted can do, but he must release some of his adrenaline or he'll burst a capillary.

Gone is the restraint with which he'd planned to slip in the sword. Now, Theodore Lively is ten years of age, coming off a poor night's sleep and nothing for breakfast but weak tea and stale biscuit, with no hope of lunch in sight.

"You are such a fool! No wonder your wife chose to vanish off the face of the earth rather than spend another eternal second with you!" Ted spits, shoving the folder at Wally. "There are some rather long words herein, so allow me to translate. It appears your late wife is alive and well."

Wally is opening the folder, reading what Ted has wrought. Ted's hastily written narrative connects the dots:

> On March 30, three plus years ago, Mary Kate Gold was lost in a tragic river boat accident. Or was she? The attached medical records, showing the dates by which a forty-year-old white female received several surgical procedures designed to change her appearance, document the slow metamorphosis from mother to maiden. The patient, Dolores Johnson, now forty-three, waitresses in a gentleman's club called Naughty Nelly's. She is known to be a recovering alcoholic. She is also said to entertain herself during meal breaks by reading Cornell's famous anthology of the Knights of the Round Table.

Underneath this is the information broker's initial summary, and the medical records received this morning.

Wally's brain is a half-step behind his vision, which is pulling the letters and numbers along too fast, a train at full tilt, headed for uneven track.

Ted stands over the larger man, who has sunk into his desk chair. "By the way, I'll be needing my payment in full before we leave tomorrow. And unless you wish your daughter to get a copy of this, you'll need to reimburse me for my stock losses."

Wally forces his brain to take in this threat, sheltering his brow in his massive hands. Then he stands, suddenly, stumbling to one side like a wounded animal, before he pulls his mouth into a semblance of humanity. Without any direction from his brain, Wally's fist takes on a life of its own and connects with Ted's beautifully sculpted cheekbone. The punch lands with a sickening *thud*, not unlike the sound of a butcher's hammer on the blood-smeared counters of the Covered Market, where Ted had so contemptuously placed Wally the day they met.

"You liar!" cries Wally, even as he is doubled over with the sickening intuition that there is a twist of logic to this tale, a possibility that no one, not even the last great optimist like himself, could completely deny.

* * *

WHEN Ted has the courage to raise his head, peering up from behind the wrists he's brought into a protective headlock, he sees that the Neanderthal has left the office. Rising from the floor, Ted gingerly makes his way to the washroom, where the mirror confirms Wally's left hook. The skin under the professor's eye is swollen, with violet and yellow undertones.

Fearing damage to the optic nerve, Ted drives himself to the hospital emergency room.

By the time he's been treated and released with an eighty-dollar ice pack and a two-day supply of painkillers, Ted has realized that Wally's assault is actually a gift. He now has the perfect excuse for insisting his family return to Oxford without delay.

* * *

WALLY—having gotten into his car with Ted's papers—is completely alone. Wally cannot say the words out loud, he cannot form the syllables, nor can he move his cheeks around a vowel. He cannot let go the fact that this person Ted's discovered, she's the same age Mary Kate would be if she was alive. He can't blot out the way his wife had lobbied for plastic surgery, against his repeated objections. He can't dismiss her habit of reading while she ate, especially books about Camelot.

Wally's mind feels like a huge black moth has settled in and is beating its wings against the walls of his skull, its dark wings admitting just enough light to remind him of the brightness he has lost.

Destroying the papers is futile, there'll be more where those came from, this he knows, even as he begins to tear the folder into smaller and smaller shreds, grinding his teeth as he presses his meaty fingers together in rhythmic denial. As long as it takes him, he will isolate the hieroglyphics of his betrayal until they are nothing but a string of crazy mixed-up letters, so small they won't obey gravity and settle, but hitch a ride on the twill of his empty lap, twitching, impervious to the slap of his hand, inadequately substantial to adhere to any surface for long.

The car drives itself to a gas station, to a seventy-five-cent vacuum that pulls the shreds into a roaring hole of sound. If it would work to hold the attachment to his ear and remove the text that will not relinquish its meaning, Wally would pay all the money in the world, but alas, as blind as he's been, oblivion is no longer an option.

There is no hope for him, that Wally understands, king of a now useless empire, but there is his daughter to think about. Just this morning he'd been counting their blessings: the park Audrey wanted, a job for Diana, a chance for Humphrey to work his magic in the concessions, everything they'd wanted.

Victory for the Good Guys. Now, out of nowhere, here came the real surprise. The shock has clobbered the Good Guys, even the concept of Good Guys, and that is the worst part.

If you'd asked him five days ago what he'd do to bring Mary Kate back, he'd have said, "Anything." When it had come right down to it, though, as he's now discovered, Wally must not have wanted her back, not on these terms, not if it meant losing his idea of who she was.

The pain of being deserted, of having gone through so much

sorrow, of watching Audrey suffer, all that is horrible enough for Wally. But almost as painful is the loss of something he thought he'd discovered from the depths of despair, the developing impulse to trust, to open himself up to Good, to signs from the Great Beyond. The exhilaration of believing, the sheer high he'd gotten from stretching his brain beyond his imagination, he'd never been quite so happy, not before his wife had died, and now, he fears, as he races home to protect his daughter, never again.

* * *

TED, on his way home from the hospital, dials 911. Accusing Wally of assault will accomplish several things, not the least of which is preventing any further contact between the families. The dispatcher takes his address and tells him she'll send a deputy along as soon as she can.

When Ted walks in the front door, he is anxious to get to his computer and printer, anxious to reprint the hard copy he's left in his mad dash from Kristen's apartment. He does not wander into the kitchen for a drink, he does not say hello, he simply rushes through his study doors and slams them behind him.

"Must you?" asks Diana quietly. She is sitting in the dark, in a leather club chair. In front of her is a large black suitcase, the significance of which escapes her husband.

Ted has thrown up his hands and shivered, he is so flummoxed. Truth be told, the day has been rather a bit much, with a death threat from Kristen, a staggering investment loss, and an assault from Gold. Ted reaches his finger to caress his damaged cheek, waiting for his wife to notice his bruise.

"Why are you lurking here in the dark?" he mutters, turning on the light and swiveling forward in his chair towards his screen. "What is it, Diana? I'm quite behind, so if it could wait—"

"I'm afraid it can't."

"Well? Have at it because . . ." Ted's words trail off as he squints at the emerging screens, looking for the folder. Logging on to the records, Ted hits print, then looks up at his wife.

"I've packed your things," Diana continues. "You might want to check upstairs if there's anything else you'd like to bring, but I think I've gotten it all."

"Have you gone psychic or have I? How did you know we were flying out?"

Diana just sits and stares at him.

Ted can't help thinking that it's not like Diana to fail to notice that a member of her own family has received a black eye. "Be a luv and fetch me an ice pack, will you?" he asks, clicking into his main directory. "And a drink? I've had a horrid morning, in case you haven't noticed."

Diana's refusal to respond is lost in the simultaneous sounds of the doorbell and Eleanor's screech from the living room. "Mummy! The Man in the Yellow Hat! No, William!" She and William race for the door, colliding and causing no end of wailing from the younger competitor, who has growled and bitten her brother's elbow to keep him from being the one to turn the knob.

The man standing there is indeed wearing a cowboy hat, khaki uniform, boots, holster, and badge, very much like the kindly hero in stories of Curious George. The Man in the Yellow Hat pulls out a wallet and opens it to Diana, who has left her husband pressing buttons and squinting at his computer. "Sheriff's office, ma'am. I'm here to see a Ted Lively."

Diana pulls away the children from the door and backs up into the foyer. "Come in," she says. "I'll tell my husband."

When she returns, the sheriff's deputy is kneeling on the floor so that Eleanor can get a closer view of his badge. The man stands up quickly, looking sheepish. "I got a little girl her age."

"Shall we?" asks Ted, gesturing towards the dining room table and pulling shut the French doors for privacy. Diana is left to deal with William's complaints that his sister's bite has broken the skin. By the time she has assuaged him by suggesting he invite Adam to play, she sees that Ted is still talking and the deputy is still writing. Diana occupies herself with composing a lecture for Eleanor, who has scampered into her father's office and is playing at his computer. "Elly!" Diana scolds. "You mustn't bite your brother! Ever!"

Eleanor ignores her mother and continues to hit the top row of the keyboard in a frenetic crescendo that monkeys at typewriters would find daunting. "Stop that!" Diana adds, pulling her daughter away from the seat and carrying her upstairs.

"But Elly helped you pack, Mummy!" her daughter is screaming, the tears already springing forth to put out the flames of her mother's anger. Today, though, such strategies are doomed, for Mummy is not quite herself, or maybe she's more herself than she's been for years. "Stay here!" Diana warns, and she slams the bedroom door behind her, off to find William so he can restore whatever it was that Ted had on his screen before Elly turned it into jibberish. All of this while she's rehearsing her speech to Ted, who is still locked in the dining room with the Man in the Yellow Hat. "I want our passports," Diana threatens silently, having woken up last night with the awful realization that Ted has the family's travel documents. He could conceivably take the children back to England without her permission, a scenario which, until she'd seen the letter from the solicitor, had seemed completely preposterous, given Ted's disinclination to spend time with them. Boarding schools and the money to keep them there, however, would allow Ted to have his cake and make sure his wife couldn't have hers, too.

"William," Diana instructs, when she finds him in the kitchen pressing ice on his arm. "I need you to fix Ted's computer."

Fixing Ted's computer is well within his son's powers, and in the course of doing so, William cannot help but notice the details of the folder his father had left open. William, whose video-game prowess has enhanced his ability to register several visual phenomena at once, notices many things. He sees the folder icon, flickering in the bottom task bar, named StripperSurvival. This flies into the boy's vision first thing. Next, he sees the name of Adam's aunt Dolores. He reads the summary that had been text-messaged to his father yesterday, then the medical records that had been saved as attachments this morning. For William, none of this makes any sense, particularly the question of why his father, who's never met Adam's aunt Dolores, would be snooping into her medical records. William is tempted to delete it, but before he has a chance, he hears his father opening the doors to the dining room. He returns the screen to where it had been earlier and jumps from his father's chair.

"William? What are doing in here?" Ted asks irritably.

"Eleanor was on your computer, so Mum asked me to fix it."

"You didn't touch anything did you?"

William, trying desperately to maintain an innocent demeanor, finds salvation in the form of a large cowboy hat. The ten-gallon, attached to the hand of the deputy, leads the long arm of the law into the study. The Man in the Yellow Hat, six-foot-seven, is ducking under the jamb of the study door. "Sir," the man is saying to his father. "If you want to file a restraining order, you'd need to come to the station to file some papers."

"I don't have time for that!" Ted snaps, gathering up papers from the printer and snapping them together. "Just leave then, and submit what I've given you. My attorney will be in touch shortly. William will show you out."

William knows better than to ask his father about the documents he's seen, but after he watches the deputy get into his car, he cannot help but return, just to see what his father will do next. His father, who is furiously typing a new note, does not see William watching him from behind the doorjamb.

I meant what I said. From you, by six p.m., I will need the following: a checque for $70,000 in salary, and $900,000 for losses suffered on the market. Oh, and by the way: Don't even think of hiring my wife, or interfering in my family's return to England, or your precious Audrey will receive a flurry of unwanted information.

After Ted has printed it out, he places it in an envelope. Using a fountain pen, Ted writes in large italic print: To Wally Gold, Personal, Confidential, and Urgent, from Theodore Lively, Ph.D. "William!" he shouts, startling his spying son. "I'll need you to run something to Gold's for me."

William waits the requisite seconds it would take him to appear from anywhere other than right outside the study door, and pops his head around its jamb.

"Chop, chop. Take this and put it in their mailbox."

"But Adam's coming over."

"Just do what I say, William. I don't have time for this. And fetch your mother."

William takes the envelope from his father and dutifully locates Diana, who is upstairs in her closet, searching for the children's passports. "Dad wants you, Mum."

"What's he want with the police?" Diana asks, rising. "And what's that?" she asks, looking at the envelope Ted's handed him.

"Something he wants me to take to the Golds'," William says. "Will you watch for Adam?"

"Of course I will. But William, save yourself a trip. Audrey's in Humphrey's room. Just give it to her. But knock first, all right?"

"But Daddy said to—"

Diana shakes her head. "Don't worry. What he doesn't know won't hurt him." Diana pats her son's shoulder, pushes him towards Humphrey's room, and hurries downstairs to finish a long overdue conversation with her husband.

As he is accustomed to doing, Ted interrupts his wife before she's had a chance to speak. "I suppose you've heard by now about— what's happened with Gold's park."

Diana shakes her head. "No—"

"Well, long, long tale of woe, cut short. He won't be building after all. Which releases me from my contract, even if this didn't." Ted stops and points to his black eye, giving Diana a final chance to notice his wound and emote accordingly. "Between you and Humphrey, we should be prepared to leave tonight. There's a nine o'clock flight and they have seats. You should be able to find a takeaway sandwich shop for dinner. You know they aren't serving food on the airline these days, and it's quite expensive if you buy at those airpark restaurants—"

Diana is holding up her hands and shaking her head.

"For God's sake, Diana, it's not as though I'm asking you to walk on bloody water. I'll have to go to the bank and to the stockbroker's. I need to clear some things from my office at work. All this with a headache you can't imagine," Ted says, pointing again at his cheek, despite his resolution to let his wife suffer if she hadn't had the sensitivity to notice his injury right off.

"Ted, we won't be going with you."

"Come, Lady Di. Gold assaulted me. He could have killed me. The man's a gun owner, for Heaven's sake."

"You go, Ted. But we'll be staying. I won't have William pulled out midterm."

"You cannot stay, Diana. That's the thing."

Diana shakes her head, as though trying to shake it free of the image of a long-haired pregnant undergraduate. "I think I can, Ted. You see, I know about—your paramour."

The thought of Kristen brings Ted's hand up to cover his crotch. The movement is involuntary, as is the rictus of dismay that has blossomed under his discolored left eye. Ignoring these physical slights, however, he cannot help but focus on the further injury Gold has done him by breaking his word about showing Diana the videodisc.

"Diana! That meant nothing. Gold will pay for exposing you—!"

"Wally had nothing to do with my seeing it. Humphrey found it."

"He showed that *thing* to Humphrey! I'll sue him for everything he's got, for invasion of privacy, for slander! That's an actionable charge."

"I can't believe you would stand here and heap blame upon him when you were willing to do this to me!"

"It wasn't *to* you, Diana. It meant nothing to me."

"Nothing."

"Gold gave me his word he wouldn't give that to you."

"He didn't! Until this second I'd no idea he knew about it."

"Well, he did, you know. He's been bloody well blackmailing me with it, too, if you must know. The man has no honor."

"For the last time, I'm telling you. It wasn't Wally."

"How did Humphrey have it, then?"

"Eleanor had colored it."

"Eleanor! Oh my God! That's despicable! She might have thought it was Telletubbies and popped it in to watch! For God's sake!" Ted holds his temples with his forefingers, a suffering stance with which his wife is overly familiar. "That's it! Gold's daughter'll have quite the surprise herself when she finds out what he's kept from her."

"What *are* you saying? Eleanor didn't know what she was looking at. Your—" Diana stops for a moment, trying to think of a word that expresses her husband's calculation in hiring a solicitor, in plotting to bring her and the children back to England under false pretenses. Diana tosses the word towards her husband with pointed significance: "*acrobatics* are beyond the understanding of a child. For that I'm grateful."

"Mummy!" Elly cries from the stairs, and it is then that Diana realizes she's overheard the whole argument. Racing up to her daughter, reviewing the conversation in her head, Diana is trying to think of how she will explain it. By the time she's gathered Eleanor into her arms and collected the tiny stuffed animal Elly insists on fitting in Ted's luggage, the doorbell has rung three times, insistently. Diana deposits Eleanor on the couch, flips on the television, and proceeds to the front door to let in Adam.

Standing there, instead, is Wally. Perhaps it's the surprise of seeing him, or the ravaged look on his face, or maybe it's the battle playing out in his eyes, somewhere between anger and fear, but something causes her to take his hand and bring him across the threshold.

* * *

Upstairs, Audrey is using Humphrey as her very own La-Z-Boy. Her head is on his chest, her arms are draped over his bent knees and Humphrey is braiding her hair. William, having knocked at the door with trepidation, is relieved to find no kissing going on. William holds up the envelope. "Mum says to give this to you."

Audrey leans forward to take the package, reading the front. "What's Ted got to tell my dad that's personal and confidential?"

"William?" asks Humphrey, for he can see by William's expression that he knows something more.

William shakes his head. "I saw some of it, but it makes no sense."

Audrey is already delicately pinching the clasp, releasing the unglued flap. There inside, following Ted's threatening note, is his narrative. Audrey is a quick study, too quick. She scans Ted's note, then reads his introduction out loud until she understands the meaning of the words. "On March 30, three years ago, Mary Kate Gold was lost in a tragic river boat accident. Or was she? The attached records—" Here, Audrey breaks off, flipping the page back to see the summary, the attached charts. She pulls away from Humphrey, who hasn't yet gotten the meaning of this sheaf of paper. Still, he can tell that something's gone very wrong, for even though Audrey's back is to him, her posture conveys disaster. He rushes forward, cradles her in his arms, takes the papers she is clenching between her fists, and places them on his rose-covered comforter. "What is it, Audrey?"

"He's saying my mom's—she's not—"

William, who is feeling terrible for having made Audrey cry, picks up the document that has so upset her. He turns the pages, in order, and says, "Audrey, these papers: They're about Adam's aunt Dolores. I don't know why Ted's got them."

"What do you mean?"

"You know Adam's aunt. The one who's sick? What's a dob, anyway?"

"I don't know, I don't know!" Audrey's panic so upsets Humphrey that he wants to help her, but he also wants to stop this enquiry before things get any worse. "William!" he snaps, grabbing the sheaf of documents from his brother. Then, only because he cannot think of what else to do, he straightens the form to be even with the edge of the bed, catching sight of the acronym causing William's confusion. "Date of birth!" Humphrey murmurs, as an afterthought.

"January twenty-third," Audrey whispers fiercely, her fist against her forehead as if trying to cram it back into her brain.

William mumbles. "That's not right, then! January would be month one, but that date of birth is number eight. As in August: 8-23-75."

"What?"

"Look at these pages. They all say 8-23-75."

"My mom, a Virgo!" Audrey snorts, laughing out loud, blowing a small balloon of snot out of one nostril. "What kind of asshole would believe that?"

At this, William and Humphrey cannot help but meet eyes, raise brows, and exchange a meaningful nod. Their patriarch, plunderer of neighbouring lands.

"Don't you see what this is about, Audrey?" Humphrey responds. "Ted wants to ensure we all return home with him. Otherwise, who'd take care of the children while he's off with his Sloan Ranger?"

"I thought her name was Cheswitt?" Audrey asks.

Humphrey, searching for words to explain British slang, is stopped at the sight of Wally walking through the bedroom door.

Wally looks as though someone has tied him to a car and driven it hard. He turns to his daughter with a look of despair.

"Dad! What's the matter?"

Wally gestures at the display of papers he has run upstairs to intercept. He clenches his fist, his body lurching to one side as though it is going to follow his hand to the floor and pull him with it. "Audrey?" he pleads, summoning the strength he'll need to comfort his daughter, but instead, Audrey is now scanning Ted's documents with the bemused outrage she might accord to right-wing propaganda. "God, Dad!" she laughs. "Wait till you see what the Evil Stepfather's cooked up now. He's trying to slip some Virgo chick's medical records past us, saying they're Mom's. What a complete asshole!"

Wally's just stares at her with a confused look, trying to sort out the girl who seems so unharmed and the distracting patter of her words that he can't tie together in any sensible way.

"Look," says Audrey, waving the papers in her father's face. "Look at the date of birth. And, Dad, how tall was Mom?"

Wally is not a detail person. He hasn't scrutinized the dates in Ted's proffered documents, hasn't even thought to. Why would he look for more evidence that his wife had deceived him? The data summary had said the woman was forty-three. And the plastic surgery fit: A year or two before she'd disappeared, Mary Kate had started lobbying to get "work done" against Wally's vehement objections. He hated that over-stretched appearance of women trying to look younger than they were, to say nothing of the danger of anesthesia. Ted's narrative had just seemed to add up, a storyline that turned back on itself, hinged by Mary Kate's alcoholism and quirks of her personality like her King Arthur obsession, her habit of reading while she ate, her insecurity about the way she looked. Wally's reaction has come from the gut, striking a core that he's struggled against his whole life, a core of anger and disbelief, not just at his wife, but also at his mom. Much as she had loved him, his mother had chosen to lose herself, chosen to leave him, time and again. This is a double-edged blade that separates Wally's emotions, between the love he insists on holding tight and the anger he wants desperately to bury. All his life, especially in the war, Wally has practiced this categorical separation, looking at people with a lens that would get fuzzy around the edges, blurring the faults. Better to focus on the kindness, the smarts, the goodness, better to resist any sort of hate that might accompany a more clinical view of human behavior. Now, he is so dismayed by what he's done, betrayed Mary Kate in accepting Ted's accusations at face value, it doesn't occur to him that Ted's weapon—his threat to tell Audrey—it's been defused. The sound of a car pulling into the driveway, it's engine revving loudly, prompts William to plead, "Can you not tell Adam my dad stole his aunt's report?" Shame on William's face is transparent. Wally is overcome by sympathy for the boy, whose father's transgressions dwarf the inadvertent harms visited by mere mortals from Wally's past. "You kids stay here for a minute," Wally urges. "I'll send Adam up."

No matter what he does now, Wally thinks, rushing downstairs to confront Ted, he's in a lose-lose situation. If Ted's right, then Mary Kate had been too cruel to be forgiven. If Ted's wrong, then Wally's failed his wife after all his ostensible devotion, by believing for a second she could ever be so cruel.

* * *

VALEEN'S Trans Am idles too high, but with Dolores being so sick, she hasn't had time to get it to the dealer. She's been parked around the corner from the Livelys', waiting until she saw Ted's car pull in, waiting until Wally's Suburban came barrelling into the driveway. The pretext for waiting is getting Adam's homework done. The truth is harder, a shaking Valeen can't get rid of, the world coming down around her.

When Kristen called, Valeen was reading a story to Dolores where Arthur was grieveously wounded, holing up in an old hermit's hut, waiting for a magical salve that might save his life. "Don't answer it," Valeen had said, but Dolores had seen the caller ID and reached for the phone. Valeen could see by the way her lover said "hello" that something was up, but what she'd heard after Dolores hung up was so much more than she'd bargained for.

Valeen can't get it out of her head that if they'd just been able to finish the story, Dolores might be healed, too. She can't stop focusing on that, despite all the other stuff she's got to keep in her head, and for this, she needs a salve of her own.

"Okay, sweetie, you can do the rest later," she says to Adam, pulling the car into drive, pulling her belly button into her spine, calling on her Pilates "powerhouse" for strength.

Showing up like this, at the Livelys' front door, it's not something she's used to doing. Fact is, ever since Dolores figured out that Ted was the Customer from Hell, Valeen's taken pains to avoid him. Now though, she will carry herself up this walkway, she will introduce herself if she has to, and when she's done, she will hurry home.

* * *

DIANA opens the immense wooden door, squinting at the sun. Valeen blinks.

"Oh, thanks for bringing Adam, Valeen," says Diana. "Do come in. Adam, do you remember Wally?"

Diana moves back to reveal the man hovering behind her. Even though Valeen has tried to prepare herself for this, even though this is why she's standing here now, Valeen is still shaken to see Wally Gold in the flesh. It's not Wally's height; he's not that tall. It's something else: a sense of power he gives off. Valeen thinks this even as she notices a wariness in his stance that reminds her of ex-cons, notices how tired he looks, the circles under his eyes, the shadows of his cheeks.

Wally reaches out, shakes Adam's hand. "Hi, Adam. Listen, they're all upstairs in Humphrey's room. Why don't you go on up? I just have to talk to William's dad."

Ted, who is sweeping into the hall from the back of the house, a mantle of dry-cleaned clothing draped across his shoulder, spits, he is so angry. "I'd have thought you'd done quite enough talking."

Diana clears her throat, finding her voice. The tone of warning is unmistakable. "Ted, this is Adam's mother, Valeen."

Ted appraises Valeen and turns his head to one side. "Have we met?"

Valeen points at her son's disappearing back and cocks her forefinger against her lips, gesturing for silence. Only when the door shuts behind him does Valeen turn back to Ted and answer his question. "Yes, as a matter of fact, we have met. I work down at Naughty Nelly's."

Ted's eyes reveal a quick cross fire of disapproval, prurience, and guilt. He covers his embarrassment with a cough.

Wally pulls away from Valeen, leans against the wall. The words are out of his mouth before he understands he has spoken. "Naughty Nelly's?"

Valeen nods. "Well, yeah. I work there. That's why I stopped over." Valeen takes a breath, her eyes suddenly fixed on Wally, whom she hadn't expected to feel quite so sorry for. "See, I didn't want any of Adam's friends or their moms to know what—that I— serve drinks for a living. So I go by Dolores when I'm working."

"You're Dolores?" cries Ted, who comes on slow, as he comes on fast. In an instant he sees her as she'd been that first day, wearing chaps, a small vest, and a sheriff's badge guarding the gates to Heaven. The look on Ted's face, to which all of them bear witness, shows that he remembers her and better yet, that he's perplexed by this revelation, which it hasn't occurred to him to question.

In fact, it is Ted's most execrable traits that have played directly into Skygyrl's hand. First off, he's a man who would never trouble himself to remember a waitress's name, so he's deprived of the recall that would counter Valeen's claim. Second, Ted's miserly nature blinds him to the fact that his tip, which he recollects perfectly, was, in that sort of establishment, an insult. Instead he recalls that he'd given the girl a full fifty cents more than the ten percent he's somehow convinced himself is sufficient in the States, notwithstanding the many times he'd been told of the fifteen percent custom. Third, because he's so frequently been surrounded by adoring undergraduates, Ted considers himself quite the catch. He recounts his masterful caress of this young lady's breasts, he remembers his intricate (if fictional) anecdotes about being knighted at Buckingham Palace. In fact, he is so ridiculously self-assured that he does not question the otherwise ludicrous notion that a waitress who'd had the dubious pleasure of serving him food while he felt her up and tipped for shit might later pay large sums to Kristen, just for the sake of pursuing him. Ted, being who he is, does not look for motives: He accepts her patronage with the careless acknowledgment of a courtier. "But Kristen said—"

"I'm so sorry Kristen got you all mixed up," Valeen says. "She's right, I did have a drinking problem and I did change my name to Dolores. I didn't want anyone to know about Adam, so I told her my kid lived with my ex." Valeen pauses. Her eyes sweep the floor before she raises them again and sighs, still looking at Ted. "I had to come over here because Kristen called and said you wouldn't leave her alone. And my manager says you came to the bar asking about me."

Ted shakes his head, processing this new information. As of now, he is so gripped by this attractive young woman's admiration, he hasn't had time to deduce that his extortion campaign has taken a swift turn for the worse.

"But you collect books about Camelot?"

"Yeah. I wish I'd known you were some Arthur expert. I'd of

talked your ear off!" Valeen says confidently. This last is, in fact, true, for Valeen's caught the bug.

"But I don't understand, you're Adam's mother?"

"Yeah, how weird is that?" Valeen sighs, neglecting to mention the flyers that Dolores had placed on Ted's windshield. "And please, I'm begging you. Don't take this out on Adam. He doesn't know what I do for a living."

Valeen turns to Diana. "I'm sorry I didn't tell you."

"No need," murmurs Diana, placing her hand on Valeen's shoulder. Her eyes narrow in concentration as she asks, "That name: Dolores—"

"Well, my cousin's named Dolores," Valeen nods, her eyes unexpectedly welling over. She has a sudden keen need be home again, to find out what happens to Arthur. "She's the one who's been sick. It was her idea I use her name instead of mine so Adam wouldn't get picked on at school. Then I could get my checks mailed to our address and since we have the same last name . . ."

Now Valeen turns back to Ted, with the confused tone of someone delivering a message she doesn't quite understand. "Oh, geez, and speaking of mailing, I meant to tell you, Mr. Lively. Kristen asked me to give you a message: She FedExed some videodisc today, to your friend, in England. Farina or Fiona or something?"

For a moment, all of the parties stand frozen in this foyer, locked in their own separate conclusions. No one seems to know what to say. Finally Valeen, who's had time to rehearse her exit, says, "So, can you not—?" Here Valeen clears her throat, her expression hesitant. She pulls her hand through her luxuriant chestnut bangs and starts again. "Could you please not say anything to Adam?"

Diana reaches out to place her hand on Valeen's shoulder. "Of course."

"I better go then."

"I'll walk you out," Diana offers, taking Valeen's elbow and accompanying her to her car. "Adam's a good boy. He's so helped William to fit in here."

Valeen smiles. "Ditto," she says, at the same time wondering whether her act of charity that day, inviting William over, had set into motion the whole mess she is now trying to sweep under the rug. Even though Dolores has assured her that Adam and William's friendship was never part of her plan, Valeen can't help but feel responsible, this premature loss her son could face, a quick rejection from his New Best Friend, on the heels of which, he will have to say goodbye to his favorite maiden aunt, whom they've both grown so fond of calling Dolores.

Wally stands at the front door, watching Diana walk Valeen to her car. Even as he steels every molecule of his body to be careful, to resist this overwhelming temptation, Wally cannot help but find in Valeen's words a confirmation of what Audrey has suggested, that the Evil Stepfather has concocted this story to prevent his family from staying in Arizona. For one thing, Ted's done nothing but lie since he got here, especially when it meant undermining his wife's success. Even more important, Wally can see from the pain in Adam's mom's eyes that it took something out of her to come here today and tell the Livelys the truth about working in a strip club. Why would Valeen place her son's social status in jeopardy, unless she was telling the truth? Why indeed, for women who love their children, they'll do anything to keep them from harm's way, as every imperfect but only partially vanquished mother knows only too well.

Nineteen

Ted rummages quickly through his drawers, collects his and Eleanor's tickets, and thanks his lucky stars that Diana has had the foresight to pack his bag. It has taken very little time for Ted's razor-sharp intellect to run through a quick series of logical operations, ending in the conclusion that he is, however he looks at it, deeply and completely buggered.

If that slut Kristen mailed the disk today, and he leaves tonight, he can arrive at Fiona's with just enough time to intercept. Eleanor will provide a buffer, and besides, he cannot bear the thought of her remaining here, under the influence of a man who'd find his way into Diana's heart by any means necessary, of that Ted is certain.

Ted quickly slides his loot into his briefcase and takes the handle of the large black valise. He slips out the study door, into the hall and past Wally, who stands mooning out the front door at Diana's willowy figure, oblivious to everything on Earth but her beautiful spine.

* * *

ELEANOR—having heard her mother and father arguing about returning to England—has taken matters into her own hands. Having followed her siblings and Audrey as they marched across the greenbelt to the Golds' house for foodstuffs, Eleanor grows impatient with their indignant review of her father's crimes. She slips into Wally's office and puts herself at the helm of his empire.

On the right side of his desk is Wally's homemade Father's Day present, a replica of a Japanese garden. The cedar box is sixteen by eighteen, five inches deep, and filled with soft white sand. A cunning copper rake allows for the illusion of mastery, creating smooth, even lines through the sand, promoting contemplative repetition: a mindless, calming stewardship. Zen, Wally proudly said, when showing the box to Eleanor.

This toy of Wally's: It is one of Eleanor's favorite places to play.

The sand is softer than the crumbles in Mummy's shiny egg, but the look on Wally's face when he's grooming the sand, it's like the one Mummy gets when she thinks no one is looking. Eleanor unfolds the pretty boy's picture, opens the small bronze orb, and rubs the ashes between her fingers. Elly knows Mummy needs her golden egg, the one she hides from Daddy. She knows that once it's gone missing, Mummy won't leave Arizona without it. Then Daddy will go by himself and Humphrey can cuddle Audrey, and Elly will be able to come and play in this Sin box whenever she likes.

While her brothers waste time chatting up Audrey, Eleanor is a child of action. She buries the urn well beneath the sand, and places another object there, too, its hard metallic glint disappearing quickly as she carefully combs the infinite grains to cover her tracks.

* * *

TED knocks at the Golds' front door, looking for his children. When no one answers, he lets himself in. He can hear the sounds from upstairs, Humphrey's voice shouting "Eleanor Lively! Come out this instant!" Gold's daughter is making a sound with her mouth that sounds like a cat mewing. Someone else is opening doors and slamming them closed, and then William's voice shouts "Adam?" Were Ted to inquire what they were doing, he would find that they are genuinely worried, but Ted is not about to reveal his presence, especially when it's not required. His daughter, when she is playing hidey-seeky, she is quite predictable, thinks her absentee father. And better yet, if she's in the garden, they can steal away with no one the wiser.

* * *

"Mᴜᴍ!" Humphrey pants into the phone. "Where have you been! Elly's gone missing!"

"What! Humphrey, you said you had her."

"Mum, she's not here. We've searched the house."

"Look, we'll find her. P'raps she's snuck back here, Humphrey."

"But Ted, is he still there?"

Diana yelps and hangs up the phone. "Eleanor! Eleanor!" she cries, running up the stairs, two at a time. "Come out this instant!"

Wally combs the downstairs while Diana searches the bedrooms. He checks the study, he checks the kitchen. When the phone rings, he picks it up.

"Mr. Lively?" asks a deep Southern accent.

"No. He's not here."

"I've been trying to reach him. I— Is there—look, are their kids okay?"

"Who is this?"

"Deputy Bentley. From the sheriff's office. I was there earlier to-day and I— Look, I don't want to worry you, but I think I may have left my gun there."

"Slow down. What are you talking about?"

"I've looked all through my house and my car, you see? I swear, I'd have heard it or felt it, if I'd dropped it at their house. But I can't find the damn thing, so I just thought I'd call and see—"

"Is it loaded?" Wally asks, closing his eyes to think.

* * *

"BANG," Eleanor mouths, her hands clapped over her ears. She is hiding in Audrey's garden, waiting for her father to disappear. She is murmuring her own sweet elegy, the sound of a big engine roaring to life, taking her daddy up high. Eleanor imagines herself in her pirate costume, with her hat and eyepatch, her ragtag skirt, and a new addition: the gun of the Man in the Yellow Hat. In Elly's ship, there's only one boss, and the ship will not be used to be mean at Mummy. "Bang," she mutters, cocking her finger out ahead, her aim dead straight at her father's back, which, in her perfect universe, should grow smaller and smaller until he disappears from sight. Such is the stuff that dreams are made of, and to prove this maxim right, Miss Eleanor, unused to the silence and the heat, lets down her guard and falls promptly asleep.

* * *

WHEN it occurs to Diana that she hasn't thought to check the swimming pools, she almost loses her balance, gripped by a sudden, awful certainty. Her fear of water: It's been about this moment, rushing to the edge, seeing the blue envelope open in front of her, crushing her lungs with the sight of a small still form at the bottom. The pool, though, when she crawls to its rim, it swells with nothing more than the empty green clang of the gate swung wide. Diana mews her thanks, taking a deep breath, before hurrying on toward the back garden. Wally is already ahead of her, opening one latch and then the other, shepherding her past the patch of dying sugarcane, past the cabana to check his pool, to sink to his knees and dip his hand into the gloriously vacant wet. He looks up at Diana, and she nods, not trusting herself to speak a single word.

* * *

IT is Audrey who finds Eleanor, prone, in the midst of the maze of her ailing sugarcane. Audrey's crop has succumbed, not to sandmites but to Sonoran jackrabbits, who've ignored the stench of human urine for the tangy flavors of sugar, jalapeño, and tequila. The leftover leaves have turned a translucent brown, the color of Elly's khaki dress, camouflaging the girl from prying eyes. Audrey lifts her tiny disciple into her arms and carries her through the back gate, towards her father, towards Humphrey and his very frantic mother.

* * *

WILLIAM and Adam have been told to stay at Wally's, for their own safety while the search for the gun is being conducted. They are playing a medieval war game on Wally's computer. Adam squints at the screen and takes the mouse from William's hands, along with his friend's warning to watch for the knights in the corridor. William moves out of Adam's way, the better to allow his alter-ego to maneuver past the waiting ambush. William takes up the copper rake solely as a means of making time go faster until his turn comes again. *Clink*, goes the sound of Adam's sword on enemy shield, *clink* goes the rake of copper on metal, as William is tugged by a dizzying sense of déjà vu. He pulls the bronze urn and Johnny's silver framed picture from the sand, and wonders if Elly will even get punished for all the trouble she's caused.

* * *

ELEANOR, for her part, is content to snuggle into her mother's armpit, feigning sleep. "Wake up, my sweet child," her mummy insists, until Elly complies.

"Milk!" she cries, causing her eldest brother no end of relief.

"You minx!" he sings, leaping up to find her favorite sippy cup. "Where in God's name did you put the cowlad's gun?"

Hours later they are no closer to an answer. William has rushed in with Johnny's ashes, and his framed picture. When he tells his mother it was buried in the sand, she insists they return to search for the gun. After all, what was the point of her dream, the one in which Johnny is teaching William to dig in the sand, if not to warn her? Especially when the dream had been so taut with her dread of the hunting party, on its way to mow him down?

After combing through every centimeter of space, though, both within the box, in the houses, and even outside in the gardens, no firearm has been uncovered. Finally, when it's time for William and Adam to go to soccer, Diana asks Humphrey and Audrey to take Eleanor with them, for it's clear the child cannot remember, or will not disclose, where in God's name she has hidden the cowlad's gun.

Wally stays behind with Diana to help her search Elly's bedroom one last time. They've pored over boxes of toys, folded and unfolded clothes, pulled every stuffed animal down from the closet, and checked shoes and boots for a lurking weapon. "Maybe he didn't leave it here after all," says Wally.

"Possibly," says Diana. "But I do hate worrying about it."

"Let's take a break. You're exhausted."

Diana shakes her head. "You rest. I'm fine."

"No way would I rest while you're still working. What kind of guy do you think I am?"

Diana takes him into William's room, too tired to object. The sun is lower in the sky by the time they've finished searching the house, but whether the job takes hours or minutes, Diana cannot be sure. All she can know, is that by the time Wally suggests they go out to eat, she's found herself immensely buoyed by his last rhetorical question because its answer, unlike the missing gun, is as plain as the helping hand in front of her face.

* * *

As Humphrey maneuvers through traffic, heading west on the Paradise Valley Parkway, Audrey finds herself drifting off to sleep. She's forgotten her sunglasses and the six o'clock sun is so bright that even with her lids shut, the light pervades her dreams.

This afternoon, searching for Elly, Audrey had felt the panic come back, not into her head, where she's developed ways of defending herself, but in her stomach, where it had clutched at her, bent her over, the knowledge she has tried so hard to forget: Bad things happen when they're least expected.

The bleak space she'd cleared in her heart, an aching emptiness of disbelief, had opened up again. It had remained with her even when she'd figured out where Elly might be, even when she'd found her in her garden.

Just for a second, time had stopped, just like they said in the books, but this wasn't a good standing still: It was more like falling into that horror of disbelief, remembering exactly how alone she'd felt when she finally realized her mother wasn't coming back.

Audrey's body had gone on automatic pilot. She'd carried Elly inside, adjusting her brain to the fact that the child was breathing, had only fallen asleep. Still, even after Eleanor had woken and demanded her milk, Audrey had been visited over and over by the terrified snatches of time in which today's search was illuminated by a knowledge she'd not been equipped with during the first days of her mother's disappearance.

Wally had insisted they let Brenner lead the search teams, insisted they stay home, in case her mom was trying to reach them. Audrey, fourteen, so clueless; she hadn't even argued. Later, though, in her worst moments, Audrey had been plagued by the notion that if only she'd gone out there in the wilderness, her mom would have felt it, would have fought to stay alive.

This remorse has never been voiced out loud, never even put into words of the unspoken sort, but it has remained, lodged, in the deep of Audrey's being. Audrey's eyelids flicker with it now, this need to find her mother. She struggles to wake up, but the world of her dream is pulling her down. She is reaching over to collect her mom. She is lifting her up, poised to hear a pulse. As soon as she hears it, she knows it is fading fast. Her mother is going, but somehow, in the shift of time between finding her and losing her, Audrey's bleak and barren landscape is swept by a gust of breath that carries with it the reassurance she will be able to hear over and over again from this day forward. Something out there, it has no name, but it is so large and so convincing, this whispering hush, like that of the old lady in *Goodnight Moon*, except instead of putting her to sleep, it causes Audrey to smile even as she keeps her eyes closed to hold on to the sound.

* * *

MARY Katherine Gold is under, submerged in a morphine sea. She is carried along by the current, beyond the banks of the Dreamy Draw, over the jagged peaks of the Superstition, to a place she's never before been. Now she is looking up from rocky ground, seared by the endless sky of the desert, then sheltered by the heart of her daughter's face, closing in. The girl is bending to revive her mother's sleeping form, lifting her as though she'd never been lost. Audrey is carrying her home, out of the dun-colored wasteland, into a field of green.

Falling water drowns the sounds of wrongdoers, soothing regret, washing clean their cells.

In times of peace and plenty, never-never land remains true to its name. When love is scratched from the parched scars of unrequited yearning, however, absence turns back on itself. What hatches from this final, bereft, and irrevokable depth is a glorious mercy. From a well gone dry or a bottle drained eons before, a bubble rises to catch, in its jagged panes of refracted sun, the most astonishing alchemy. It is only atoms, the elements, it is only volume and mass, but the colors are dizzying. Their spectacular warmth pulls Mary Kate towards the dazzling, incendiary light.

As she gives in to the pleasure of her daughter's embrace, to those capable seventeen-year-old arms rocking her like a baby, Mary Kate abandons herself to this beautiful river of grace. Falling back, she surrenders to its deafening hush. The pain is gone, her daughter's heart beats close to the surface of her mother's breast. The sound of that heart is so clear, so deep, so vast, that Mary Katherine Gold will no longer fear that her long-awaited dream of reunion might be a tale just too good to be true.

Twenty

By the time Ted arrives at Gatwick, he has constructed a cover story, one in which he's staged the Golden Showers as performance art, a kinky valentine to Fiona. That's it, he is telling himself, at the same time as he unzips his valise for the customs inspectors. Ted is reassuring himself that such alibis won't be necessary if he arrives in time to intercept the post, and thus his body language expresses more than his usual dose of impatience with the idiots searching his bags. For the new inspector across the counter, who's just seen a training video profiling terrorists, Ted's nervous energy is a bit worrisome, but still, when she reaches below the stuffed bunny to extract the muzzle of an unusually clean handgun, she is nearly as shocked as the passenger himself.

* * *

WITHIN the four days it takes the Cheswitts' solicitors to straighten out the mess and begin the convoluted process of returning the gun to the Maricopa County sheriff 's office, provincial abode of Eleanor's Man in the Yellow Hat, Theodore Lively has lost three pounds and the endowed chair of Arthurian studies. St. Mark's College, shuddering under the publicity of one of its Fellows having been arrested trying to smuggle contraband into the U.K., has graciously acceded to Wally's discreet request that he replace his three-million-dollar endowed chair with a more modest one hundred thousand pound scholarship fund to be named in the honor of John Humphrey Sennett and Mary Katherine Gold. The scholarship program—to be advertised in low-income communities throughout England and the U.S.—is to be awarded to promising students in Environmental Studies, Tribal Studies, or Arthurian Studies.

* * *

FROM time to time over the next few weeks, Wally finds himself bludgeoned by the reappearance of a fear that he must continually swat away. How ever much he tries, he cannot completely kill the doubts that Ted's meddling have raised. This time, instead of burying his head in the sand, Wally forces himself to pursue the truth. He hires two private investigators, one to confirm that the medical records actually match Valeen's date of birth, height, and blood type, another to trace the money that had disappeared shortly before the rafting trip. The second man turns up a lead that rings true. A substance abuse center in Tuscon admits they received a generous donation from Mary Kate shortly before her death. Though the center is unwilling to state the amount they'd gotten, this explanation makes more sense than the financial acrobatics Mary Kate would have had to go through if she'd wanted to change her identity. Besides, it wouldn't be the first time she'd written a large check to charity without consulting Wally. Mary Kate had never been one to look before she leapt. Moreover, she felt, as did her husband, that their money belonged to them both.

This constant struggle to resolve the mystery, to know for certain, without a single doubt, this occupies more than a little of Wally's energy. It will continue to do so, for he's discovered an unfortunate paradox: No real exhilaration attaches to certainty, only to risk. This paralyzing gamble, of believing in his late wife, is a ledge he will continue to force himself towards, even as he struggles for balance.

When Valeen drops by the Gelding Drive house some weeks later, Wally finds himself happy to see her. He opens the door and takes her hand without thinking. Her palm feels chalky, with sand or something gritty, but that, too, he figures, can be explained. As he'd watched her from the livingroom window, Valeen had come up the flagstone path and knelt, to smell the blossom of a small Bird of Paradise, planted only three years before, and blooming well before the decade it should have taken the plant to bear fruit.

There's not much of a scent, as far as Wally has ever noticed, but then again, Mary Kate had always laughed, when he couldn't smell her saffron or the subtle hint of ginger, it was a good thing he'd not been born a bloodhound. He can almost hear his late wife's voice, as he leads Valeen into the noisy house, cajoling him, *You just need to relax, mister. Lean in,* she'd say, *close your eyes and let yourself go.*

* * *

By January, when the digging begins in Dreamy Draw, many of the complex details of Diana's legal status have begun to be sorted out. As a British subject, with highly sought technical skills, she has been fast-tracked for a green card, with the help of the Legal team at Gold Industries, whom, having put the Huntington buyout to bed, have had plenty of time to argue her merits. As regards her marriage contract, Diana's attorney has proposed an exchange: Diana will forfeit all claim to Ted's future income if he'll abandon custody of the children. Although Ted's solicitor has yet to respond, being tied up with the draconian prenuptial Fiona is insisting upon, Diana is hopeful that pressure from his fiancée's parents—eager for their grandson to enjoy all the benefits to which his great-grandfather, God rest his Presbyterian soul, had intended—will hasten his decision.

As for the requirement that Diana be supervised until she's become licensed as an architect, Diana finds no shortage of firms wishing to put their imprimatur on her designs. After all, it's not often that an English housewife specializing in dollhouses is suddenly "discovered" in the *New York Times'* Sunday Supplement on the Environment. Tom Peterson, to whom Wally had sent Diana's drawings, has written a four-page story on Diana's visionary blend of rooftop gardens and grassy swales, her internal maze in which children of all ages might find themselves embarking on quests that simultaneously reward individual initiative and social skills. The fact that this park would be one of only a handful of structures built of entirely nontoxic materials didn't hurt, either.

TechGreen—the maker of these building products—has seen its stock explode in value since the passing of the Colorado River Protection Accord and the City of Phoenix's SafePlay campaign. Though jurisdictional appeals have already been filed by the manufacturers of treated wood and PVC, among others, enough orders have already come in to create four hundred new manufacturing jobs at TechGreen's Yuma plant. The purchase order from Phoenix alone—which is procuring new wood for the dozens of carpenters who'll rebuild the city's playgrounds—has handed TechGreen an economy of scale on a silver platter. Now their wood almost competes with the cost of CCA-treated wood, and the company's other products are flying off the shelf faster than you can say "invisible hand of the marketplace."

Humphrey, who's been reenlisted to create concessions that satisfy Crazy Martha's organic muster, has spent not a little time cursing himself for having deleted the recipes from Skygyrl's school when he'd extricated himself from working on the project. In the meantime, though, Audrey, still guilty over having misplaced Humphrey's raffia-tied menu of starters without ever having looked at it, has become obsessed with a new brainstorm: that of debriefing Brenner to resurrect her mom's best dishes. These foods will be served at the end of each questor's journey, a lovely reward, in a restaurant named Mary Katherine's.

Indeed, in this ambitious endeavor, Audrey finds Humphrey a most willing accomplice. Though he never, ever, not even once, mentions the similarity between what he's lost from the computer and the culinary grail sought by his cherished Audrey, Humphrey is a dab hand at helping the girl recreate the best of her lost mother's legacy.

In fact, when Audrey tastes Humphrey's dishes, unveiled at a lovely buffet, after the construction project's ribbon-cutting, she cannot help but feel a shiver of delight, and even a small amount of wonder, at the taste of such wonderfully familiar food magically reappearing just when she'd wanted it most.

Wally, for his part, is similarly cheered. These recipes, they are unmistakably, uniquely, and absolutely Mary Kate's. Of this Wally is certain, even before he picks up a fork. For once in his life, Wally Gold has acquired a potent sense of smell and he can hear his wife's voice, too. She is calling him *loco. Lean in,* she is saying, *close your eyes,* she is saying, *and let yourself go.*

* * *

STILL, it is not until some months later, on March 30th, the anniversary of Mary Kate's death, that her words begin to put down roots. Wally is over at the Livelys', sitting by himself at the dining room table. Diana is upstairs, saying good night to the children. In the first quiet moment he's had all day, the man formerly known as Arizona's Ammo King sits in the dining room he'd built, drinking a beer, and waiting. He is moving his fingers over the surface of the table. *WS,* he traces, with his workman's hands, over and over, pressing the crooked letters. W. S. Wally Sell, or so he'd thought, before the unhappy question of his wife's whereabouts had surfaced, only to be buried again, but not completely. Hey, though, he tells himself, even if Ted's story was true, no way Mary Kate could have snuck in there and carved a message onto a table bought after Wally's trip to England. The house was never empty. Too risky. There'd be no percentage in it. Besides, how could she possibly predict her fond husband might get drunk, get coloring, and the next day, get Jesus?

It had to be one of the kids, Wally reasons. William, maybe, though he wouldn't have a clue how his mischief might be seized upon as a sign from Heaven by an idiot looking for company. And the king on his passport, that had to be Elly, not Mary Kate or—God help him for hoping this—a spirit of some kind, helping him find his way in the dark. The idea that someone might be out there, on his side, watching over him, helping him succeed, had he made it all up?

These "signs" he'd felt so sure of: the broken reading glasses, the king on his passport, the WS carved into the table, Diana's being an architect, even the helter-skelter of characters on her drawings, had they been anything more than a random set of accidents he'd stuck together to distract himself from loneliness?

He does not hear Diana's steps on the stairs, nor the whisper of her hands as they cover his eyes. He reaches up and swallows her hands in his own, diving into the soothing darkness made by their overlaid palms. He pulls her elbows forward until he can feel her heart beat behind his ears. In the artificial night created by the warmth of Diana's fingers, he sees the random accidents of her children's play as white streaks of light that are gone before they've moved from one star to the next. The pattern he detects is not something he can describe, nor could he draw its shape. Where it came from, a dead wife, a wife alive, a source within himself that wanted to make sense of things, or simply the lovely slipshod interplay of a family connected to him and to each other by the merest of chance, none of this he knows, but for just a moment, Wally gives himself over to its blinding beauty. He pulls himself up and turns to face the woman whose small and muscular hands have brought him right.